BEHIND THE FORGOTTEN FRONT

BEHIND THE FORGOTTEN FRONT

A WWII Novel

by

Barbara Hawkins

Behind the Forgotten Front
Copyright © 2014 by Barbara Hawkins
Exclusive of U.S. Government Maps
Cover Design by Aidana WillowRaven

This is a work of fiction. All of the characters, organizations, and events portrayed in this novel are fictional re-creations of actual events, practices, and people - drawn from diaries, biographies, period publications and the author's imagination.

Edited by Monica Buntin

Library of Congress Control Number 2014913395
ISBN: 978-0-9915984-1-0 paper
ISBN: 978-0-9915984-2-7 electronic

First Edition: 2014
Published in the United States of America

BEHIND THE FORGOTTEN FRONT

is for all those serving in the China-Burma-India theater but in particular the men who built the Stilwell Road between Ledo, India and Kunming, China; Merrill's Marauders; and the Mars Task Force, including my dad, Dick Hawkins.

Your contributions are not forgotten.

ACKNOWLEDGEMENTS

To Monica Buntin, my editor, for cutting and
adding in the right places

To the Berkeley Writers Group, whose comments were painful
and uplifting when I needed both.

CONTENTS

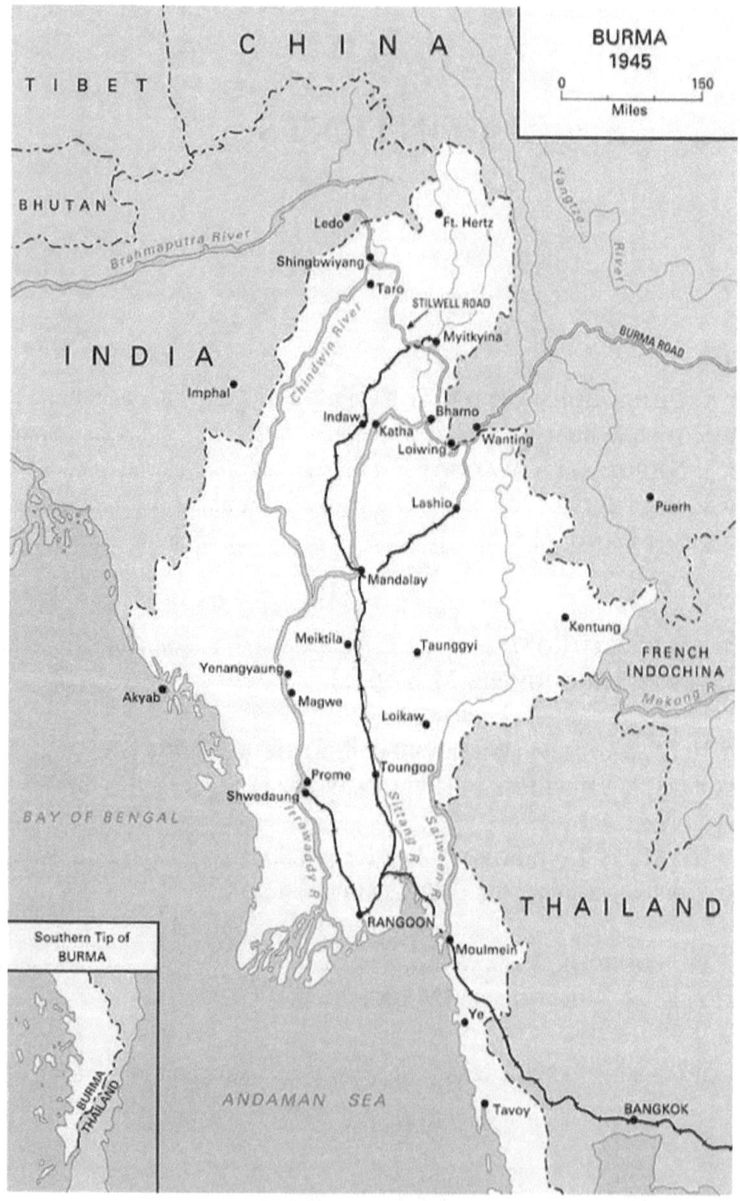

US Government Map

MAP 2
WALAWBUM TO SHADUZUP

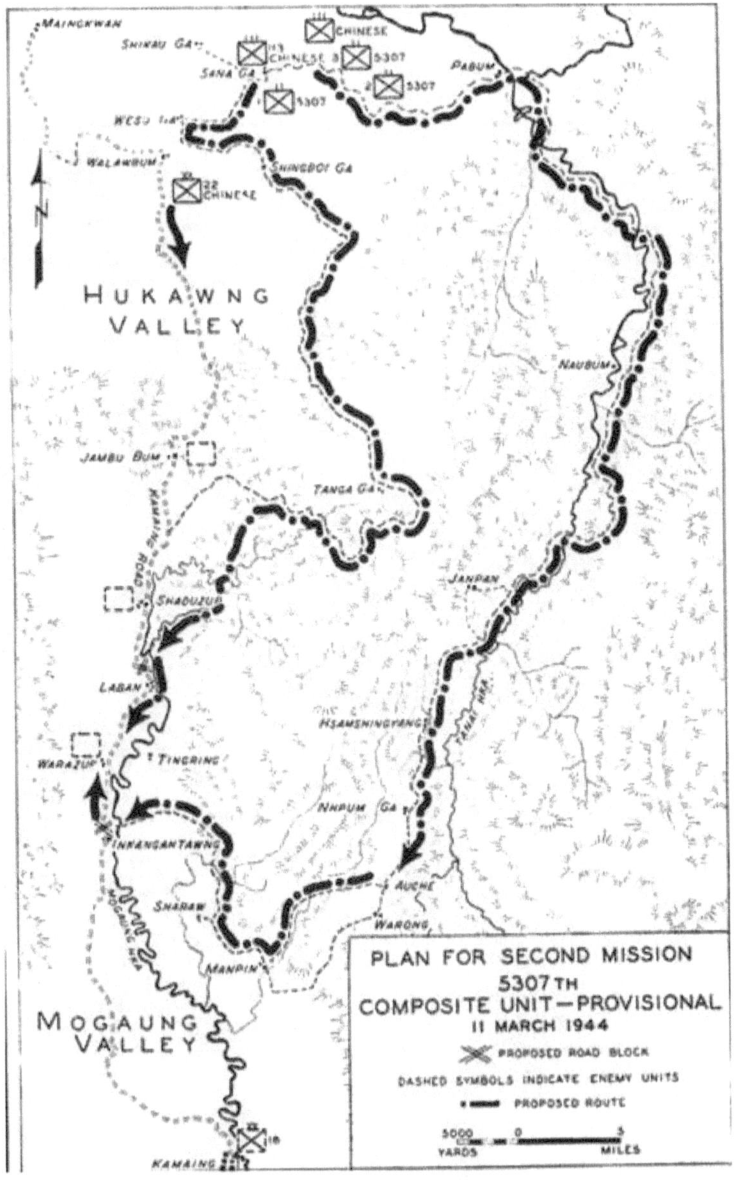

US Government Map

MAP 3
NHPUM GA – MAGGOT HILL

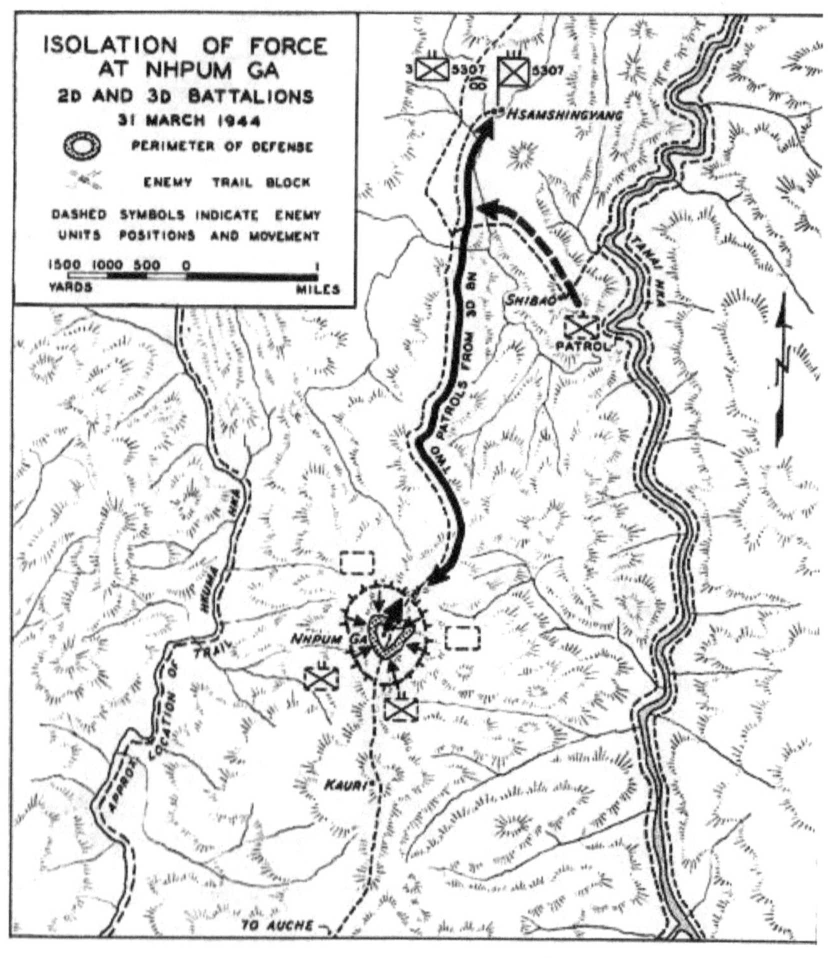

US Government Map

MAP 4
MYITKYINA

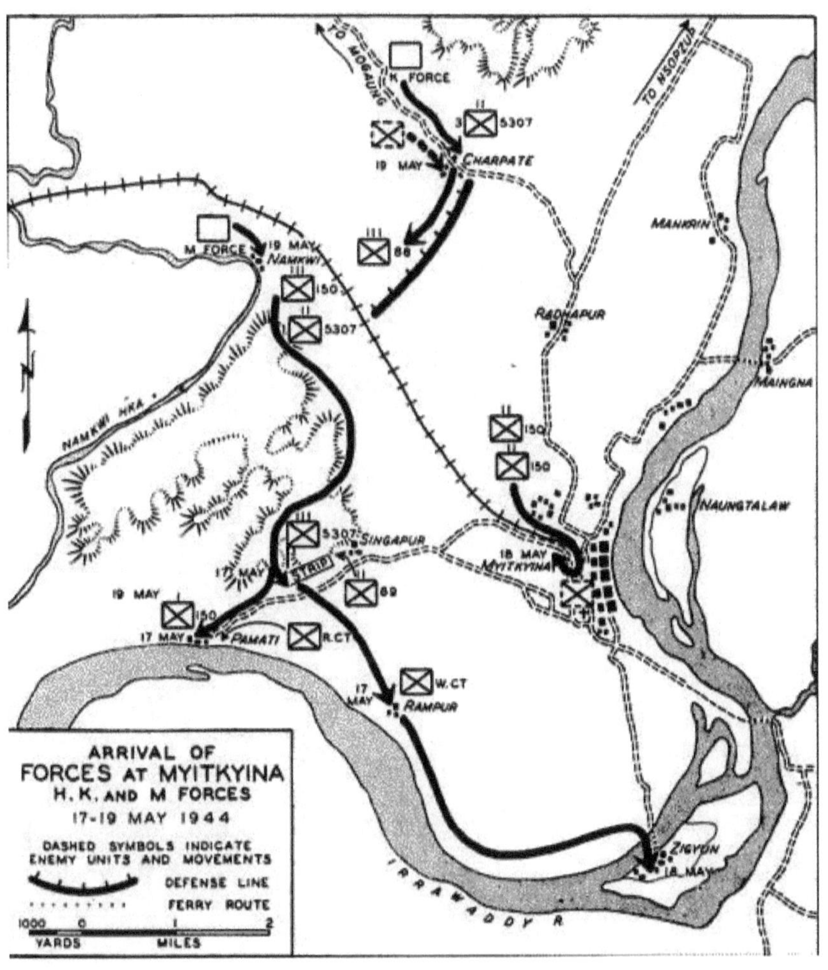

US Government Map

MAP 5
LOI KANG

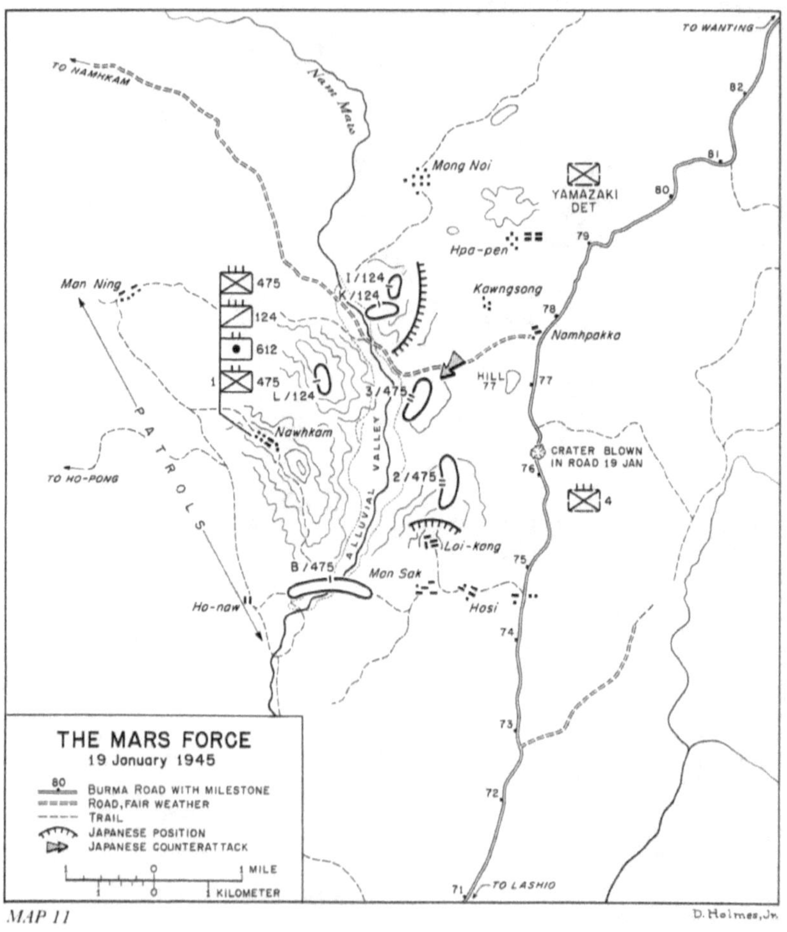

US Government Map

On the now-yellowed paper from 1945, the following words were written. *Below is my diary, kept while on tour of duty first as a Services of Supplies officer building the Stilwell Road through the Himalayan Mountains, later in jungle combat as one of Merrill's Marauders, and finally in Burma, with the Mars Task Force. Some people think history is only about facts. To me, it's about the driving passions and sometimes the mistakes of men and women made of flesh, blood, bones, and hearts who were at that place at that time.*

PART I

STILWELL ROAD

CHAPTER 1

May, 1942

How could life be better? We just declared War on Japan and Germany six months ago, and I'm ready to fight. I walk to the edge of the diving board, peer down ten feet, then take a step back. Without any effort, I swing myself up into a handstand at the tip of the board.

"Hey Harry, stop showing off," an army officer calls up to me. "You're going to make us all look bad in front of the gorgeous dames down here."

The other fellas watch me as I release my grip on the board. Slicing cleanly into the still water, I feel the molecules part like lightening in a thunderstorm. Seconds later, I surface at the edge of the pool, where my buddies nurse bottles of Coca-Cola.

"Who's next?" I challenge, then hoist myself out of the swimming pool in one easy motion. Spotting the young officer whose army cap shades his face while he bends over to fill his pipe, I yell, "Hey Bob, is it really you?" I push through the others, wet suit and all, then grab my best friend in a relaxed choke-hold. "When did you get home from the front?" I shake the water out of my hair, showering the others.

Bob Clarke good-naturedly flicks drops of water off his uniform, then resumes lighting his pipe. In between puffs, he quietly asks, "So, when are you going to join me, Harry? Hitler's making a mess of things over there. We need men like you, who are ready to take control and make decisions."

Randy Polowski, a tall, lanky Polack from the east side, complains about the water I splashed on him. "Hey, I got a dog at home that's better trained than you." He throws me a towel, then turns to Bob. "What about the rest of us?" he asks. "We're not good enough to keep you company on the front?" He looks to the others to back him. "Well, make room for me, anyway, because I got my Navy letter last week." He boasts while upturning imaginary lapels on his t- shirt.

Nothing beats pledging your honor to your country and fighting side-by-side in a foreign country with your buddies. The thrill of it makes life worth living. Even Marco Fazio and Joseph Graf, two Richmond boys with parents from the mother countries of Italy and Germany, didn't let paperwork get in the way of patriotism.

"When they heard I visited relatives in Germany every summer, they sent me to the front of the recruitment line," Joseph brags.

"Didn't even know I could speak Italian," Marco jokes, "until the conscription jockey asked me, 'En che anno nato?' Talking just like my grandma. It felt like I was in the old Sicilian village. I expected him to show me where to start chopping onions."

At the mention of Uncle Sam, I decide it's time to go. I edge to the back of the group while war talk hypnotizes the others. I haven't told anyone that I've been forced along a different course, and I have no intention of sharing that news now.

Bob grabs my elbow as I try to slip away. "You can't sneak out that easy. You never answered my question. When are you going to sign up?"

I swallow a laugh. "Can't you let a fella change out of his wet clothes without interrogating him?" I shake my head and try to push the uncertainty from my voice. "I asked for front line duty. You'd think they'd give anyone a rifle to kill those Krauts and Japs. And I'd be good at it!" Knowing I can't lie to Bob, I add, "But they found out about Ma's polio."

I resent being treated differently, so I continue complaining to Bob. "They're pampering me like I'm a wimp. I got a desk job," I feel my face flush with embarrassment. Clenching my fist, I look for something to smash. "But I haven't given up. I'll get a piece of the action one way or another."

Bob slings a fraternal arm around my shoulder and says, "They put you on an office track because they saw something in you that the rest of us don't have."

"What's that?" I ask, still annoyed and shrugging off Bob's support. "A father who sleeps it off curled up in the back hall, bottle in hand, locked out of his own house? I didn't get to be a kid because of him. Now Uncle Sam's trying to steal my right to be a real man. Will I ever get a say in how my life is run?"

"I'll bet it has nothing to do with your mom," Bob answers, then puffs on his pipe.

If Bob is right, it means I got shanghaied from active duty because of something else.

Why didn't they give me combat duty like all the other guys?

"Get this." I throw the wet towel on the ground. "When I went to sign up at the induction center, some clown came out of his office and called out for Harry Flynn. When I raised my hand, the joker said, 'Son, you have mighty fine handwriting. That's a talent we need.'"

My body blocks Bob from escaping my tirade. "Handwriting?" I sneer. "While you're putting your life on the line, I'm going to be a Goddamn secretary."

For a long moment, silence stands between us. I feel humiliation strain through every muscle, then I relax as I see a way I can twist this to my advantage. I wrap my still-wet arm around Bob's shoulder, relieved and smiling for the first time in days. I say, "On the other hand, he who holds the pen holds the power." It doesn't occur to me how the truth in those words could stalk me for the rest of my life.

CHAPTER 2

December, 1942

A sturdy desk with an Underwood typewriter waits patiently for me. After three hours of work in this roasting temperature, I need a break. So I slump in the hard wooden chair, stretch my legs out in front of me, and let my head drop back. A single, naked light bulb hangs from the center of the ceiling. My tired eyes close, refusing to let me be the creased-to-perfection soldier. I wait for anything that could remotely be considered a breeze to relieve the heat in this sweltering, military supply office.

The mud-plastered, bamboo walls of this hut they call a basha let the midday heat seep through, and, like a bubble, trap the scorching air in the room. My flesh feels like an added layer of clothing. It's so hot that even the katydids take a nap.

Since early this afternoon I typed pages and pages of requisitions: Spam for the Americans, rice and taro root for the Chinese, and curried lentils for the local Indians. The hay on the list could be for a horse or a mule, but it ends up being for the elephants every time. The other Service of Supplies—or SOS—men received an emergency shipment late last night, so they'll start their shift after dinner. That means I'm alone with nothing to keep me awake but the sorry-looking Underwood. Dying of boredom seems to be the biggest danger in Ledo, India. My mind wanders back home.

"No End in Sight for Marines at Guadalcanal" had been the headline that day in September when I received my official letter. Rain pounded on the metal roof of Tillie's Diner, where I waited in the back booth for Ruthie to get off work. Like usual, my knees bounced with nervous energy.

Ruthie works in an ammunition factory where they recycle scrap metal to make bullets for the boys overseas. A blue cotton blouse, dungarees, and bandanna have replaced the pink, well-fitted suit she wore when I first saw her. Even so, all I see is my Ruthie: a princess dressed as a factory worker.

"It's so cold, I wouldn't be surprised if this rain turns to snow!" she shivers as she slips into the other side of the booth and pulls off her rain bonnet. Then she stops abruptly. "What is it?" she asks.

My rigid posture and clasped hands resting heavy on the table must have alarmed her. "I got my orders today. I'm shipping off in three days," I say, staring at the rivulets of water coursing down the blurred window pane.

She puts her hand over mine and says, "We knew that was going to happen." Then she leans closer and demands, "There's something you're not telling me."

"It's not about me," I say, and pause to study the checkered table cloth, then momentarily let myself become distracted by a rip in the booth's leather upholstery. "Joseph Graf was killed," I finally tell her. "And he didn't even have to go; he volunteered." I chuckle humorlessly at the horrible reality. "We always called him helium hand. Damn him. No one was supposed to die."

She holds my hands for a few moments, then asks, "What will you do when your life is on the line?"

It's not as if I hadn't already asked myself that question. I pull one hand away and fumble in my pocket for a smoke, but pull out an empty pack. Squashing it, then tossing it on the table, I say, "I'd either want to cry or wake up from a bad dream." I wrap both my hands around hers.

Then I whisper, "I feel like a coward because I want to live."

Instead of scowling in disappointment, she smiles. "Sounds smart to me." She caresses my cheek with the back of her hand, then says, "Do me a favor; don't come home to me in a box."

My mind snaps back to the present and thoughts of my gut-wrenching sea voyage across two oceans to Bombay, followed by a hemorrhoid-jarring land journey of two thousand miles. Early this morning, I arrived in the town of Ledo in the state of Assam. *Where in the hell is Assam?* I wondered.

"Northern India—somewhere between Delhi and Burma," a returning soldier had told me on the train as we bumped along on a narrow-gauge rail. Outside, terraced fields of rice stretched to the horizon. "Assam has nothing but abandoned tea plantations. They call it the chicken neck of India; it's beyond the boondocks. You've heard of head hunters?"

I nod.

"That's the Naga tribe," he continued. "So, you must be going to headquarters in Ledo. It's where the railroad stops. It's nothing but a squalid bazaar town with trash in the gutter and bone-thin mutts wandering the streets."

But it's also the China-Burma-India (CBI) Northern Command Center, and the base for my first army assignment. The Underwood stares up at me from the desk, looking as forlorn as I feel. Behind me, the bamboo door on the basha slaps closed.

"The chow they serve up here sucks," offers the Captain as he saunters over to my desk. I saw him on the train from Delhi this morning. He drops a thick manila envelope on my desk with the word 'Requisitions' and the date stamped in bold letters on the front. "But the mess hall is a helluva lot better than sitting in this sauna." He looks at me like I'm half nuts. "You can stay here and die from a heat stroke or tempt the fate of your bowels by trying curried egg-foo-yung or some other local delicacy. I suggest you get something to eat."

I jump to attention. "Yes, sir!" I salute.

"Schmidt." He offers me a handshake. "Captain Peter Schmidt." He looks at the pile of requisitions I completed and the taller one yet to be started. "Forget the formality. Just remember, the reason you're here is because supplies save lives. So don't plan on impressing anybody with spit and polish, unless it produces results." He grins, then adds, "And you've got to have a pulse ticking to do that. So go eat, Lieutenant."

CHAPTER 3

I expect to be blinded by the tropical sun as I push out of the basha, but a searing orange sunset is melting into evening. Still, it feels like I'm breathing baked vapor. I feel too stupid to ask for directions to the mess hall, so without a guide or crowd to follow, I'm lost. I wander around row upon row of barracks, but everything looks the same.

I track loud talk floating around the corners, which bursts into raucous laughter as I get closer. It feels good to be walking, even if I am trapped in this rectangular maze of identical, tin- roofed huts. The fourth bend of dirt paths opens into a clearing, where a string of Negro soldiers slowly inch towards a basha emanating a vague, unidentifiable odor. I'm just a country boy, so I was never around Negroes much back home. I feel a little out of place.

With my hands stuck deep in my pockets, I walk towards the men. The joking stops as soon as they see me, and it's as though I am taking my last steps towards the guillotine. "Hi, fellas." I try to sound friendly, but my voice cracks. "Where can a new guy find a meal around here?"

The men look at each other oddly, as if I had just challenged them to a fight. There's no invitation in their eyes and no answer to my question—just dark, suspicious glares.

"My mistake." I attempt an apologetic wave, then turn to go. "Could be I'm going crazy with this heat, but I thought I smelled chicken." My stomach is so jumpy that anything I eat would most likely bounce right back out. And if I was hot before, I'm sizzling now. "Sorry if I barged in on you guys."

I walk away. Any direction will do. Then I hear a deep bass voice call after me: "It's pork chops and grits."

I stop and look back cautiously. Their tightly coiled fists persuade me to be on my best behavior.

"There's a heap load of food." The deep voice comes from a tall, skinny black man with skin like sun-beaten leather and a wide, mostly toothless grin. "But if you ask me, it's chops and shit. They plum forgot about the pork."

I pull my shoulders back, brace my heels, and keep my fists ready in my pockets before I answer. "Yeah, it's probably not like home-cooking. But it wouldn't make sense for Uncle Sam to starve anyone."

The weathered man shakes his head in contempt, then gripes, "White men always have an answer." No one moves. "Like you said, got to feed an animal to get him off his ass."

There are more than a dozen of them, and they all look like the boxer, Joe Louis. "Aren't you getting paid to be here?" I ask, sounding cockier than I feel.

"Not as much as you," he answers.

"But I'm an officer." I know I can play this card only once, but feel I've walked into something beyond me and need a way out. "I think you'd best show me some respect."

"No disrespect intended, sir. But we ain't on duty. We're just minding our own business, waiting to be fed, like a pack of dogs." He laughs like it's a joke, but it's clear he doesn't think it's funny.

"Do I need permission to walk around these barracks?" I haven't done anything wrong, and it seems like they have it in for me just because I'm white.

"You ain't got no business coming around here to eat." I can see the mental boxing gloves being pulled off and the men positioning themselves to watch a fight.

"You got a better suggestion?" I ask, palming the sweat off my face as the sour taste of acid rises from my stomach.

Like the eerie stillness before a storm hits, there's just silence. As I wonder whether he'll throw a breath-sucking gut punch or KO to my head, I instead see the men look at me like I'm wacko. One second, they're ready to kick my ass; the next, they act like I'm mentally unbalanced.

"Lordy, this kitchen serves only us folk," the lanky black man confesses. I shrug. "I don't think I'm hungry anymore."

"I ain't never hungry for this food," he grouses.

The men shake their heads in solidarity, complain about the gristle and watered-down slop, then josh each other. They pretend to ignore me, like I'm a mutt waiting for scraps.

"Guess we weren't none too friendly, you being a stranger and all." His smile now seems genuine. "This shit may not be poison, but it sure tastes like it." Their grumbling escalates into lucid descriptions of rotting garbage, vile enough to make any man gag.

Thinking it's better to make a strong first showing than be remembered as a coward in the months to come, I decide to brave the group and move to join them. I pull out my cigarettes—an international equalizer—take out one, stick it in the side of my mouth, and offer the pack around until they're gone. With the smell of sweat heavy from a hard day's work and mud caked on everything—boots, army-brown pants, and even their arms—the men from the 823rd Regiment don't have to tell anyone they've been assigned to slave labor.

"What happens around here at night?" I ask.

The smiling soldier's expression turns grave. I should know I'm in trouble when he raises his eyebrows and warily lights his cigarette before drawling, "You'all come in on today's train?"

I rock back on my heels and take a long drag on my smoke, stalling for time to think, then say, "I must look like the kid who ran the touchdown to the wrong goal post." I hear polite chuckling. Fortunately, nobody tries to make me feel like the knock-kneed klutz who always has the ball stolen from him. "Yup, I'm new in town, if that's what you want to call this place."

The soldier nudges the next one in line to get his attention, "Why, Earl, wasn't it just last weekend we decided to call in on the Taj Mahal?"

Earl considers the question for a moment, rubbing his chin. "You're dang right on that one, Reginald," he answers with a reserve saved for swearing on the Bible. "And what about those snake charmers in Calcutta? They had mighty fine looking vipers coming out of those straw baskets." Earl imitates a chicken jerking its neck at feeding time.

Reginald places his hand on Earl's shoulder and interrupts: "And what about the yogis, practically butt naked on the steps of the Ganges River? They've sure got balls. Shit, the snakes had more to show than those diaper-wrapped skeletons. Should've been ashamed of themselves."

Reginald takes the first bold step and moves to shake my hand. It takes every ounce of courage I have not to flinch and trust that I'm not getting set up for a side punch. He guides me away from the others and, in barely a whisper, asks, "Would you like me to get you a ticket to the Taj Mahal for this weekend at my special rates?" The sincerity in his voice is as smooth as Jack Daniel's.

"That sounds swell," I splutter, loud enough for everyone to hear, even though I have this feeling like I'm about to get swindled. "I...well, hell, I just don't think I'll get leave any time soon. Can I take a rain check?"

Reginald backs away and doubles over. A burst of laughter catches fire and spreads through the ranks. Some of the men, with tears in their eyes, almost choke. They carry on, slapping each other on the back, as though I don't understand English. I feel riled at being the butt of their joke, but, really, I want to kick myself for being stupid enough to be set up.

"A rain check?" Reginald wheezes, then wraps his arms around his sides and takes in a deep breath to regain some composure. "If you haven't noticed, this town ain't no desert." He giggles in a way that only a man confident that he won't be teased for being silly can. "Shucks, a rain check's what you'll get every day up here. As a matter of fact, during the monsoon, you'll be checkin' for a foot a day."

Earl, a man of imposing muscles, grabs my hand with a lock-breaking grip. Lester, whose surly look first sent my mind spiraling into red alert, surprises me with rowdy laughter like you'd hear from the boys back home after a long day during harvest season.

Overhead, monkeys throw hollowed fruits at us and screech for attention. The banana palms hesitantly begin to waver with the evening breeze, still not ready to release the energy- zapping heat of the day.

Then a hand digs into my shoulder to spin me around. "What the hell? Did you get lost, boy? Or do your tastes lean towards southern well-done?" I twist to see Captain Schmidt, his lip quivering with disgust. He grabs my collar, then propels me out of line. I trip, but quickly catch my balance.

"When I'm hungry, I follow my nose," I say, and shake myself away from his control, wondering who the hell this guy thinks he is and not wanting someone to make my decisions for me.

"Ah, I guess you Yankee boys can't tell a dining room from a pig trough," Schmidt digs, looking at Lester with a dare in his eyes that shows he doesn't expect to be challenged.

Schmidt adds, in a voice loud enough for all to hear, while jabbing a pointed finger at me: "And you probably think *darky* means a farm hand after a day of burning a field. Let me suggest that you will be judged by the company you keep around here. *Our* mess hall is over there." He flicks a condescending farewell wave to the colored soldiers.

I do my best to keep my emotions off my face, but the mere fact that it's devoid of any reaction should be telling. This guy must have his conscience up his asshole. I brush imaginary dust off my pant legs, then, as though Schmidt just arrived and nothing has happened, I say,

"They're serving pork chops and grits here tonight. Thought a farm boy like me should give it a try."

"Like I said, boy"—here, he shoves the palm of his hand against my shoulder. I resist, but he doesn't relent. Then, in a low, cutting voice, he says, "I suggest you do as I say…"

Schmidt's back is to the Negroes, who say nothing, but pack together to form a barrier several men deep. Moments earlier, Lester's hearty, contagious laugh had disarmed me. Now, he's seething as if in a poisoned trance. Earl holds him with an arresting grip.

Schmidt spins me around and pushes me forward.

I look back, torn between what I want to do and what I've been ordered to do. The sign on the aging basha reads: Negro Kitchen. The monkeys still bounce up and down on the branches, screaming frantically, but the chain of black soldiers are deaf to it and instead concentrate on Schmidt, a bigger lurking threat.

CHAPTER 4

Schmidt sets a slow, deliberate pace away from the Negro Kitchen. "Hey, don't worry," he says to me. "It's your first day. We all make mistakes when we're tired." He sounds congenial, but his eyes whip me with repulsion. "You must be color blind. That can be a real problem in the army. Something you'll need to change."

Grub for white officers is on the bottom floor of a wooden, two-story tea house. The upper level sits on stilts with peeling plank boards and shuttered windows, while the bottom floor is wide open. I grab some food, and look in the opposite direction for a place to sit, hoping Schmidt will find someone else to terrorize.

"Attention!" A soldier in a crisp, clean uniform stands at the entrance to the mess hall at full salute. A General and Colonel enter the building.

Chairs tip over and tin cups drop to the floor as everyone pushes themselves to standing.

The joking banter silences.

"I don't give a damn if the Brits think building this road is a laborious task, unlikely to be finished until the need for it has passed. We know how to win wars. And flying the HUMP just isn't enough. Who do they think we are—one of their bloody colonies?" The grizzled General, sporting a razor-edged crew-cut and biting down on a long, black cigarette holder, barks at the younger, pipe-smoking Colonel. Both are absorbed in their heated conversation and walk past the soldiers as though they're ghosts. They go to a corner table. Coolies rush plates and bowls spilling over with curried rice to them. "At ease, men," the older general says as an afterthought. "We're fighting a war. So dispense with all the jumping up and down business."

Chairs scrape the floor and the conversation volume goes up as the men sit down to finish their meals.

I find an empty seat at a table with a couple of soldiers. "This spot looks like it's reserved for greenhorns," I say as I sit down, then nod my head in the direction of the two officers. "Who are the bigwigs?"

A polished-looking soldier leans over and whispers, "The grey-haired guy is the one and only 'Vinegar Joe' Stilwell. Merrill's the Colonel. You won't have any problems around here if you do what they tell you. Stilwell's the kind of guy who'll join you at the end of a day with his bottle for a few drinks and a story or two, then, in the morning, ask pigs to fly."

"Yeah," a buzz-cut redhead, chewing with his mouth wide open, agrees. "Ever since the Japs humiliated Stilwell by booting him out of Burma in '42, he's been looking for revenge. So the Bible according to Stilwell has us winning this war through Burma with guts and determination. I'm voting on it being someone else's guts, not mine." He wriggles his eyebrows up and down, so I can't tell if he's joking or hiding behind his clown act.

"If they just used fighter planes to protect the boys flying supplies over the HUMP, then we wouldn't need to rebuild Marco Polo's trade route to China. But I'd never say that to Vinegar Joe," the first solider says.

An image of the mud-caked Negro crew comes to mind. Always one to take the side of the underdog, I suggest, "Isn't it murder if we send unarmed road workers up against Japanese troops in Burma? The only sure thing to come from constructing that road is a lot of dead men. Somebody should do something about that."

I'm met with silence. Then the redhead reaches out with a rough handshake. "Bernard Roman. Call me anything but Bernie, and I'll ignore you. I'm the guy who keeps the rigs running. Bribes of cigarettes and booze are always welcome." He jerks a thumb towards the first soldier. "Charles Olfson—one of our best radio operators. We call him Charming Charles.

You'll see why when we're around the ladies."

Olfson takes the jibe in stride, then adds his own editorial. "He's called Hot-Blooded Bernie—because of his hair, not the dames. Or, call him Stubby if you want to make him mad." Charles points to where Bernie once had a finger. "He says it was the carburetor's fault. By the way, rumor has it you're Harry Flynn, the rookie in our barracks. Welcome to the other side of the world."

CHAPTER 5

Bamboo-and-rope cots line the walls of our barracks, a tin-roofed basha. Our gear and personal belongings, including photos and letters from families, get stashed under our beds. We bathe in open-air showers with water that tastes like sweet rain on humid days, but the relief lasts only as long as it takes to put on a shirt. The latrine system makes for a neverending job of shoveling crap out of a ditch. Everyone sees the cruel signs of dysentery and thanks the coolies on shit duty with cigarettes and gum.

It's dark outside, the work day is over, and there's nowhere to go. So why is the guy next to me shaving? Shaving without a mirror make men who've never gone to battle look like they should be getting a purple heart after a few minutes with a razor. Watching the blood dribble from his cheek reminds me of one time when my old man raced out of the lavatory, wearing his best trousers and shined shoes; blood dripping from his neck and soaking his white undershirt.

"Let me help you, dear." Ma limped over with a wet dish towel. "And where will you be going this time of night, all decked out?"

He let her fuss about him until the bleeding stopped, then pulled on a freshly starched shirt. "You're always on me to be getting a job, woman," he said. "So don't be standing in my way when I'm looking to make some money." He slicked back his black hair; his deceitful eyes, an innocent shade of baby blue, already showed the signs of drink.

"Ah, but you're a fine-looking man." She admired her husband, holding his arm as long as he'd allow. "I wish ye luck." But her voice dropped with the last word, knowing, as I knew, it wasn't a job he'd be searching for. Soon he'd be back, owing money rather than earning it.

To change my thoughts, I ask others in the barracks, "What movie are they showing tonight?"

There's a movie every night in the mess hall, usually a rerun so old that the film splinters, and, when the frames blank out, gurgles and cackles from night birds fill in the gaps. Unless it is a popular rerun, the men kill the night's boredom by trying their luck in a poker game in one of the barracks.

"Why would you care?" Bernie asks as he sits down on his bed, crosses his arms, then plants his feet flat on the floor, his face as red as his hair. "You'll be gone."

Charles shrugs his shoulders in response to Bernie's sullen mood, but keeps moving towards the door. "No one's stopping you from going," he tells Bernie. "Harry's been pushing requisitions for almost a whole month and hasn't seen any of the sweet little temptations in Ledo. Why be in the army if you can't live it up? We'll be back before dawn. See you then."

I follow Charles out of the basha. The GIs on base don't have curfews, but the town of Ledo is off-limits. I light up a smoke, like any other night, to relieve the tension. "What's up with Bernie?" I ask as the two of us hit the dirt path. "He doesn't strike me as a goody-two- shoes."

Charles waves away my cigarette offer. "Bernie got caught sneaking out to Ledo once.

Hell if I know how he did that. Must've been talking more than watching."

Charles indicates a move to the left, so we turn away from the front gate, and then he says, "Someone may be on the lookout for roaming GIs. No sense in announcing our plans." We walk away from the light of the barracks towards the blackness of the headquarters buildings. "If you can't beat 'em, join 'em," Charles laughs. "The muckety-mucks have their own private gate up here. I learned about it when a radio operator read me the riot act for almost blowing a secret delivery. As if, by intuition, I was supposed to know the gate existed." He rolls his eyes.

I hear a rock skip across the gravel path up ahead. I try to stop Charles, but he nonchalantly shakes free from my hold. "We haven't done anything wrong…yet." We continue walking.

More gravel grinds, but this time it comes from behind us. Charles pushes me to the right at the next corner. Our pace increases to a fast clip. Our breathing becomes heavy. "Turn left next corner," Charles hisses.

The huffing behind us gets louder. We increase our stride. Then a flashlight, dead ahead, blinds us from where we were about to turn. We freeze.

"Identify yourself," a gruff voice orders.

We block the beam of light with our arms. Brilliant, I think. First time out, and we get caught like we're leaving a trail of beer bottles.

Charles's strong radio voice answers, "Olfson and Flynn."

The shaft of light illuminates us up and down for confirmation.

"And you?" I ask, thinking it only fair that the bully at the other end of the beam identify himself.

He circles the flashlight like a car making a U turn and ignores my question. "Authorized personnel only. Turn around." Then the floodlight is redirected at us so we feel like prisoners under interrogation.

I recognize the nasal voice—the one I always hear accompanying a whiny complaint— and dish out a harsh laugh, "Schmidt. Buddy."

No answer.

"This area is no more off-limits than the crapper," I continue. "Are you trying to hide something from us, buddy?" My first days of intimidation by Schmidt have grown into revulsion over how he treats others, and he knows it. "Now, turn that damn thing off if you don't want to find it shining up your ass."

"There's no reason for you to be here." Schmidt regains his confidence, but redirects the floodlight.

"Looking for someone to torment?" I shoot back, remembering Lester's black eye from when Schmidt "accidentally" tripped him, belittled him with, "If you're not careful, you're going to get hurt, boy," then kneed him.

I can tell that Charles doesn't want to battle with Schmidt. His placating voice interrupts: "There's no reason why we can't be here, Schmidt. It's Pete, right? So go have a nice walk, and we'll do the same." We make the turn we had intended, leaving Schmidt alone with his flashlight marking the spot as he receded towards the barracks.

Now, cold with sweat from an anger I hadn't felt until I saw Schmidt, I apologize to Charles, "I guess we can't choose which roadblocks stand in our way. But that guy's rubbed me wrong from day one."

"Schmidt!" Charles huffs in disgust. "It's because of jerks like him that we're at war in the first place."

We approach the south exit and catch a glimpse of the guard at the VIP gate dozing off. I watch the sentry's head slowly drop, then jerk awake. Poor guy – it's a boring job. A radio transmission slaps him alert, and, just our luck, the night's stars are as bright as a torch.

"Now or never!" Charles pulls me towards our escape route.

With our backs flattened against the concrete wall, we inch along the face to the gate. Threatened by the surveillance beacon surrounding the guard shack, I suck in my gut to make myself small and avoid its circle. I feel my heart beating against my chest like a trapped, coiled spring.

At that moment, I realize I really don't want to go into town. What has Ledo got that's worth this trouble? An image of flat-footed Bernie back at the basha comes to mind. Beer and a poker game sound pretty good right now. But it's too late.

The guard puts down the radio receiver and stands up. He makes a three-hundred-sixty- degree inspection, then halts. His posture says he registered a sound, and he pauses, looking in our direction.

I force my breathing to be shallow, almost noiseless. Focused on a distraction in the distance, the guard is about to leave his shack when the radio squawks. He shakes his head and goes back to the transmission. We run like hell across the grass field.

Barely able to catch our breath, we almost pass out when we finally stumble onto the unlit road. My stomach and chest ache. Ahead, the road blends into a ditch, where the jungle canopy encroaches onto the thick brush border. I trip several times in washouts along the path, and the pungent smell of jasmine flowers is sickening. We put some distance between us and the base. The only things we can hear are the crickets chirping and banana palms flapping.

"Schmidt's worse than a spy." I whisper. "He actually has authority to breathe down my neck." We continue down the road. Then I hear the huff huff huff of panting closing in from behind. "Hell, I think someone's on our tail."

Charles grows rigid. We listen to soft thumping in the dirt grow closer. Who'd be dim- witted enough to make so much noise if they're following us? The thudding gets louder. It sounds like he's sprinting along the edge of the road. Then I realize he's going to run right into me.

As this thought strikes me, a knee jams into my thigh. The runner topples over me, knocking me flat on my butt. Sounds of breaking branches come from Charles ripping into the bushes. I push myself up, then crash into the tangle of vegetation. With each snapping twig, I flinch, expecting the hiss of a viper.

"God damn son-of-a-bitch!" the runner explodes.

Charles and I stop. I feel blood trickling down my face from the sharp stems. "Where the hell are you guys?" Bernie shouts into the darkness, pulling himself up.

Charles extracts himself from the noose of branches and, with long strides, moves in on Bernie. "You little shithead." He bops Bernie on the back of his skull. "How would you prefer to die: snakes or Schmidt?"

"Hell, they cancelled the poker game tonight. What was I supposed to do?" Bernie whimpers, rubbing his crew cut where Charles whacked him.

"Sometimes you act like you're the same age as your shoe size, Bernie." Charles doesn't wait, but shoves off along the perfumed road. Bernie scratches his chin, giving Charles's words some thought, then kicks up a wad of dirt as he races to catch up.

Leaves rustle along the side of the road. Bats swoop in and out of towering trees, snatching insects midair. An expansive sky, filled with stars, lights our path. We continue our walk to town in silence. The evening has all those earmarks of becoming a memory. As soon as we reach the village, we give each other space and follow different passageways in the market- lined streets.

CHAPTER 6

Ledo at night reminds me of a manic-depressive on the uphill swing. A diffused glow from flickering gas lamps lights the streets. Droves of women in brightly colored, intricately wrapped sarees blossom after dark, like night flowers. Bodies smelling of cumin and garlic spill out onto the street from stalls, selling fresh fish. Respectable men in their loose-fitting dhoti pants, followed by their wives with flowing dupatia veils, walk about, unrushed. Clusters of locals pause to chat while they wait for vendors to wrap their goods in newspaper. I walk among them, catching fleeting moments in their personal lives, not even noticed.

Transportable vegetable stands, covered with canvas tarps, hold shallow boxes of green and red chili peppers; mounds of translucent rice; and plump, purple eggplants of all sizes and shapes. A merchant in a palm-thatched hut sells goats that decorate his booth in layers of bloodied corpse: they're sickening. My eyes significantly influence my stomach, so I decide to drink my dinner tonight. Within ten feet, they sell whiskey that tastes like rum. I buy some, then wander the bazaar for hours. Or is it minutes?

"Well, lookey who's come out to play," a southern drawl remarks. My gut twists the way a dish towel is rung dry.

"My man, looks like you're hungry for something a little special tonight."

I strain my eyes, adjusting to the shadows in the night, until I see Reginald's toothy grin. "I know just where to find young, juicy meat to satisfy every aching part of a man's body." Reginald leers at a petite, childlike girl, the red dot on her forehead as riveting as her lustrous black eyes. She passes by, giving him a knowing smile. He arches his eyebrows, which ask me whether I'm interested. "They sure know what a man wants a girl to do."

Alabama Earl and Lester have their arms around two young women—if they are old enough to be called that. They're pretty, but I've never taken to a woman who paints herself to hide her real looks. "I'd like you to meet Deepa and Mira," Earl says, always the gentleman in the group.

Lester, shy on words, beams, showing his satisfaction with the night's conquests.

"We heard from Charles that you had a little run-in with our favorite bully tonight," Reginald cuts in. "And I thought he had it in only for us." He turns so only I can hear. "Today he got all chummy with Lester, then says, 'Tell me what it's like to fuck a bitch?' And he wasn't talking about no woman. That man is sick. Some day he'll be in the wrong place at the right time, and not even God will be able to stop me."

Behind us, Earl lets out a soft, appreciative whistle. "That boy is a magnet for a storm." I follow his gaze.

A gaggle of clucking girls floats towards us like a cloud. In the middle, Charming Charles surrenders to their preening; each vying for him as though driven by a nesting instinct.

"Harry, what do you think?" he asks, spreading his arms wide to display his winnings.

One would have thought he'd want to share. But his eyes tell me to find my own party. "Impressive," I say, without envy. "Catch you later after you've worn down your admirers." Then I stick my hands in my pants pockets and wander into the thick of the crowd.

Spellbound, I watch the bickering of sellers and buyers the way one follows a political debate, back and forth. The smell of incense draws me towards a thin line of snaking smoke that dissolves without a trace into the night. Underfoot, blending into the ground, a woman sits cross- legged with a child cuddled tight in her arms. Her eyes beg as she reaches out to me with an upturned palm. I walk away, embarrassed.

All I can think about is when the night will be over. I see Bernie's red crew cut bobbing above the others. In curt English, he barters with a Hindi speaker who sounds like a grieving parent unwilling to part with his only child. I push my way through the crowd just as Bernie takes possession of a Gurkha knife.

"Isn't this a beauty?" Bernie asks. His eyes travel the length of the sickle-shape blade, swiping it through the air. A man with clenched fists hides his family behind him as he scolds Bernie in Indian dialect, most likely for almost decapitating his wife. Bernie wobbles but regains his balance, then, with the smell of undiluted alcohol on his breath, says "Jack off" just before he collapses to the ground.

I want to leave him there the entire night to sleep it off, but it would be inconsiderate to the others. With the same intensity of enthusiasm I'd have for cleaning out a latrine, I bend over to drag Bernie somewhere decent.

From above, someone offers, "I may not be able to give you a hand, but I do know a proper place for that young man." Looking up, I see Reginald. Under the crook of one arm, he's protecting the young girl with the red dot, and, possessively wrapped within his other arm, is an older woman, wearing experience in her face and body.

Reginald sees me studying the red dot, a third eye, on the girl's forehead. The local brew leaves me squinting and refocusing on the young girl's face, then moving down her body.

"Tell me these young little creatures don't move a man," he says.

A fuzzy memory of a night I hate to remember plants itself in my mind. I heard my ma screaming in their bedroom. We'd just gotten back from visiting the farm. My old man had stayed back to "look for work," but I was afraid he'd drank what money he had, and knew what he could do to Ma in that condition. I wanted to go to bed, but knew Ma'd expect help. So I barged in on them—all three of them. I had never seen young, bare breasts before, but I knew what they did to men.

"Darling, she don't mean nothing to me," he pleaded with Ma, who went silent when I entered the room, tears streaking down her face. "You know there's no woman for me but you," he flattered her. "It's just the drink and, and, sometimes I feel so lost."

I grabbed his pants and shirt, stuffed them in his hands, then pulled him from the room and pushed him out the door. By the time I got back to the bedroom, the young girl had thrown on her clothes. "Get out!" I said, more calmly than I felt. "And tell him he's never to come back, or I'll kill him." At the time, I was only ten years old. It was the height of the Depression, and the Dust Bowl took away the farm jobs we once had. I hated my old man for being a taker, but deep down I resented Ma equally for what she made me become.

"They move you into action," I hear myself slur, and, with Bernie under one shoulder, I grasp his waist and drag him, half-walking, towards a side street.

We follow Reginald. At a plank-boarded building where loud, arguing soldiers are being calmed by soft-spoken men, we stop. A frail woman—or is it a man?—with bold, red lipstick and thick, fluttering eyelashes, leads us to a solitary cot in a back closet. When I turn around, only the young girl remains. There is something attractive, yet vulgar, about her.

CHAPTER 7

The stink of the room has soaked into the walls and mattress; a single pad on a utilitarian frame hugs the corner of the room. The filaments of the one bare bulb lighting the space dangle from a frayed wire. She confidently takes my hand and leads me to the bed. I kick off my shoes and step onto the cold, sticky concrete floor.

The thumps and moaning on the other side of the decrepit walls make me sick. This isn't a place of romance.

"Why big man always shy?" the girl with the red third eye asks, sitting down on the bed and pulling me towards her. I teeter, then fall less than gracefully on the mattress, getting a coil in my ribs. She giggles as she props me against the wall. For an instant, through my blurred vision, I see both a sweet child and a woman resolved to seduce me. It's not only the discomfort of the bed and whiskey that make me feel ill at ease. Thoughts of Ruthie confront me.

"Your blue eyes like sun-bleached flowers." The girl rearranges loose strands of hair on my forehead. Her soft, massaging fingertips soothe the throbbing at my temples. "Your black hair twist like tail of pig: boing boing," she jokes, but then smiles sympathetically as my inebriated eyelids try to block out the circling room. "And what muscle!" She growls like a kitten while squeezing my biceps, deflated by my liquid dinner.

I feel her methodically rubbing my head and neck. Then she carefully unbuttons my shirt. At this point, I don't care what she does. Someone could be arching a hatchet over my head, and all I would think is: it's a good way to get rid of this headache. I am sweating so much, it feels good to have the soaked t-shirt pulled off. As she rolls me over, the pressure on my gut almost forces my stomach to do a back flip. She sits on the backs of my thighs, stretching her arms long. With the palms of her hands, she pushes up the full length of my back, then her knuckles drag down, opening up tight muscles. I succumb to her strong, kneading fingers. After some time, she stops, and, like an acrobat, slips to the floor. I check to see if she leaves the room, but she stays.

She studies me, calculating. I think about my money, but know I couldn't protect it against a flea in my current state of mind. Squinting at this woman whose mahogany skin and soothing onyx eyes leave me tied by invisible bondage, I give up worrying before I can even start.

Slowly, she unbuttons her blouse, button by button, waiting for me to watch. The cheap yellow cotton slips to the ground. She is no child. Instead of looking ashamed, she closes her eyes and seems to melt as she fondles her firm, flawless breasts. Her nipples harden. I feel a warm, tingling sensation surge through me.

With a look of satisfaction, she unties her loose pants to expose her sinuous curves. The downy hair on her bare legs emphasizes her natural beauty as the cloth slides down her sleek, muscled thighs. My chest feels heavy with desire; blood courses through my veins, ready to burst with the pressure. When I reach out for her, she issues a simple command with the tip of her finger, pushing me back on the bed.

"Such a big, hairy chest," she says to herself more than to me as she releases the dagger- like clasp holding back her glossy black hair. Her fingers snake over my shoulders, down my torso; her long nails dig welts into my skin until she reaches my pants. My heart thumps so loudly in my ears that the noises from the next room disappear.

As she loosens my belt and reaches for my zipper, she lets her breasts rub lightly against my chest, teasing at first, then rubbing hard as she slips her hand into my pants. I smell the perfume in her hair and the musk from her body. "You not slimy and greasy like Japanese," she whispers.

Her words slowly register in my cluttered mind. I'm drunk, but not stupid. "Japanese men?" I ask, hoping she will tell me I heard wrong. I feel sick at the thought that she may be fucking the enemy.

"You no worry." Her breath, sweet and fast, is warm as she begins kissing my body, inch by inch. "GI Joe best. Not like Nip. Aim – fire – dead."

In a moment of alert separation, I realize that under this warm, soft façade is a stranger who I know less about than the GIs at base camp that I've never spoken to. "Where are the Japanese in India?" my foggy mind is shocked into asking. An emergency dose of adrenaline surges through my body.

"No, silly boy. Japanese in Burma. I in Burma last year." Lost in her own performance, she continues her act. "You the best," she licks around my ears. "No one like you."

Like a nail in a tire, all the air of my desire goes out. Her flattery is a screaming siren to me. The room is hot and smelly once more. At an early age, I learned smooth talk and a good heart do not usually come in the same package.

I'm sickened by myself and at this young woman, for she is no child. She carelessly plays her beauty like a winning card.

My longing for her plummets, and I grab her by both shoulders, wishing I could shake the little girl back into this prostitute. Fear wells up in her face, and I feel her muscles tighten as she strains towards her barrette, which now looks like a knife, not a hair clasp.

"How old are you?" I ask gently, searching for a tolerance I can't find. "I forget," she answers, struggling to pull away.

"Don't you care what others think about you?" I hold her wrists tight, knowing her nails are weapons, disappointed in her and—more honestly—in myself.

"You crazy, man? Why you not let me go? I tell you Japanese in Burma, not here. What you want to do to me? You no like the way I look? Maybe I find you boy," her voice is nonchalant, but underlined with tense alertness.

I don't answer.

Her aloof stare, looks for a way out, and leaves me feeling beaten. "Why you care about me?" she asks.

I don't care about her. So why does she make me feel like the sands anchoring my life are slowly eroding away?

"Others no think about me—too important. But men need women. I pretty. What wrong with that?"

"Do you like your life?"

Her expression of irritation surprises me. "What wrong with my life? I happy with myself." She frees herself from my grip, swings around, and ties her hair up in a ponytail. She decides I'm not a threat, after all, and sits back down on the bed. "People believe woman like me weak because I buy pretty clothes, have nice things. They have nothing. Want to hear story that make them good, me bad."

"Aren't you hurt by what others say?" I realize it's not just her I'm asking these questions. "Hurt by what? Words? Words just noise to me." There's a dull grief in her voice.

"Work as pretty girl, or no work. You think it better I sit in street and beg for food? No, I make decision to live with nice things." She gets up and walks toward the door, then turns around and sneers, "Why so many questions for me? Why you not feel guilty 'bout ripping my country apart? Why you not fight in your own country?"

I'm thrown off guard and don't know what to say. Finally I answer, using the party line. "We're fighting for world peace, and the Japanese are here, not in America."

She tilts her head back wistfully and says, "Fight for peace, no make sense." Pulling out a cigarette from my shirt pocket, she lights up, then continues. "War just excuse. Big America kicked in ass by tiny Japan," she taunts. "You hypocrite, no look for peace. No care about people like me. But man who want honor back, you look to settle score." She takes a long drag on the cigarette.

"You think I devil girl?" She spits in disgust. "My only sin is I daughter of poor man." A dirty ray of light filters through the windowless opening above the door, highlighting a scar running the length from her ear to her collar bone. "My mother and father, they sell me to buy food. I dead to them. I cry no more." She looks like a cold, dry, porcelain doll. "Our bad luck make our character. Push us where we must go. It women like me, who not behave, you not forget. It men who listen to heart of enemy who lead us to peace." Then she stubs out her cigarette and pulls me down. "We sleep. Just sleep."

We lie on the lice-infected mattress. I begrudgingly respect her understanding of her limits; her acceptance of her choices, or, really, her lack of them. My eyes focus on a hole in the ceiling, but my mind can't be tied down. Why *are* we fighting here? Is it just self-righteous pride?

I awake before the roosters. The cooled air pricks up and down my exposed arms. As I leave, I mentally trace the outline of her supple body. Doubled over in a fetal position, like folds of silk, her lean legs lay relaxed. Her hair cascades loosely down her back and veils her face.

Like fresh berries, her lips are young and full. The hard life she has ahead of her saddens me. It's the image of her slightly separated lips, sighing in wisps, that I keep as I close the door.

I know I'll never see her again, but she's opened a door that I wish I'd never even knocked on. It's like I've been betrayed by my own beliefs. I always thought of myself as a good person, even though I'm not the most tactful. And I thought I championed all underdogs, until now.

When I reach the outskirts of the sleeping town, halfway to base camp, I realize I am being followed.

"You're going need me to get back into those barracks." Reginald sprints the last few steps to catch me. "And how was your amorous night in Ledo, my man?"

I don't answer.

"I see," he says, his profile a silhouette against the sieve of sunlight pushing up from the horizon. "Passion without the fireworks." We walk on in silence.

CHAPTER 8

February, 1943

"COX BAZAR to TIGAR," the radio screeches.

Charles straightens up and focuses on the transmitting box as though he's talking face to face with COX BAZAR, a British unit stationed in East Bengal. "TIGAR to COX BAZAR, copy."

I wonder if the code name for Ledo, TIGAR, was a deliberate misspelling of tiger to mislead any spy decoding our documents. But really, even with a name like TIGAR, it can't be too hard to place our headquarters in India or Burma.

"Chindits need clothing and food." The English accent on the line sounds self-assured, almost casual.

Charles covers his microphone and whispers out of the side of his mouth, "What a bastard. He's sent his boys out to be slaughtered in central Burma, and it just occurred to him *now* that they'll need supplies?" He suppresses his anger to respond. "Copy, COX BAZAR. Happy to help you out in an emergency. Flying boxcar's ready."

"Thanks, mate. Will send coordinates shortly. COX BAZAR out." The radio buzzes like a swarm of insects.

"You're welcome," Charles says to no one, then takes off his headphones and looks up at the clock, which is hanging on a sagging nail in the bamboo hut. "Harry, be a buddy and help me out by pulling together whatever you've got in the supply depot, like boots and k-rations. These are Wingate's boys, and I don't want those guys to think we're just a bunch of office wimps, letting them take all the fire for us."

"We're building a road, not fighting the war. Wouldn't those boys need more than food and clothes?" I lean back in one of the rattan chairs commandeered by Charles, who has tried to make the radio shack into something more than it is.

Charles grabs my shoulders, pushes me out of the chair, and steers me towards the door. "I know you have a good heart somewhere under that self-righteous veneer. But just get what the man asked for."

An hour later, I hand him the requisition list. "You're a real hero," he says absently before starting his transmission, not noticing my sheet-white face. I just found illicit ammo stored in the stock room. It definitely looks like the start of a smuggling operation, but maybe it's to help the boys flying the HUMP. I want to tell someone, but, unlike me, everyone's a road cheerleader, and only a traitor would dare suggest there's anything more important.

"TIGAR to COX BAZAR." He releases the radio button to receive, then silently reads off the list of supplies. "Whiskey? What the hell do they need whiskey for? The Chindits are conscripts from the Nepalese and Burma rifles. They'd probably do the service for free if you told them they'd get a commendation from the queen." Then he stops, reevaluating his words. "I take that back. There are some Brits in the Chindits. The Liverpool infantry battalion owes you. Good move, Harry."

"I found the stash of whiskey salted away for a VIP rainy day. When will a guy be more important than right before he says adios for his country? Or, in this case, someone else's country."

The radio on the water-stained teak table vibrates with a response. "COX BAZAR to TIGAR, copy."

"COX BAZAR requisition list ready for transport. Do we ship to ROMULUS? Over." Charles can't help showing off that he's on top of all the operations' names.

"Negative." The cool British accent puts out the fire under Charles's victory dance. "LONGCLOTH is en route. Wait for further directions. Over."

Stunned by the news, Charles looks comatose. Then, recovering, he closes out the transmission, "TIGAR to COX BAZAR, copy. Over and out."

Catching Charming Charles in a less-than-charismatic pose is payback for my efforts that day—maybe even for the last week. "Don't worry, Charles. I won't spill the beans that Operation LONGCLOTH slipped past you. By the way, how are they going to get their supplies if they're already marching? Is there a base in Burma where the flying boxcars can deliver the goods?"

Ignoring me, Charles pulls out a set of notebooks and flips through the last few entries. "This isn't normal," he finally shares. "Harry, there's a rumor that Wingate wants his Chindits to use experimental guerrilla tactics in Burma like the ones he used in Africa."

"Wingate?" I ask. "Never heard that name before today."

"He's a Brit. I've been told General Wingate's either batty or brilliant – at some level, it's impossible to tell the difference. They say the guy walks around stark naked while gorging on raw onions hanging from a rope around his neck."

He adds, "In Africa, he sent small columns of men into the desert behind the enemy line, where they sabotaged communication lines and ambushed supplies. Very nasty business: no backup, only air-dropped supplies. Here in the CBI, they'll be in tropical forests with an enemy to fight. And we all know the Japanese are masters at jungle fighting."

After five boring minutes of watching Charles, spellbound in his research, I get up to leave. Just then, the radio crackles: "CHAMPION to TIGAR." Charles, still in a trance, is deaf to the call.

"CHAMPION to TIGAR," an irritated voice repeats.

Charles is totally lost in his cryptic notes. So I hold one of the earphones to my ear and push down on the transmit button, "TIGAR to CHAMPION, copy." Charles isn't the only one who knows how to play with the radio, I tell myself, then realize CHAMPION is Delhi Headquarters. Charles's eyes meet mine.

"Rommel's last stand in Africa. Repeat. Rommel's last stand in Africa. CHAMPION, over and out."

We took down the bastard that killed Joseph Graf; such sweet revenge. "Hitler and his gang of bullies seem to have a hole in their amour." I slap Charles on the back. "And we're about to rip it wide open." Charles glares at me, but I couldn't care less. It's not my fault he was too lazy to do his own work and I had to get the call. It's a powerful feeling, being the bearer of good news.

When I leave, instead of going back to the barracks, I turn towards the supply hut, hoping no one spots me. I've got to find out why there's a new horde of illegal boxes.

Walking between the radio hut and supply depot when it's a part of my regular routine is as natural as breathing; I don't think about it. But now it feels like every clod of dirt I kick up makes me look like I am rushing into trouble. So I slow down. A couple of soldiers by the water spigot seem to watch me too closely. I struggle with my key chain, testing every key as though I'd never opened the door before. Finally, with hands shaking and sweat blurring my vision, the door slips open.

"Hey there," I call out as a precaution. Thankfully, no one answers.

Curiously, several shipments have been separated from the other supplies and purposely mislabeled. I would never have uncovered the diversion, except I knew the ration for Indians was not the same as that for Americans or Chinese, so I opened a few boxes in the corner to make sure I'd grabbed from the right stack for the Chindits. Instead of ration staples, I found Thompson sub-machine guns, Browning Automatic Rifles (BARs), M-1s, colt hand guns, flamethrowers, dynamite, and a wide assortment of knives. No one had to tell me this wasn't a shipping accident. But why was someone deliberately hijacking arms?

I'm torn between exposing this undercover operation and buying in to it, but the perpetrator and I may not be fighting for the same cause.

I decide to see how tight of a tracking system this covert operator has by lifting a few pieces out of each box. I try to deny my fear, but feel myself hyperventilating. My hands work without direction from my consciousness. I deliberately empty my brain and refuse to take responsibility for what I know is wrong. But it looks like no one is minding the store on the CBI front, so I convince myself I should.

In less than ten minutes, I've created a pile by the door that looks more like discarded trash than a horde of arsenal. Dreading the possibility that someone may notice the weapons cache had been uncovered, I reseal the boxes, leaving the arms inventory where it was, in a corner against the back wall.

Then I turn my focus back to finding the right set of boxes and closing up the Chindits' order as fast as my sweaty hands allow. I re-inspect the boxes of staples I had set aside, labeling them Operation LONGCLOTH. With one ear open, I listen to the sounds outside. Scurrying lizards and muffled conversations beyond the basha walls rebuild my fragile confidence. My breathing returns to normal. There is no excitement or suspicion in the voices beyond; they speak as though there could be nothing more boring.

I almost laugh out loud, like a madman. Instead, I reward myself with a thin smile of satisfaction, pleased with my easy deception.

Without warning, I feel the light pressure of five fingers on my shoulder. "What the hell," I barely whisper as I abruptly turn and find Schmidt. His steely grey eyes and curled sneer let me know this is no chance visit. Fortunately, I hadn't thrown an instinctive punch.

Schmidt eyes me with mistrust, his body pulled tight to full attention, leaving me feeling exposed. "You look a little nervous, Lt. Flynn. Is it the heat of the room, or is there something we should talk about that has you sweating like you just signed a contract with the devil?"

"You scared the shit out of me," I complain, then release an involuntary sigh of relief.

Schmidt smiles, thinking he has the upper hand. "Flynn, if you are doing what I think you're doing, you should be petrified."

Remembering it's only Schmidt, I look around the supply room to see if we're alone, then point to the cluster of boxes marked Operation LONGCLOTH. "This order, for the Chindits, has got to go out immediately. Do you mind if I continue with business?" I head over to the boxes, but he doesn't seem satisfied. Neither am I. "By the way, why did you drop by?" I ask.

He waits a moment, deciding whether or not to answer. Then he relaxes and lets the truth be his excuse. "I heard another arms shipment arrived. Came to check it out." His eyes make me feel dirty; guilty without a trial.

"Really?" I keep packing, and my faked surprise sounds authentic. "What'd you find?" He doesn't hesitate: "You."

Why do I feel like I'm hanging, ready to drop into his un-cinched noose?

Instead of crumbling, I gamble my death warrant into a chance to partner with this enemy. "Did you come up empty-handed? Let me know if you want me to keep an eye open for you." My glare shows him I know something, and, as my prime suspect, I'll be tailing him like a hound on a jackrabbit. I say, "Is it possible someone's been shipping arms to help the boys flying the HUMP until—or maybe I should say if—the road ever gets done?"

CHAPTER 9

"Down with Hitler! Down with Hitler!"

Chants erupt, overpowering the crackle from the slowly rolling black and white news reel that announces, "German Operation HERKULES scrapped."

Enlisted soldiers and officers alike crush against each other, elbow to elbow, on benches on the bottom floor of the teahouse to see *Casablanca*. But the deafening response to the news bulletin nearly cancels the showing. "Keep it down, boys, if you want to see more than your own dicks tonight," the projection operator calls out.

In a melodious baritone, the broadcaster excitedly announces, "The Allies have just learned that Operation HERKULES has been terminated. Nearly one-hundred-thousand Axis troops were to storm Malta's limited force of twenty-six-thousand men." The movie shows a backdrop of grounded German DFS-230 assault gliders. "The plans included five-hundred German aircraft and two hundred Italian gliders supported by amphibious craft. The attack on Malta would have blocked the Allies on the North African front and given Rommel unlimited access to military supplies and oil. Fortunately, Rommel siphoned off too many men to support his attack on Egypt, leaving Malta a secondary target. This could be the biggest blunder of the war by Germany and Italy."

"So even the Krauts are incapacitated by their own testosterone," Charles remarks in his understated demeanor.

"That'll teach those perfectionists that they're not as smart as they think they are," Bernie says and clinks beer bottles with Charles.

"You're the experts," I agree, taking a swig of beer while

wondering where we would be if stupid luck hadn't corrected the course set by our so-called intelligence specialists.

Bernie, wiggling his eyebrows in mock Marx Brothers style, says, "Gentlemen, I've had a perfectly lovely evening. But it was another night. Now, would you shut up? The movie's starting."

Instead, another snippet, this time on the CBI Theatre, squeezes in before *Casablanca* can begin. The room goes so quiet it would wake a baby.

"Out on the Orient Front, General Stilwell and his troops are pushing the Ledo Road closer to China." The black and white tape shows a photo of Stilwell with his trademark cigarette holder in hand. "General Joseph W. Stilwell, the U.S. Army's newest four-star general, is as regular and down-to-earth as the scuffed GI shoes he wears when tramping through the jungles. He's no glamour-boy general. He's a tough, frank old army man who hates Japs with an unwavering intensity." The film switches to a photo of Stilwell and a young Punjab Indian. The broadcaster continues, "Dara Singh, a twenty-seven-year-old born in Malaya, is among Stilwell's personal body guards. The young man worships Stilwell."

In the news reel, Singh says, "Stilwell's the grandest man I've known. I'd follow him to the end of the earth."

With that, booing erupts, spreading from one side of the room to the other. By the thinnest of threads, those supporting Stilwell grab control of the grumbling before the undercurrent turns into an outbreak of soldiers slugging it out. To some, Stilwell's the hero they need to convince themselves to charge forward. Others find the General prickly and fractious.

The movie reel slows, and the sound drawls into a low, unintelligible message until it stops. Silence takes control of the room once more, until the Warner Brother credits fill the screen.

Later in the night, we walk back to the barracks, discussing the movie in the freezing night air. "Rick was a gutsy guy," I say of his contempt for the Germans. "'I'm on their black- list...their roll of honor.' But that French policeman, Renault, was a jerk."

"Oh," Charles raises an eyebrow. "He seemed to be the only one who knew it was a game: 'I'm only a poor, corrupt official.' Rick felt too sorry for himself to know when he was being played." Charles' tone suggests his superior intelligence meant he'd never be a Rick.

"Harry, your hero, Rick, wasn't as clever as you think," Bernie chimes in. "And he wasn't exactly a great gambler, either—winning at roulette, but running guns for the wrong guys." Bernie gives me a look, like, "Now, tell me that wasn't stupid."

"The winning side would have paid you much better," Charles's radio voice mimics Renault.

"Besides, Rick was a sucker." Bernie elbows me to get a reaction. In a wimpy, mocking voice, he repeats a line from the movie: "You better hurry. You'll miss that plane." Then he gets serious. "What kind of a guy lets a drop-dead gorgeous woman use him like that?"

I agree with Bernie: beautiful women can make a fool out of a man. But my Ruthie never would. She may look like femme fatale, but she's got substance in the right places. My mind goes back to the day we first met.

Bob's round-roofed Studebaker with its shiny grill and chrome bumpers pulled up in front of the Cotillion box office. The Andrew Sisters harmonized *Boogie Woogie Bugle Boy* on a Victrola. A crowd, all ginned up in their finest threads, milled around outside the ballroom.

Under the yellow bulbs that circle the marquee featuring Tommy Dorsey, a sailor and army private tried to outdo each other, performing jitterbug twists and turns. Seeing the two hoofers, I straightened my double-breasted suit jacket, then hammed-it-up by belting out, "He's the boogie woogie bugle boy from the Company B, toot toot toot." My long arms imitated a trombone player, then I clapped my hands to the syncopated rhythm. God, I love to dance.

Tommy Dorsey's Orchestra started with Opus I. The maestro's brass instrument reached for the sky while the piano player dragged his thumb down the pearly whites. I waited patiently—beer in hand, toes tapping, fingers snapping—but my feet itched to get out on the floor.

As I searched through the crowd, hoping to see someone old or luck upon somebody new, I watched a young lady at the front entrance as she attempted to push her way onto the dance floor. She tried to thread her way beyond two jokers, whose animated conversation blocked her.

First, she backed up, then advanced forward, like she had caught a swinging bar door at the right moment.

After the first song ended, I scanned the crowd for an old girl-friend. But my eyes were drawn back to the entrance where the petite, dark-eyed beauty smoothly pushed on to the parquet floor in her pink, well-fitted suit like she was parting the Red Sea. With a little sway in her hips, heads turned as she sashayed across the floor, heating up the room. And she knew it.

Now, *that's* a woman who can hold her ground, I thought. But can she boogie? My eyes followed the black-haired Sheba to a table of girls along the dance floor. The only way to find out would be to ask. So I opened my suit jacket and casually made a move towards her table. I had previously discovered that if I think twice about talking to a girl, I back out, so I learned to act without thinking.

"Can I ask you to drink or offer you a dance?" I asked. From the girl's bewildered look, I realized I had just tangled my 'come-on' into a double-bend fisherman's knot. Pulling down on my suspenders so hard they almost snapped, I leaned back, then let out a hoot. "I really dance better than I talk. You won't need your combat boots."

One of the girls at the table nudged her out of her seat. "Go on, honey. You deserve a good time. And if we're not here when the music stops, it means we were lucky, too."

The black-eyed Sheba held back for a moment, then tentatively offered her hand as she quietly confided, "Don't worry. I'm wearing steel-toed heels."

And then I'm back to the present, trying to hold my own against Bernie and Charles, who gang up against me. I suggest, "War can change a man. Force him to do things you'd never expect. Like Rick running weapons and being a chump for the enemy. They were probably duds."

"Who? The weapons or the enemy?" Charles jokes.

I listen to Charles and Bernie continue to one-up each other with movie quotes. But the thought of Rick trafficking ammunition nags at the back of my mind. I'm trying to find a likely explanation for the build-up of weapons instead of road equipment in our own supply hut, but the gossip line isn't floating anything yet.

As we huddle against the cold and retrace our steps to the barracks, I shut out the sounds of the night and try to remember yesterday's conversation with Schmidt. I feel like there's something I'm missing.

"Somebody's getting demoted for this," Schmidt warned, jabbing a finger at me.

Other botched orders had come in since Operation LONGCLOTH, but I didn't let on that I knew. This went against everything I'd been taught, but I secretly thought the mistaken swap of ammunition for supply parts brilliant—a way to support the boys flying the HUMP and delay Stilwell's road at the same time. Now, it seems this was no oversight. Someone's actually trying to fight this war rather than build around it.

He checked off the supply list, then flipped through the pages of receipts. We were the only ones in the supply room, and I had that ugly feeling of being contaminated by his presence. I wanted out.

"Shit happens," I said, trying to protect some unidentified chump. "Besides, that road is killing more soldiers than the Japanese. Maybe this mistake is a life saver."

Unfortunately, Schmidt's one of those guys who has a radar for apprehension. He looked up from the paperwork, distrust in his eyes. "Are you suggesting someone may be altering the orders to shut down the road?"

My throat felt dry, and I'm sure my face radiated guilt, even though I'd done nothing wrong. But I knew, without admitting it, that there was something strange going on that was beyond my rank to solve. I turned towards the door, as though I hadn't heard Schmidt, and left without answering.

A red blinking star in the sky pulls me back to talk of *Casablanca*. Up ahead, lighted by a dusting of the Milky Way, Reginald, Earl, and Lester stroll at a relaxed pace. They're too deep in their own conversation to notice we're closing in from behind. I put the troubling thoughts of Schmidt aside.

Hemmed in by looming barracks on both sides, Reginald starts to whistle, and Earl's deep singing voice spreads up through the stark, night air. "You must remember this: a kiss is just a kiss, a sigh is just a sigh. The fundamental things apply as time goes by."

A voice calls out from one of the lightless barracks. "Shut up out there. Some of us gotta work tomorrow."

Bernie gives the anonymous soldier a raised middle finger. It's then that we notice the path is deserted and most of the kerosene lamps in camp are out.

Earl scowls, so I saddle up to him.

"You look like you're itching to kick a cat. Something's on your mind." I say to him. He shakes his head as though nothing's bothering him, then changes his mind, "Harry,

how can those boys back there at the movie criticize Stilwell, an officer who is trying to do good?" In Earl's world, there is a right and a wrong, and he won't ever burden anyone with his misgivings if there's gray in his mind.

"I ain't saying Stilwell is perfect," he confides. "Hell, we all screw up now and again. The only ones who don't slip up are the ones doing nothing at all. But who's born a General? Lordy, he has too much on his mind to do everything right."

"It's a matter of him knowing what will win the war," I say. *And what will get us nowhere*, I don't say.

CHAPTER 10

"Give me a Goddamn D-7," demands a mud-caked equipment driver from the 45th as he bursts into the supply hut. "That puny D-4 I was driving just rolled down a two-hundred-foot drop-off. One of you trying to kill me? We got the enemy picking us off in the field, those blood sucking leeches and mud-floods. Hell, I'm lucky I'm alive. So do me a favor—buy me some time to die and get me a motherfucking D-7."

It's past midnight. The day's inventory count is logged in and coolies wearing baggy dhoti and loose-fitting tunics are loading the stock onto elephants to be transported to the construction site about seventy-five miles northeast of the base. I've been in Ledo four months, and only seventy-nine road miles out of one thousand have been built.

"Boy, calm down," a supply officer drawls. "You think I got a D-7 I'm hiding from you?" The man turns in circles, faking an inspection of the inventory piles.

The sallow-faced equipment driver, fueled with anger, slouches, resigned to being demeaned like so many of the colored soldiers stationed at Ledo. But something is burning in his belly; he cocks his head one last time and spits out, "Get me a D-7, or this road will never get built." Then he stomps out of the supply office.

"Was that a threat?" The officer laughs. "I sure hope it's the first and last time I see that boy, for both our sakes."

With my back to the supply officers, I ignore their harassment and continue to direct the coolies, who patiently wait outside the basha walls. There are too many fronts to fight around here. It seems one war should be enough.

When the others aren't looking, I whisper to the lead coolie, "Is there room for me to hitch a ride?"

The man's dark face is barely visible in the shadows cast by the flickering light bulbs in the supply hut. "Sahib, where you go?" he asks in a sing-song voice.

"I want to see the front—where they're breaking ground for the road," I say as quietly as I can without raising suspicion. "If we get there in five hours, I can be back in time for tomorrow's shift." I listen to the mercurial laughter in the hut over the D-7.

"Sahib, it is cold at the pass, and the rivers have begun to swell from the early monsoon rain. We may not be back in time. It is much nicer here with your sturdy huts and hot food."

I want to puke at the prospect of being trapped in Ledo as the war marches along the road into Burma. I know I'm taking a chance by going to the front without orders, but I'm ready to accept the punishment if it means I can see more than warehouses, barracks, and a typewriter. "I have a warm hat and jacket. I'm ready. When do we leave?"

"This gaja's shipment may depart." The coolie pats the elephant on the rump, then shrugs his shoulders. "I will tell the others you will replace one mahout tonight. You may go now."

I hear the other SOS men closing down for the night. In a hushed voice I say, "Give me five minutes before you leave." Then I make a scene of getting ready to hit the sack, but slip away at the last minute.

Swaying atop a male elephant makes it hard to concentrate on anything but its pungent stench. There is nothing but the black night to draw my attention away. I bob at the nape of the giant mammal's neck, while the goods stored in netting across its back shuffle in sync with each large stride. I stare into the impenetrable forest, hearing more than seeing; coarse foliage rustles.

Unsettling screeches from night birds and muffled animal grunts catch my attention, but neither the elephants nor the coolies take note.

I wind the rope from the elephant's nape around my hand, then nod off, periodically blinking my eyes open to soft murmurs from the Indian mahouts coaxing their elephants to move forward: "Aye ah ha ha." Rising and falling in and out of sleep, I finally awake in a fit. The air has cooled as we climb from four hundred to four thousand feet. Feeling the nip from the night wind, I pull on my hat and thick jacket, hoping we'll see a snowy pass.

Settling into the gaja's rhythm again and listening to the coolies' mesmerizing whispers, my mind wanders. Although there has been little talk of fighting, the war is taking its toll. I laugh to myself at memories of my early, innocent days in Ledo. My grin turns grave, and the price of war sobers me up. I think back to that first night trip into Ledo, returning to the barracks at the early hour of dawn.

That morning, lost in my own self-pity, I had assumed I was alone until Reginald sprinted up to my side. After guessing my night had been passion-filled without fireworks, he said, "Harry, don't get me wrong. I'm like any other red-blooded man. A woman of charm can make me feel like Tarzan. But I got a girl back home. And I do believe the most romantic thing about a relationship is friendship." We had walked most of the way back to the base in silence.

If it wasn't for the days when the road crews from the 45th and the 823rd came into town,

I'd have gone crazy and hung myself with one of those light bulb lines from the thatched roof to get some amusement. Sure, I'm entertained by Charles's radio stories about espionage on the European front and Bernie's disparaging sidebars as he reads letters from back home 'If my family didn't argue, we wouldn't have anything to talk about," he'd say,' but Reginald, Earl and Lester are the natural storytellers. One time, Reginald brought back a shrunken head from a Naga tribesman.

"I went to pee and get a little bit of an unscheduled R&R, you know what I mean?" he asked in his storyteller's voice. "But when I looked up, this butt-naked man—well, except for a cloth wrapped around his cock—was staring at me. He had a string of what I thought were beads around his neck, bracelets on his arms, and a bone tied in his hair. But believe me, that man's masculinity was not in question. Did I mention his legs and arms were tattooed, he had boar tusks in his ears, and he held one of those crescent blades long enough to slice me into bacon?

He looked like a sumo wrestler with muscles; woulda made Superman think twice."

Reginald made eye contact with everyone to check that we were all listening. Then his voice geared up for more of the story.

"Now, I wasn't in the most negotiating of positions, so I decided to be polite and demonstrate my good manners. Still, I had this feeling talking to him in English wouldn't buy me my way back to my dump truck. I was secretly hoping the crew chief would be pissing mad and come looking for me—I'd've rather dealt with him. As my luck would have it, there was a mud slide, and they had to stop work. So no one even knew I was gone." Reginald threw his arms in the air as though he was begging for the sweet Lord's intervention.

"I opened my hands for the naked wrestler to see I didn't have a knife or one of their— daos, you know, those hatchet machete things. But he just kept staring at me. So I checked my pockets, thinking maybe I got a rupee or two to buy me my freedom, but all I found were chili peppers. Every time I go to Ledo, I stock up on peppers. The food here ain't fit to feed a pig, but at least the peppers make it not taste like crap."

Earl twirled his finger for Reginald to speed up the story.

"You should have seen that tribesman's eyes light up, so I gave him a couple of peppers. Like I said, the food here is Godawful, and I was not ready to deprive myself of my only luxury. Then he grabbed me by the arm like he was marching me to the firing squad. He dragged me to his village, bobbing along in a dog trot." Reginald mimicked a loping canine and giggled at his imitation, while flashing a smile as wide as his face.

"Get to the point," Earl pestered.

"Let me paint you a picture of this Naga village," he waved his arm as though, by magic, an invisible movie screen would appear. "We stumbled through that jungle, tripping over knee- high roots and splashing into puddles swarming with insects, me praying there's got to be somebody on my heels ready to save me. But oh no, it was just me and this ugly midget—a mighty muscular one, all painted up like he was going to some fancy Halloween party. You can not," he said, "You can not *imagine* how a man will react when he's dragged into a Naga village."

Earl became very serious. His eyes lit up with questions, especially since we knew the Naga were headhunters.

"This one was fenced with sharp bamboo sticks topped with decorations. It wasn't no Christmas tree lights sprucing up that fence, but heads: shriveled ones, new ones still a little bloody, young and old faces of both men and women. Hell, I messed in my pants right then and there and prayed my fastest prayer, not knowing how much time I had left.

Women with black teeth and naked children snuck out of their huts, blinking at the sunlight like vampires, wondering whether to cook me medium or well-done. But instead of killing me, the decorated wrestler offered to trade me one of his shrunken heads stuck on the bamboo fence for my peppers. They were going to let me live." Reginald got down on his knees and kissed the ground in front of him.

"They think the heads protect them against their enemies, the Sing Pho." He got up off his knees to regain his storytelling pose, "The Sing Pho are the tribe letting us build the road on their land. I'd say the heads scare the shit out of 'em. And there just ain't anybody else out there to fight, except the Nips." Then he slapped his thigh. "Ooh wee, do they hate the Japs!"

Now, this Naga wrestler wanted all my peppers. I thought long and hard, until he pulled out his dao. So I decided I'd take a couple of heads for my peppers, and we'd call it even."

Reginald could tell a tale like a preacher; every yarn was like opening up a new present; it's why he always had a captive audience. Then there are fools like me, who got suckered into picking up the pepper deal with the Naga midget that Reginald started. Each month I make the delivery before they can think about using my head as an ornament on their fence post. But rather than trading peppers for heads, I give the Naga a bag of chilies to stop building their camouflaged pits with poisoned poles on the bottom and to stay away from the construction work. We both think it's a good deal.

Thinking back at how easy it had been to get a blazing smile from Reginald, I let my consciousness fall into that border zone between sleep and reality.

Who knows how much time passed when suddenly the elephant high-steps one leg after the other over a fallen log. I grab the gaja's flabby, wrinkled skin, my upper body rolling off to one side, until the multi-ton monster drops back to an even step. Awkwardly, I pull myself back up on the nape of the five-ton giant. My heart's beating all the way to my palms. I remind myself to pay attention if I don't want to be smashed into an elephant pie. But once we're back to a gentle rocking rhythm, I close my eyes and remember the day Earl came rushing into my basha.

A couple of the other guys had complained. "Hey, no niggers in here."

In my heart, I knew something was beyond wrong. "Fellas, I've got it handled," I said to calm down my bunk mates, then pulled Earl towards my cot.

"It's Reginald," he said as I threw on my pants and slipped into my shoes. We rushed out of the basha. "Those Japanese left booby traps in the road, and it blew him to pieces."

I stopped. My heart thudded like a baseball bat. This was one of Earl's jokes, I hoped, but usually Reginald told the jokes. I didn't trust myself to breathe my next words. "He's dead?"

Tears rolled down Earl's mud-crusted face. "I don't know, Harry."

Although he said nothing else, I heard fear in his voice for the first time ever. That was also the first time I felt the pain of war.

We rushed to the infirmary basha. Reginald wasn't the only one waiting on a stretcher. "Get out of the way or help," one of the doctors yelled as he pushed past me. "We got a live one over here; get him into surgery." Men and women in white shirts rushed anxiously in crazy circles.

They don't know what to do, I thought. This isn't a practice drill; it's the real thing. It's not just bug bites and dysentery.

Reginald lay on a cloth litter with its sides wrapped around two bamboo poles. I grabbed a medic by the collar and forced him over to my friend.

"Hey, Doc." Reginald gave a weak laugh. "They told me back home when I came over here, 'Don't you let those Japs kick your ass, boy.'" He grit his teeth as a shudder wracked his body.

Blood dripped under Reginald's stretcher as they lifted him to a table.

"Well, I kept my promise. They done not kick my ass." Reginald's face softened with sadness. "They done blow it off." His eyes willed Death to reconsider playing his losing card.

I didn't realize I'd dozed off until the elephant's rocking stops. I open my eyes. The chill from the wind that's lashing over the unprotected peak has frozen the tears on my face.

We crest the Pangsau Pass at sunrise, where the colorless, foggy switchbacks are transformed into a pink-fringed horizon. A grove of rustling, lacy pine trees ridge the summit. I shiver, cold and sad. Thick, grey clouds cling to the spine of the snow-capped Himalayas.

Scattered streams groove the thickly forested hillside, then gather at the base of the mountains where a tumbling, gushing river runs.

At the summit, the blustering cold whips through my hair and chews my face. Ahead, a recently posted sign reads: "Welcome to Burma. This way to Tokyo." We're almost to the construction front and halfway to Tagap Hill.

Before I look around for Earl and Lester, I need to understand what compelled me to make this trip. Through my windswept tears, all I see is Reginald's trademark smile. He believed that life was too beautiful to let bullies like Schmidt or Stilwell's Road bring him down. With his death, I truly know: "One man can make a difference."

CHAPTER 11

The road to Tagap Hill hugs a precipitous overhang. As we travel the final few hundred yards to the construction site, I pat the elephant's thick skin, grateful for its large, padded feet on the rain-slicked road. Turbulent water roars below. I lean to one side, trying to catch a glimpse beyond my ride's enormous, flapping ears. When I see the crumbling rock face plunge dangerously down into a virgin valley, I quickly pull back, breathless.

Once we arrive at the site, I slide off the gaja in search of Earl or Lester. The crew has finished eating breakfast, so I decide to look for Earl's famous bulldozer—the one with the bulletproof blade. But first I see an SOS truck parked outside construction headquarters. So I walk over to ask for a lift back to Ledo later in the morning.

"There's room in the back, but I'm leaving in an hour and I won't wait for you," the driver warns, then walks away to finish his business.

So I stomp around in the mucky road, flanked by sturdy ferns and palm fronds, looking for Earl. All around me, the road crew skirts tire gouges as big as small lakes. Carrying freshly skinned logs, the men ignore the tree trunks that dangle above them, rooted in the crumbling, water-soaked hillsides. Woody vines cover the eroded escarpments and tenuously strap the trees in place. I peek over a sheer drop-off where fields of yellow mustard plants bloom downhill.

Further down, in a thick, uninviting tangle of vegetation, tigers, wild elephants, and snakes wait. But our worst enemies are the blood-sucking leeches, malaria-carrying mosquitoes, and typhus mites. Then I hear someone call my name.

"Harry, my man. What the hell you doing here?" Alabama Earl yells good-naturedly across the road bed.

"Looking for the Japanese," I shout back. "I came to see why I was sent to India. Except it looks like the enemy is sleeping the day away." Slipping on the slimy mud, we look for secure footing on the bank side of the road. We step back and watch a truck drop gravel to be spread in the wet sludge. "Where's Lester?" I ask.

Earl points down the road at what looks to be a chain-gang crew throwing pickaxes into the side of the hill. "Last time I saw him, they'd just dumped a load of rock by those fellas." We walk the site looking for Lester, dodging trucks, logs, and dozers. With such chaos, I can see why progress is so slow.

"Have you ever found yourself doing something for the wrong reason, but it turns out to be the right thing to do?" Earl asks, looking ahead at nothing. His soft-spoken manner always surprises me, a contrast to his wrestler's physique and basketball player's height. "I came here to run away from trouble. Yeah." He smiles in that mocking way. "Another name for trouble is the law. I ain't going try to convince you I was innocent. It don't matter no more. But the right thing now is to kill these here Japs like they killed Reginald. And I'm gonna work day and night to get this road built, because we got to win this war. We got to stop the Nips. Or lives— his life— would've been worth nothing."

The engine in the pickup truck—my ride—coughs and belches black exhaust out the tail pipe, as the horn honks. "Damn it. I got to go." I reach out to shake Earl's hand, but something pushes me to also blurt out, "I have no idea what your life was like before the war, but you're a good man. And I expect to see you in Ledo on your next leave, or I'll just assume that gambling debt I owe you is gone."

Earl shakes his head as though he didn't care. "I don't need no leave time. I just want to win this war."

I punch Earl's arm. "Don't go killing yourself by working your life away. You'll be doing the enemy's job for them."

Earl hesitates, then decides to ask: "There's something you *can* do for me, Harry." "Name it."

Earl beams like he's about to ask me to smuggle whiskey out to the site. But instead he says, "Well, I ain't the best at writing. Just something I never thought was important, until now." He looks down and fiddles with his hands like he's trying to clean out a wound.

The pickup honks again. But I wave them off and wait for Earl to finish.

He clears his throat, then asks, "Would you do me a favor and write Reginald's family? It just don't seem right getting a telegram saying, 'Sorry your son's dead. Thanks for raising him, loving him, then sending him to help Uncle Sam. But he's dead, and we got to move on.'"

I can just imagine Reginald dancing around in Earl's mind, and all those times he made this huge black man in front of me red with embarrassment or frustration. "I don't know Reginald's folks," Earl's voice falters. "He was from North Carolina. I'm from Alabama. But let them know he worked like an ox. They'd be mighty proud to see how fine he looked in his uniform. Why, Reginald, he had us laughing until we forgot we was at war."

Choking at the thought that Reginald will never go home, my words get trapped. So I nod my head. Earl climbs into the bulldozer and starts the engine.

On the return trip to base camp, we backtrack along the slimy, serpentine trail. As we drop in elevation, wild orchids sway on tree limbs, and the brisk air pulses with songbirds' warbling. Alone, bouncing in the bed of the truck, I consider what I'll write in the first of many letters; this will be the only one to Reginald's family.

We are sincerely sorry for your loss. Your son was like our brother. Reginald would not allow us to surrender to despair and reminded us to look for joy in every corner of each day. We are proud to have served with him and will honor his memory in how we live our lives. Reginald was buried in the Himalayan foothills, shaded by a giant Halong tree. He died with a photo of his family in his breast pocket.

Iridescent blue butterflies, bathed in the filtering dawn, spiral on air currents, then drift aimlessly, finally alighting in bamboo thickets. The truck slides sideways, then rights itself, around every curve. The warmth of the morning and the heat I know I will get from Schmidt is settling in. But nothing can thaw this mounting, irrational notion that the big boys are only playing a game of marbles, each taking turns with the steely, picking off one country after another.

Why am I the only one to see that Stilwell doesn't give a damn about any of us? He wants his road built at any cost, including Reginald's life; maybe even mine. Earl, Bernie, Lester, and Charles have all been brainwashed with rah rah rah for the stars and stripes, but I've become jaded. Still, I'm afraid to stand up against the likes of Stilwell. I could lose everything, and everyone I care about could be hurt. But I'm starting to wonder whether I have any other choice.

"Life may not be fair, but I'm going to beat the shit out of anyone who tries to take it from me or my friends." My words dissipate in the tropical subcontinent air; far from home.

The lighthearted laughter of schoolchildren erupts as the truck bounces into Ledo. The boys and girls squeal in delight as they slip away from our barreling pickup. The thought that had been refusing to surface is rupturing. Stilwell's senselessly getting men killed building his road to nowhere. Someone's got to blown it up. Hell, I've got the arsenal. Guess that someone is me.

CHAPTER 12

"Flynn!" a crisp, decisive voice barks. "Where the hell've you been?"

From India's eastern horizon, the intense sun starts its rise. Through squinting eyes, I see Schmidt, hands on his hips and extremely pissed off.

Jumping from the bed of the truck, I adjust to a full salute. "Escorted supplies to field site, Sir." I say with little enthusiasm. I hate the chain of command kiss-ass routine, especially when it comes to Schmidt. If he wants another excuse, then he's out of luck.

"Escorted?" Schmidt, who has no interest in men at the construction site other than making sure they receive their supplies bellows. "What kind of a jackass needs to show coolies how to do their job?"

"In my humble opinion, I thought a first-hand observation of the site conditions would help me—uh, us—understand where the supplies are going, including any illicit arms." I add, "Sir."

"Flynn, you wouldn't log in the extra hours just for that. There's something you want to tell me?" Schmidt's voice is thick with disbelief. "I'd hate to see where they'd have sentenced you if Stilwell found out you'd hijacked an elephant for a joy ride up and down the mountain. You don't think Ledo's hell enough?"

I take a different tactic and remind Schmidt of our little secret. "Didn't we agree to work together to track down those," I cough to show my discretion, "misdirected orders, Sir?"

The stash of confiscated ammo comes to mind. I still haven't devised an inconspicuous way to get back into the supply hut so I can find out who really is diverting ammo instead of supplies to Ledo.

Visualizing the abandoned vehicles that have slipped off the road by the Pangsau Pass from this morning's "joy ride" I add, "It's a burial ground out there. They just ditch equipment over the side when they don't get replacement parts. Don't you want to know why your orders are getting screwed up? Won't it reflect poorly on you if you don't?"

Schmidt scratches his head as though an answer will loosen up. "You're right," he concedes, begrudging our accidental partnership. He tries to take control of the conversation. "We're nothing but a forgotten front—the stepchild. No one listens when I tell them the vehicles shipped to the CBI theatre don't work here. The humidity's rusting the crap out of everything.

And they're sending all the spare parts to Europe." He curls his lip, then adds, "They're setting us up to fail."

"So now aren't you happy to see me, Schmidt?" I follow him as he tries to escape the unwritten contract he just metaphorically signed. "I'm trying to help you."

"Let's just say *happy's* not a word I'd associate with you, Flynn." Schmidt glares at me with a resigned acceptance.

I keep pace with him, loving his discomfort. "At the Pass it looks like a mudslide carried the whole fleet downhill."

"So I've been told." Schmidt walks swiftly towards the mess hall for breakfast, arms swaying in sync with his rapid pace as he tries to leave me behind. "The road's not going to get done if this continues." He stops abruptly, then asks pointedly, "Does that bother you, Flynn?"

I don't trust Schmidt. He hasn't shown all his cards, and his interest in the ammo doesn't seem to have anything to do with the road crew. The sorry sucker who's smuggling the ammo instead of ordering supplies will not be popular on base, especially if he's trying to sabotage the road. Schmidt will decorate the base with posters of him. And without lifting another finger, the men will quarter the traitor into pieces that are so small even an ant would need glasses to see them. That guy's going to pray for the fastest ticket to hell. I wince at the thought of being caught with my little stash.

"Until that road's built, our boys out of Barrackpore need to keep flying The HUMP." Schmidt checks the skies like he expects a plane to fly over any minute. "They've got to be crazy to take planes over those peaks since they could be chased by Jap fighter pilots or sucked in by windstorms during the monsoon. But," Schmidt sneers, "someone's got to get those supplies to Kunming, or else our deal with Chiang Kai-shek is off and *we'll* be the ones fighting the Japs in China."

"Why does China need our boys flying the HUMP or a new road?" I ask. "What've they ever done for us that we should be losing lives for them?"

"Ask the Chinese. Their 10th Regiment is being flown in next week."

"I'm asking you." For once I can pull some useful information out of Schmidt.

"The Japanese occupy China's ocean ports, and they've blocked the land route to India. If the Japanese keep moving west and connect the Axis Power's Pacific front with the Atlantic, the Allies may as well give up. *That's* why China's problems are ours." He looks at me like he shouldn't have to educate me on world politics.

"Stilwell asks 'How high?' when Generalissimo says 'Jump.' Until the road's built, our boys will keep delivering supplies over the HUMP. And they'll be no more than target practice for the slant-eyed Nips out of Myitkyina." Schmidt leaves abruptly, ending our conversation.

I don't let my conscious wonder if I'd be issuing a death warrant for the boys flying the HUMP if I blew up the road. I feel justified in my actions, knowing the thing our fly boys really need is more help from our fighter pilots.

Overhead, clouds move in quickly. I hurry over to the communications shed, hoping to find Charles.

With only one foot across the basha threshold, I hear, "Harry, you're just in time." Charles pulls off his earphones, then points to the radio, indicating I should take over for him. "Duty calls, if you know what I mean."

Charles rushes out of the shed faster than an iceberg melts in the Sahara, leaving me to wonder what to expect. I plop in Charles' chair, look for one of the girly magazines he has stashed in a secret spot, then lay back. The radio erupts in static.

"COX BAZAR to TIGAR," a barely audible, frantic voice calls out.

I put the headphones on, realizing this is probably not a routine call. "TIGAR to COX BAZAR , copy," I answer.

Relief spills through the radio waves, "Operation LONGCLOTH needs immediate drop. Downpour of Kawasaki blocking glider touchdown. Need FLYING BOXCAR at Indaw. Over."

I know the objective of Operation LONGCLOTH is to demolish the Japanese rail lines and ammo depots in central Burma. It's supposed to confuse the enemy and prevent them from attacking our construction work. With knees jiggling, I close my eyes and ask myself whether we should help LONGCLOTH now or stall Stilwell's road and redirect support to the HUMP. Choosing between one life and another is a decision that should not be left to any one man. But the thought of our boys either being bulleted out of the sky while flying over the Himalayas, or leaving the Chindits mired in the jungle with at least a fighting chance helps me make my decision. Eventually I answer, "COX BAZAR. NEGATIVE. No BOXCARS. Over and out."

Then I hear Charles: "HELL, Harry. Are you crazy? Indaw's behind enemy lines. Are you trying to get the Brits killed?"

CHAPTER 13

Earlier in the week, when the 10th arrived, I stared at them, not sure if I should trust my eyes. I'd never seen a more sorry-looking unit. Some wore remnants of uniforms with no country insignia. Others looked like they were plucked straight from the rice paddies and would feel more at home harnessing a water buffalo than carrying a rifle. Surprisingly, only every third Chinese soldier carried a weapon.

Chiang Kai-shek, Generalissimo, had sent them to protect the advancing road crews. But shortly after they arrived, they were diverted to construction work where they clear mud slides, knock out four-wheel-drive trails, and build temporary log bridges. They do as commanded without question, but boy, can they eat! Their gaunt bodies can put on an extra twenty pounds in a month. No one, except me, begrudges them a single crumb. Only I find the road a threat, and recognize that without the Chinese helping out, the road effort would be at a stalemate.

Leaning against a pole supporting the tin awning we call the fleet garage, I watch in wide-eyed amazement as the Chinese soldiers load field supplies into overflowing bamboo baskets balanced on bians or shoulder poles. They're moving to the construction front, and I'll be following them shortly. Bernie, busy in his element, slides under the bellies of trucks perched on well-used hoists, then sticks his neck deep under the hood to check greasy casings, oblivious to anything else. The hand with the stubby finger grabs the fender, and he pulls himself out.

"If my Uncle Eddie could find anyone who'd work like these Chinese, I'd be out of a job during the harvest season," I tell Bernie, who now leans over the hood, and, having just released a clamp without being electrocuted, raises a questioning eyebrow without answering. He drops the cables to grab a different hand tool and ignores me.

At the mention of the farm, I reminisce about the harvest moon rising early in the evening and the taste of salty beer at the end of the day. It brings back good and bad memories.

Uncle Eddie, my ma's brother, who now owns the family farm, was more like a father to me than my old man. Every time I'd leave the city to help out during harvest, I'd try to imagine my Uncle Eddie, Ma, and old man growing up in that Podunk town, the place where I was born. My ma and old man met because he was pals with Uncle Eddie, but how could they've ever been buddies? They had nothing in common. I guess my uncle, a take-charge kind of guy, made my old man look good by telling him what to do and letting others think he had his act together.

And my old man, good-looking and full of stories, just reeled in the women, which is why the other guys liked having him around. Unfortunately, Ma was one of the fish he caught. She was a plain farm girl and he was filled with dreams. When she got pregnant, her older-brother, Uncle Eddie, saw only one solution.

I turn my attention back to Bernie as he swipes the sweat that's beaded up on his forehead. Finally, he answers, "The Chinese aren't the only ones who work hard." He sticks his head back under the hood of the next Jeep, twirls the wrench like it's a baton, then pulls out and slams down the hood. Eventually, he grabs a rag and tries to scrape off the black smears that cover his hands. He takes his time examining his nails for remnant smudges before he hesitantly asks, "Harry, is it true what I heard?"

The procession of Chinese soldiers continues to march by, bians sagging across their shoulders. "Could be," I answer without really hearing him, still thinking about the farm. I watch the 10th as they passively set pace along the newly built portion of road towards the construction front. I'm not sure if I admire their blind dedication or feel sorry for them.

It poured rain only a couple hours earlier, and the paths around the barracks are like pig sties. Bernie and I walk over to the water spigot to wash off the clammy sweat from the smothering humidity. I replay Bernie's question in my mind a second time. "What are you talking about? Is what true?" I ask.

"You leaving," Bernie turns the faucet off and shakes the water from his soaked crew cut, but doesn't look at me.

My transfer orders arrived only the night before. Schmidt told me if someone was trying to sabotage the supply system, he needed help out on the front to track the arrivals and find out where they were going. So I'm his man. This is also my chance to transport the ammo supply I've built up to blow the road to smithereens before we lose any more men on the "road to nowhere." Bernie and Charles are my closest buddies in Ledo. Not telling them when I got my orders is probably my way of not admitting our differences.

"Yeah," I answer, hoping someday he'll understand that a man's got to be true to his beliefs, or he's no man at all.

When I loaded the supply truck the night before, I was scared shitless. Labeled as cleaning supplies, my ammo went unnoticed. The boxes were plausible, though; they will sanitize the road.

Bernie gives me "Do I even know you?" kind of look. "What's come over you, Harry?

Whose side are you on, anyway?" Bernie's not one to be fooled. He may not have the brains of a surgeon, but he's been on the street and can read people. It's a skill he had to learn if he wanted to survive back home. I should know; we're a lot alike that way.

"The right side," I say, and hope it's true.

Bernie slaps me on the back, purposely leaving a permanent black handprint on my shirt. "Then this is it, Harry," he says. "Charles is on radio duty. He says to wish you good luck and keep him informed. Not sure what he thinks you're going to tell him when you can't even say goodbye." We shake hands, then he walks away.

Doing the right thing doesn't always feel good.

CHAPTER 14

I roll up the CBI newspaper, *Roundup*. It's April, 1943, and Stilwell's Road doesn't even make the back page. The road crew has advanced only one mile in one month, but that doesn't mean it's been slow at the construction front. Schmidt dropped me in the middle of nonstop confusion here at Road Headquarters, and it's hard enough to keep track of your own shoes, let alone trace any illegal ammo. Unexpectedly, the one thing that's a constant is Nazir, the Naga headhunter, and his monthly ration of chilies.

I had been on the road front for less than a week when he found me. One minute I was alone, checking to see if there were any new equipment carcasses in the graveyard, and the next I turned to find Nazir with a rope bag of blue-throated barbets slung over his shoulder.

"Why you no bring peppers?" he asked, legs rigid and rooted to the ground like tree trunks.

No one can get my hands shaking faster than Nazir. "How did you find me?" As soon as the words were out of my mouth, I knew it sounded like I was running from him. "I mean, I was just transferred here and haven't had time. So I was planning on doing it later."

The relief on his face said he didn't want my head decorating his fence post. "I wait here while you get peppers." I found myself nodding and backing away, almost in a run.

When I returned, Nazir had already started to pluck feathers from and gut some of the birds. He sat on a boulder at the edge of the road, entrails intermixed with blue, red, and green feathers at his feet. I had never noticed before, but with his boar-tusk earrings and tattooed arms and legs, he blended into the jungle better than a shadow.

"You couldn't wait?" I asked, handing him the bag.

He took the peppers and inspected them. "You move away. Need take longer path to find you. Make me late. So I fix birds be ready to cook. Birds no good with no peppers." He stood to leave. "Harry come visit village. Children ask to play with white man who act like little boy."

Nazir has become a part of my monthly routine and not the most unpleasant part of life on the front. The sixteen-hour shifts are enough to shatter anyone's will. I push my way out of the barracks into a drizzling morning. Rain splashes mud against my already-damp clothes. I pass a soldier who stops, reaches down into his pants, and wrenches out a blood-dripping leech. Pissed at the mud, the rain, and the leeches, and now wondering if Schmidt got me out of Ledo to frame me, I stomp through puddles looking for Lt. Lin. I feel the tension in my neck with every step.

Off in the jungle, quarrelling birds skitter about in the undergrowth, taking advantage of the light sprinkle. They'll probably be glad when we give them back their forest. I search for Lin as I walk past the Chinese road crew. Their broad, triangular, straw hats rise and fall in rhythm with picks and axes. One man, taller than the rest, stands with his hands at his sides. His jet- black hair is rain-slicked to his skull, and his legs are spread apart to secure his footing in the mud. His voice grates in response to a younger man, who reluctantly lifts a sledgehammer and looks back with sullen disinterest. Without even knowing the language, I understand their one- upmanship pattern of quarrels. Unlike with the Americans, where clashes became a nose-to-nose, chest-to-chest act of defiance, Chinese use incessant nagging to wear down their rivals.

Further down the road, I hear, "Damn it! Get the fuckin' dynamite wedged in tight before you blow it." Lester calls over his shoulder as he and several men scramble towards the detonation box and away from a bulging boulder, ready to be blown to smithereens, that blocks the road passage. The dynamite drops from the rock ledge, sinks into the mud, splutters, then dies. The men tip-toe back to the dead dynamite, sinking to their knees in the sludge and mud.

"Maaaaaaan, if you got a better way," the soldier shivers, "show me how you'd do it. I'm just lookin' to serve my time here and go home alive." Lester shrugs, rolls his eyes, and plucks the dynamite from the mud soup. He's looking in my direction, but doesn't see me when I wave.

Putting one foot in front of each other each day is the only way to keep your sanity out here. If you could go backwards in time, you'd wish you could re-live your worst day before the war rather than face this endless future.

I look away, knowing at least one of the men in Lester's unit will soon be left behind. At the current rate, we're losing a man a mile to malaria, typhus, and the crumbling, waterlogged mountain slides. The number one assassins—mosquitoes, mites and mud— never take a break. There's so much senseless death. I wish I could follow the popular path rather than question the Stilwells of the world; it's so much easier to follow blindly. But I'm not going to go quietly.

No one knows that I'm stockpiling an arsenal of explosives. It gives me a sense of some control in my life. My stash grows each time another shipment of dynamite is delivered for the road crew. It shouldn't be hard to place the dynamite at night so it won't hurt the crew, but will wash out the road. I hope it's enough to make Stilwell give up building this impossible road.

I trudge towards the supply hut, leaving the road crews behind, expecting to run into Lin. Along the road, trees rise hundreds of feet, and a dense undergrowth of palms and vines form a tangled green barrier, making it difficult to see the sky. I look up through the network of branches, hoping to see blue patches. Instead, I find dark, heavy clouds. Frustrated, I crunch the incomplete requisition list into a ball, ready to toss it in to the brush.

It's then I see the tiger, with bold black stripes and golden fur, only a few feet from the edge of the road. My breath is sucked out of me; I'm fascinated and scared shitless.

Remembering what a man dismembered by a tiger looks like paralyzes me, and I'm not sure if I should run or freeze.

He sees I'm his only audience. I watch the thickly muscled, golden predator bat an unsuspecting trogon from a lower branch. The bird's turquoise wings flail as the giant cat stuffs them between his immense white fangs. Satisfied, the cat slips away.

Lightening, obscured by the clouds, flickers; it's followed by muffled, then crashing, thunder. Moments later, I hear scampering in the brush. Small rodents and dusty green birds rush for shelter under clusters of broad leaves to wait out the imminent deluge. Avoiding the ravine on my left side where trucks have lost the battle to the muddy mountain, I pick up my pace. With my crumpled wish list in hand, I duck my head into the small, leaky basha used for road headquarters to wire that day's requests to Base Section Three, Ledo headquarters. Lt. Lin is waiting inside, not late like usual.

Pissed at myself for wasting my time looking for Lin just so I don't have to place two orders, I recklessly grab the headphones for the radio. The gentle, polite nature of Lieutenant Lin Tien-Kuo hasn't blinded me to his sly ways. Every day he wants something new, right after the day's orders have been sent. Yesterday afternoon, he cornered me in my basha. Outside, the rain drove down like bullets, but he needled me into action.

"Lt. Flynn." Lin started, like always, with his goddamn bow. "Men with no jacket in rain, no help to road if dead." His gaze concentrated on the tears in his boots, exposing his dark, leathered skin. I felt no pity for him. He knows how to get what he wants and plays his part well. "Elephants leave Ledo in one hour. Radio talk with Ledo take only five minutes. Jackets here tomorrow if radio talk now."

Like any good officer, Lin takes care of his men and wheedles away their opposition by handing out tokens of goodwill, be they bigger servings of rations or better clothing. I admit the Chinese are hard workers, but their bickering is like a static transmission that you can't tune out, and it drives me up one side then down the other.

Rainwater puddles at my feet. "ROAD HEADQUARTERS to TIGAR," the radio squawks as I push down the transmit button.

"TIGAR to ROAD HEADQUARTERS," comes back the fuzzy response, crackling from interference caused by the weather. "Ready to receive."

When my transmission is almost complete I reluctantly reach out for the paper Lin waves for my attention. "Just a few more items," I warn base camp, then release the transmit button and glance over his scribbles. "Carrots? Onions? Peas? Out here?" Rolling my eyes, I let the sarcasm ooze with each word.

"Yes, most honorable Lt. Flynn." Lin's face shows no sign of emotion. "Chinese eat vegetables. Americans like meat. Chinese get sick from only meat."

I say nothing, letting the drip drop of the leaking rain express my thoughts. "If you get fresh vegetables, then I'm asking for whiskey," I say to him. Then I turn back to the radio and punch down on the transmit button. "Send me all the vegetables you got for the 10th Regiment. Our men want Jack Daniel's. ROAD HEADQUARTERS out."

The radio squeals a high pitch buzz, "ROAD HEADQUAR-TERS. Can do on vegetables.

Jack Daniel's? In your dreams. TIGAR out."

"I'll be damned." I toss Lin's list across the table in frustration. "When I ask for simple things, like axle grease, carburetors, and bread, what do I get? Shovels and noodles. You ask for vegetables and you'll probably get a shitload of every color." I lean against the radio table and light a cigarette. I don't offer one to Lin. After releasing a long drag, I spit out, "What makes you so special?"

Lin looks straight ahead, beyond me, as though I'm not there. He offers no apology. I notice the elbows in his jacket are worn thin, making it hard to believe he's an officer. "I ask for what can be had," he says.

I flick ashes on the wet floor. "Hmm!" I grunt, take another drag, pinch out the cigarette's fire, and pocket the butt. "Why should we build a road for you if you won't even fight your own goddamn war?" Unloading on Lin for his underhanded ways feels good.

Lin's jaw is rigid. A stern glare is his only response.

This infuriates me further. "How come our boys are dying for you here in Burma? Can't you and the Japanese fight your own battle and keep us out of it? If it wasn't for China, we wouldn't even be here."

Without remorse or incrimination, Lin speaks quietly, "If Japanese not kill in China, then Japanese kill in Australia. Kill in Philippines. Kill in United States." Lin bows, which I see he uses to define his strength, not subservience. When he looks up, he says, "Where Japanese troops be now if not battle China? Japanese hate of Chinese blind them to bigger treasures in Australia and America. We not give all our soldiers in Burma. We fight in China, too. Protect our children, our women. While Chinese families die, America homes are safe."

CHAPTER 15

The other day, my explosives ripped out a couple more culvert pipes. Brown washouts fanned the road. I should've been happy, but in the back of my mind, I kept wondering whether blowing up the road would stop Stilwell or if his stubbornness would just push the men harder.

As I leave my temporary barracks—a leaking bamboo hut holier than a Bible—I notice the leaves overhead in the towering jungle act like funnels, channeling rain in but blocking out the sun. Forget about having clean, dry clothes. Like a thirsty straw, the hems of my pant legs stay soaking wet from the ponds of water in the rutted road. It seems senseless to change clothes every day since washing off the mud is about as effective as scraping tar off a fender.

A growing rumble shakes the ground. But when I look up, I am surprised to see a bleached-blue break in the clouds and no lightning. Then, like a stampeding herd of cattle, the construction crew runs towards me from the gully around the bend. They pass me without a word, sprinting toward the barracks. Chinese soldiers carrying logs drop them in place, not looking back. Trees on the hillside sway as pebbles and dirt sift out from cracks in the earth. Another mud slide.

The supply hut is just on the other side of the ravine. I want to get there before my shift starts to see if my order for ammo was discovered in the night. If anyone thought I was smuggling ammo to the road site I'd just deny it, anyway. "Get out of my way," I shout as men rush towards me from all directions. "You're afraid of a little washout?"

Everyone's seen slides before. Most of the erosion stops up in the narrows of the canyon.

But sometimes new valleys are gouged into the hillside, laying to waste work that takes hours upon days to rebuild.

"You Goddamn fool," one man screams at me. "The whole hill's washing away." Hesitating to take a second look, I shrug my shoulders as though everyone is overreacting but me.

As I continue to move forward, he looks at me incredulously, then starts running in the opposite direction.

Within less than five steps, the sound of tree trunks snapping cuts through the air.

Vegetation is ripped from its roots by an invisible giant. The earth splits open. Out of the mouth of the gorge, a gurgling waterfall explodes. Fragments of fractured stone fly in every direction while a cascade of rocks tumble. Ten-foot-tall boulders, Neanderthal giants, soar like freed birds, demolishing the road bed as they bounce down the eroding hillside. A runaway boulder, dead ahead, bounces towards me, smashing trees, shaking the earth, and throwing up lifeless chunks of dirt. I turn, but it's too late. The ground crumbles under my feet.

A terrified face, drenched in muck, screams soundlessly nearby as the rock kicks him off his feet and flings him into the mud flow with the rest of the debris in the quagmire. A shower of rocks and mud sprays over me. I wait for the thumping, ripping, and rattling to stop, but more weight piles on top of me.

I cup an opening around my mouth, creating an air pocket so I can breathe. Rocks pound all around me on their way down the hill. I strain every sense, listening to tree roots as they're sucked from the earth. Every neuron in my fingertips is charged, wanting to connect to something solid. But, blind with claustrophobia, I do nothing.

The ground around me finally stills, but I can still hear the muffled static of shifting earth nearby. Viscous fluid has filled every opening around me. I force my muscles to move, but nothing budges. How deep am I buried? If I live—no, no, no; I will live. I will...I will. But my mind races forward, and I see the worst. I slide in and out of panicked unconsciousness.

In front of the stove, my mother looks over a steaming pot. I'm standing in the doorway. "Ah, sure, lad. Truth be known, you've not been dealt a royal flush. But seeing as you've got what you got, you're to be smart when playing those cards." Then she walks away. Wait, I need help, I think. Can't you see how hard it is to be strong all the time?

Then Bob tosses me the football. He says, "Harry, there are two kinds of people in life." I run deep, then curl in on a hook pattern.

I catch the ball, then sprint back. "Yeah: those who want to win, and those who want you to win for them."

Bob gives the field a hard eye, then says, "No—those who make promises, and those who keep them." He throws a long pass.

I want to ask Bob, Aren't I keeping my promise now? Aren't I saving lives? But he looks away, disappointed. I'm crushed.

Next, it's Ruthie's sweet face searching mine with a puzzled look. I say, "You know, you can tell a lot about a person when you first meet them…maybe more than what you know about someone you've known for years." We're dancing a slow, close number. She smells like Palmolive soap. "You're curious about a stranger, so you study them. Then, voila, you get what you see."

I find her plucky disregard for hoity-toity airs a breath of fresh air. "On the other hand, you think you know your buddies as well as you know your own social security number. Like, what kind of dame turns their head. So when they do something screwy, you do a gut check and ask: Do I really know that guy?" I don't know why I'm telling her all this, but it's bothering me that my buddies think I'm a daredevil with nine lives and expect me to go to the front when I'll only be sharpening pencils. She waits for an explanation.

Maybe the truth is, *I'm* not the guy I think I am. "The mistake is, you see what you want," I finish.

Ruthie wraps her hand around my neck. "That's only a problem if you don't like what you see. Now, what can you tell about me?" she asks.

"First, I know you're a hard worker." I open her hands to look at her calloused palms. "You don't get these by sitting on your duff all day." She tries to pull her hand back, but I hold firm. "And you only spend your money on necessities."

Her face flushes. "You mean I don't buy hand cream," she says, unable to hide the hurt in her voice.

"No cream, no make-up, no perfume. Because you don't need it." We stop dancing, and I grasp her hands with both of mine. Her high cheekbones tighten as anger swells in her eyes, but what I say next softens her again. "I'm dancing with the sweetest girl in the ballroom, who's as pretty as a sunny morning at Fenway Park on opening day."

I feel Ruthie slide the back of her hand along my cheek. At first, it calms me. I had forgotten how she made me feel confident. But I slowly come to, alone and scared.

Muddy grit seeps into my eyes, so I clench them shut until flashes of white streak behind my eyelids. I feel each molecule of my body being flattened, slowly, pore by pore. I want to open my mouth to inhale big gulps of air, but the force on my body is crushing me.

In this lightless tomb, I remember my father cupping my face between his palms. "My spitting image. Like father, like son." Flattery was his good luck charm. But goddamn it, it's not mine. My anger explodes. I'm not like you, and never will be, I yell at him in my mind.

I start churning like a washing machine. Within seconds, the taste of gravelly mud in my nose and mouth intensifies. It takes all my energy, and I lose my air pocket. I twist and rock, twist and rock, pull my knees towards my chest, hunch my shoulders and thrust out like an exploding volcano. But I sink deeper. There's no air in my lungs. I'm swallowing mud, drowning in mud. No, I silently scream. I won't give up. I'll never give up.

Then, layers of mud seem to slide away. A breeze tickles the hairs on my arm. My thoughts waver between blackness and nothing. Calm yourself; easy now, easy now. It feels like someone is grabbing my ankles and crushing my bones, but my heel is probably just wedged between two rocks. Then there's the sensation that my body is being sucked out, feet first.

Instinctively, I try to say something, but muddy gravel totally fills my mouth. I'm suffocating and going crazy with the loss of oxygen. My eyelids feel like sandpaper. "Damn it; now's not the time to lie down and die," I tell myself. So I start twisting back and forth again like a rotary blender. My closed eyes see light, electric signals from my brain. Or, maybe…

Daylight! Air! My body is dragged up, slow at first, then faster. I spit out mud. I'm trembling and my eyes are blinded. Tears of relief well up, but the mud jams my ducts. I blink and blink. Then shades of light break through the blackness.

"Nasty time to be taking a break." I hear Lester's deep, familiar voice. A blurry Earl and Lester drop my legs. Their biceps, slicked with sweat, are bulging with exertion. "You ain't settin' a good example as an officer." Lester stretches out an arm and pulls me to my shaky feet.

"I thought being buried alive and walking away would be one hell of an act to follow," I say before I stagger and drop back to the ground. A visceral hatred of Stilwell and his damn road penetrates every nerve in my body. I vow that this road is not going to kill me. Then I vomit.

CHAPTER 16

June, 1943

Life went back to normal—if that's what you want to call it—after the slide. It's a war zone around here, but we've only battled the weather.

The sky is thick with rain clouds, making the jungle smell like an old, musty cellar.

Construction has come to a halt except for a last-ditch effort to save what's already built. Most of the road crew was sent back to base camp knowing the monsoon season will win. Earl and I are on clean up duty.

"Well if it ain't my man," he shouts, as he slides out of his bulldozer. "What gifts of glad tidings is Harry boy bringing me today?"

"Not what you're expecting," I answer. "There's to be a little VIP visit from Colonel Merrill. You know the name?"

"Yessiree, do I know that name," Earl answers. "They say he's Mr. slick-as-ice. You don't get to be a colonel at his age with just luck."

This visit from Merrill is about as welcome as a hangover. Last night I inventoried my stash of explosives and ammo. I was tired, so I just threw a tarp over the boxes instead of packaging them. Now I have to worry about Merrill snooping around. We talk on our way to the mess hall.

"Now don't go bullshitting me that someone like Merrill is here because he cares," Earl gripes.

"Probably wants to know why Stilwell's Road's not done.

Rumor has it we'll be gearing up to push the road to Hukawng Valley by January."

"Hell," Earl punches a fist into thin air. "I hope that man's as smart as they say he is. We're moving mountains out here. In the states it'd be like building a dirt wall ten feet high, from Frisco to New York. Someone plumb forgot his brains if he thinks we'll be that far by January."

Monkeys in the overhanging branches howl and screech nervously, tossing their stinky durian fruit onto our path. "Some day I'm going to get my hands on one of those pesky critters." Earl watches them swing away in search of cover as the sky opens in a thick downpour. We stop talking and hurry to the mess hall basha.

Dodging the rain water dripping down from the poorly thatched roof, we slide into a corner table. Earl props his elbows on the table and clenches his hands together, looking weary.

"Lester Jones done get hauled back to base camp by the porters yesterday. He got the fever real bad. It was mighty painful watching him drag himself out of bed each day. He'd just take his time, real slow, like he was letting the day move him along. Then one day, he dropped to the ground; his eyes went swimming in the back of his head. He was so hot with fever it done steal the cold out my hand."

Earl sighs, resignation plastered all over his face. "Harry, I been thinking. You did such a fine job writing that letter for Reginald's family. Well, I may be asking you for another favor soon." He waits, then adds, "I'm going to do everything it takes to get this road built for men like Reginald, and I pray the Lord spares Lester."

Outside, the warm monsoon rains pour down like it's been building up for weeks. Inside, I'm torn. Earl's dedication to building Stilwell's Road is as great as my determination to destroy it. How many men will die if it is built? How many will be saved when I blow it up? I feel so lonely; I can't talk to anyone about my plans, so I think about the young prostitute in Ledo.

"I am loyal to no one but myself. It is the only way to survive," she had said.

The rain slows, but the steaming humidity it leaves behind is so thick, you practically need an oxygen tank to get enough air. With rain fifteen hours a day, the men have little to do except wait as the days and the nights blur together. It's mind-numbing persecution with no end.

Lt. Lin scurries in to the mess hall, and I wave him over to our table. We reached a tenuous truce after we learned we had a lot in common. It's as though I'm looking at a different man, although nothing has changed about him since that day several weeks ago.

"I not take their religion," he had told me that morning, about the evangelists in southern China who schooled him before he became a soldier. "But I learn from missionaries so I may eat." Lin took off his flat Chinese uniform cap and shook the rain off it. I'm always surprised at how young he looks when his thick mop of black hair is let free. "Their teachings most useful. I learn English so I make officer in army."

"I thought you went to a fancy school in Shanghai," I said, pulling out a chair in the supply hut and offering Lin a smoke.

"Thank you. Most high praise." Lin nodded slightly to my compliment, but declined the cigarette. "I from family of farmers and soldiers. Father leave I only eleven. Fight Japanese with Mao Tse-tung in China north. I not want to be soldier. I not want my son be father for family like me. So I not go when Japanese invade south."

I had leaned back in my chair and whistled in admiration. "And you didn't get into trouble for not joining the military?"

"I only simple farmer from south." Lin explained that Japan first invaded northern China for iron to make machinery. "Sell to United States. Give Japan much power. But when Wall Market fall, no money. No need machines in America. No work for Japan."

My heart felt vacant, remembering that time. I added, "We called it the Great Depression."

"Then America get mad at Japan. No send food to Japan. So Japan send soldiers to steal China food." Lin's lip narrowed in anger, reliving a private pain. "Before Great Wall fall, my father go north, fight war for others. Never see again. Then Japanese come south for rice. Japanese take all I have. Find mother, find sister, find child, no head. Find wife," he turned away from me, "no clothes. I left with nothing but hate. So I become soldier."

I told Lin things I never told others. "The drought came right after the stock market crashed. I was on my Uncle Eddie's farm, digging row upon row of ditches to catch rain for the corn. But it never came, and the dirt blew away. That's when my father gave up. He drank himself into a hole, hiding like a rat." I swallowed the bile in my throat, remembering the terror in Ma's face as she wondered how she would support us. "One good thing came out of the Depression," I grinned. "Everyone wanted to read about everyone else's suffering. Newspapers sold like water in a desert. We moved from the farm to the city, where I hawked papers at the corner delis and Ma washed floors. We learned how to survive."

Lin tilted his head back, surprised. "You man of family at young age, too?"

"Yes." I stood up, feeling a little uncomfortable with these memories and ready to end the conversation. "And you were a farm boy, too."

We tried to cover old wounds from childhood with a few moments of silence. "I think we more alike than different," Lin answered. "Now I older," he continued. "I wonder if father bad or like young man, follow dreams. I often see same look in men from Chinese 10th."

Surprised at having shared my thoughts with Lin, I remember putting on my cap to leave the supply hut and brave the rain. I told Lin things I hadn't even told Ruthie. Now, there was so much I couldn't tell her.

Lin joins me and Earl at the corner table, where the three of us sit in comfortable silence.

There'll be an afternoon game of cards, later. Before Merrill comes.

CHAPTER 17

"No. I don't understand. You got a road to build, but you're playing cards." Colonel Merrill clenches the stem of his pipe between his teeth as he talks. Rainwater drips from his razor-edged crew cut down to his glasses.

Earl slaps a fan of five cards down on the table and stands up abruptly, tipping his chair over. The other men at the table, including myself, do nothing.

"Sir," he starts with a contained southern drawl. "Have you been given a full tour of this here construction site, including what we call the graveyard?" Placing a hand on his hip and throwing his muscled shoulders back, Earl looks at the Colonel as though the word insubordination is not in his dictionary. "I think you'd get an understanding of what'd happen if we fired up our equipment in this here rain."

Leaning forward, Merrill folds his arms across his chest and waits, eyebrows furrowed. "Now, don't go blaming me an' the rest of these men because the road ain't done." Earl's voice drowns out the rain. "But since you is an officer of far-reaching reputation, maybe you can tell us whether someone up high thinks we can fix these here trucks with duct tape an' run them off rainwater, because that's all we got."

Merrill shakes his head, unwilling to surrender. "Maybe you should show me that cemetery you're talking about," he offers with a sweeping gesture towards the entrance of the basha.

Earl pulls on his cap and leads the Colonel from the mess hall, shadowed by a thick- skinned, pock-marked, teenage Kachin scout. Earl's not taking this heat alone. I push myself around the table and out the door. The others at the table watch in silence.

I chase after them, splashing in the potholes. My boot gets stuck in the clay, locking me in place until I wrench it free. The others walk further away, through the muck of the thirty-foot-wide, recently-cut road, unfazed by the dense rain.

To their right, the trees have been cleared, and a storm-capped Himalayan chain rises as a sentinel in the distance. They stomp towards the canyon that separates us from the mountains.

Slipping in the slimy clay from the unfinished road, they finally stop at the edge of the gorge. Merrill looks down over the rim at the sediment-laden river. The rushing river below and the pounding rain has silenced everything else. They don't even notice me when I finally catch up to them.

In the narrowest section of the path, Earl stops and shouts, pointing at a junkyard of abandoned equipment. "This here we call the cemetery." Rolled dump trucks, mud-caked yellow power shovels, and an assortment of other trucks lay strewn along the banks, submerged in the reddish mud that was once a part of the road bed.

"Now, I ain't never been accused of being any more than a smart ass," Earl grins, "but we boys in the south know that if you pull down them trees and clear the weeds, that dirt ain't got nothing to stick to if it done rain."

We march further along the road to where the thick jungle meets the open road cut. At the edge, Earl's dozer sits, waiting to smash through the unexplored vegetation. A rock outcrop blocks further movement on the rig's left, and, about fifteen feet to the right, a steep drop-off is hidden by hundred-foot-tall hardwood trees. Their wet canopies blend in with the bamboo shrubs along the perimeter, forming a green wall. Slash marks blazed in the tree trunks and survey sticks hidden in the undergrowth trace an outline or mark the spot where the future road is to be built.

Merrill examines its precarious alignment. Bending over, he fingers the thin film of soil that will be the road's only support. He looks to the right; the defiant jungle towers over a sliding slope. To the left, bedrock refuses to budge. "It's a landslide ready to drop." He turns to look us in the eyes, then says, "This is shoddy work."

The distrust in Earl's face turns into outright disregard for authority. He marches over to his bulldozer, swings up—rain trickling off his cap and into his collar—then calls back, "You want to see how easy it is to follow orders from someone sitting at a nice, dry desk who ain't got any idea what problems we got? You wondered why I ain't workin' on the chain gang today.

Well, you got it now. Follow that trace. I'm not the one who marked it, but I've been told to track it." He rams the switch up and the engine growls to a start, then snorts as he lifts the blade, slipping, wobbling, but eventually inching forward along the marked trail.

The bulldozer grazes a shale rock ledge on Earl's left. The equipment tilts to the right, where a stand of supple, slimy, bamboo shoots reaching fifty feet are flattened by its massive metal blade. The green mat forms a wet, unsupported base. The big rig lurches, shakes, then pitches towards what we now see is a fissure in the trace—an earthquake fault line ready to split the road open under the dozer.

Slowly at first, crumbling mud clods separate along the trace. Each lump tumbles down the gorge, dodging trunks and vines. The rift grows, and the lithe bamboo stems cannot buttress the swelling avalanche of mud or the big rig. Earl, in a rage and unaware that the ground beneath him is flowing downhill, forces the coughing machine forward, smashing a tunnel opening in the jungle, and destroying the virgin forest.

Doubt paralyzes the three of us watching the bulldozer sputter and lean towards the incline. I recover and dash towards the slide, screaming "Earl, get off the motherfuckin' machine!"

Merrill chases behind me. "What's that man thinking? Is he blind?" he yells.

Along the side of the road lies a fallen tree covered by a thick rug of vines. "Grab the other end of the trunk," I shout to the Kachin. "The best we can do is wedge that log downhill and prop up the dozer to keep it from sliding any further."

The wiry, muscled youth pulls at creeping vegetation to free the tree pole. Finally, the wood, freshly felled and heavy, releases. Merrill and the Kachin ranger follow my example and encircle the log with their arms, their faces red as we lift it. We haul the log towards the rig, our vision obscured by the rain.

The bulldozer teeters to the right. Earl turns off the machine and heaves himself out of the cab towards a rock on the uphill side. It's then he realizes the danger. Guilty fear clouds his face and renders him immobile. "Harry, what should I do?"

Merrill shouts to him, "Bounce the machine towards the outcropping. Jump up and down and use your weight to tilt the rig upright."

Earl nods numbly, then throws his whole body into propelling the equipment away from the drop-off.

Clutching the log like we're ready to ram a wall, the rest of us reach a point where the ground starts to slip away under us. We stop, unable to move any further. Without hesitation, Merrill commands, "One, two, three, heave!"

As the log flies through the air, its bulky, wet weight propels it forward.

We turn to see the dozer lean towards the ravine. Drenched in sweat and water, Earl bounces up and down on the cab's foothold until a loud crash grabs our attention. We look back to see the front tip of the log we had just thrown gouge deep into the downslope mud. Oozing clay cements the log in place against a giant Halong tree.

Angling deep into the uphill ground, the dozer finds a shaky equilibrium. From the corner of my eye, I see Earl lose his balance, fall against the rock ledge, and smash his head. His limp body slips out of sight beneath the dozer. Then the underbelly of the rig—and Earl—slide towards the gully until the log wedged in the bamboo thicket arrests its advance downhill.

The young Kachin runs around the bulldozer to find Earl. He holds up a hand to stop us before we try to dig Earl out so we don't trap him further. Wordlessly, he grabs my arm and drags me to help roll a huge rock under the engine. We fix it in place, stabilizing the metal hulk. The muscular native and I pull a dazed Earl free. Then the tribesman slides his shoulder under a half-conscious Earl and drags him to dry cover.

Out of breath, I'm barely able to hold up my own weight. I'm sick of this: the road, the rain, the deaths. The washouts where I placed dynamite are nothing more than obnoxious bug bites compared to this. I've been wasting my time; not even Mother Nature can stop Stilwell. I slump to the ground and let my head drop, close to vomiting with exertion. I hate this feeling of defeat.

My head is level with the underside of the dozer, where the rusted bolts on the tracks have popped. "This shit's as easy to snap as a toothpick," I sneer. Then I remember Schmidt saying the equipment rusts from humidity. Turning my attention back to the belly of the dozer, I wonder how easy it would be to sabotage all these construction rigs until there's none left.

Dynamite may not be the most effective way to derail Stilwell's Road.

CHAPTER 18

As the pock-marked scout leads Earl away from the teetering bulldozer, Merrill surveys the wreckage. I hear him swear under his breath.

Soaking with sweat and the rain, I lash back at Merrill. "Sir, you told the men to stop playing cards. Earl did as he was told."

"Who asked for your opinion, Lieutenant?" Merrill's anger found a target.

"These men never make decisions on their own," I snap back. "They're not allowed to think around here. Didn't you hear Earl? He does what he's told."

"Did someone tell him to drive that rig off the road?" Merrill points at the tractor, barely visible now in the downpour. His glasses are splattered with rain and mud. "If either of you had a half an ounce of sense…"

Ready to go toe-to-toe with Merrill, I shout, "You calling somebody brainless? I ain't the boss. And Earl's only mistake was to obey your order."

Merrill looks once more at the hulking piece of road equipment sinking deeper in the mud before he squeezes his eyes closed. "I'm mad at myself, not Earl," he admits quietly.

"Nobody in their right mind would dig up a mountain in this kind of weather," I holler. The wet wind pelts me with rain. "I know what happens to the land when you don't treat it right. You lose it all. By the time this road is built, the war will be over and the only thing to come from it will be a bunch of gravestones."

Slamming his fist on the upturned dozer, Merrill yells back. "Well, Lieutenant, you're obviously so smart—how would you build a road to China? The Japs have cut off all the eastern sea routes. And I'm sure you've seen the picks, hoes, and axes the 10th regiment use as weapons against the Japanese army. How the hell do you suggest we get help to China?" Out of breath, Merrill sucks in a lung full of air.

"You can't even get us the right equipment or spare parts to construct this road. What makes you think we can help China?"

"Because we have to." Merrill's jaw tightens. "Can't you see? No one's stopping the Japanese in China." The rain beats down on both of us. "China is our wall between the Atlantic and Pacific. The road is the only way we can supply their troops and stop the enemy."

I feel like I'm ready to explode. "If you really want to win this war, you've got to stop thinking like an American. Kill the Japanese by taking away their honor, not building Stilwell's Road."

Merrill hangs his head, takes off his glasses, and shakes the water from them. "Lieutenant, meet me at road headquarters in one hour so we can finish this discussion." He turns to go, then looks back at me, "And I have questions for you about the supply hut."

The rain and road are erased from my mind immediately and replaced with nervous fear.

What did Merrill find? Once he's out of sight, I beeline to the supply basha.

I scan the room as I enter. It smells like moldy bread. Spare equipment parts are piled high in the back of the shed. It's hard to tell what we have and what's missing, with stacks of motor parts and spark plugs mixed in with the electrical gear. I shiver, but rather than turn on the generator, I light a kerosene lamp.

Smoke follows the lantern's arc as I swing it around the room. Nothing seems to have been opened. The boxes of oatmeal and coffee are stashed in a corner, safe from roof leaks. The typewriters and sheaths of paper sit on the makeshift tables of bamboo and plywood, ready for the next order.

POP. POP. My shoulders tighten at the noise, which sounds like distant gun fire. My eyes inch around the room, searching for the sound, while I feel like a target with the lantern as a beacon. Finally, I notice it's coming from a leak dripping on a tin can.

Strangely, none of the illegally stockpiled guns in Ledo that Schmidt sent me out here to track have made it to the construction site. Did Schmidt have something up his sleeve by sending me out here? Now's not the time to brood about that. I laid most of my dynamite stash earlier in the month and made mud soup of the traces. They'll have to start from scratch, setting the schedule back months. My satisfaction is fleeting. I still have grenades, a couple of Thompsons, and a belt of ammo to ditch. And there's only a half hour before I'm to meet with Merrill and the guillotine falls.

When I enter my barrack, it's empty. My guess is the men are still in the mess hall. It's better to be playing cards, ready for action, than to be sleeping on the job. I lie down on my rope cot and pull my pillow over my face so I won't be disturbed.

In thirty minutes, I may be thrown out of the army for defying an officer. But I don't give a damn. No one even remembers we exist. We're the forgotten front.

Bob, Earl, Charles, and Bernie would never understand the logic behind my thinking. But nothing great comes of doing what's expected unless you're the enemy and can take advantage of it.

"Most honorable Lieutenant," Lin squeaks as he enters the barracks.

Peeking from under my pillow, I see him hurry into the basha out of the rain.

Lin bows up and down like a bobbing sandpiper, trying to stir me from my isolation. I know it's more out of habit than respect.

Water drips from Lin's jacket as he bends over to rouse me. "Go away," I answer, then turn on my side towards the wall.

"Lieutenant Flynn, may I have moment of time?" he says in staccato English.

I toss the pillow away, swing around, and sit up. Without saying anything, I glare at Lin, jaw clenched.

"I hear you to speak with Colonel Merrill." Lin waits for an answer. It seems he mistakes my anger for fear. He tries to console me in his gentle sing-song voice. "In China, we say: cannot catch bees with vinegar."

I say nothing.

Lin continues. "Colonel knows one word of advice from man with wisdom is better than a hundred from man who only read books. Like young boy, your words of passion miss target." Before he goes, he adds, "You brave man, Harry Flynn, but you dream like poet."

Thirty minutes later, I don't even feel the water sloshing in my boots as I ascend the steps to road headquarters. I push through the door, heart pounding in my ears. I walk to the front desk and am relieved and irritated to find it vacant. The soldier on duty appears while I'm studying the envelope on the desktop addressed to Harry Flynn.

"You Flynn?" he asks. I nod. "Merrill got called away. But he left this for you." Nonchalantly, the soldier passes the letter to me, then goes back to his business.

I rip open the seal. The letter reads, *Thank you, Lieutenant. I got what I came for. You and Earl helped me figure it out. Colonel Merrill.*

Eyes closed, I roll my neck to release the tension. I feel the cracking all the way down my spine. "Thanks, buddy," I say to the clerk.

My foot is halfway out the door when the soldier adds, "Oh, yeah—Merrill said to clean up the mess in the supply hut."

CHAPTER 19

August, 1943

A fresh crop of GIs step from the cars onto the train platform. I'm stationed back in Ledo until September, when the dry season should start. Today I got hospital duty, and a rush order of quinine for malaria and typhus just arrived on the last train. I get to visit Earl after I drop the medicine off at the hospital. That place gives me the creeps, but I guess I should be happy it's only a day's job and I'm not stuck in there.

Knowing I had the hospital run today, I stuffed a few sticks of dynamite in my rucksack, cushioned them with a few old 1943 *CBI Roundup* newspapers, and threw it in the back of the Jeep. The 14th Evacuation Hospital is about five miles out of town, and Jairampur—or Hell's Gate—is fifteen miles further. It's at the beginning of the switchbacks up to Pangsau Pass and a good spot for a washout. No one knew when the train would arrive, so they shouldn't notice if I take an extra hour. Earl doesn't even know I'll be dropping by. I hope I don't look nervous, but I'm already on edge after reading the letter I got from Ruthie.

Dear Harry,

Some of the injured boys are returning home already, needing someone to keep them company in the hospital. So I go visit them with a couple girls from work. I know what it's like to feel lonely; I haven't heard from you lately. But since I can get letters from Bob, I can't help but wonder whether you still care.

All you have to do is drop me a line, and I'll know everything is okay. I miss you.

Love, Ruthie

"Yeah, I've got something to say." I scrunch up the letter. "Get off my back." She doesn't know what it's like to be here, fighting for what you believe in, alone.

Package in hand, I start the Jeep in neutral, then quickly change gears. I feel like I'm in a washing machine; the wipers barely keep the road visible. This is a nice stretch of land. Lush, terraced fields rise up along the mountainsides until it's too rocky and there is no soil.

I go through my mental checklist for the fiftieth time today: dynamite, fuse wire, cap, detonation box. Wound tighter than an alarm clock, my mind can't settle on anything. My overstimulated nerves scream until the blood vessels in my ears are ready to burst. It's not like when I was out on the construction site and I could easily slip away. Pilfering the few sticks for today was like lifting a wallet from a pickpocket.

The culvert under the road where I want to stick the dynamite is in a draw just around the bend. I park the car facing the direction of the hospital, ready for a quick getaway. I slide out of the Jeep, my jacket and pants immediately drenched. Luckily, the CBI magazines kept the ammo dry, and I have a change of clothes. I check to make sure none of the local villagers are out in this rain before I hunch over the rucksack and hurry to the ravine.

The mud squishes into my socks, down my pants, and up my shirt as I shimmy down the slope. Only a few feet further to the edge of the pipe where I'll stick the dynamite. The culvert flows full with cold water. Preparing the fuse wire in this cramped position is the pits, and the splicing knife slips from my hands. "Damn it." My foot blocks it before it tumbles into the current. I twist my body and reach downhill, trying not to fall head-first into the stream. Slowly, I inch the knife up my pant leg until I have a good hold. Sweat and rain blur my vision. The knife is dull. Why didn't I check it before?

I look up towards the truck where I left the detonator box, hoping the length of wire I cut is long enough. With the way this mud is running, there's no room for second chances. Pressing my face closer to the ground to block the rain, I try to work faster. "Damn it." I hold up my hand. Blood drips steadily from a chunk of skin hanging off my thumb. My hands are slippery, and the damn cap doesn't want to stick in the dynamite. "Calm down," I coach myself. "You're almost there."

Finally, after what seems to be a whole afternoon, everything is ready. I scramble towards the road, grabbing at roots, barely noticing the thorns in the branches as I slip down a half foot for every foot of rise. At the top, I spit out mud and wipe if from my eyes.

Only the igniter connection is left. Months ago, when I first tried to connect the fuse wire to the igniter box, I must've spent an hour trying to get it right. Now, after several dozen blasts, I can practically connect it with my eyes closed. Today's not my lucky day, though; it's like peeling carrots with a butter knife. The metal wire is exposed, sliver by sliver. With a questionable connection, I call it quits. My patience is running on empty.

I strip down before getting into the truck, knowing that a muddy bench seat would lead to questions. After a deep breath, I go through my checklist: dirty clothes, unused fuse wire, rucksack— all stashed on the floor. The detonator box is ready to be plunged.

I push down on the T-handle and listen. Nothing happens. "For Christ's sake." I grit my teeth. A second look at the muddy slope doesn't bolster my hopes. I finally admit it's too wet today and detach the wire from the detonator and stick it in my sack.

Just as I get back into my truck, I see a little girl with a wicker basket balanced on her head about two hundred feet down the road. Her physical details are shadowed by the overhanging tree canopy, but I can see she's young and drenched. She stops and stares at me.

As soon as she realizes that I see her, too, she turns and disappears down the slope, almost like she's an illusion. Now I'm grateful the blast was a dud. I drive past the child on my way out; she plods along a lower path towards the ravine in the wet, thick vegetation. Her neck is bent downward, avoiding my stare.

On the drive back to Jairampur, my hands on the steering wheel shake. Today was a big waste of time. My muscles are cramping, but I ignore them and let myself be comforted by the gentle patter of a million drops tiptoeing on the roof.

A dull WHOOPH, like the release of an air vacuum, sounds from the gorge behind me.

I'm afraid to look back, but I can't resist it and whip my head around to watch the chocolate brown chunks of mud and rocks begin to fill in the gully. From the bowels of the crevice, the watery stream thickens into sludge. I slow down and look back to see if the girl is ok, but she's nowhere in sight. I convince myself she made it to the other side before turning my attention back to the road and accelerating.

I veer into the curve. It's then I see her basket in the rearview mirror. It's upside down, caught in a branch, on the brink of the ravine. There's no girl. I look harder. Still no girl.

Shaking my head in disbelief, I lose control of the wheel. The Jeep hydroplanes, and I brake hard until the truck fishtails. Mud splatters across the windshield. For a moment, I'm blinded. The tires teeter off the edge of the road until I throw the wheel in a wild arc and it rights the truck.

Within minutes, the slushy rain grows into a torrential flow, and I can't see beyond the front of the Jeep. I drive faster, as though getting away will erase what just happened.

"What did I do?" I ask myself. Staring straight ahead, I try to reassure myself it was just a trick of my eyes. But the rain can't wash away what my gut says happened. My eyes dart from one side of the Jeep to the other for confirmation that this is really happening. My mind screams,

"Stilwell's Road is the cause of all of this. It's the murderer." I'm panting. My anger at the road feels safer than the truth.

"Give me a sign that this is right. Anything," I hiss between gritted teeth. I look for a bolt of lightening, a thundering voice. The swishing of the windshield wipers back and forth is what I get. Like a ping pong ball, my mind bounces between "you killed her" and "no, she's safe."

"Damn it," I scream, slamming my fist on the dash.

The rain pounds on the roof, and bone-chilling air seeps through the vents. My temples throb like they're going to explode. I briefly close my eyes. When I open them again, a blurry image in the side window mirrors my face: gaunt, creased, and sad. It's then I start to face who I've become. Am I willing to live with his decisions?

CHAPTER 20

Falling off the dozer was the best thing that could've happened to Earl. It forced him to see a doctor. The concussion he got when his head hit the rock isn't his biggest problem; it's the ulcerated leech infection. His leg's swelled to the size of an elephant's. The thought of his red, oozing sores is enough to make me reconsider my visit, but I have no excuse. I run my hands through my hair, feel the stubble from my recent crew-cut, and push open the flap to the hospital basha.

I gag at the stink from amoebic dysentery. It practically knocks me over. If anything can take my mind off Hell's Gate, this is it. Silky parachutes white-wash the hospital walls and create a barrier between the patients and the malaria-carrying insects. They also trap in the heat and the stagnant air. I walk towards Earl's cot at the back of the hospital, looking but not seeing.

Unblinking men, the whites of their eyes dried open and bodies wasted down to the bone, lay lifeless, except for tremors in their hands and feet. I ignore the clawing and incoherent whimpering punctuated by vulgar outbursts from men flushed and steeped in sweat. Most of the patients in the hospital have typhus or malaria, like Lester. Blinders on, I head straight towards Earl, wondering how he has survived in this hot bed of infection, especially with Lester's cot next to his.

Lester lays curled up, fast asleep or delirious with fever. Given the sweat on Lester's face and the bedclothes that stick to his once-burly body, now shriveled and sagging, I'd say the fever is winning. Malaria is a tough enemy. Whenever I come here, I ask myself the same question every other soldier wonders: why him and not me?

"Lester has got to stop losing weight, it just doesn't look good on him," I say. I've always found it easier to joke than face the truth.

Earl slowly shakes his head, resigned to God's decision. "My man, my man; Harry boy.

You feeling a bit guilty, coming to visit me two times in one week?" Earl asks with a disheartened cheer. He props himself up against the wall, then points to the end of his cot for me to sit.

"I thought if I didn't stop by to shake things up around here, you might skip out on me." My laugh is stiff. I sit down, refusing to look at the gentle, unassuming man who practically pulled my leg out of its sockets until I surfaced from that mud avalanche.

"Now, where would I be going if it wasn't back to my rig?" Earl winks.

I don't feel comforted with what I see. "The only reason we need this hospital is that road.

I think it would be patriotic to stop construction; quite a few lives would be saved," I say, mentally including that little girl at Hell's Gate.

It only takes Earl a fraction of a second to change gears from mischievous invalid to ball- busting patriot. "Boy, what you talking about? That weather must be molding your brain. If that road ain't built, Reginald will have died for nothing. An' I ain't going let that happen. Without it, we ain't going win the war. Now stop talking that treason, or you're going get both of us in trouble."

A petite Burmese nurse wrapped in a long, brightly patterned longyi and weighing no more than a hundred pounds tries to slip by like a shadow.

"Maran Lu, Maran Lu. Ahhhh, what a pretty little creature be you." Earl flashes her a huge white smile that could be intimidating, but Maran Lu ignores his come-on and responds with a tolerant sigh as she drops a bed pan by his cot.

"Still not walk," she scolds in halting English. "You pick at leg?" She gives him a scolding look, hands on her hips.

"Honey child, I'd do anything to get you back by my bed, singing those sweet hymns about baby Jesus."

A strand of shiny black hair slips from her severely wound bun as she shakes her head in disapproval. She whips out a thermometer. "I know how keep you from talk bad about Jesus." Her sweet young face scowls, then smiles triumphantly as she jabs the instrument in his open mouth. "I tell Daddy you pinch me if you not zip lips." She looks to me conspiratorially.

"Why you not keep mouth shut like your friend with—" she turns her head and boldly examines my face—"sky blue eyes and black long lash." She teases me with a caress to my cheek. "Harry, your girlfriend like blue, no?" She isn't the least bit embarrassed by her lack of timidity.

Maran Lu lost all fear when the Japanese burned down her Kachin village, killing everyone in her family, and changing her life forever. When we first met, she told me how she had quickly scrambled up a nearby tree and hid when they invaded the cluster of bashas along the stream in central Burma she called home. The Japanese left, assuming they had eliminated another clan of informants. She wandered the jungles, hoping to live out the war in hiding, but stumbled upon a mission hospital where she was drawn in and protected by the doctor and his staff. That doctor was Gordon Stifler Seagrave, or, to Maran Lu, Daddy.

"Don't get me in trouble because Earl's misbehaving." I take a step back, feigning fear of being infected with whatever insanity Earl contracted. "This is between you and Earl. You're not going find me messing with you or your 'daddy'."

From the room on the other side of a parachute flap, I hear: "Goddamn, son of a bitch.

Where's my scalpel? If I see another one of these Chinese come in with one of their filthy, homemade leaf compresses, I'm going to ship them back to China." Giggles in the background punctuate his grumbling.

"Speaking of Daddy," I grimace, teeth bared in mock alarm, "Sounds like Earl isn't the only one on his shit list today." I say this in reference to the physician, otherwise known as the Burmese Doctor.

I admire Seagrave. He told his parents, Baptist missionaries in Burma, when he was only five years old that he would become a doctor. Twenty years later, with a bucket of discarded surgical tools from Johns Hopkins, he made good on his vow. His foul language is as strong and legendary as his belief in God.

"I not know these words," Maran Lu comments as the profanities continue to stream from the surgical ward. "But make Daddy feel better." She artfully extracts the thermometer from Earl's mouth while completing other tasks simultaneously.

Earl rolls his head back and laughs, "Boy, you should've seen us last night. It was Daddy, me, Maran Lu, Little Bawk, and Snowball making music like God meant our voices to praise the holy Lord. Even Lester joined in with a couple Amens."

"He not sing bad," Maran Lu compliments Earl begrudgingly, then gently pats his cheek. "You not get big head cuz God give you deep voice." As she walks away she adds, "But you got rhythm."

"Honey, all God's children got rhythm," he teases her. "You just like mine." She blushes as she leaves.

Earl's look becomes serious and, quietly, he confides to me. "I think Lester's 'bout ready to go home." He looks over at the quivering body in the cot next to him, slick with perspiration, and begins to sing. "I'm just a poor, wayfaring stranger, travelling through this world of woe.

But there's no sickness, there's no toil, nor danger in that bright world to which I go."

CHAPTER 21

"Go get 'em boys." General Joseph Stilwell good-naturedly smacks a stocky private's back. In response, the surprised soldier grimaces an uneasy smile. The rest of the enlisted men dutifully continue to unload the recent shipment of food, construction material, and equipment parts onto the rail platform. Awaiting my own delivery of medical supplies, I shield my eyes and look up at the unrelenting midday sun. There are no promises of mercy, only more sweat and fatigue. The dry season can be as brutal as the monsoon.

Conspicuously lacking his insignia and rank and looking more like a severe Oklahoma dirt farmer than the highest-ranking commander of the US Forces in the CBI, Stilwell bites down on his long-stem cigarette holder. He leaves the services of supply soldiers and walks over to Colonel Merrill, who's just arrived from Delhi. "Got a report for me?"

Standing at ease, arms behind his back, Merrill jokes with an easy smile, "Things couldn't be better, Joe. Or could they?" He pulls out his pipe, pointing it at the piles of discarded supplies. Quickly reinserting the pipe between gritted teeth, he reaches out to shake hands with his commanding officer and friend.

The two scrutinize the growing disarray of boxes, dented canned goods, and broken equipment in the center of the station. Along the curbside, a line-up of soldiers heft supplies on to the coolies' heads, which are to be hiked to storage bashas on base. The clanging rail cars and black soot snorting from the steam engine force the officers to leave the platform.

An army staff car, parked in front of my tarp-covered Jeep, waits for them at the entrance of the rail station. I walk a safe distance behind the two officers, followed by coolies carrying the special shipment items to be packed in the bed of my Jeep.

Glancing back at the rail platform swarming with soldiers and merchants, Stilwell says under his breath, "Looks like Larry, Moe, and Curly have joined the unit."

"Give me the Three Stooges any day," Merrill says. "At least I'd be laughing."

"I got your letter," Stilwell says, unable to hide a look of concern. "The road's that bad?"

Merrill nods, "It's not the Japanese blocking construction; it's the damn rain and mud. If you think it's a mess here, go to road H.Q. There's a cemetery of everything that doesn't work in Burma buried out there. Hell, I saw more ammo than spare parts in the supply hut. Joe, the road's not going to get done unless you pull rank."

"No Nips?" Stilwell asks Merrill quizzically. "But ammo?"

Shocked that Merrill found my ammo in the supply hut at road headquarters, I hesitate. One of the coolies, head down, plows forward and rams me from behind, so I whirl around. His box slips from his head, and I grab the cargo before it hits the ground. Together, we readjust the load, but not without shouting and dirty looks from the other carriers. I notice Stilwell and Merrill have reached their car. After settling the yelling and accusations among the coolies, we continue towards my Jeep.

I let them load the goods while I listen in on the conversation between the two officers. An image of the ammo supply at the road site, heaped in a pile looking more like garbage than shelf-ready goods, sticks in my mind. Why didn't Merrill question me, then, if he thought something was wrong?

Last week, a shipment clearly labeled as ammo arrived in Ledo. Later in the day, I looked for the boxes. It was as though the whole truckload disappeared. When I checked the requisition tag, it had been signed by Schmidt. Guess I need to do a little reconnaissance on that before Merrill starts snooping and someone, like Schmidt, plasters my name all over something. My trip to Hell's Gate and the little girl with the wicker basket convinced me to kick the dynamite habit. Thanks to Bernie, I found another way to do my duty.

In a barely audible undertone, the two officers continue their debriefing. "The Japanese are farther into Central Burma—the Hukawng Valley." Merrill looks around as though he wishes this conversation was not out in the open. "And the enemy has good air coverage just south of there at their Myitkyina base. How the hell are we going to stop those fighter pilots from mutilating our boys flying the HUMP?"

The General looks over his rimmed spectacles into the distance as though he's inspecting the supply operation. I move around to the other side of my Jeep to get within better hearing distance. Old Vinegar Joe crosses his arms, then drops the bomb: "I've got an idea: Code name Galahad."

"Really?" Merrill asks, then takes the pipe out of his mouth. "What is Galahad?"

"A counterinsurgent, long-range penetration unit. The President's put a call out to the Allies. He wants to talk when we meet in Cairo." Stilwell shifts his gaze from the rail station to the street, observing the honking cars weaving around overloaded bicycles that dominate the road. "Roosevelt and Churchill will both be there. Rumor has it Mountbatten—what a sap—will be given the head CBI post instead of me. Most likely some inside work by my Chinese cry- baby friend, Generalissimo."

"Chiang Kai-shek's got nerve, throwing his weight around," Merrill says. "He's constantly bellyaching, even though most of his men are still in Kunming." He, too, shifts his attention, suddenly finding the sirens and blare of street traffic interesting and probably a better place for his words to vanish.

"I just want to squeeze the brass enough to get some help and push this road through." Stilwell says, brushing off Merrill's sympathy with an annoyed wave of his hand. "Mountbatten ought to be feeling a little guilty if he gets the post and not me, so I expect he'll cut me a few breaks. Wingate's under Mountbatten, and he's also supposed to be there."

"Now there's a loony toon," Merrill laughs, filling his pipe with tobacco.

"And a genius," the General adds. "He's always boasting about his Chindits slipping behind the enemy line and sabotaging the Nip communication lines. I want to pick his brain and find out how to form our own commando unit, Galahad."

Out on the street, horns honk. I move closer to the front of the Jeep, adjusting the tarp's ties.

Stilwell's thin lips are barely moving. When it quiets down, I hear, "I want an American team leading the guerrillas in Northern Burma. We need to wipe out all the Japs in Myitkyina to build the road. So I'll ask for the commando unit to be shipped to India in a couple of months, November at the latest. By spring, they'll infiltrate Burma and disrupt enemy operations; then we can send in the Chinese X Force combat battalion to clean out the site for the road crew."

"Galahad will land in India in two months, and then what?" Merrill's skepticism hangs between the two men.

"Mountbatten will want Wingate to train them with his Chindits," Stilwell says, his hawk eyes narrowed and jaw set firm. "But I want you in charge. You know Northern Burma.

Wingate can work the south with his Chindits. You'll have until February to get them ready. I want Myitkyina before the end of the next monsoon season."

Merrill's only answer is raised eyebrows and a lot of tobacco smoke.

I move back towards the rear of the Jeep. The suffocating smell of rotting fruit and human sweat wafts in from the train station as this news shakes me. I gasp for air as I re-arrange goods under the Jeep's canvas tarp.

I remember Charles's quick research on the Chindits a few months ago when Operation LONGCLOTH penetrated the Japanese line in Burma and blew up a few railroad bridges and ammo piles. They're a tough bunch of Brits, Burma Rifles, and Gurkhas. They travelled light, so they were fast, but they had no artillery cover, and all supplies were air-dropped. So during the monsoons, when rains grounded the planes, they were literally abandoned.

Now Stilwell wants an American version of the Chindits—Galahad—to start right before the monsoon season. Seems like a risky idea. How does Stilwell think a group of American-led guerrillas—hell, any group with only a few months of training—can take down the whole town of Myitkyina? It's swarming with the enemy. But Stilwell's so thick-skinned, he doesn't think twice about sacrificing young men.

Stilwell stands transfixed, as though he sees his plan in action. "We've got to get behind enemy lines and wipe out the Myitkyina airfield by next April. I'm calling it Operation END RUN."

"Joe, be realistic," Merrill interrupts. "It's taken us eight months to get fifty miles.

Myitkyina is another two hundred miles. At the rate we're going, we'll get there in three years. There are ten major rivers in the way, with more rain than you'd ever see in the Everglades. Then, as if that isn't enough, the Himalayas are the toughest mountains in the world. Oh, and by the way, did you forget the Japanese are waiting for us in the Hukawng Valley and…"

"Okay, Okay," Vinegar Joe answers, slamming an intolerant fist into the car door. "But we need a man in charge of the road, not that insect we have there now. I want someone to get this road built over that mountain range between India and Burma so we can catch the Nips with their pants down. I want to get to Shingbwiyang by the end of '43."

"What the hell?" Merrill argues. "That's almost sixty miles in four months. Besides, there's something screwy in SOS."

"Colonel Lewis Pick." Stilwell answers. "He's a can-do soldier. We need men who can help us win this war. Except for the Chindits, we've got enough British pansies who'd prefer we never get to the front, and the Chinese are such cowards; they won't fight unless they're sure they'll win."

Still hidden behind my Jeep, I stand motionless as perspiration rolls over my eyes.

Sounds like Stilwell wants to fly solo.

"Joe." Merrill grabs Stilwell's arm. "We're all Allies. I know

I'm your subordinate, but I'm also your friend. Get a grip on your emotions. You need the Allies' help to build this road. So, don't alienate them. You've got to have patience."

"Patience. I hate that word," Stilwell answers. He pauses, then shrewdly asks, "So is Operation END RUN by next spring really asking for too much?" Vinegar Joe doesn't wait for an answer. "Get me Pick. I'll pull rank if I have to."

The train, next to the nearly empty platform, belches another cloud of grunge and grime.

The officers' chauffer finally arrives, and Stilwell and Merrill hop into the waiting staff car. Sounds like big adjustments and a little drama are in store under the name of General Lewis Pick. I slam my door shut and head to the supply station to drop off the goods, then find Bernie and Charles.

Bernie thinks I drop by the garage after work each day to wait until he's done so we can grab Charles, then hit the mess hall together. He doesn't watch me as I wander in and out of the hulking masses of metal, not so much to inspect their condition, but to make it difficult for someone to observe me. During my first month back from the construction front, Bernie introduced me to my dynamite substitute.

On my first day back from the construction front, I had singled out Bernie from a circle of mechanics, whose expressions said they wanted to tear me to shreds, slowly. "Hey, buddy, isn't it closing time?" I asked as I joined the group.

"You're not actually a welcome sight around here, Harry," Bernie warned, holding up a spark plug clearly having seen its full life. "We need parts that work."

I threw my hands up in surrender. "Don't shoot me, boys. I suggest you take it up with Vinegar Joe Stilwell." I nodded towards the door as a hint for Bernie to stop. He ignored me.

The whites of Bernie's eyes and his red hair stood out in stark contrast to his oil-smudged face. "Looky here." He held up a bottle that looked like it belonged in a chemistry lab. "HCL.

Now, what can I do with hydrochloric acid?" He pronounced

hydrochloric as though it was four separate words, then looked me straight in the eye. His sarcasm would have soured water.

Knowing Bernie's volatile spirit, I suggested, "It's probably a mixup with the medical supplies. I'll check it out." I reached out to grab the bottle, but Bernie held tight.

One of the other mechanics nearby overheard us talking. Before Bernie could respond, the old guy was looking over our shoulders. "Hey, I hear you can use HCL as battery fluid when you're out of sulfuric acid." In his strong Brooklyn accent, he continued, "Since your buddy here won't send us new batteries, we may as well doctor up the old ones we scavenged from the cemetery. One of the SOS typos may have been a brilliant accident." He laughed with more disappointment than humor.

Bernie looked skeptical. "I thought that stuff only rusted metal."

"Full proof with no dilution, it'd eat metal like sugar dissolves in water," the mechanic answered. "You've got to mix it with water, like you do your liquor." He gave Bernie a good New York ribbing, then grabbed a discarded battery and placed it on a bench. In a glass container, the older mechanic carefully mixed a solution of HCL and water. He poured the mixture into the battery's opened caps. Within a few minutes, several other mechanics surrounded them as they placed it in a vehicle, and waited for a resurrected battery.

While they played scientists, I pretended I wasn't interested. Hydrochloric acid, I repeated to myself. It eats away metal. Sounds wicked, I thought. Why would anyone need to rust metal away unless they wanted to destroy it? That's when the idea popped, just like the rusted pin in Earl's overturned rig. The chain separated from the dozer's track because the rusted pin snapped. Without the pin, the rig was useless. Without the rig, there'd be no road.

Since that day, I'd been adding a drop of HCL to all the pins and bushings my eye- dropper could reach. Bernie thought I was just lazy, wandering around the garage with nothing to do.

Today, after having eavesdropped on Stilwell and Merrill, I

have no time for doctoring the machines. Stilwell's obsession with winning the war with his road has left him blind to the real reason for war, which should be to save American lives. I grab a rag and walk in between all the vehicles floating on hoists, looking for Bernie. "Go wash your face, then lets pay Charles a visit before he's off radio duty." I thrust the rag at Bernie. If he's stubborn and says he wants to tune up a couple more vehicles, then I'm out of here without him.

"Sure, Harry." Bernie cocks his head back and eyes me with irritation. "I see there's something burning a hole in your brain." He lowers the hoist and grabs the rag, then tosses it on the bench in three smooth moves.

"I just got a tip that's a real cliffhanger," I taunt in singsong. "Let's get Charles to check out Lewis Pick and Galahad."

CHAPTER 22

October, 1943

We snooped around for dope on Pick and Galahad in September. Charles's usual genius in finding the impossible was stymied. The only thing we learned was that Pick had an anal obsession about punctuality. Leads on Galahad were even colder. It seems Stilwell didn't have the strategic muscle I thought he had.

"CHAMPION to TIGAR," the radio squawks. Charles drops the deck of cards he's shuffling, scrambles over to the set, and pulls on the earphones to receive the call from Delhi headquarters.

"TIGAR to CHAMPION, copy." Our charming radio operator gives Bernie and me an "I'll kill you guys if I get caught" look, then shoos us out of the radio room with his free arm. We don't budge. Bernie puts his feet on the table where we're playing cards and closes his eyes for a cat nap. I tilt back on my chair, showing mild curiosity about the incoming call.

"TIGAR, Pick arriving at 18:00 hours today." Charles mouths to us, "I thought the Colonel was to show up tomorrow."

He answers the radio with, "Copy. 18:00 hours. QUARTERBACK in line." "CHAMPION, out." The buzz and crackle of the disconnected line grates like nails on a chalkboard before it goes dead.

"Those guys in Delhi," Charles sighs. "Talk about throwing a grenade. I hope Quarterback Stilwell knows who'll be knocking on his front door later today." A twitching eyebrow signals Charles's building panic attack. "Harry, were you assigned as Colonel Pick's driver?"

"Nope," I answer. "Our friend Schmidt has that honor. And if I know the Captain, he'll be decked out for a presidential ball when he meets his new boss."

Charles nervously taps his toe until I'm ready to sit on his leg. "Harry, you don't happen to know where Schmidt is?" he asks in a tone I don't like.

"Hell, I'm not his keeper," I answer.

Our charming radio man scowls as though pouting will get him what he wants. "Since you and Schmidt work together, I thought you may watch out for each other. I mean, cover when the other's busy. Harry, be a pal. Go look for Schmidt."

"No can do," I answer. "Saw him heading towards Ledo on my way over here. He probably went to the station early so he'd be ready to kiss Pick's ass."

Bernie opens one eye. "No one knew when Pick would get here. I bet Schmidt's up to no good, like usual."

"What do you mean, like usual?" I ask, dropping my chair forward and trying not to look too interested. I thought I was the only one with suspicions about Schmidt.

Bernie pauses to consider his words, then says, "There's one truck that's gone every other day about this time, using up a ton of gas. But no one's been signing it out."

"So how do you know it's gone?" Charles asks, clearly not convinced of foul play. "A man may lie, but an odometer won't. I keep a record of the mileage for all our trucks."

I wonder what other information Bernie's not sharing and who else he's tracking. "Why d'you think it's Schmidt? And what's he doing with the truck?" I ask, thinking Schmidt is probably busy cleaning up his ammo stockpile before Pick arrives.

Bernie sits up and starts putting the cards back in the pack. "I've no idea what he's up to. But he's the only one who smokes Cavaliers. I've been cleaning out the ashtray before the truck goes missing. When it returns, there are always a couple of butts in the tray." He turns to me, thinly veiled distrust clouding his face. "Frankly, Harry, I thought it was you copping the truck until the butts showed up. You sure have been acting squirrely lately, sneaking around the garage. But I know you hate Cavaliers."

"And I hate it when guys you think are your friends don't trust you." I can't look Bernie in the eyes without verbally grinding him into bone meal. I feel my face turning red. "You think I'm crazy because I don't act like a jackass and refuse to look like one? Try getting buried in a mudslide. See if that changes your perspective on things. We got soldiers dying in a war we're not even fighting. You don't think there's something wrong with that?" I bump into the poker chips. They fall to the floor and roll in all directions.

Charles adds, "Harry, I've got to agree with Bernie. You've done some pretty stupid things lately, like calling off the flight to Indaw when the Chindits were in the middle of Burma on Operation LONGCLOTH."

"You forget the FLYING BOXCARS were grounded that day. I can't believe my two best friends are turning on me."

Bernie looks down at the floor rather than face me. "Hey, buddy, sorry. But you haven't been the same since you came back from the construction front. Hope there's no hard feelings."

From that moment, I start to see them all in a different light. What hits me is that I should have seen it sooner. I'm so convinced that the road is the enemy that my I've been blind to the people around me.

Charles breaks, emotion rising in his voice, "Can we hold the kumbaya until later? We all agree Schmidt's an asshole and nowhere in sight. So right now I need someone to get Pick from the train station."

Fighting back burning indigestion at the sight of Bernie, I stand up to go. "No problem. I can motor to the train station to pick up the new boss. I'd like to meet this fella before he gets his ass kicked by the QUARTERBACK when he can't get us to Shit town by January." They laugh at my reference to Shingbwiyang, but I'm serious.

Charles looks at his watch. "It sure would be swell if you left right now, Harry." He pats his perfectly groomed hair just as the radio screeches. Before he takes the call, Charles lifts his boot as though he's ready to literally kick me out.

CHAPTER 23

The train chugs out of town as I motor up to the station. A tall, broad, silver-haired officer with the refined look of an executive, stands at the end of the rail platform. He is flanked by two small leather cases, looking like he could be anyone's grandfather.

Colonel Pick catches sight of the staff car as I roll to a stop. I jump out of the sedan and rush to open the passenger door. "Sir," I salute.

"Ledo appears to have a relaxed schedule," Pick teases as he slides into the car and lets me load his luggage. "Old Stilwell must be getting a little lenient with age." I notice how he watches me for a reaction when I start up the engine.

"No, Sir." I won't let myself get trapped into betraying my opinions. "Lenient is not a word I would use to describe the General. He demands strict obedience."

The car bumps along the dirt road. I try to dodge the deep ruts but can't miss them all. "Obedience?" Pick chuckles. "I knew Old Joe laid down the law, but I also heard he respected his men, Lieutenant…" Pick fishes for my name.

"Flynn, Sir." Still wired with anger at the hurtful accusation from Bernie, I find it hard to stop myself from spitting out my thoughts. "General Stilwell's a straight shooter. But he expects a lot out of his men, and if you get on his bad side, well, I'm told he remembers."

"Sounds like you're not a great fan of Stilwell." Pick doesn't beat around the bush. I feel his gaze waiting for my response.

Cold fear washes through me. I know I'm not making a good first impression, but my bet is he'll be gone before the next monsoon. The bigwigs around here appear to be almost as dispensable as the enlisted men. Besides, if I can't be true to myself, how can I call myself a man? I let my rage answer. "Some say Stilwell's here to build his road, not win a war. It appears we're fighting the road, not the enemy."

"Son, that road's why I'm here. I believe it'll help us defeat the Japanese." Pick sounds sincere, but the insignia ribbons and badges don't encourage my trust.

I shift in the driver's seat and roll my neck to release the tension. "It's hard to beat the Japanese if our men are dying on the road before the fighting even begins."

Without turning, I sense Pick's tension as he straightens his shoulders. "So you don't trust your commanding officer?" Pick asks bluntly.

"I'm here to fight a war." I pause because I want to say that Stilwell doesn't give a rat's ass if we die. Instead, I say, "The General asks for the impossible, only faster. Some guys like the way the General dishes it out to the Brits and how he throws his weight around with the Chinese. Others say he's got a way with words, and I don't think they mean he's tactful." With my left hand, I point ahead towards a series of tin-covered bashas spreading out on both sides of the road, "Ledo base station."

A red sambur bounces out from the brush, hesitates like any cautious deer, and bounds back into the forest. The Colonel doesn't respond to me, choosing instead to study everything we pass: buildings, ditches, the invading jungle. The conversation dies, and we drive in silence to the gate.

As we enter Base Station Section Three, General Stilwell and Colonel Merrill stand in front of the chow hall yakking it up. They seem surprised by Pick's early arrival. Stilwell motions to stop the staff car.

Stilwell reaches out to shake Pick's hand. "Glad to have you on our team. We weren't expecting you until tomorrow. We work, eat, and sleep—mostly work—around here. Hope that matches your expectations."

Pick responds to Stilwell's hint of the daunting task with a wry grin. "General, I'm honored to serve under you. I love a challenge."

Stilwell lifts an eyebrow in response. "Is that so? Then can you cut me a fifty-mile, four- wheel- drive road up through five-thousand feet of limestone, then down into mud and quicksand? I can take a no as well as I can take a yes, but I can't stomach a maybe."

Without hesitation, Pick answers. "I can't build you a road for a civilian car, but I'll build you a truck route. Tell me when you want it."

"By January?" Stilwell asks. "Yes," is Pick's only word.

I turn my head so they can't see my reaction. I want to puke—another puppet.

Stilwell takes a deliberately long drag from his cigarette, sends out a victory smoke circle, then beams. "Glad to see you're willing to roll up your sleeves and crack the whip."

The following morning, in the quad fronting the H.Q. offices, I stand at attention with other key staff reporting to our new road officer. Pick's not a man to preamble with insignificant gestures or words of tribute. I can tell he's here to get a job done, one that's already behind schedule.

"Men," he starts in a tough but confident voice. "I've heard the same story all the way from the States." Wrapping his arms behind his back and clasping his hands, he parades before us. "It's always the same – the Ledo road can't be built. Too much mud. Too much rain. Too much malaria. From now on, we're forgetting the defeatist attitude. The Ledo road is going to be built, mud, rain, and malaria be damned." He scans each man's face. "I know there are no other soldiers as far from home as you. You'll be asked to live in jungles never before penetrated by civilized people. But we've got work to do. That's all, men." He finishes with an encouraging smile.

Disappointment overwhelms me. I walk to the barracks with my head hanging. I'd fooled myself into hoping they'd send someone with the right vision.

CHAPTER 24

November, 1942

On Stilwell's road—newly dubbed Pick's Pike—officers throw orders twenty-four hours a day, seven days a week, at every able man. Colonel Pick has us attacking the road as though it's our enemy, but we're making good time. Construction is moving forward at an unprecedented rate of a mile a day. But the sixteen-hour work days are brutal.

Scalding heat replaces the monsoon rains, reminding us we're far from home. Even at night, the heat doesn't dissipate. To keep the midnight road lit for construction, I pour kerosene oil into buckets hung on each side of bian poles carried by the Chinese.

Nearby, a big rig rolls in reverse. The driver thrusts the gears back into drive to send the dozer forward into the unexplored jungle. Giant virgin trees fall. Their canopies, silhouetted by the oil flames, crash into black holes.

I wince as sweat runs into a patch of peeling sunburn on my forehead and scratch unconsciously at swollen mosquito bites along my forearm. The evening air is thick with the buzzing insects. I hate the night shift.

Sunrise breaks a thin line on the horizon. All around me, men pass tools to each other as the shift changes, and the construction motion doesn't skip a beat. I sag indecisively, not sure whether I should try to get some sleep or doctor the machines.

As I return to the supply hut by the newly built air strip, the night crew walks away, groaning with relief. I duck inside. Although the supply office is away from the hub of road work, I always feel watching eyes hiding. Someday I'll probably get caught. I grab my HCL, then take an alternate route towards the vehicle yard.

The night transitions into the morning's stuffy, thick smell of dust, rising with the inevitable climbing temperatures. Hands thrust deep in my pockets, I walk behind the morning- shift mechanics deeply engaged in friendly banter. As they turn towards the hoists, I detour in the opposite direction. While pretending to scrutinize the rows of equipment, I dig in my pocket for the HCL. The bushings and pins only need a single drop.

The airless heat and now-glaring sun leave me dizzy, colors dancing behind my eyelids.

I'm tired, stressed, and paranoid. I put the vial back in my pocket and leave.

In the center of the road, silver-haired Colonel Pick sits patiently in a chauffeured Jeep, trapped by eager, ass-kissing soldiers. I can't fault Pick for the Ledo Road. It's Stilwell who's flying solo, throwing away the book while no one's watching. Someday, it will come back and bite him. I hope.

Without warning, a staccato of bullets trace a line of flying dirt, and shattered equipment is hurled into the air.

Sunlight reflects off the Frank, a Japanese fighter plane, as it comes into view a couple hundred feet off the ground. I taste bile as I lunge into the brush and listen to men race about, screaming obscenities. Within seconds, a line of freshly slaughtered bodies litter the road by the Colonel's Jeep.

Pick dives and rolls towards the thicket. His Jeep bursts into flames, the driver still inside. An explosive boom and cloud of black smoke hide the confusion. The deep hum of the swooping attack aircraft drowns out angry shouts and cries of pain.

"Radio for help," Pick shouts from where he lays tangled in the weeds. His pants are torn, and blood courses from his hip.

I rush to Pick. "Let me help." I pull him to his feet, and his face goes white with pain. "Goddamn it, Flynn. They need your help. Not me." Pick pushes me away, sputtering nonsense…like a drunk without his bottle. He limps towards the carnage.

I heave the closest mutilated body over my shoulder, refusing to look into his face. And what have these men died for? I ask myself.

"No." Pick shouts. "Find the live ones." He stoops to turn over mangled bodies, looking for a puff of breath. "Where's a Goddamn radio?" the Colonel screams, checking corpse after corpse.

Waving a radio high in the air, a private dodges among the billowing Jeep and the screaming live or silent dead bodies.

"Give me that!" Pick snatches the radio from the young man before yelling, "They're coming back."

I look up to sight the plane circling back, like a maggot on an infected wound. I drag a barely live soldier to the side of the road, then shout, "Take cover!"

One of our single-engine supply planes taxiing for takeoff is too tempting for the Japanese pilot to ignore. The tarmac is defenseless, with the soldier manning the air strip's anti- aircraft gun slumped over the mangled barrel.

"The air field," I shout. But the construction crews just shove each other out of the way as they drag the injured to the edge of the road, sometimes stopping in shock and dropping to the ground at the sight of dead friends. No one thinks about a second attack. They're building a road, not prepared to fight in the war.

Instinct takes over, and I race for supplies, charged with adrenaline. Within minutes, I emerge from the basha, stuffing my pockets, half running and half concentrating on the pineapple hand grenade ringing my finger. Charging forward, I don't hesitate to study the pull mechanism. A new trail of bullets ricochets off metal and thumps into bodies.

Feeling crazed and out of control, I sprint towards the air field, aiming the first of the grenades at the tail of the dipping Japanese plane. I throw without aiming, again and again and again. Not a single grenade connects. Fast fusing blips, like firecracker duds, are the only show for my efforts.

In blind exuberance, the enemy pilot almost catches the top of a giant teak tree, throwing his plane off balance. He lifts higher for another assault.

I drag myself back to the hut for a better weapon, ignoring the blood oozing from my ripped pants. There's no time to dig through the supplies, so I have no choice but to rely upon muscle memory to find the bazooka. Smoke and oil fumes hide the road crew from the unearthly screams as I exit the hut.

The Japanese plane banks, then turns for its third assault. I imagine the pilot's exhilaration as he propels the plane forward and sit the bazooka on my shoulder. I wait for the target to soar over the treetops.

Colonel Pick stumbles in the direction of the air field, weaving between injured soldiers fleeing for safety. "This is insanity," Pick yells.

"Come on back, you bastards," I holler encouragingly to the approaching plane still high in the sky. Our Piper Cub is on the runway, ready to lift off.

"You reckless bastard!" Pick grabs my shoulder. I try to free myself, but only wobble in place on unsteady legs. "You want to kill us with the shrapnel? You're a moron if you think you can blow up that Frank with a bazooka."

I clench my jaw, and ask, "You have a better idea—Sir?"

"Your rash behavior is going to kill more men than that damn Frank," Pick shoots back. "We don't need heroes—use your brains." Disgusted, I shake loose from Pick's digging hand. For a second, he struggles to keep his balance, then splutters, "You're a self-serving ass hole."

Without budging, I shrug my shoulders in frustration. "You still haven't answered my question—Sir."

But Pick's focus shifts to the airborne supply plane in the distance. I aim the bazooka and fire at the incoming Frank. We wait. The Frank soars to the end of the runway, then careens across the tropical canopy towards the east. The supply Cub picks up speed and altitude, banking to the west. The distance between the two aircrafts grows. Although the Japanese fighter's altitude doesn't drop, it continues to veer away from the Piper Cub, tilting in the opposite direction.

Pick frowns at me suspiciously, then glances back at the enemy plane. It looks like it's been hit. Eventually, he says, "Naw, that's not possible—Is it?" On the road, soldiers throw buckets of water to control the flames and busy themselves with anything but fighting a war.

I lower the bazooka and shout, "You're not going to win this war with a pick and a shovel."

The Colonel looks up into a cloudless sky, then answers. "Soldier, you got assigned to the wrong unit."

CHAPTER 25

December, 1943

Reluctantly, I return to the 14th Evacuation Hospital, this time to patch up the hole in my hip from the grenade blast on the road front. When I enter the hospital, I think of Lester, who, in a malaria-induced delirium, picked phantom bugs off his skin with ferocious intensity until blood trickled down his arms, determined to "kill the bastards." Instead, they got Lester first.

Stitching me up, the doctor says my wounds will mend and instructs me to put on some weight. I may be getting lean from the long work hours, but I'm not complaining after what some of these guys have been through. And so, as much as I want to run out of the place, I drop in on Alabama Earl.

He's sitting upright in bed, looking off into another space, another time. His once- muscled body looks soft and vulnerable, and his will to live seems uncertain. Next to him, in the bed where Lester died, a soldier lays motionless. His entire head and most of his body are bandaged. I'm nauseated by the smells of thickened blood, anesthetics, and diarrhea. Pointing to the end of the hospital bed, I break Earl's trance and ask, "Are you saving this spot for Maran Lu, or can an injured buddy take a seat?"

Earl shakes the cobwebs out of his head. "That girl is goin' be the death of me. I've been waiting for her all morning, and all I get is, 'You not sick. I busy.'" A broad smile lights up Earl's face. "I sure am going to miss my little honey when they send me back to the road front, but I'm willing to make that sacrifice."

Earl watches the men around him suck in air, and his body sags again. "That tuberculosis is like puncturing a man's lungs with a meat cleaver. And these poor boys with malaria get plumb wore down fighting off demons more real than life."

I ease myself down on the corner of Earl's bed. "I wanted to stop by and give you this before I head back to road headquarters tomorrow." I pull a sheath of paper from my pocket and hand it to Earl. "It's the letter for Lester's family."

"Read it to me, my good man. You do a fine job of writing pretty words."

I hesitate, wondering whether a hospital full of dying men is the best place for this. But then I recognize the message is for them, too.

> *We are so sorry for your loss. Life does not come to us tied up in a bow, but it is a gift just the same. Lester gave his life so that we may live. What greater honor can a man give?*

"Praise the Lord." Earl bows his head and remains silent for a few moments. When he looks up, he uses the back of his hand to wipe away a trace of tears.

"I bet that someday, Stilwell's road will be constructed," I say. "But we'll all be dead by then. I'd rather get a purple heart fighting a real war than get paid to be brainless."

"Harry, we've had this conversation before." Earl's voice is adamant. "And I never want to hear it again." Without skipping a beat, he adds, "I see my little Angel of Mercy coming to my side." He waves the petite Burmese nurse over to him. "Maran Lu, Maran Lu, stuck in the jungle, pretty little thing like you. What'll I do when I leave my Maran Lu?" he sings, then reaches out as though he's going to pinch her behind.

"You have claws like crab and brains like one, too." Maran Lu raps the side of Earl's head like she's knocking on a door. "No, I wrong…you have less." Then she offers him her warm smile of support. "Why you still here? Road work started. You big man on road job."

From behind the parachute partition separating the surgery room from the hospital ward, Dr. Seagrave calls out to his assistants, "Another meat wagon. Prepare for surgery."

I'm always surprised at his callousness. But a clean, sterile word like ambulance is inadequate for a war. The graying surgeon pushes aside the partition and ambles over to Earl's bed. While he keeps watch for the incoming wounded, his shoulders slouch and eyeglasses slide down to the tip of his nose. Oblivious to the unflicked cigarette ash hanging precariously from the butt in his mouth, he asks Earl, "What the hell you still doing here?"

Earl splutters, "My good doctor, say the word and I'll be out of here faster than a fox on a chase."

Seagrave flicks the cigarette ashes into his hand, then answers, "Earl, you know I like you, and you're my best baritone singer, but I need that bed. I'm not discharging you so you can go home. You're going back to where we need you: on top of that bulldozer."

"Well, you're the man." Earl swings his good leg and drags his bad one to the side of the bed. "Where are my clothes, Maran Lu?" he asks, then winks at the little nurse, who is adjusting bandages on the patient in the next bed.

"She isn't your Goddamn mother," the doctor grumbles. "Find them yourself. She's got real work to do."

A growing sound of men arguing at the hospital entrance grabs our attention. Medics carrying blood-dripping stretchers jockey to get through the door. Frantically, they bump into wash basins and chairs as they stumble towards the surgery wards.

"What the hell?" Seagrave throws the cigarette butt on the floor. Hurrying to the surgery room, he shouts, "Hang some lamplights in the corner to keep the bugs from falling on the operating table. We need hot water. These instruments are coated with blood…Jesus Christ." The only other sound is mumblings from medical assistants rushing behind the hushed curtain.

Maran Lu shadows the doctor, and Earl withdraws back into his bed. I'm pushed aside, as inconsequential as Seagrave's smashed cigarette.

The man on the first stretcher has two legs blown off at the thigh and ulcerating burns all over his torso. His scream is continuous and shrill, as though he's giving all his energy for one last plea. I can't speak Chinese, so I can only guess he's begging: "My legs, my legs. Give me back my legs."

The left half of the next patient's skull is blown off. The beating gray and white mass of his brain lays exposed. Lifeless arms flop over both sides of the stretcher. He can't be more than fifteen years old. I close my eyes, but can't erase the sight.

Shrapnel slit the next patient's stomach wide open; organs are pushed back inside by a Kachin attendant as they rush towards the operating room.

I need to get out. As I stumble towards the entrance, I bump into a Chinese officer, dazed and unaware of anything around him but his men. Without his cap, the officer's thick, black mop is wild and unruly. Lt. Lin, his uniform shredded and stained, stands rigid, mechanically supervising the treatment of his brigade.

Mistrusting my own eyes, I mumble, "Lt. Lin?" I squeeze my eyes closed and will my gut to be calm at the sight of more butchered bodies. "These are your men?"

The medical ward whirls as men caked in mud and drying blood cry, scream, and whimper. A rushing medical staffer whips past the billowing parachute walls. Stretchers bunch up, filling every aisle to the operating rooms.

Lin hyperventilates. His clammy skin and darting eyes worry me. He strokes the cheek of a young soldier lying in a litter, ignoring the blood dripping from the boy's nose, ears, and mouth. I am frightened by his blank expression and his rapid, incoherent barking of orders to the stretcher bearers. I pull him to sit down.

Lin sinks onto the edge of a bed and lets his head drop into his hands. I wait, desperately wishing I could leave, but feeling compelled to stay. I'd want someone to do the same for me. If only he could cry to release the stress. But Lin refuses to break and slowly lifts himself up, respectful of his men.

"Lt. Flynn," Lin says, weakly, barely acknowledging me.

"Japanese hold hill in Hukawng Valley. My men ambushed." His look says he's seeing the battle again. "For your road, American road, Stilwell Road." There's bitterness in his voice and resignation in his eyes.

"Chinese not afraid to die. But no honor in dying poorly fought battle. We have too much ammunition from your General Stilwell." Lin looks down, struggling with the guilt that overpowers his quivering face. "Unfortunately, we not learn how to use American weapons in time to live. So many die." Lin is obedient to Chiang Kai-shek, who is a man in search of power and willing to expend any life to reach that goal. The Chinese lieutenant straightens, suddenly proud. "But now Japanese know we worthy enemy."

Abruptly, he stops talking and looks out the door to see how many more of his men have come to die. "I must leave. Do my duty," the slight, Chinese officer says as he straightens his hair, puts on his cap, adjusts his torn jacket, and disappears into an increasing horde of Chinese soldiers.

I feel despondent at the thought of all my friends, batty with red, white, and blue Stilwell fever. Charles and Bernie talk about me when they think I'm not around, and Earl is obsessed with righting Reginald's and Lester's deaths by finishing the road. What is the point of dying to build a road that won't be done in time? "Damn it!" I curse under my breath. "*They* may not care if they die, but no one's going to cheat me out of *my* life."

CHAPTER 26

CHRISTMAS, 1943

Christmas is no exception to the daily construction routine. Work is non-stop, come rain, shine, or Jesus. The guys roll out of their cots to the same smelly, humid heat, unconsciously scratching legs, arms, anywhere that got a bite in the night. But not me. Early this morning, I caught a truck into town. Seagrave needs help at his Christmas shindig in Ledo.

When I walk into the supply hut, Schmidt's already barking orders like a rabid dog. I can't help but think of him as Satan's offspring, with thin skin stretched taut across his skull; pinched features; and colorless, greased-back hair.

I move out to the parade ground and start opening boxes. "Christ, there must be a dozen bottles of beer here for every enlisted man. And donuts?" I tell the helpers where to stack the cases of the booze. "Is that barbecue I smell?" Suddenly, I'm starved.

Schmidt can't stay away from me, and I feel him staring down my back. "Flynn, quit goofing off." I want to bash in his teeth.

Without a second thought, I toss him the package I'm holding. "Empty handed?" I ask. "I know you like to keep busy."

He catches the box and winces as the cardboard slices his fingers and draws blood. "Try that again, and I'll let slip where some skeletons are buried," he snarls.

"I'm glad you brought that up," I say while directing the coolies. Schmidt stands idle. "You sent me to the construction front to watch for hijacked ammunition. None showed up. And you never asked me a thing about it when I returned. Sure seems like you just wanted me out of your hair. Makes a fella wonder."

A triumphant smile lights up his face. "Flynn, don't ask questions." "I just don't like being set up. Would you?" I ask.

His confidence falters for a moment, but just as quickly he dismisses my threat with another smile and patronizing sigh. "You don't have anything on me. Besides, I've been reassigned to Dinjan, so if there's any dirty laundry here, it's all yours." Smug as usual, he strolls away to inspect the other men.

Dinjan is base camp for the boys flying the HUMP. As soon as I can, I need to find out if Charles knows about Schmidt's transfer. He hears all the gossip.

Up front, by the mechanic's shop, Bernie ratchets a bolt into the makeshift stage he and his crew are rigging for the Christmas show. Nearby, Charles unwinds a lasso of microphone wires roped around his arm for the sound system. Red and green streamers hang limply from bamboo poles. I can't ask about Schmidt with everyone around, so I slip away to my barracks. Sitting on my cot is a letter from Ruthie. When I open it, a newspaper clipping slips out.

Dear Harry,

At work they asked a couple of us girls to dress up like Santa's helpers so they could include the photos from our company's newspaper in the GI magazines. If only there was more we could do for our fighting boys overseas. I hope this gets to you before Christmas.

Every day I wonder when I'll see you again and hope you think about me. Whatever happens between us, don't give up on happiness, or you'll give up on life.

Love, Ruthie

I look at Ruthie in a short Santa's skirt and red, tailored jacket fringed in white fur. On bent knee, she's handing out a wrapped present from under the Christmas tree. I wish she could jump in that box and get shipped to me, and I bet a lot of the other guys who see her photo will think the same.

While the others eat, I lay on my bed. I'm not hungry any more.

After dinner, the microphone system on the concrete slab buzzes. The real party's ready to begin. I find Earl, Charles, and Bernie by the stage wearing dumb grins on their faces, compliments of the beer.

A big band ensemble, tuxes and all, is spread out on Bernie's platform. The trombone kicks off "I Wish I Could Shimmy Like my Sister Kate." Earl grabs the hand of a reluctant but curious Maran Lu, and pulls her out on the concrete slab where, hours earlier, batteries and engines sat.

"I not dance with longyi – no move knees," Maran Lu complains. The tinsel interwoven in her braid sparkles like her cat-like eyes.

"Well, baby, roll'er on up that skirt so I can show you how we do it." Earl teases with his broad, promising smile.

Following Earl's lead, other soldiers coax the remaining Burmese nurses to dance. They tiptoe onto the dance floor like delicate flowers. Within minutes, their thick, black braids unwind to the rhythm of the jitterbug as they dance with soldiers whose faces they'll never remember.

Ties are loosened, then wrapped around the girls' longyi, cinching bodies together, belly to belly.

American nurses, whose only curves have been dangling intravenous tubes in the past, sport body-hugging tops that swell and ripple in the right places. Like caged animals, everyone's wiggling, bumping, and writhing: nurse with soldier and soldier with soldier.

Of course, charming Charles found himself a girl, but Bernie and I stand like wallflowers on the side. The parade ground spills over with happy drunks.

"I never went to bed with an ugly woman," one soldier says to another. His dance partner responds, "But I bet you woke up with more than one." Beer spills down their chins as they laugh.

Merrill's voice behind me breaks through the music. "We lost a couple of our Chinese scouts the other day." I glance back to see Merrill, Stilwell, and Seagrave standing together a few feet away, cupping glasses of something stronger than beer.

"Good." From the corner of my eye, I see the eagle profile of Stilwell. "I'm sick of pointing out their poor performance to Chiang Kai-shek, that peanut sized twerp."

What a caring guy, I think as I watch him sip from his glass.

"Did you hear what Churchill's been saying lately?" Stilwell's voice carries despite the officers huddling together. "'You can count on the Americans to do the right thing after they've tried everything else.' Now, doesn't that sound like typical Limey crap?"

"What has Mountbatten said about Galahad?" It's Merrill's voice.

"He's a dumb bunny like the rest," Stilwell grunts. "Mount-battten wants to welsh on the 14th British artillery he'd promised me. He's nothing but a double-crossing bastard. But I don't give a damn. Wingate's playing it straight and has three Chindit brigades ready to back me up at Myitkyina." I see the smoke rising from his cigarette as Stilwell pauses.

Two soldiers, leaning against each other for support, stagger in front of me. "Remind me to kill you tomorrow for letting me make a pass at that dame."

His buddy answers, "That was no dame. Next time look for the tits." "Remind me anyway," the first soldier says.

The dark night and loud music hide me as the officers continue to argue.

"Joe, won't our guys need support from an artillery battalion? Rifles are no match for tanks and mortar." Merrill's voice sounds more defiant than questioning.

"Merrill's right," Seagrave's gravelly voice interrupts before Stilwell can answer. "Central Burma's swamped with the enemy. You've marched through that elephant grass and know the Japanese could be waiting beyond any blade. Our boys don't know the jungle like they do."

"I know. It's a cockeyed setup but it's all I've got to push that damn road through for the Peanut," the General says. "Besides, the Chinese X Force training outside of Bombay will soon be ready, and the Generalissimo has agreed to give me fifty-thousand more of his Y Force."

"You think marching the Y Force from China is going to get you anything more than fifty-thousand hungry stomachs to feed? And they won't fight unless we're already winning. They're not like the Japanese…they don't attack; they only know how to defend themselves." Seagrave's not intimidated by Stilwell's bullying.

"What do you want me to do? Sit around and go crazy until the Brits decide to join the war?" Stilwell snaps, then stomps away.

Unexpectedly, one of the American nurses, a sassy-looking redhead, grabs my hand and drags me onto the concrete slab. This girl looks like she's ready for trouble, and after a few beers, I'm ready to dish it out. At first, I think her seductive, smoky eyes and the unfastened top button of her satin blouse are saying something to me. Then I realize I'm only her prop. Still, I don't mind. With legs like that, someone's got to know the jitterbug throws so the other guys can get a thrill. "Doll, let's boogie?" I see I have a live one on my hands.

I whisper in her ear, "You know, I think you're the most beautiful woman in the world." A soothing, deep-throated laugh escapes. "Really?" she asks.

"No, but I don't mind lying if it gets me somewhere," I say with a straight face. Bernie, wearing a red sock on his head and beard made of palm leaves, shouts, "Hey,

Harry, where'd you find Rita Hayworth?" When he wriggles his eyebrows like Groucho Marx, I can understand why women go the opposite direction. Suddenly, the beer bottle in Bernie's hand shatters when a couple of soused privates smash him and his bottle against a wall.

It doesn't take a genius to see Bernie's short fuse is about to explode into flying fists. I elbow my way through the crowd and hand him over to Rita Hayworth's double to rescue him from a black eye. The two look at each other, surprised but not disappointed.

I slip away to a corner by the shop, hidden by a clump of bushes. I lean against the wall and light up a smoke. The funk from Ruthie's letter still eats at me.

The band starts up another tune but quickly peters out, one instrument at a time, as Stilwell takes center stage. "Testing one, two, three." All eyes are on the General. Offstage, Merrill and Seagrave wait.

"I hope you're having a good time. Merry Christmas." The men give Stilwell a whooping cheer as his eyes skim over the crowd. "It's a helluva job, fighting a war, but I want to let you know, I'm proud of you. Not being with your families has got to be tough. I know it is for me." The crowd goes silent. "The life of a soldier isn't an easy one. But there are kids back home saying a prayer for you. Remember, you're here for them." Stilwell salutes us. Before he leaves the stage, he adds, "Now, here's the Colonel you can thank for tonight's booze."

A pack of soldiers push a hesitant Pick towards the stage. We can also thank him for getting the road to Shingbwiyang's doorstep so rapidly. Hell, I should hate him, but I kind of like the guy.

Colonel Pick motions for quiet.

"It is indeed a privilege and pleasure to officially recognize your hard work. You battled flash floods that rose three feet in fifteen minutes. You worked sixteen-hour days without relief and slept without cover. You deserve the highest commendation. One-third of the Chinese road to freedom has been built. With such dedication, I have confidence the Ledo-Kunming Road will lead the CBI Theatre to victory."

"Hell, we're only one-third of the way?" A voice on the other side of the bushes startles me. It's the QUARTERBACK. "Am I the only one pushing to get this war over?"

"Joe, you've got a great plan, but I don't see how you're going to get Galahad, the Chindits, and the X Force to Myitkyina by next Spring. So there's no reason to sit on the road so hard." The younger Merrill humors his boss. "If Operation END RUN doesn't go like clockwork, the monsoon will kill the road and a lot of men."

"But the Japs will never expect us right before the monsoon. That's why it's the perfect time!" Stilwell explodes.

Merrill presses the General further. "Wingate's guys and Galahad have had guerrilla training. But you can't send the X Force out yet; they just arrived in India. Besides, they're a bunch of punks still in training pants, probably no more than fifteen years old. "

The General juts his chin out in defiance. "Christ, if that's the answer you're going to give me, then good night!" Stilwell barks. "You sound like you got your dink cut off."

No one talks, but I see smoke, like war signals, rise from the famous cigarette holder and pipe. The music winds down, and men are being hauled back to their barracks.

Merrill takes in a big breath, releasing it like he's trying to blow out a campfire. In the faint night light, his graying temples show his age. "It's your call."

"Glad you see it my way." Stilwell sounds satisfied. "Hey, your parties are getting better, Seagrave." Their voices fade as they walk away.

"Kee-rist," I mutter. My back slides down the wall until my butt hits the ground, and I slump over my knees. "Galahad's a suicide mission. That heartless son-of-a-bitch is desperate."

Clicking heels stop in front of me. I lift my head to see red fingernails on an outstretched hand. My eyes inch up the sleek, shapely legs. It's the redhead, short a couple more buttons.

"Thanks for the hand." I grasp her soft, delicate fingers. But she doesn't pull me up.

"It looks so—lonely down there." She unbuttons a couple more buttons, exposing more than cleavage. "I thought you may need some holiday cheer."

CHAPTER 27

February, 1944

Waves of heat rise from the barren, scorching ground. Floating dust particles reflect multicolor rays from the setting sun. I drive a food truck through the listless jungle to the construction site. The humidity drains my body and leaves my mind numb.

Before I throw the door open, I wrench the stick shift from low to neutral. The construction crew moves at a dazed, mechanical pace. Still, the road continues to inch forward towards Jambu Bum in the Hukawng Valley. Grinding gears from thumping power shovels and front end loaders momentarily stop for the dinner break. On my truck's tailgate, I set out food and jugs of water. Men shuffle to where they've stashed their mess kits, then wordlessly line up, either too tired or too hot to waste energy on anything more than what's absolutely necessary.

The lineup is a hodgepodge of Negro equipment operators; Chinese laborers wearing broad-brimmed bamboo hats; and ragtag, uniformed Chinese soldiers who guard the road front. They jam up the line, filling up their canteens and drinking deeply multiple times, until the water drips from the corners of their mouths. Only then do they spoon the stew into their plates. They sit along a row of trees, hoping an afternoon breeze will pick up. After ten minutes of rest and provisions, small talk breaks the vacant air.

Out of the corner of my eye, I see a battalion of soldiers and their mules spill out, single file, from a well-concealed animal trail. The headlights of an earth mover spotlight the column as they approach us.

Limp with heat exhaustion, and seemingly rooted to the ground, the road crew watches the procession of war-bound American soldiers. Grinning, some of the GIs nod at the staring workers. A dust screen envelopes the road bed; dirt clouds rise and fall to the rhythm of their shuffling feet. Helmets, leather boots, rifle butts, and a pyramid of provisions piled on the backs of mules peek out here and there from the billowing haze.

Most of the troops just plow forward, but a few drop out of rank, pull their canteens from their belts, and unscrew the caps before they tramp over to the tailgate. I shove my hands in my pockets and lean against the side of the truck, curious about the parade.

I open the spigot on the water jug as a soldier, red-eyed from dust, thrusts his canteen under the spout. He barely notices me.

"Thanks, buddy," the tired young man mumbles when he leaves. He lifts his canteen in the air and lets the water spill over his face. Most of the clear liquid drains down his throat.

"Hey, you guys look a little thirsty. Where did you come from?" I ask. They aren't wearing any insignia, so I don't know who they are, but I'm not too proud to be nosey.

The soldier stops his makeshift shower, looks at me with suspicion, then walks away without another word. I shrug an apology. By now, other soldiers, faces crusted with dirt and stained from coursing sweat, crowd around the back of the truck, canteens in hand. They slowly come to life.

"Nice looking road you have here," a man with a slow, steady smile says. His gaze takes in the road, the crew, and the equipment. "We've heard about you and this road of yours." His New England accent slips in on the vowels.

I can tell that the sergeant—I can tell his rank from his lapel—wants to make small talk, but his voice is slightly anxious, as though shooting the breeze is not a luxury he can afford right now.

"Got shipped out a year ago. What about yourself?" I ask, pulling out a cigarette and offering it to the soldier.

The soldier's helmet slides forward as I light the smoke for him. He inhales deeply. "Deogarh, India, a few weeks ago. We took a train up to a town just south of Ledo, then hit the dirt. It's been mostly uphill since then, and our feet are sorry little puppies. Been bivouacking along the side of the road every night." He takes another drag and throws his head back as he exhales. Then he rolls his shoulders back and forth to unwind. "If I didn't have this sixty-pound pack on my back, and my leg muscles didn't cramp up every night, this might be a nice place to visit." He stares off into a stand of giant Halong trees. Absentmindedly, he smashes a mosquito on his forearm. "No, I take it back," he grimaces. "I hate bugs."

I make a quick check of the supplies. It looks like they need more water, and I pull out another jug. "Why the surprise party out of nowhere? Someone should get the benefit of this road we're building to nowhere."

The sergeant considers my question, but answers with his own query. "Seen any fighting in these parts lately?"

"I wish," I answer too quickly, then try to backpedal. "Well, no American troops have seen any action. They've sent these Chinese boys, but they're about as experienced in combat as I am in brain surgery."

The middle-age soldier offers a comforting nod of agreement, "Yeah, I've heard the Chinese X Force is supposed to be our backup—just hope they don't back up so far that we're left facing the enemy alone."

The other soldiers drop in and out of their columns, fill up with water, then rejoin the march. They're like nomadic herdsmen, wild-eyed and set on survival. A colonel, younger than the sergeant by about twenty years, steps up to join our conversation. He guzzles water from his freshly filled canteen, but fixes an eye on me with a manner that tells me he's on a fishing expedition. His youthful looks do not camouflage his commanding countenance.

"A few days ago, a British brigade passed through," I say, reaching to pull out a cigarette for myself and offer one to him. "Looked like an infantry unit."

He ignores me and instead he tells his men to hustle with their canteens and drop back in line. By now, a swarm of the American soldiers are jostling the truck like they want to tip it over and drain every last drop of the provisions inside, just for fun.

"Don't worry about our guys." The older sergeant sees my concern. "They're just a bunch of high-spirited boys too tired to do much damage. They'll settle down in a few."

Then the Colonel asks, only partially interested, "How much farther does the road hold out?"

I close my eyes and consider his question, hoping I'll get more information from them before I give away the store. "There's the trace, cleared road bed, excavated dirt, gravel track, then tarmac finish. Which section are you talking about?"

He takes my holdout as though he suffers it every day. "The trace will do."

"Two miles up," I offer, wondering why the hell they're so secretive. Then it hits me: this is Galahad.

"Appreciate the help," the colonel answers. "Mr. Doyer, we best be on our way." "Sure thing, Colonel Hunter," Doyer says, but he holds back for a few minutes more.

Wheels squeal and motors rumble. I check over my shoulder to see the road crew back on the clock. Through the last bits of daylight, I watch a dozer battle a tangle of vines and hundred-foot-tall trees. My shoulder muscles are tight as Hunter walks away. I feel defeated at the thought of letting Galahad slip by without passing on what I heard from Stilwell.

Doyer looks at me expectantly, as though he knows I have information. "Rumor has it the Brits were Wingate's Chindits," I say.

He nods, but says nothing.

"You ask me, you're all on a suicide mission. No heavy artillery to back you up. Just your own rifles and machine guns. The Japanese mortar and tanks will wipe you all out before you're within firing distance." I expect to see alarm or anger in Doyer's eyes, but his passive lack of response tells me nothing.

He instead screws the cap on his canteen and nods his thanks.

"It's all a matter of fate," he finally answers with an invincible confidence that seems to be founded on ignorance.

I catch Doyer's glance back before he turns to catch up with Hunter. "You're Galahad?" I ask, hoping for at least one answer.

"Something like that," he says. "We're the five-three-oh-seventh." He pauses for effect, then adds, "Provisional."

When I get back to my barrack, there's a note waiting for me. "Flynn, meet me at my field office, 08:00 hours." Signed Colonel Pick.

I've got a bad feeling that I'm finally going to be buried by my own stupidity.

CHAPTER 28

"Flynn, you're late." Sitting behind a desk in his spartan office, Colonel Pick frowns at his watch. Bright sunlight illuminates the room.

Confused by this greeting, I stammer, "Yes Sir." Then, with barely a moment's hesitation, add, "No, Sir." I straighten, confident that I'm actually five minutes early.

"Are you calling me a liar?" Pick stands up, towering over me even though I'm no slouch at six feet. "Because if you are, that's insubordination. Do you know what happens to soldiers who are insubordinate?" He walks around his desk, ready to give me a full grilling.

"Sir, my watch must be wrong." I know it's not because I've become a clock watcher lately, ready to quit as soon as my shift hits the hour. "I'll make that correction."

Pick grunts in response. I don't like the way he's scowling and attacking me. He must know about my dynamite or the HCL. My neck knots up and stomach twists.

"Flynn, I get the feeling you don't like being in the Army." Outside the office, drawers slam, no-nonsense voices chatter, and feet retreat, but the Colonel seems oblivious to anything but me. "I had a little chat with Captain Schmidt." He checks to see how I react. It wasn't a question, so I stand erect, looking straight ahead.

"What do you think of Schmidt?" he asks, his tone encouraging me to trust him.

I hear every miniscule noise: the fan blowing behind his desk, the swish of a gecko's tail climbing up the wall, my watch ticking. I swallow to clear my throat and say, "Captain Schmidt is the SOS field director. Sir." And he's a fucking bastard, I think to myself.

Inches from my face, Pick circles around me, inspecting my uniform as though any crease out of place will be reason enough for me to get slammed. "That's not what I asked," he whispers a hair's width from my ear. "Soldier, go ahead. You have my permission to speak freely."

The sun streaking in from the window practically blinds me. What the hell is going on? My mind spins like a whirling roulette wheel waiting for the ball to drop into place. Pick knows how to push my buttons, and he's jamming them right now. "What do you want me to say? I don't like the guy. But I'm doing my job. Okay?"

"Not according to Schmidt," Pick shoots back. "We need soldiers who are team players, not loners."

I throw my head back a little too defiantly, wanting to brace myself with both hands on my hips in preparation for the next punch, but I don't move. "Well, if I want to live through this war, it ain't gonna be because of the likes of Schmidt. Sometimes you just gotta take control of things; otherwise, you're stuck holding the bomb they've left ticking in your hands. Schmidt's in it for Schmidt. And if there ain't anything in it, there's no Schmidt."

"So you're the kind of guy who goes off half-cocked, not giving a damn what your supervising officer or anyone else thinks." Pick mirrors my stand off, still not explaining why exactly I'm here.

I slap the back of the chair in front of me; it tumbles over onto the desk, "If it means survival, yeah." I wait for another smart-ass remark from Pick, but he just studies me. "I may not always make the right decisions, but I make them. And I own up to them." As soon as I say this, I think of the girl with the bamboo basket and pray that she's still alive.

Pick knows he's got my goat. His thin smile tells me he's toying with me. "You're the kind of guy who calls himself a leader, but you just like to defy authority to get attention. If..."

"That's not true," I interject. "There's something wrong here, but nobody cares enough to notice. I like to make things right. I'm good at it. I've had to fix problems my whole life."

Images of the past hit me: my mother hunched over the table

so we couldn't see her fears of eviction; peddling newspapers to condescending businessmen; scrubbing toilets in military school before all my friends, who didn't have to work for their tuition, arrived.

"So you've been in tight spots before?" Pick's gaze softens; the caring grandfather side of him baits me. "Doesn't seem like a good place to come from."

"No, it's not. But our bad luck is what pushes us forward. And I've come a long way." My jaw clenches; I'm determined not to be trapped.

"Seems to me you have a little difficulty deciding who's right and who's wrong. Whose side you're on and whose head you want to bust open." He leans against the edge of his desk.

"You're right. I don't always know who I can trust. So I don't trust anybody."

"Well, then I'm glad we haven't put a rifle in your hands. You'd probably shoot anything that moved." The Colonel resumes his authoritative stance and begins circling me again.

"You're wrong. I respect a gun. It isn't a toy. It's a tool."

"So you've used a gun before? How many Japs have you killed?"

"None, Sir. But I grew up on a farm. So I know how to use a gun." I close my eyes to find strength; memories of dried leaves crunching underfoot as I hunted pheasants back home flash before me. But never have I shot a man.

"You know how to use it, but are you any good?" "Some say I've got a talent."

"And others?"

"They're jealous." I grab the fallen chair and slam it back upright. "You sound like you're a crybaby if others don't see things your way." "I don't cry." That's a lie.

"Well, we'll see about that after I tell you what Schmidt's recommended." Colonel Pick's steely eyes tell me the other shoe is ready to drop. "Got a talent for cleaning toilets? What about digging out latrines, shoveling manure? You're an old farm hand, after all. Or would you rather be doing what we came here to do: win a war?"

"Give me a gun and the enemy any day. And get Schmidt the fuck out of my life." "Son, I have always thought I could do everything ten times better than any boss I've ever had, and that's the way it should be. But orders are orders. I'm not sure who you're fighting, but it should be the Japanese, not us." The Colonel sits and swivels in his chair, his back facing me. "Pack your bags and get out of here." I've just been dismissed.

"Sir?" I feel like I've been pummeled.

He turns around and looks up, extending a paper in his hand. "You have fifteen minutes to get your gear together. They're waiting for you."

"Who? Where? Sir." I reach for the paper, but I can't focus to read.

"Hunter told me he had a little chat with you on the road." Pick checks for realization in my eyes. "You just volunteered to join the 53-07th."

"Provisional?" It comes out as a whisper, a question, disbelief. I don't know whether to be happy, mad, or scared.

"Their SOS man broke down sobbing, and they haven't even seen any action. We can't send them out with somebody they've got to babysit. Everyone has to hold his own." The game's over. Pick's smile tells me I passed the test. "Soldier, you'll have to learn to trust Galahad, or you'll go home in a box."

Stilwell bursts into the room—no knock or cordial interruptions—and strides over to Pick, ignoring me like I'm a fixture, not a person. I salute, then turn to leave. As I walk towards the door, I glance back and hesitate.

"I just got the dope on our airboys," Stilwell says. "They got pounced because the Chinese X Force was caught napping." The General grimaces, then swipes his fist at an invisible opponent while looking out the window for the next taker. "The Peanut's men have got a lot of pep when they talk, but they're cautious movers. What saps. I bawled them out and told them to buck up or get out."

"So now what?" Pick stands up. Stilwell takes a seat, crosses his legs, then throws back his head in reflection.

"We wait for Galahad."

The door clicks softly in place behind me.

PART II

MARAUDERS- WALAWBUM,

SHADUZUP, MYITKYINA

CHAPTER 29

We stop along the banks of a tributary draining into the Chindwin River in Northern Burma. Some of the guys go swimming; others wash clothes before we bivouac for the night. Wet fatigues and t-shirts form a camouflaged carpet on the boulders and along the shores of the stream. Plopping down, I unlace my boots and empty the sand that has been grating my flesh all day.

A scrawny soldier, looking no older than fifteen, jokes, "Hey, Harry, I have a uniform for every day of the week." Looking down at his attire, he continues, "and this is it."

It hasn't always been so lighthearted in the couple weeks since I joined Galahad. If it wasn't for Stilwell wanting to build his damn road, we wouldn't be on this suicide mission. So the General better do his job and help us do ours, then get us out of here, because the alternative is grim. It's been impossible to ignore the bitterness the men of Galahad feel towards Stilwell and H.Q.

As I strip down for a swim, a captain, red-eyed from kicking up dust all day, gives me an earful. "At least we have a name now: the five-three-oh-seventh. Hell, we didn't even have a proper designation until we hit India." He spits out the words with disgust. "We were just a soon-to-be something. Do you know what it feels like to wake up each morning not knowing what you are? Especially if you're a volunteer on a mission that you're not expected to return from. It's like they didn't know what to do with us, so they pretended we didn't exist." He wades into the stream, exasperated.

On shore, another soldier picks up a stone and skips it over the clear running water. "They think we're outlaws, outcasts. Maybe we are." He's a long-jawed soldier with a wicked grin straight from the Wild West. I feel my stomach turn when he boasts, in his machine gun staccato, "I relish hand-to-hand combat. It's pure joy, hearing them squeal like puppies as you slit their throats from their neck to their skull and watch the blood spurt." Looking down at his scuffed boots, he nervously digs out chunks of earth with his toe. "Guess that doesn't sound very healthy, does it?"

It seems their isolation and this refusal to conform is what welds them together. Instead of just taking in the strangeness of India and maybe even finding it fascinating, they fight it like they fight everything. The men in Galahad see the turban-headed porters and their stick-like limbs as threats, ready to rob them. For these men, the smells of curry and aromatic wood smoke can't stifle the stench of the open-drain sewage. Rather than being swept away by India's flowing silk and vibrant jewels, they focus on images of rag-torn beggars. From the soldiers in Ledo, who don't give a damn about anything, to Galahad, who only give a damn about themselves, what have I gotten myself into?

Downstream, Winton Steinfeld, nicknamed Doc, floats on his back in the glittering current, soaking in the filtered light and indulging his playful love of life. His wet, black hair shines blue in the afternoon sun. Cloaked by a canopy of overhanging trees and vines, the stream would have been idyllic had we not been alert to the poisonous vipers hidden in the branches.

Doc responds nonchalantly to the complaints by the men: "He giveth and He taketh away; both very inadequately." Then he sings out his own rendition of things.

"The Five-Three-Oh-Seventh Comp. Unit Provisional
Has come to battle for CBI on the basis of one conditional
They not be scorned for being themselves, which one may think is too original
For they have sinned as one may judge on a scale that is beyond super divisional."

At night, we camp uphill, away from the beach, to avoid the sand flies. Lt. William Woomer...or Woomer the Boomer, so named for his exploits in the South Pacific…and I take our rifles and try our luck at a little hunting. Woomer is in it for the meat. I need the target practice. Even though I'm assigned to supply duty, everyone carries a rifle and is expected to fight.

"Harry, over here," Woomer whispers, then motions towards a clearing ahead with his long, lanky arms. Barely visible in the night's fading light, a tiger stalks an unsuspecting marsh deer. The tiger's yellow stripes are illuminated by a rogue ray of light, and its amber eyes are intent on the kill. Each limb of the cat moves in stealthy, synchronized motion; every muscular molecule is activated in sequential order at the precise time. The deer looks up, alert and sensing trouble. But the smell from our bodies, combined with that of the tiger, confuses it. Instead of loping off towards safety, the doe jumps directly into the claws of the leaping tiger. The brush thrashes.

"I think I'll let him have that one." Woomer turns instead towards the animal trail that leads to the stream, then ducks under the draping branches. Within the hour, we're hauling a dead deer, legs tied to a bamboo pole and head dropping to the ground, towards camp.

We skin and roast it for dinner. We haven't had a food drop in two days.

As the supply officer, I work with the radio crew to pinpoint the coordinates for our food drops. The flight carrying our drop two days ago was cancelled because of a torrential downpour. Flying low over the mountainous treetops through clouds is the best way to crack up a plane. No sense in adding to the death toll. The next day, in agony, we watched the white, green, and blue billowing parachutes plummet into the one-hundred-fifty-foot-tall jungle canopy. I still can't figure out how they missed the co-ordinates I gave them. We shot our rifles to dislodge the bundles and even tried a mortar or two, but our only reward was shattered branches and bits of food blown to bits. With the road crew, talk of dames enlivened our evening poker games; in the far reaches of this Burma jungle, our nighttime conversation turns to fried chicken and apple pie recipes.

CHAPTER 30

The morning dawns with another grueling march ahead of us. We're barely out of the sack when we hear a gunshot. Ahead, our scout races back towards us. Men slip off into the forest, aiming rifles down the road. We hear a rumble, and the ground shakes. Trees bounce. Birds alight from branches, screeching. From a bend in the road, a wild baby elephant charges towards us. Yet, no one moves. How do you control an elephant gone berserk?

The soldier next to me raises his rifle. "Stand back," he shouts, then fires once, twice.

The calf stops. It looks surprised, hurt, and frightened. It wobbles, then kneels down, as though it will rest a bit. It rolls over and blinks its large, wide eyes to study a platoon of soldiers grasping guns, smoke still rising from one barrel. It never gets up. I think of the gaja I rode to the construction camp; its leathery skin, flapping ears, and gentle gait, burdened with our supplies, patiently carrying me up the steep slope. I feel pity for this dumb, juvenile beast, probably left alone by its mother for but a moment. Then, alarmed, I yell, "Let's clear the area. Where there's a baby, there's a mother." I needn't say any more. We hurry along the trail, not looking back.

It's then I realize I never loaded my gun. What kind of a soldier am I? From behind, I hear a trumpet wailing.

We begin our steep ascent by crossing the hundred-foot-wide Tanai River over a native bridge. Five bamboo poles plank the walkway. Men grab the hemp handrail and lead their unsteady mules over the river. When I turn back, the bouncing bridge is holding twenty soldiers, each carrying sixty-pound packs. I feel a rush of relief that the hollow shoots held while I was trapped in the middle. It seems we're always one step away from disaster.

Ahead, we take turns fighting a thicket of the willowy grass. When it's my go, I hack with the machete until it's dull and my arms burn. I move towards the back of the line, limp from exhaustion. The next guy slips, and his machete slices through his pants. "Get him out of here.

Next!" someone shouts.

While the others work, I grab bamboo shreds and stick them in my sack for dry kindling.

Even if we don't get our food drops all the time, I save my packets of coffee and like it hot.

On the other side of the Tanai, we make a clearing for a light plane to land. It's something Galahad has become experts at, so brass can be flown in and wounded—like the machete guy—flown out. When the piper cub lands, I'm struck by the appearance of its only passenger. I never noticed before that Merrill wore the same combat hat and faded fatigues as the rest of us. The only thing out of the ordinary is his pipe.

Colonels Hunter and Osborne approach the plane as Merrill jumps from the door. Even without hearing their conversation, it's easy to see the friendship among them. Though shorter than Merrill, Hunter's broad chest and sturdy build equalize him. And Osborne, a slight-framed intellectual—more the professor-type than a combat battalion officer—is no slouch, either.

Men busy themselves with chores close to the headquarters tent so they can learn more about Merrill, who everyone knows has a direct line to General Stilwell. The wireless radio sits at the edge of the tent's canvas flaps, where I crank the generator. I give the code clerk an enciphered message to base H.Q. for our next supply drop, as the officers convene in the tent to review topographic maps and decide upon routes.

"Your boys look ready for the job," Merrill says, a satisfied smile inching around his pipe.

Hunter folds his arms, then, in a crisp, low voice, answers, "Glad they meet with your approval. We do our best to please."

Osborne adds, "Merrill, they'd like to hear that from you."

"Then let me tell them right now," Merrill offers. As he exits the tent, he looks in my direction and, with a friendly smile, quips, "Flynn, why am I not surprised to see you here?" The officers approach a group of soldiers cooking over a campfire.

Woomer defiantly jumps up from the fire, long arms swinging like an orangutan. "Colonel Merrill, the men would like a straight answer. Where are we going, and what's our objective?"

Merrill eyes Hunter. Hunter shrugs his shoulders, and gives Merrill center stage.

Without further encouragement, Merrill walks over to the campfire and asks, "If this isn't a private war, can I join you?" He waits for a nod from Woomer, then describes the plan. "Your mission is to wipe out the enemy on the Kamaing Road. It's the north-south axis for Japanese communications through the Hukawng and Mogaung valleys." Merrill reaches out to shake Woomer's hand. "Thanks for asking."

By now, the men are gathering to meet Merrill. He walks among the ranks, answering questions. His unassuming demeanor gives the men confidence that someone cares, and we're happy to finally have a leader. After he talks with a number of the men, he boards the plane and leaves.

The plane left a full food drop, but, unfortunately, the mail run wasn't loaded. Galahad hasn't received mail since last fall, and the disappointment is thick. These men's unshaven appearance and disdain for life led me to believe they didn't give a damn about anything. But they do.

After bushwhacking through fourteen miles of jungle and up thirty-five-hundred feet of sheer cliffs, I'm exhausted from the day's brutal beating, but my body refuses to relax. Lying on the hard ground, I look up and follow the luminescence from a shooting star until it fizzles into the horizon. My wish is for immediate sleep to wash away the pain from today's march. On top of everything else, breaking in new boots has been murder on my feet. I'll have to do a better job of wrapping them tomorrow. Now I'm thinking; my poor GI back.

Laughing aloud as I recall one of the mule skinners coaxing—or, more accurately, harassing—his pack animal today, I force myself to sit up before I cough to death.

"You need a drink or a shrink." Joe Doyer's New England accent catches me off guard. "You don't mind if I join you, do you?" He sits down and lights cigarettes for us both.

"Thanks." I take a drag, and it shoots a little energy into my numb body. "Did you see that guy this morning chewing out his mule?"

Doyer nods.

"My feet hurt, too." I mimic the soldier's sarcasm. He had shoulder-pushed the animal's rump, cussed him, tugged his rope raw, and whispered sweet nothings to try to get his ass up a finger-clawing steep slope. "This is my second assignment in Burma, and it's only your first, you son of a bitch. Blah blah blah. You volunteered, too, so shut that hee-haw of yours, or I'll have to call you Jack, cuz you won't have an ass after I'm done kicking you up this here hill."

Mr. Doyer, which most men call him instead of Sarge, was my first Galahad friend. Like me, Mr. Doyer, a Chief Warrant Officer, is an SOS man. More than twenty years my senior, he can out-march me and most of the other soldiers. As the story goes, Colonel Merrill assigned him to the rear echelon. But Joe, having fought in the first war and knowing how the game is played, was not ready to be put to pasture. He bet Merrill he'd out-hike and outshoot the Colonel.

Needless to say, Mr. Doyer got front line duty.

"That mule may have a direct line to God. If so, we're in for shit." Mr. Doyer's down-to- earth tone makes the listener believe in what he says. "Maybe we ought to make him General.

We got enough other asses with brass."

He stubs out his cigarette, rubs the back of his neck, and lion yawns. "Think I'm going call it a night, Harry." He stands to go. "And don't go laughing to yourself too often. The other guys will think you've got a screw loose."

As I lay back on my blanket, wind rustles the trees overhead and the stars slowly disappear behind the developing clouds. The long-range radio plays a soft refrain in the distance from *Aida*. The music is so incongruent with the surroundings, infusing the primitive wild habitat with a crystal-clear aria—whether the voice cries out passionately in pain or pleasure, I don't know.

My mind returns to Stilwell's Road—that broad gash through the jungle, undulating up slopes and down ravines, disappearing behind bends and fading in the distance. Now that we're deep in the jungle following uncut paths, I feel lost without its constant presence giving me a reason to fight. Instead, I'm stuck with a bunch of suspicious, trigger-happy guys. And these are the boys Pick told me to learn to trust. I got what I asked for; a gun in my hand. But is it what I really want?

"This is radio KXKY, signing off from Darwin, Australia."

CHAPTER 31

I wake to the babble of monkeys and the chafing cry of hornbills. Wild elephants trumpet, deep within the jungle. As I roll over on the hard ground, I notice the other men have eaten and are packing up. Disorientated by the unannounced wake-up call, I throw on my clothes and pack my poncho and blanket. Breakfast will have to wait.

We hear a rumble in the distance. Someone jokes, "Let's hope it's artillery and not thunder."

We're ordered to shoulder our packs, and, without further delay, the column pushes forward towards our first objective.

We march in silence until the morning's sun wears down our caution.

Finally, my feet force words out of my mouth, "Can someone explain to me why we can't use that perfectly good dirt road about a mile to the west?" The sand eats away the soft flesh on my soles, and this new fungus infection makes me want to scratch them raw.

Mr. Doyer slips back in the column to hold position a few paces behind me. "Harry, we're playing a game called hide and don't seek. The Japanese don't know we're here. We want to keep it that way."

Seems to me like common sense is not something taught by the military, so I say, "As soon as I see a down slope, I know I'll be squishing through a stream and then hiking uphill again. All I'm suggesting is that it's easier if we stay near the ridge top."

"And how would you hide almost three-thousand men from those Japanese Franks patrolling the skies?" Doyer's patient voice is irritating only because he's right. "Besides, we have another rendezvous later today with the brass outside Ningbyen. So we *have* to trek down because we can't build them a light plane landing in these here steep hills."

On our descent, the stench hits us before we're out of the elephant grass. Dilapidated bamboo bashas sit on stilts at the edge of rice paddies. Mutilated bodies, swarming with insects, remind us why we're here. Most are women and children within an arms reach of each other.

Rabid dogs, bloody and growling, threaten us to keep clear as they paw, rip, and disembowel their meals. As we march on I wonder if this is what they did to Maran Lu's village.

Within a quarter mile of the road, at the edge of the river, we're ordered to stop. We drop down and lean against the bank, letting our feet savor the few moments of reprieve.

I close my eyes, then think aloud: "Let's call it a day, boys. How's about a beer?" I hear restrained chuckles, warbling birds, and the sound of the rushing wind that has been concealed by the repetitive thudding of mule's hooves. I open my eyes, breaking the spell.

Downstream, where the shallow sandbars flank the widening river, we see a procession of men crossing to our side. One of them wears a Chindit hat and shorts. I recognize him and groan.

"Stilwell sure has skinny legs," Doyer says. We both know this is no indication of his tenacity. Still, his wiry body and ordinary looks are less than awe-inspiring, and it's rumored his lack of negotiating flair isn't lost on the high-ranking brass or political puppeteers.

Sunburned and stiff, I begrudgingly prepare to stand at attention. For all the times I've seen the General, I've never spoken with him. This seems to be a strange place for him to finally welcome Galahad. The other men ready themselves, too, snarling at their leader, who has abandoned them until he needs them.

"Men," Stilwell says, parading in front of us. "You've been told by Colonel Merrill that we need to push the enemy out of Burma. We're starting here in the north so we can clear a path to connect our headquarters in India to China. Your first objective is Walawbum. It's the northernmost tip of the enemy's control, just outside Jambu Bum Pass." He speaks simply and quietly. "In eight days, your job is to sabotage the lines, put in a road block, and ambush the scouts so they're caught with their pants down. Our Chinese X Force will press the advancing Japanese back and keep them busy, while you infiltrate from the rear." Sweating in the midday sun, his energy seems to increase with each word. "You won't be alone on this mission. Further south, the British Chindits will take out rail tracks and destroy communication lines to eliminate the possibility of Jap reinforcements moving up. I want you in and out before the Chinese infantry and tank units attack from the north."

Lt. Sam Wilson, a lantern-jawed, fair-haired southerner and, our personal Civil War historian, states, "Sir, the men are in great shape. We can get it done in less time."

Stilwell's naturally gruff nature returns. "Soldier, this is no cake walk. I want you to fan out into the Hukawng Valley, then surprise them from the east. That's a lot of marching. Do I make myself clear?"

"Yes. Sir!" Sam's young face exudes an idealism that's hard to supress.

Pleased with the reception from Galahad, Stilwell bites down on his cigarette holder, then confides, "Men, your role is critical to the success of the CBI Theater in Burma. We need to build that road to China so they'll get off their butts and help us win this war. I'm looking at a well-trained, hard-hitting unit. I know it will be rough going for you boys, but you can do it."

The General's made a good first impression on the men, as evidenced by the way they swagger back to pick up their packs. But I know Stilwell's too busy being a political butterfly to really concern himself with us.

Looking satisfied, Stilwell turns to Hunter before re-entering the stream. "Tough-looking lot of babies you got here."

In keeping with Stilwell's orders, we march east into the valley until it's dark. We grope around boulders, find places to drop our packs, unload the mules, set up communication lines, then eat a cold meal. The skies are clear, so rather than pitch tents with the supply drop parachutes, we lay out our ponchos and pull our blankets over our heads. It's only the first day of this mission, and we're already exhausted. Still, unworried, sleep seeps in immediately.

We're not out of the valley in the requisite eight days. The long, less-than-scenic route has been a tip-toeing nightmare. Small parties of Japanese hold the high ground, so at every bend we prepare for an ambush. Galahad's suffered its first causality in-action today, Pvt. Robert Landis.

At camp, I sit on a rock, killing time, hoping I'll soon get a response regarding the next supply plane. Yesterday, we abandoned the food and ammo drop when we received an emergency call from Galahad's blue platoon in the 2nd Battalion. By the time we arrived at the coordinates, a sprawl of dead Japanese bodies told the story. But now, we're low on supplies. Thankfully, we can harvest water from bamboo shoots, but manna isn't floating down from heaven.

We wait nervously for the intelligence and reconnaissance platoons to return with news of Japanese locations before we press ahead. Sam and his team are the first to drag themselves back to Galahad's command post.

Sam, at nineteen years old, leads the 1st Battalion's I&R platoon. "Every step, I expect to hear something behind the thick elephant grass. But how can you hear a Jap waiting silently with his rifle aimed at your head?" Sam wormed his way out of shooting range after taking down a roving enemy patrol. The relief on his peach fuzz face turns authoritative when he orders his men to turn around and retrace their steps in the morning. "What is courage when you're risking the lives of other men?" The guilt on Sam's face shows the toll this operation is already taking on him.

I'm still waiting for static from the radio to send us news of our next drop when the Orange 3rd Battalion's I&R platoon returns. Lt. Logan Weston, the team's officer, who was a divinity student in the states, drops to the ground and begins his story while he unlaces his boots and rubs his feet.

"Our corporal in the lead was immediately suspicious, scouting a village a few miles south from here. Unlike at other Kachin sites, we were not greeted by timid native women or racing children. He lifted a hand to halt our platoon. I finally caught up to him, but the foot path was thick with vines, and slowed me down.

"I had heard sounds ahead," the corporal chimes in. "Weston thought they may be Chinese. He wanted me to make sure they were the enemy before I shot. So we moved forward towards a bend in the road to get a better look. Weston covered me from behind. I yelled back, 'There's two Chinese. They're smiling and waving us forward.'"

Fear still hangs in the guarded expression on the scout's rugged face.

"Weston followed, still in firing position, when the Asian man's waving hand went down and two machine guns broke loose. I hit the ground firing, and a bullet grazed my cheek. But I could see one dead Jap sprawled out. After diving into the brush, Weston and another soldier covered me so I could scramble back to safety."

"We could've knocked them off," Weston boasts, now within the comfort of the camp. "But our mission was to find out if there were Japanese in the area, not take them down."

After dinner, I make it a point to find Sam, who you'd never guess was distressed from his perpetually bright temperament. Next to Sam sits Weston, whose gentle appearance could mislead one to underestimate his nerves of steel. They're sitting on the ground outside the H.Q. tent where, with the aid of a Zippo lighter, Hunter finishes going over tomorrow's route.

After Hunter leaves, I stoop to join them. "I hope you don't mind me asking, but how did you guys choose the men on your I&R teams?" I'm not ready to give up supply duty yet; just curious.

With his normal youthful exuberance, Sam lights up, ready with his answer. "I went into the guardhouse looking for the guys I had seen stand up to authority. The ones annoyed when someone told them what to do. Men with the gut instinct to react without my direction. My theory is, men who don't give a damn if they live or die will survive, and they'll hold anyone trying to stop them from doing it their way in contempt."

Weston laughs as though he's heard it all before. He begins his explanation like he's preaching to a congregation. "I'm a man of God," he starts. "I went through the ranks and asked for all the men who had been in a hopeless combat situation before. I chose the men who told me that when they couldn't advance a step further, they'd dropped to their knees and trusted in the Lord."

Later, I learned Weston was thought of as the *Fighting Preacher*, which is why everyone calls him Preacher.

Expecting only three days' travel time to our objective, we receive the order we're waiting for from Stilwell. Strike! We begin a forty-hour nonstop march to Walawbum, out of food and low on ammunition. In a typical, cocky, Galahad fashion, one man boasts, "We're gonna decimate those yellow slant-eyes."

With a distinct disadvantage going into this operation, I have a visceral urge to jump ship. But I remember once having said that it's easier to judge a stranger the first time you meet them than someone you've known a lifetime. In front of me is a group of men with no other alternative than to win. Whether we're right or wrong, we've had to convince ourselves we're invincible.

At dawn on March 4, with only fifteen miles to go, Galahad's three battalions split up. Orange moves south to set up a roadblock. White heads north to secure the high ground. And Blue Battalion will cut a jungle trail due west and march into the heart of Walawbum.

CHAPTER 32

March 5, 1944

Last night, to the north, we heard the staccato of machine gun fire and mortar shells. The Chinese X Force kept the rear of the Japanese 18th occupied. Hoping to surprise the Japs' front line with unexpected visitors, all three Galahad battalions move in quickly. What a coup if we can corner General Tanaka.

Supply drops have been held up until after the attack, so I've joined Preacher's I&R platoon as the portable radio carrier. We're tasked with setting up a roadblock. Unencumbered by mules or heavy equipment, we advance ahead of the infantry, who carry machine guns and mortars. We're protected only by our M1 carbine rifles, grenades, knives, and a couple of Tommies. I lag behind with the added forty pounds of the SCR-300 radio.

We wade across the hip-high Tawang River, blinded by the fog-cloaked morning.

Immediately upon entering the forest on the other side, we encounter an enemy trail-block of crisscrossed logs. Crawling over the recently felled trees, I expect to hear gunfire, and my back crawls with the sensation of penetrating eyes. But all is quiet.

The Japanese advance ahead of us through the jungle, leaving booby traps in their wake.

We're forced to stop and disable them before we move on, and I feel the tension building in every nerve. Ahead, the enemy moves at a leisurely pace, overconfident from running circles around the lethargic Chinese in the past. They don't know Galahad's on their tail now.

With such dense foliage, it's hard to tell how close we are, but we keep finding Japanese boot prints filled with fresh water. We press on to our objective, keenly aware we may be walking into an ambush but knowing we have no other choice.

A burst of fire from the trail warns us of impending action. Preacher turns back to look down the line of taut, frozen faces. We wait for his command to commence standard operating procedure. "Get in position," he barks. The lead squad plunges for cover, then returns fire. The other two squads drop into the woods on either side of the trail. Remaining with the lead squad, I slip the radio off my back, then ready my carbine.

Harry Flynn, this is it, I think, then suck in a lung full of strength before I squeeze off my first shot. Adrenaline courses through my body as more Japanese round the corner. Pumping the trigger on my M1 is the only thing that relaxes my nerves.

A bullet slams into the soldier next to me. He winces, calls out, "I'm hit," then drops to the ground. Shots fly everywhere.

The enemy hears our flanking units approach and stops firing. They race ahead, shooting randomly and wildly. My pulsing heart stabilizes while we regroup.

"They'll probably set up more ambushes," Preacher cautions. "Try to delay us. Our job is to get that roadblock in. Now that they know we're here, it's critical to get it done fast."

The Japanese continue to play cat and mouse with us for several hours. When we reach our objective, we work together silently like cogs in a machine. This won't stop the enemy, but it will slow down their artillery and give our Chinese X Force a chance to catch up. Preacher orders the retreat while I help place the last log on the roadblock, fingers trembling.

We race back to the bend in the river, chased by gunshots. The river looks wider than it did when we crossed it this morning. We'd be sitting ducks if we tried it again now in the daylight. The ground is higher here than the surrounding area. It's a good defensive position, but I'm not looking forward to an overnight stay. The clock is ticking, and my survival instinct tells me to get out now.

"No time to cross the river." Preacher's dark eyes focus on a plan. "Dig in," he commands at last.

We drop our packs. I pull out my shovel and dislodge clods of dirt and wet sand. Others had abandoned their shovels early in the march to ditch some weight, and now their faces are twisted in regret and sinking fear. They drop to their knees and furiously scrape at the ground with their knives and scoop earth with their helmets. We have to open up foxholes for the inevitable onslaught.

"My God," a man screams. One of our guys has been shot in the head, and his friend stands over him, paralyzed in disbelief. Our holes are barely deep enough, but we jump in. I hear Japanese voices approaching and bullets whizzing from the north. Another sergeant drops when a bullet severs the artery in his arm.

Next to me, under a crisscross of flying lead, I watch Preacher scramble over and pull the sergeant back into the relative protection of his own hole. "Give him some water," Preacher orders me. I uncap my canteen and moisten the wounded man's lips. The Japanese are only twenty yards away.

"More are coming," our Nisei interpreter calls from two foxholes over. "They'll circle us."

"They can't," I yell back, sounding braver than I feel. "We've got the river to our backs." I load my M1, and fire as fast as I can pull the trigger.

Preacher had the foresight to set up the platoon in a three-point star with two Tommies in the front. Their rat-a-tat-tat stops the advancing Japanese. We hunker into position, dirt flying, bullets whizzing, and men screaming. But I hear none of it. I'm enveloped in an unreachable cloud.

More Japanese arrive and hover along the fringes, thirty yards away, under the cover of the brush. Everything moves in slow motion. A bullet misses me by inches; I fire back and see my target recoil. Overhead, I hear the rustle of leaves in the softly swaying trees. But the shrieking enemy face in front of me is soundless. I rise out of my foxhole, disconnected, as if I'm watching myself from above. My rifle's smooth metal calms me as I squeeze the trigger. I fleetingly think I'll live forever, and then wonder if I'm going crazy. Without any sense of urgency, I drop back into the foxhole to load more bullets. After that, I lose track of time.

American Tigercat bombers strafe the surrounding area. Their bombs drop over enemy- occupied villages. Smoke rises, swirling into the drifting clouds overhead. Breaking my trance, a man shouts over the barrage of fire, "Our fighter planes found us. Where the fuck is the support from the tanks and the X Force?"

In the trench next to me, the wounded man drifts out of consciousness, a relieved smile on his pained face. I expect to feel sad, but I'm on autopilot: fire, load, fire, load, fire.

"Banzai!" A feral, guttural chorus bellows around us from all directions. The Japanese rush out of the woods with bayoneted rifles, their eyes grotesquely distorted by their thirst for blood.

Preacher screams, "Down. Now!" We duck below the tops of our foxholes as bullets stream by overhead.

It's suicide above. The area's so small that, as the enemy converges towards the center, they're just shooting at each other. A young Japanese soldier—just a boy with broken glasses— flops in front of my hole, eyes open in surprise. I close mine.

"Flynn, set up the radio," Preacher yells. "Now!"

I hesitate, then set my rifle aside. My face burns with anger and fear. There's nothing to do but hunker down while the enemy charges, killing each other, so I do as I'm ordered and struggle with the antenna and knobs. There's squawking from transmission conflicts between the diving planes and infantry. From the radio, I hear Stilwell's voice saying, "This is a damn mess. Where the hell is Merrill?"

Downstream, from the other side of the river, a bang marks our mortars letting loose on another advancing Japanese battalion. There's Merrill, I think to myself. Where's the X Force, is what Stilwell should be asking.

"Radio for help!" Preacher is out of sight, but I hear his command.

I switch frequencies and get the 3rd battalion's heavy weapons unit. They're on the other side of the river, about three hundred yards upstream. The ear-splitting din makes it difficult to hear my own voice. I pull out my compass, take a bearing off a smoke shell to identify the target coordinates, and shout into the transmitter, "Due west seventy yards."

Woomer chuckles over the radio. "Harry, we got a mortar in position. Ready? Fire!"

The earth around us shakes, and two Japanese bodies fly twenty feet in the air right in front of me. The Nips run back into the woods as the shelling throws their retreat off balance.

"Get back," Preacher orders. Men slip out, one by one, to the river. The shelling continues to throw up dirt and smoke in front of us.

I pull myself and the radio out of the hole and stumble around piles of Japanese bodies I can't look in the face. Nearby, a cheap, gold-gilded Buddha has slipped from the hands of the dead Japanese boy. I pocket it. A corporal and I tie our fatigue jackets to bamboo poles to create a makeshift litter. We slip back to Preacher's foxhole and heave the injured sergeant onto it.

We're the last to leave the mound, save for Preacher, who pushes us out. The shelling has stopped, and the Japanese will soon charge. Crossing the river, knowing we're as vulnerable as naked babes, I feel my courage drain. Behind me, on the bank, an enemy gunner sets up a Nambu machine gun.

On the opposite side of the river, one of our men takes aim while we're in the middle of the current, hoisting the litter as high as our tensed muscles allow. The radio on my back makes the effort even more tortuous. My heart is beating in my throat and bile rises from my stomach.

Right as my sodden boots hit the dry bank, our side fires, and the Nambu gunner falls over his weapon. As we rush for cover, a chill ripples through me. I'm still alive.

We return to the protection of the wet rice paddy where we spent the night before, and I set up the radio. Next to me, the corporal snaps a twig, tosses each half into the distance, and fumes. "What happened to the tanks? Where are the artillery and the

Chinese X Force? Are the Chindits going to stand us up, too? It sure looks like we're in this alone."

Preacher looks up to the sky, then answers, "Hunter said two brigades of about ten- thousand Chindits, are being flown in on gliders tonight. Operation THURSDAY is launching from Imphal, India right now." We're out of food, and Preacher has forbidden us from lighting up any fags, so our hopeful eyes and ears are on him.

The brilliant setting sun paints the western horizon, while a full moon rises in the east. Preacher pulls off his ripped shirt; lays his poncho over the squishy, wet field; sits down; and continues, "Michael Calvert's 77th Brigade will land on a rice field south of the Mogaung Valley tonight; the site's code name is BROADWAY."

He rolls his neck around, and it pops with released tension. "Ferguson's men just arrived at Aberdeen, and Masters' brigade's to be dropped on the other side of the Irrawaddy River, then march to BLACKPOOL. So the bottom tip of the Mogaung Valley will be covered by the Chindits. Sure hope Masters' men get across that river before the monsoon floods start."

Suddenly, there's a crackling sound next to me. I reach for my rifle, but relax as the radio static continues. The Orange combat commander is on the line. "Where are you guys? Over." Explosions erupt in the infantry's background, reminding us we can't let down our guard.

Preacher jumps up and grabs the earphones. "We're holed up on a soggy field, east side of the river. Hey, we're waiting for the tanks and Chinese. What happened? Over."

We listen as raucous laughter breaks out on the other side of the line. "The tanks took a wrong turn. They're camping for the night. And the X Force got lost on the other side of the river." His laughing turns to coughing, so he signs out. I think about all the smoke and dust in that crossfire and wonder whether I'd rather be here or there.

We all bed down for the night, happy to be alive for the moment. No one's to talk, walk, or smoke. "I'll grenade anything that moves," Preacher promises. "If you've got to go," he says, "pee in your helmets."

CHAPTER 33

Before dawn breaks, we're marching toward a nonstop baptism of shell fire back and forth across the river. The Japanese artillery has been shelling the 2nd and 3rd infantries for more than thirty hours. I trudge on, reassuring myself that it's better for our I&R platoon to be with them than away from our combat group. Unlike in typical warfare, where battles are fought with a front line dividing the two sides, we've penetrated into enemy territory and need to get back to our main line of resistance.

Palm leaves and bamboo shoots slap me in the face as we weave through the dense brush towards the protection of our command post. It's an eerie feeling, knowing the leafy layer hides us but also sets us up for exposure at every bend. Ahead, we hear nervous chatter. "Kore wa nan desu ka?"

"Wakarimasen,"

Our lead scout drops a hand to silently halt us. The lead guy peels off, away from the Japanese voices. We follow, edgy and tired after no sleep last night.

I had lain on my poncho, closed my eyes, and willed my thoughts to be soothed by Ruthie's voice. As soon as I relaxed, the fallen Japanese boy with broken glasses stared back at me. To avoid his face, I spent the entire night wide-eyed; fireflies flickered above, while the full moon rose in the east then settled to the west. Now I march mindlessly, eyes gritty with dust and exhaustion. I finger the gilded Buddha in my pocket. It's terrorizing to fight the insensitivity of a bloodthirsty enemy. It's worse to fight their humanity when they're dead.

Most of the group is several yards ahead of me, and I try to adjust the weight of the radio to give me comfort so I can catch up.

But my back is raw all over from the backpack straps, and, as I hoist the unit in search of relief, I'm thrown off balance. I try to brace myself, but branches rip at me, stealing all my control. While I'm falling, I hear a crack, and fragments scatter where a bullet hits the radio casing. My face smashes to the ground. This is bad.

"Susume! Susume!" The Japanese call is spine-tingling. Bullets scream above. Japanese soldiers advance. The Galahad soldier behind me falls forward as he's readying his gun.

Camel-toed Japanese boots and harsh voices rush towards my face. For one last instant, I reach to hold on to everything I love. I taste the grainy dirt and inhale its pungent, moldy smell. The faint whistle of birds continues. Oh, Ruthie! I don't want to die.

A laughing Japanese soldier kicks the man sprawled next to me. I cringe inside as cleats pound the fallen man's back. The canvas-covered boots twist, then stomp in my direction. One toes my shoulder, cleats digging into my back, but the radio protects me.

"Nani o shimasu ka?" An angry voice challenges the soldier booting me.

Muddy water splashes in my eyes as he returns to the other soldiers. I'm blinded, but can hear them arguing on my other side. I blink the clods loose and search desperately for an escape when they're not looking. We're surrounded by bushes, but I can't roll or lunge for cover under them with the radio weighing me down.

"Doko ka?" The voice is incredulous.

"Koko!" Someone pats the walkie-talkie on my back.

"Grab the Japanese's arm the next time he reaches for the radio," my mind screams. Then use him as a body block. But my muscles are frozen with indecision.

One of the Japanese soldiers sets his rifle against a tree trunk before he reaches to roll the fallen Galahad soldier over. His smile turns to streaking blood as bullets from the downed Galahad's Tommy shatter his teeth. Holding his gun in position, half-standing and half-kneeling, the American soldier mows down the other two, then lifts me off the ground by the radio's shoulder straps.

"Let's get out of here," he says, then pushes me hard to pick up my pace. As we hurry away, he nervously jokes, "That's my sleeping dog trick."

Ahead, Preacher rushes towards us, "What the hell happened?"

"Three Japs on patrol," my companion yells. "This is a roving no-man's land. We've got to get away from here, and fast."

As we race to catch up with the rest of our platoon, raw pain shoots through my back. "Ah, does that feel good," I say, thankful to be alive.

Near noon, we reach the rear of the 3rd combat battalion. Japanese shrapnel has killed quite a few of our mules, so they now serve as a perimeter barrier for artillery fire. The men in the front are dug in, and the major in charge orders the Galahad soldier who saved me to move up front.

After taking off his helmet and wiping the sweat from his balding head, the soldier—his name is Pfeifer—nods and moves towards his position.

I grab his arm. "Hey, thanks for…you know, back there." What do you say to a guy who just saved your life?

He gives it only a moment's consideration, then, with a wry smile, says, "It's all in a day's work. You work supplies, right? 10-in-1 rations for the rest of the war sounds like an even swap to me." He sobers, adjusts his helmet, and runs to the battle front.

I post myself outside the H.Q. tent, ready to take my turn at the SCR-284 crank as soon as Sergeant Roy Matsumoto is done with the radio. Wearing the only set of headphones, he furiously decodes a message. All around me, runners leave for the infantry fronts and others arrive with updates.

Merrill's standing at ease, hands behind his back, puffing hard on his pipe. Hunter, arms crossed over his chest, looks pensively towards the fireworks. Colonel Osborne debriefs them on the 1st Battalion's position.

"We're outnumbered and surpassed in fighting power. Also, they were waiting for us. I think we've got a mole in our midst, but we could use that to our advantage and feed him bad information if we find him."

Matsumoto rips the headphones off and interrupts, waving the message in the air. "Sir, I don't know how—maybe the enemy has gotten sloppy—but I've tapped into their line." The officers look skeptical.

"Sir, there's a Japanese ammunition dump guarded by only three men. I got the coordinates when they radioed for help." Matsumoto's dependable reputation leaves little room for doubt. "I don't think it's a set-up," he continues. "General Tanaka's head-quarters responded that they have heavy losses and couldn't help. I think they plan to retreat."

"What have we radioed out?" Osborne interrupts.

"Tanks and artillery are arriving. But we didn't say when," Matsumoto answers

"Let Tanaka and his men think we're bigger than we are. This long-range penetration strategy behind their lines seems to be scaring them off," Hunter says, relief softening his jaw.

A sly smile blossoms on Merrill's typically reserved expression. "Call in the bombers.

We'll help the ammunition dump."

Roy salutes his understanding. "Yes, Sir."

Within two hours, the American tanks and Chinese X Force arrive, effectively relieving us of our duty. We can't call out on the long-range radio, but we hear Stilwell's tirade from base camp. "The tanks are there. The X Force has arrived. Where is Galahad? What is Merrill thinking? Did he lose his nerve? Just what I need before Mountbatten arrives. Thank God for Operation THURSDAY. At least the Chindits are in position and we've taken Walawbum."

CHAPTER 34

We laboriously retrace our steps to a bivouac along a quick-running tributary of the Tanai River. I listen to it gurgle over rocks and watch the sun dance on the water where it peeks through the fluttering leaves. If we weren't at war, I'd say this is idyllic, but it's impossible to shut out the reality around me. Already a dozen men have been hauled out with shattered nerves. Fortunately only eight have been killed. But our numbers continue to drop from malaria, typhus, and the Japanese. Disease is the biggest threat to our strength. We started with twenty-seven- hundred men. Only twenty-five-hundred remain.

We'll camp out here for a couple days, so far out in the boondocks I doubt anyone could find us even if they tried. And after two-hundred-sixty miles of bushwhacking, I'd say we deserve a break. There's not a plane in the sky, a single engine sound, or even a baby crying out in this wilderness. It's only us and the wind.

I haven't eaten a full meal in a week or bathed in two. I stink, but we all do. So I strip down to swim. Swollen, black ticks speckle my body. I'll have to burn out their heads before the sores turn into ulcers. My uniform is shredded, and my boots are holier than heaven. Hopefully they'll send fatigues with the food and ammo in tomorrow's drop.

After I wash my clothes, there's nothing left except bare threads. I lay them out to dry and find a place to relax. I doze off, thinking of Ruthie. She hasn't written to me since I got her Christmas photo, and I haven't sent her a response. The deeper I get into Burma, the more distant she becomes in my life. My eyes are heavy, and even the pebbles under my back feel good.

Our long-range radio buzzes distantly as I drift in and out of sleep. "The Japanese in Northern Burma received a solid body blow this week from Galahad," Radio station KQKY out of Perth Australia announces. "Once again, General Frank Merrill's Yanks are heroes. Sergeant Oliver Pung climbed up a tree to a perch fifty feet off the ground and kept his unit posted on Japanese activity via walkie talkie. Merrill's Marauders killed eight hundred desperate Japanese. We're proud of those boys."

A blanket of near-naked GI Joes lay sunning along the rocky bank in the late afternoon rays. In a lazy, contented voice, our best shot in the outfit apologizes. "I guess me and my Betsy must've gotten nervous. I thought we took out more than that."

The news turns to music. It's the first I've heard in over a month.

Next to me, Pfeifer burns away his own ticks with a red hot knife. He releases the parasites' burrowed heads and bloated bodies from his skin, then flicks them onto a nearby rock and squishes them. Blood runs down the rock. "So, Harry, what's for dinner tomorrow night?" he jokes, knowing damn well I have no control over what actually makes it on the plane.

"You name it," I answer, feeling the warm sun bake the aches out of my muscles. "And did you remind them about our Christmas packages?" Now his tone is serious.

I push up to lean on my elbows and tilt my head to keep the sun from blinding me. "I told them we're all starting to doubt Santa."

"I've doubted Santa since I was in kindergarten. I never got a thing I wanted. Neither did anyone else in my family. Our problem was if we wanted to know what anyone wanted, we'd have to talk to each other," Pfeifer flicks another bloated tick onto a nearby rock.

"In our house, Christmas was a battle ground; when family gets together, you always have to take sides." I lay back down. "So, if you didn't talk to each other, who'd you talk to?"

"No one."

"Come on, you had to say, 'Who left the empty bottle of milk in the ice-box?'" "Actually, no. We were very polite to each other. "

"Those must've been *some* Christmases."

"At least there wasn't any fighting. That wasn't allowed either."

"Yeah, but we had fun."

"We didn't. Breakfast at 6 a.m., dinner at 6 p.m., and lights out at 10 p.m." Pfeifer torches the little buggers on the rock for more revenge. "Kind of like under the Stilwell regime— do as I say, not as I do," he mutters under his breath.

"You're preaching to the choir on that one," I agree. The relief of having another person to talk to gives me more of a kick than a shot of Jack Daniel's, though I wouldn't turn down the latter if it was offered.

With one smooth motion, Pfeifer wipes his sweaty, bald head. His glasses slip down his nose as he concentrates on each black bubble. Watching him remove the ulcerating bodies before they attract flies should prompt me to sit up and pull out my Zippo, but I just close my eyes and enjoy the moment.

Thinking back to Stilwell's conversations with Merrill, I want to test the waters with Pfeifer, but I'm still not ready to lay it out on the table. I hedge around it. "He treats us like we're pawns in a chess game. No, actually, the Chinese are the pawns. Still, we get our share of his dirty work."

Pfeifer puts his knife down momentarily, as though he's imagining the chess board. "And Stilwell's the king."

"Ah." Without opening my eyes, I point my finger at Pfeifer. "That's the problem. There are too many kings in the game: FDR, Churchill, and Chiang Kai-shek."

"So, who's the boss?" Pfeifer puts away his knife and stands to stretch.

"That's it: none of them. They're fighting among themselves instead of together against the Japanese. 'Who gets Hong Kong?' 'Give me the Philippines.' 'I want supplies to win our civil war.' And we're just chips in their game."

CHAPTER 35

March 11, 1944

Less than a week after we secured our first objective, we begrudgingly backtrack to Walawbum. Instead of Santa, Stilwell and two Brits, Mountbatten and Wingate, have come to town. The last two food drops didn't include clothes or razors, so we look like a bunch of hobos. Still, they want us on show for *Roundup* magazine.

Its midday by the time we straggle into the clearing where they've set up a wooden box for Mountbatten to stand on for his "Do it for your country" speech. The area is bare of brush, and we're far from any mosquito-infested rice paddies. Only a few desolate trees remain after the Chinese infantry and Brown's tanks barreled through. It looks more like a desert than a jungle. The press swarm like bugs.

Mr. Doyer, with his understated New England accent, joins Pfeifer, Sam, Preacher, Doc and me to watch everyone scramble in preparation of the wartime newsreel. "They've flown in more than the regular handful of reporters for this performance," he comments. We watch as they unload plane after plane of press.

Out of nowhere, a crass voice calls from behind. "I'd know that bald head anywhere." Zimmerman, one of the photographers who felt the whiz of bullets and went hungry with us early on in our march, readjusts his camera and pulls a deck of cards from his pocket.

"Here." He hands the pack to Mr. Doyer. "If you can't use these, pass them on to your boys." Then he worms his way through the mass of khakis and helmets, up to the glittering buttons and insignias.

In response to waving hands, we line up. Photographers shield their lenses from the dust clouds kicked up by the assembling mass. None of the Galahad force is in the front line; our fatigues would be an embarrassment back home, but we serve as a good backdrop. Someone's planted about a dozen clean-shaven boys for the traditional handshakes.

As the other soldiers move forward, I drop to the back row with Doyer and Pfeifer. Sam and Preacher end up a couple rows in front of us with Doc Winnie in between. Although they're dressed in clean uniforms and ready for the show, Stilwell and Merrill have migrated to the back, where they can talk.

Doyer cracks open the deck of cards, then whistles under his breath once, twice. "Did Zimmerman slip you a deck of fixed cards?" I ask, edging over to get a look.

Doyer pulls the cards to his chest. "I think you're too young for this." With a smile more leering then devious, he passes one to Pfeifer, whose impassive expression is clear. The deck of cards is stacked.

Doyer deals one to me. Stacked is right; she's a blonde. "Va va voom." My mind stops and, my blood rushes elsewhere.

Doc turns and snatches the card from my hands, so Doyer hands me another. Suddenly, derriere has a new meaning for me. I feel the pressure build. It's only mildly uncomfortable until I tell myself there's fifty two of them, and then I just about burst.

Within minutes, the cards are circulating up and down the rows. Men cough, doubling over to hide their reactions. Preacher sighs, "Oh, God." We all know he isn't praying.

Lord Mountbatten steps up on the box, squinting into the sun even under his Admiral's hat. He's taller than most Brits, with a long, strong face and dark hair. His perfectly creased white uniform is begging for a Jeep to drive by and kick up some dirt. We stand painfully at attention and salute, thankful we're not on display in the front.

"Men, at ease." We quickly resort to the fig-leaf pose, where we can continue to move the cards and hide our thoughts. Mountbatten flattens his uniform tails, which continue to flap in the wind. "You are facing a formidable enemy in difficult country, but you are outfighting and out maneuvering them. You have recently gained an outstanding victory in Walawbum against one of the enemy's toughest, most seasoned divisions. I shall always remember with pride the days that I spent with you." He descends to formally greet the men in the front row.

I'm sure more was said, but my head is filled with the card women. Agitated, the men yawn, groan, and moan under their breath, as the cards move from hand to hand; panting and sweating even with a breeze. Doyer hands me the last one, and, I hold on to it as long as I can, knowing the others may have already been pocketed. She looks as sweet as a baby, with rosebud lips and curves that my eyes can't leave.

"Looks like Supremo's having a good time," Stilwell says under his breath to Merrill. "He sure has the press begging for more."

We'd forgotten they were behind us, though it seems they're more interested in what the press says than what we do. Finally, I slip the last card to my right.

"Did you hear he flew in with sixteen fighter escorts? That's enough fuel for me to mount an offensive. Hell, we only had four at Walawbum." Stilwell is so focused on Mountbatten that we could be stripped naked, rolling in the mud, and he wouldn't notice us.

General Orde Wingate climbs on the box at Mountbatten's bidding. He's a handsome man, with heavy brows over piercing blue eyes and a beard that makes even the most scraggly of us look clean shaven. With the passion of a prophet, he lacks the orthodoxy of military rule.

The men like him immediately.

"Americans, unlike any other nationality, have an admirable belief that if an attack is right, one will have might." Wingate's booming voice appeals to our patriotism and honor. "This confidence in victory is your greatest strength. But your ignorance is your worst weakness. Do not fool yourself into believing that which is not true. Most of our trained men have been sent to the

European front, so you need to find where your power lies. God gives man peculiar instruments with which to pursue His will. David was armed only with a sling, yet he toppled a giant. In turn, don't let success confuse your judgment. Let it go to your heart, not your head.

You must be unpredictable to your foes but consistent to your friends. To Galahad, I say, quietness and confidence shall be your strength."

His abrupt speech had none of the rah rah rah I expected. We all look at each other, bewildered at his quirky style and quick exit. He appears to be more of a loner—like a poet, or even an artist—at war instead of the military technician his reputation has painted to him be. He steps down from the box and walks the wings to shake hands with the men on the fringes.

Stilwell takes his turn, now. "Men," he says, then halts. We stop mumbling and passing cards, and resume our full military stand. His eyes search the crowd, as though he's speaking to each of us. When his eyes meet mine, it makes me edgy. "We've taken Walawbum. Now the Japs know we're a real threat. Your job is to get to the next objective before the artillery and confuse the Japs, so when our tanks and big guns are wheeled in, we can wipe them out quickly with minimal Allied casualties."

Stilwell is articulate, but he lacks the grace of the other two men.

"The British Chindits have launched Operation THURSDAY," Stilwell says, then looks to Wingate and nods his recognition of the commander. "On the night of March 5, American gliders and Dakota transports led by Colonels Phil Cochran and John Allison dropped thousands of soldiers behind enemy lines near Indaw, Burma. I want to share with you Cochran's words to his men that night.

'Anything you boys have done in the past can be forgotten. Tonight, you are going to find your souls. Tonight, you are going to take these troops in and put them in just right. Those boys have a tough job, and we are going to do our bit to help.'"

The General gets down from the podium and walks among the ranks, still speaking. "Those boys knew they were flying into uncharted land. General Wingate's men, led by Colonel Mike Calvert, landed in a paddy field strewn with teak logs and elephant wallows so deep the first few gliders flipped. That night, those boys did their job. They'll block the Japs from the south. Let's show them what we Yanks can do and help them wipe out the Nips in the north.

Let's win this war so we can go home."

After the speeches, we're dismissed. The brass make the rounds, posing in front of tanks and inspecting shells from the various mortars and rockets from the artillery. They're swallowed up by photographers, and the rest of us are forgotten.

Pfeifer and I join the others to grab our rucksacks. We've done our duty and made Mountbatten look good for the folks back home. I guess it's a good idea to keep our families' spirits up, even if we're dragging at the thought of the eleven miles in front of us.

I need to hand out the rations before we start our march. The men line up while I break open precious food, ammo, and water. I hand them the five pound packs, wondering what the Japanese will be having for dinner tonight and when we'll meet up again.

I mark the final tally on the clipboard, then absentmindedly sigh, and pick up a loose sheath of paper off the ground and slip it in my rucksack. I pull my pack onto my shoulders while Mr. Doyer, in his indefatigable cheerfulness, asks us, "What else do you have to do tonight? Got hot dates?" He hands me a card he had saved from the deck, and I pocket it to savor later.

As we trudge past the command post, I hear Mountbatten giving Stilwell a taste of his own medicine. "I'm diverting the boys from the HUMP and some of your bombers to help the Brits take southern Burma. I know you'll understand."

"That's a dumb idea. Then the Peanut—excuse me, Chiang Kai-shek—will hold back his Y Force in Yunnan. Who's going to be covering my men in the east as I move Galahad and the construction work towards Myitkyina? We're building that road for him, not us." Stilwell's defiance doesn't hold up against Mountbatten's regal appearance.

Mountbatten has the upper hand, and he claps the General on the back patronizingly to remind Stilwell who he's talking to. "My good chap, this is a team effort. Think of it as achieving the Allied working accord."

"Kee-rist! If we keep farting around, shuffling our resources between fronts, we'll lose all the advances we've made." Stilwell spins on his heels to leave.

Pfeifer, Mr. Doyer, and I move past the C.P. tent, establishing a pace as we edge towards the clearing. It doesn't surprise me that Vinegar Joe's lack of finesse isn't confined to just his subordinates. It occurs to me that Stilwell may actually have the correct military solution, but it won't work if he's marching alone.

CHAPTER 36

It takes several days to cover the first leg through the flatland along the Tani River to our second objective, Shaduzup. The next twenty miles is all steep hills with some fifty river crossings. The sand has rubbed my feet so raw that I develop a limp every mile or so from new blisters. Rain drips down my neck from the dense, overhanging vegetation. Stepping one foot forward, then the next, I plod up slippery mud slopes. It's so steep that sometimes my feet slip out from underneath me, and I have to crawl on all fours. Vines wrap around my ankles. I rip free and keep pace with the rest. Right now, I'm resenting the weight of each meal I'm carrying. Every few feet, I inch around another soldier with dysentery who has stopped along the trail, in plain sight, so he's not shot as an enemy when he returns from relieving himself. No one wants to be left behind.

Surrounded by thousands of soldiers, I'm still alone. It's the march that can drive a man crazy. Like every other guy, I hope today's not my day to face a bullet. Thirty days ago, I would've welcomed the action. Six months ago, I would have told you how to win the war. Two years ago, I didn't even know the name Burma. I may have wanted to be a hero, but I also expected to enjoy the glory that came with it; something I can't do if I'm dead.

With an uncontrollable smile, I remember Ruthie describing Bob's perspective on the war. "He doesn't know how to complain," she'd said. "He makes the war sound like he's been sent to a resort. I'd like to see how he gets those steaks he's always bragging about delivered to the Italian Front."

If I want to keep up with Bob, I'd better start boasting about the lush river valleys and dense jungles we get paid to march through in Burma. I've got my eye opened for that out-of- the-way resort with tropical drinks and daily massages by female employees.

We've been told the Japanese are quite a few miles southwest of our position, so there's light chatter among the men. I start to whistle mindlessly to shift my thoughts.

Sam Wilson starts singing along with my tune in his southern accent. "My mama done told me. When I was in knee pants. My mama done told me, son."

I whistle a little embellishment. The other men stop their talk and listen.

"A woman with sweet talk will you give you the glad eyes." Sam waits for me to build the music climax, so I oblige.

"And what you gonna do…but give it a try?" Those girly cards must've given Sam some ideas. He tries to finish his improvised lines, but, finally, he can't hold back the fit of giggles.

"Hey," I call out over the snickers, "I wish my mama told me that." My emotions are so spent that laughter turns to tears and back to laughter.

"Don't tell me that isn't what you'd like to be thinking," he yells back at me.

Sam's right. The last card in the girly deck was a beaut. Her face would make angels sing and she wore a nighty that I'd be happy to hurry home to each night. It'd drive even the devil wild. Another soldier picks up the singing with *Paper Doll*. Others join in.

Then shouts from the front guard warn us to take cover, and we fall into position. The rat-a-tat-tat from a Tommy up ahead volleys with the tat-tat-tat-tat-tat of a Japanese Woodpecker machine gun. I look down and see the prints from the enemy's canvas boots and feel dizzy. It sounds like the Woodpecker is in our ranks, and the Tommies are aimed at us. Something's wrong. Are the Chinese gunning us because we're trapped here with the Japanese?

One Galahad column flanks to the right and another to the left, leaving my column to hold our position. Sam is confused, too. He calls for a Chinese interpreter to communicate with the gunners ahead. The Chinese soldier yells out, "Wah?....Wah?"

From uphill, we hear a hesitant answer, "Waha. Waha." The interpreter shakes his head, confirming we are not fighting a Chinese troop. That's a Japanese accent.

Without a second thought, Sam commands us to fire. The Browning automatic rifles rip the vegetation—and the men hiding within it—to shreds.

The persistence of these Japanese is horrifying. Is this a suicide standoff? Why don't they retreat? Column after column, the enemy charges our BARs and machine guns like they're doped up. I stand to fire my M1, and when I hunker back down, I'm shaking.

After eight skirmishes in less than a mile, the shooting stops. We push our position forward a few yards further, but still there is no return fire. The flanking columns have stopped shooting, as well. Crouched low, we hear busy chatter, but it isn't Japanese. We hold our positions and wait for further orders. Standing up to steal a quick look, Sam catches direct eye contact with the lead commander. "It's a bloke."

Sporting a British turtle helmet, drab khaki uniform shirt with calf-length trousers, and leather boots attached to pea-green gaiters, the chap is followed downhill by a column of Kachin rangers in brightly colored clothing with Tommies slung around their necks.

"Hello, Yanks. Don't shoot," the British captain calls out. "Looks like we trapped the buggers between us. Hope none of our Tommies caught you in the crossfire." He looks satisfied, but not smug. "We were told to look for you. I'm Captain Charles Evan Darlington." The bloke looks more like a Spanish conquistador than a Brit, with his noble brow and narrow black mustache. In an understated tone he adds, "Didn't expect you this far east. But it's splendid you've covered so much ground so soon. Our camp is in Naubum. It's not far from here, and a much better site to bivouac for the night than this hill."

Darlington salutes in parade ground fashion, then, without further formalities, about faces.

His young, innocent-looking cutthroats, wearing Aussie hats with their broad brims turned rakishly up on one side and trigger fingers positioned on their machine guns, follow obediently.

We trail the British subcontinent representative to what we learn through his colorful narrative is his Kachin wife's village.

"You learn how to walk that fine line of being a judge, doctor, and justice of the peace for the Empire if you want to return and not have a snake warming your bed on your next visit." Darlington chats as though he's having tea rather than scrambling up a thirty-five-hundred-foot incline in the pouring rain.

As we break through the vegetation and spill into the village, our bodies are so tired that our feet cross and men lose their footing. Yet, we are showered with welcoming smiles from the Kachin villagers. Their meager clothing, faded to a colorless hue and frayed beyond repair, is telling of their poverty. As we march into Naubum, the natives hand out their limited supply of food. I am moved and too tired to care if I cry.

Preacher's deep-set eyes are full of internal strength as he proclaims, "God is good." And at that moment, I am in agreement.

CHAPTER 37

I wake with my eyes tightly matted together. "Where am I?" I roughly rub the crust from my lids, alarmed at my loss of time and place. I peek outside my parachute tent, where a gentle rain splatters on the oversized elephant-ear leaves. A thin thread of grey at the horizon is the first hint of morning. The distant sound of children giggling and the murmur of excited voices bring me back in time. I feel like it's the morning before some celebration at home, a parade or the Fourth of July, and everyone's up early preparing.

I'm disoriented, so I sit up. Bumping my head into the sagging tent roof makes pooled water drain onto me. I rip myself free from the cloth, and my hopes sink. In front of me, a sprawling sea of makeshift tents covers the ground. This is Burma, not home.

While the others sleep, I throw my gear together, then tiptoe around the resting regiment towards the sounds. Everything is colorless in the early morning light, but silhouettes of bashas on stilts guide me to where I need to go.

Within the village center, the children drape small, bamboo-woven flags from tree to basha to whatever post they can reach. They argue like little adults about where to place the next ornament. Women, decorated with traditional circles of yellow-white paste on their cheeks, stoke fires. Steam rises from large, woven pots. Mothers with babies strapped on their backs and half-naked toddlers hanging on their hems stir the pots with long-handled wooden spoons. There are no young men among them. They either don't see me or are too lost in their chores to care.

Then I see an old man scramble down the ladder of his basha and rush away.

I follow him to an opening in the forest, where the elders of the village are out in force. Bare-foot and wearing the traditional longyi skirts, they wrap their arms around bundles of leafy branches. Without concern for their feet, they hurriedly carry the debris over sharp bamboo stubbles to the edge of the forest.

"Be a good chap and lend us a hand." I turn to see a sweating Evan Darlington hauling a sapling over his shoulder. What a strange person, a westerner living in a remote Burmese village.

Without questioning why, I bend to engulf a large load in my arms. The muscles in my legs spasm, and I feel a pinch in my lower back from yesterday's hike. The bundle is larger than what my arms can reasonably hold, and my ego punishes me with sticks poking into my ribs and branches scratching my face. Beneath me, the ground is level under the buildup of vegetation. It looks like it could be a ceremonial ground, but it's too far from the village.

Darlington heads back into the field, and I haul my bundle to the perimeter of the clearing. He yells to me, "We're expecting visitors—or at least Merrill. And hopefully your next round of supplies will be on board."

Colonel Merrill and Hunter stayed with Stilwell at Walawbum while we marched to our second objective. Next time I'll stick by the Colonel and fly in rather than test the limits of my body. The aches from yesterday's uphill march are slowly starting to loosen up with this activity.

We cross paths again as I return for another load. Darlington's arms are overflowing so I can't even see his face. I finally understand what I'm walking on. "This is a camouflaged landing strip."

"Of course. How would you expect us to get supplies if we advertised our headquarters to the Japanese?"

Domesticated elephants haul away downed logs while the male villagers transport more bundles. The older men taunt the younger good-naturedly, and it's accepted with respect. These younger men are barely teenagers, and they're to be our guides? I'm skeptical, thinking back to how dependable I was at that age. Was that really only a few years ago?

More Galahad soldiers appear to help clear the field. On the edge of the opening, the old men now sit cross-legged, chewing and spitting red juice from betel nut while they let us finish the job they started. Clever trick.

When we're almost finished, a refreshed-looking Pfeifer cuffs me on the shoulder from behind. "Harry, you have a knack for finding trouble," he teases. "Remind me to not follow you in the future." He joins others returning to the village center.

While I wait for the supply plane to arrive, I approach a tree full of oranges nearby.

Behind the tree, on the rungs of the ladder leading up a basha, a young woman nurses her child. I reach to pick a fruit, but my guilt is stronger than my stomach. She watches me, but says nothing. What would it be like to have a war dropped at your front door and a full battalion of soldiers sleeping in your backyard? Where could you go to get away? I wave as I leave, empty- handed. She nods.

Within the hour, Merrill and the supplies arrive. Hunter and the pock-marked Kachin who pulled Earl from under his rig are on board, also. We stack the food, ammo, and medicine along the perimeter of the field. Next to the plane, litters wait, holding men drained by dysentery or delirious with malaria. I help hoist them aboard, knowing they'll never be the same, even if they're nursed back to health.

By midday, the Kachin celebration begins. Colorful flags flutter in the damp air. Children weave in and out of the crowd of gawking soldiers. My stomach growls at the smell of boiling goat. Old men with tattooed faces sit in the center of the circle and methodically beat ceremonial drums with knobbed sticks. Others strike an assortment of gourds with their hands. The village pulsates with dissonant vibrating sounds.

Mr. Doyer cracks each of his knuckles while straining his neck to watch the show. In his plain-speaking, New England humor, he says, "If this marks the end of their dry season, then what the hell is the wet season like?" The sun has burned off the morning drizzle, but a slight mist reminds us the monsoon is coming.

"I can't imagine what they grow around here, other than rice, with all the rain," I say.

Next to me, Pfeifer snorts and lightly scratches his bare head. "Harry, I thought you were a farmer. Didn't you see those hillsides of white flowers with capsules ready to burst?" He doesn't give me time to answer, but continues in his patronizing tone. "And you've never heard of opium or heroin? Or smelled that 'funny' tobacco the locals smoke?"

"Ah," I answer, not only remembering the strange tobacco but also realizing I smell it right now. A circle of Kachin patriarchs and matriarchs—some chewing the red betel nut; others smoking through long, outlandish pipes—wait around the perimeter. The performance starts, so I say no more.

A woman with large, drooping eyes and wrinkles stretched over high cheekbones clangs a single brass triangle. The ringing sends chills up my spine. Two young girls, hair wrapped in turbans, play oboe-like reed instruments with her. Their eerie music is harmonious, but it lacks any melody and seems to ramble. Clearly, everyone is in a festive spirit, but suddenly I feel awkward around the sounds and smells, their clothes and music. The smoke, thick like incense, rises and fills the air around me. Subconscious tension reminds me we're at war and that I have been living on edge for months. Finally, I let myself relax and be pulled in by the exotically strange celebration.

A soft, little hand grabs mine. I look down at a boy, disfigured by a harelip, smiling at me encouragingly. He shows me his flag. I marvel at his self-confidence, then show him that I have a flag, as well. Next to him, a wisp of a child tugs Pfeifer's hand, too. Not willing to play the game, Pfeifer shakes his head, then passes his bamboo flag to an empty-handed Doyer. The children pull us into a ring of dancers.

At first, we all hold hands—child, adult, child, adult—half-skipping around the center in a circle. Merrill, pipe hanging from his mouth, is in the dance ring next to Doyer. Hunter, stiff and reserved on the other side of the circle, gently holds the hands of two young women. Sam Wilson mocks the dancing soldiers from outside the ring. "Have you forgotten how to have fun?"

The drumming increases in volume and speed. Chimes—a clanging, then banging, of the metal triangle—punctuates our movement. Watching from the fringe, Captain Darlington stands next to a sweet-faced Kachin girl I suppose to be his wife. Women with red-stained teeth nod their participation in the ceremony from the edges of the circle. I notice their meager clothing has been adorned with colorful belts, sashes, and ribbons.

The hollow sounds of the woodwinds rise above the other instruments. The tousle-haired children stop then drop our hands. They lift their delicate, handkerchief-sized flags by the corners, and wave them as though they're the wind, breathing life into bamboo. Their smooth, round faces with young, bright eyes encourage us to join them.

Soon, all the adult men in the ring are flapping their little flags and tiptoeing in distinct circles, each following the lead of a different instrument. Merrill and Doyer introduce a do-si-do square dance to the Kachin tradition. I think back to my jitterbug days and wish Ruthie could see me now. All the Americans are laughing, and there isn't a drop of liquor in sight.

The celebration lasts throughout the afternoon. We eat mutton, goats, chicken, mangoes and pickled tea leaves. My stomach has shrunk with our diet of k-rations, so I feel sick after gorging myself. Merrill offers gifts of candy to the children and earrings to the women. Tthey gather around him like he's Santa. I marvel at the unlikely partnership between the Allies and Kachin. Like Lt. Lin and myself, we're fighting on the same team, but this time, I don't question whether we're fighting for the same reason, I'm just relieved.

CHAPTER 38

The black curtain of night falls. Mothers carry crying children up ladders into bashas with waiting roped hammocks, and soldiers light up their Cavaliers on their walk back to our bivouac. Set among paddy fields on a ridge top, we're able to relax with Kachin rangers posted on sentry duty.

Sam, Preacher, Doc, Pfeifer and I follow Darlington and four or five Kachin dignitaries to the chief's basha. Shortly after we arrive, Merrill, Hunter, Osborne, and the pock-marked Kachin join us. Inside, women, face paint fading but still in their festive best, prepare the children for sleep. As soon as their little ones are settled on the woven mats along the side walls of the hut, they pull out their red betel nuts for energy and keep to themselves. Near the back, a long-range radio sits on the floor.

We settle around an earthen hearth, where kindling erupts into sporadic flames. A Kachin adds more wood, and the fire smolders until the logs glow. Shadow figures dance on the bamboo-latticed walls from the fire's wavering light. The Kachin smoke their black tar opium in long-stem pipes. We light up our Lucky Strikes. I lean against a pole and listen to the sounds of two languages rising and falling. The staccato joking in English intersects with languid Kachin whispers. The day's ceremonies are coming to a close with this final ritual.

My body and eyelids wants to droop, but none of us can let go of the tension that's become second nature. Night brings relief for those who can find sleep.

Darlington sits in his designated spot, reaches back, snaps on the radio, and adjusts its knobs. High-pitched whining and static are followed by, "The Japanese have attacked British headquarters in India." Our muscles automatically prepare for action, bracing us for what's to come.

"Along the southern Burma border, one-hundred-thousand Japanese have crossed into India. Imphal and Kohima are under siege." The radio sputters, and we lose reception. Today's reprieve is over, bringing us back to the ugly truth of why we're here.

Hunter, normally unfazed, bristles. His jaw tightens. "We thought we were pushing the Japanese further south. Now we know they were moving west on purpose."

"Who's tracking the air reconnaissance information?" Preacher poses the question we're all afraid to ask, because if H.Q. isn't, then no one is. "The Nips seem to know where we are. We should know their positions, too." With his long arm, he pitches his fag into the fire. "There had to be fire and smoke, unless they traveled at night when our planes can't catch them."

Merrill stays silent, loyal to Stilwell until the end.

Darlington shifts uneasily, then asks the pockmarked Kachin, "Nau, have you heard anything about the Japanese movement to India?"

We wait while Nau inhales deeply from the opium pipe. He passes the pipe to the chief, composes himself, then answers, "Chindit Ferguson tell American pilot Cochran to bomb ammo depot west of Irrawaddy. Many wonder why Japanese had ammo supply so far from base camp."

"That could be good news," Osborne says, eyes closed while he considers the enemy's tactical plans. "If they don't know their stash had been destroyed and they've unloaded a hundred thousand troops near India without enough arms, they may be handing the Brits their surrender papers."

Nau shakes his head vehemently, "I hear there ammo dump near Kohima. It belong to Americans. Why Americans store ammo near British? Unless it *not* for Americans or British."

Doc reaches for the opium pipe, "Maybe we should all smoke a bit of this. Looks like Nau is thinking more clearly than we are. We've been ignoring the obvious."

"You think one of our guys in India is stockpiling ammo for the Japs?" The flickering fire exaggerates Sam's innocent, wide eyed expression.

I get a sick feeling in the pit of my stomach as a piece of the puzzle slips neatly in place. Finally, I understand why Schmidt wanted me out of the way and reassigned to the road front. If he could push any of this on me, he would. Then they would think I'm a plant in Galahad. This is more information than I want.

Darlington takes the pipe from Doc, then passes it to the Kachin sitting next to him. "I doubt there's only one soldier in on this." He stares at Merrill. "I hope someone checks it out."

Merrill nods.

Static from the radio interrupts Darlington, who repositions himself so he can adjust the knobs better. It whines a pinning sound. I grit my teeth. Still no reception. The silence is harder to take than bad news. That must be how Ruthie feels when I don't write.

Darlington's soft monotone draws me back to the fire ring. "Your General Stilwell insisted the Chindits help you chaps in Burma. It appears that while those boys are here to help Operation END RUN, no one's minding British Headquarters in India."

Hunter, leaning on one elbow, legs outstretched, throws a twig into the fire. "So you think the Japanese know we're here?"

Darlington gets the radio to squawk. After some pinning, he fine-tunes the frequency. I recognize Stilwell's voice. "…everybody's buzzing and jumping up and down. How did Merrill get things so botched up?" It crackles and dies. Darlington answers Hunter: "They certainly know the Chindits are in Burma."

Abruptly, Hunter pushes himself up into a sitting position. "I suppose Stilwell will blame us for that, too. We've done everything by the book, but there's the Army way, and there's the Stilwell way." He looks at Merrill, who simply shrugs.

Ominous quiet settles into the basha. The Americans are as charged as a bolt of lighting with the news that the Japanese have attacked India. Panic sets in. I wish I'd gone back to my tent. We were supposed to be able to park our problems for the night, but instead, we chain smoke while our knees bob nervously. An owl hoots in the distance. Rain patters on the thatched roof. By now, the final glowing embers light only the edge of the hearth.

"Stilwell's right," I say, unable to believe my words. "Revenge or not, now's the time to act, while the Japanese are spread out and focused on India. But the Chinese were a week late at Walwabum. Will they be a month late at the next objective? If we don't have the X Force behind us, we may as well be shooting toy guns." I can't take any more news; my nerves are shot. I stand up to leave and push the basha flap open. It's pouring cats and dogs.

CHAPTER 39

The dawn sky is thick with threatening clouds. Throughout the camp, soldiers huddle around small campfires, whispering to each other as though they don't want to wake themselves. I want to take my coffee back into my tent and sleep the day away, but my gear's already packed. No one wants to be left behind when the orders come to march, so we've gotten into the habit of rising ready to run.

"Harry, I'll trade you for your candy bar." Pfeifer throws me his packet of coffee.

This decision is no simple task. Knowing I get chocolate for a midday snack makes the first thousand steps bearable. I consider whether we'll even be allowed to have fires for coffee when we camp tonight, what with the panic about India. I toss the coffee back to Pfeifer.

Merrill and Hunter walk out of the H.Q. tent, followed by Darlington. A half-dozen Kachin guerrillas, burp guns slung over their shoulders, trail behind.

We kick out fires and fold up camp. My pulse pumps. The division commanders gather around Merrill and Hunter, and we watch, anxious to get started, yet dreading what will happen next. Merrill looks like he's had a rough night.

Waiting for the men to settle down, Merrill lights up his pipe and takes a few puffs. His voice is monotone. "Gentlemen, Imphal and Kohima are under attack, but we're still moving west to the Kamaing Road so we can take our next objective, Shaduzup. We'll set up three roadblocks, then let Brown's tanks and the Chinese X Force artillery move in for the final kill."

Some of us know we'll be going into Japanese territory without assurance that the Chinese will show up. Pfeifer and I give each other a knowing look. I kick the dirt in front of me, trying to divert my anger at Merrill's timidity, but I guess a commander can't tell his men he's sending them in to die. I reach deep for Ruthie's strength to carry me through the day. It grounds my nerves.

Merrill builds up momentum and confidence. His slight smile seems almost hopeful. "I want the White combat and the 1st I&R unit to cut back into the Hukawng Valley to form the northern block out of Shaduzup. The Blue Battalion and 2nd I&R will continue along the ridge, then swing in to form the southern block. In between, half of the Orange combat battalion and 3rd I&R will block the trails along the Tanai River. The other half of the 3rd will join the Blue Battalion."

Preacher, standing next to me, throws a soft punch to my gut. "Let's give the Blue Battalion some help. Maybe we'll see some action."

I double over from the fake blow, then straighten up. Every time I look at Preacher, with his thick dark eyelashes, I think of a llama. But he's anything but a docile animal. The guy probably wakes up wondering who he's going to fight that day. "I'd like to see some action, but not the kind you're thinking about," I answer, rolling my eyes

"Harry, didn't anyone ever tell you that your pretty blue eyes would get stuck in the back of your head if you keep doing that?" Preacher sprints ahead to grab his gear. Once we tighten our rucksacks for the march, Pfeifer connects with us to join the 2nd Battalion.

Kachin mahouts lead a file of seven elephants holding tails, one with a young calf at her side. Darlington pats the lead elephant's head. "You'll find this Kachin scouting unit will help you get in and out of some nasty terrain on your march through the villages along the ridge top. Once you arrive in Janpan, Fr. James Stuart will help you from there. Not to be confused with Jimmy Stewart, the actor, Fr. Stuart still gets to act, as a man of God. So far, the Japanese believe that's all he does."

We watch, unconvinced of the value of our new mascots, as the mahouts prod the elephants into motion. Darlington continues, "I won't be going with you, but we're sending three hundred of the best Kachin rangers." The peculiar Captain walks with Merrill towards the edge of the village, where he shakes our hands as we pass him.

Near the forest border, we pass by the young woman with the orange tree. Her child is strapped on her back, limbs relaxed and deep in sleep. When she sees me, she tentatively steps down from her basha carrying a paper-wrapped package. She hands it to me, then looks at the orange tree. I nod my thanks. She smiles and returns to her stairs. I pull out my poncho and tuck her oranges into the open spot. The clouds have opened, and it's raining buckets. This is going to be a long haul.

One day wears into two, then three. Men are weak with dysentery and malaria as we climb up and down the spine of the mountain range. Thank God for the elephants. They prove to be worth ten men on these steep, slippery slopes when the supply drops get a little less than accurate. But the mules are getting thinner, having to share their feed.

On the side of the road, I hand out packages of five-day rations from a pile, as the men march by, then let my eyes rest upon the horizon. Below, a faint blue ribbon meanders back and forth across the basin in the valley to the west. Above, a cloud layer floats in line with the path of the stream. For hundreds of miles, all I see are varying shades of green suffocating the foothills. I wonder why such a tranquil part of the world had to become hell for so many men.

After almost a week's march, the Kachin in our lead greets an unofficial representative of the guerrillas at the entrance into Janpan. His nationality and official status are hard to gauge, given the widebrimmed, Aussie felt hat with a pheasant feather on the left side, turned-up British-style, and calf-length khaki trousers much like Darlington's. He leans against a tree, chewing on a twig with an impish grin, trying to act disinterested.

When he sees Hunter, his expression turns exuberant, and he reaches out a well-muscled arm. "Colonel, I see you've brought the Marauder laddies I've heard so much about. Tis grand that ye made it before the night fell. A hundred thousand welcomes. I'm Father James Stuart." His Irish accent is so strong that if I closed my eyes, I'd swear I was listening to my Uncle Danny from Galway. "Let me show ye to where yer men can camp. It's a wee bit of a walk from here."

"You've heard about Kohima?" Hunter asks the Irish priest as they walk the narrow path through the village.

"Aye. Tis a sad day when the Japanese took over in Burma. And now they're on to India! Well, if yer willin' to continue to have them, the Kachin will be your best guides." The priest is pulled aside by one of the villagers holding a small, sickly infant.

The villagers are joyous as we march through their town. Old, leathery men and women with red-stained teeth greet us with waving windmill hands. Their bashas straddle the only path through the village. Ragged children run rampant. The men's opium-clouded heads bob like they're on springs. Their faces begin to show alarm at the unending column of soldiers. This must be the biggest gathering of white people they've ever seen. They crane their necks to see how many more soldiers are coming from the ridge, then turn to each other with childlike looks of awe.

The priest returns with a permanent grin on his face—one that's ready to tease, rather than tolerate, your existence. "Sorry to keep you and your lads waiting, but when God calls, I can't say no. And how long will ye and yer boys be staying with us?"

It's obvious by Hunter's blank expression that he doesn't have a definite answer. "I need to wait for orders, then we'll move out."

"Grand. Be sure to let yer men know I'm here to listen to any of them, and if they happen to be Catholic, we can negotiate the penance."

"There are about two-thousand of us, so I don't expect you'll get to know too many of them. But my boys have been whining about a nice, long furlough. So, depending upon when our orders come, you may get the unpleasant honor of hearing more than a few of them bitch."

"I'm probably not the one to sympathize with them on that. I've spent ninety-six straight months in the jungle without leave. Let's see if they can top that."

As we walk through town, the natives try to sell us betel nuts, eggs, and rice—things we usually don't have in our food drop. But we're all anxious to set up camp. This morning, we got our first mail drop in months, and everyone has at least one package to open.

Not wanting to seem rude, I let a villager who's dangling a chicken in my face stop me.

The others march on. He opens the wings, then points to the fleshy breasts. Shaking it, he emphasizes the prize he's offering me. I hurriedly trade him an accessory pack of sugar, plus Chesterfields, and, finally, he's satisfied with two m-rations. As I march beyond the bashas and dense brush to our bivouac site, my mouth waters for roasted chicken, and my body aches, in so many ways, to read the letter I got from Ruthie.

"Harry, over here," Pfeifer waves me over to the only level spot with a grass cushion. We even have a little rain protection from the overhanging canopy of a twisted tree. He's thrown down his pack and, not bothering to set up his tent, has ripped open the first envelope in his stack of mail.

"Hell," I look enviously at his pile of at least fifty letters while I throw down my gear. "Do you have a pen pal, or is that all from your ma?" I know he doesn't have a girl, so I'm glad someone's thinking about him.

Flashing a photo of a hubba hubba, definitely not the girl next door, he says, "Dream on, buddy."

Ruthie's letter screams to be opened, but I'm not sure what will be inside. I debate whether to read it now or tonight while I enjoy my succulent chicken dinner. Eventually, I drop the chicken on the damp ground and search for the letter in my pile. Right now, there's nothing more important than her.

My hands shake as I unfold the paper full of her handwriting. I can almost smell her Palmolive soap. I sit down and lean against the tree trunk, briefly close my eyes, then tell myself I can handle anything before I begin.

Darling,

It's been so long since I last heard from you, and I'm sorry I haven't written. I know life must be miserable for you, and I hate to be the one telling you this, but there's no easy way to say what I must. My heart is breaking.

I pull my eyes from the paper, and my chest constricts. My heart thumps so hard I can hear it in my ears. How can it be that the very thing I've waited for day after day, I now want to tear to shreds? Why didn't I see this coming? Because all I thought about was me. I tell myself I can make it right later. So I read on.

You see, Bob is gone. We don't know where or when, but his mother received the telegram.

My mind flashes back to Bob, smoking his pipe and honking the horn in his shiny Studebaker, the first to wear an officer's uniform. Without warning, tears flood my eyes and blur my vision. No, I shout inside. My body shudders as I try to hold in the pain. I can almost feel his paternal arm around my shoulder and hear him saying, "They saw something in you, Harry— something the rest of us don't have." I've seen so much death already, but this time, it's Bob.

Why him, someone who was my strength when my life seemed empty?

My body convulses as I silently sob. I feel Pfeifer looking at me, but he says nothing. I push the letter back to my face so I can hide behind it. It doesn't seem possible.

Maybe they're wrong. But I would hate for you to come home thinking he'll be here waiting for you. I know you miss him terribly...like I miss you.

I love you. I always have. Ruthie

I'm surrounded by a mass of wet, cruddy, unshaven soldiers, heads bowed, absorbed in their private lives. I hear chuckling, grunts, and whistles in response to their letters. I've got to get away from this place, from my mind, from the truth, from this war.

Standing up, I knock my letters into a puddle. The papers soak up the water, and the ink bleeds until it's drained, illegible, and worthless. Right now, I don't want to read any more, anyway. Without seeing, I weave in and out of the maze of men sprawled about the bivouac and run away.

"Hey Harry," Pfeifer calls after me. "Where are you going?"

I push aside several joking soldiers standing in my way. "Sorry," I mumble. "Just a little sick."

"Aren't we all?" one answers back, sympathetic, yet oblivious. His group of friends is in high spirits, and why not? Life is good, they're alive.

My feet take me in an unknown direction. First, I follow a dirt trail, and then push into the dense jungle. I wander in circles. Why you, Bob? I retch, then let loose the tears. Branches scratch my bare arms and face, but I don't push them away; the pain is soothing. My eyes are itchy and swollen, but I can't stop crying. Gradually, I become aware of the drizzle splatting on the leaves and dripping to the ground. Rain soaks my hair and clothes, but if I stop walking, I'll have to admit that it's real. So I keep moving. Night falls before I realize I'm trapped in its darkness. I can almost touch it and smell it. The last thing I recall is crumbling to the ground in a thicket without energy to move, think, or cry.

When I wake, it's still dark. I'm in my tent, wet, with welts stinging my entire body.

Someone's thrown my blanket over me so I'm not cold. I roll

over and see light from the cigarette in Pfeifer's tent as he inhales and exhales audibly. I turn back to hide under my blanket, not ready to face the truth. But the facts are relentless.

Bob saw goodness in everything and everyone. If prayers could bring him back, I'd get on my knees. Oh, God, give me the courage to understand why you took away the only man who believed in me. Show me why I should live instead of him.

CHAPTER 40

My mouth tastes like vomit, my swollen eyes itch, and my head's pounding. I can't recall drinking any alcohol, so I wonder why I have such a headache. I remember all at once and wish I hadn't. In one swift motion, I tear down my tent. Under the distorted tree, Pfeifer holds my chicken by the claws with one hand and shakes my helmet with the other. The feathers on the chicken's limp, body are frozen in clumps. Chunks of ice float in my helmet.

"Hope you didn't have plans for cordon bleu tonight." Pfeifer eyes me for approval to toss the carcass and with concern for my sanity.

I grab my helmet. With an easy underhand, he tosses the dead bird. It lands by the tree's trunk.

Dense fog socks in our camp. My breath comes out in solid puffs of condensation, and my teeth chatter like a wind-up toy. I roll up my blanket and fixate on the comfortable routine of packing. I'm grateful Pfeifer asks no questions about my letter from yesterday.

All I can and want to do is to suffer, so I think about Bob.

It was almost midnight. The ROTC Academy had a late football game, and I was on cleanup duty. Only Bob knew I worked a late shift to cover tuition.

"Why do you work your butt off to go to *this* school, I'll never understand," Bob said while helping me bag some trash. "If my folks didn't foot the bill, I wouldn't be here."

I had just finished the latrines and was almost ready to call it quits for the night. "There's a dream inside me that says I can be a somebody. Without chasing that dream, I'll never get there."

Bob stopped tying the bag, looked at the bleachers, then the goal post, and said, "You'll catch that dream someday, Harry. You're that kind of guy."

Ahead, a megaphone-voice bellows, "Move out!" We groan, but file into a column as ordered. I'm happy to be leaving Janpan.

The day passes, monotonous and hot, as we drop from three-thousand feet to sea level. I focus my thoughts on squeezing through the pinching boulders and curse the gravel sliding under my feet. I grab branches to break my falls, then pull the stinging thorns embedded in my palms. Chattering birds battle in the air. Everything's a welcome diversion from the memory of Bob. I even push thoughts of Ruthie away.

Pfeifer barges downhill at a fast clip. I drop to the rear to sink into my thoughts.

Below, along the stream channel, a family of wild elephants weaves in and out of the dense undergrowth. Two of the full-grown mammals bookmark each end, with their calves in between. Their silver-grey skin reflects in the sun and almost looks soft. They avoid the large, open spaces where they may get attention and shy away from other animals, including us.

"What'd you think of those Kachin women?" I hear a tentative voice ask me from behind. I don't want to talk, so I act like I have cotton balls in my ears.

"I bet they wear those turbans to hide the lice nests," he speculates.

The thick skull following me doesn't take my hint. I shake my head and plow forward a little faster.

Finding solid footing on these limestone ledges is tough. To one side is a steep rock face; on the other, a precipitous, hundred-foot drop-off. Vertigo isn't a problem when I have plenty of room all around me, but with men in front of and behind me, and a solid rock wall on the third side, I feel claustrophobic. In some spots, the mules have chiseled the path down to only a few feet wide. So I study the path ahead, placing one foot in front, then the other, pretending I'm alone, and inhale the comfort of isolation. It doesn't last long.

"Hell, I'm stuck," comes whining from behind.

The gravel crunching underfoot and grunts from trekking

men soothe my jagged nerves and do a pretty good job of blocking out his bellyaching. I've got my own problems to worry about. He can piss on his own.

"I need help." Without looking back, I keep marching. "I said I need help." The panic in his voice grates on me. "You bastards, I wouldn't leave you."

Guilt gets me every time. Irritated, my shoulders slump, and I glance back just in time to see the Boy Scout lose his balance. Alarmed, I yell, "You moron. Grab the branch."

Instead of hugging the boulder side of the path and turning his pack towards the drop off side, his rucksack bumps against the rock. While I'm watching, he teeters off the edge of the cliff.

At the last minute, he clings to a weather-beaten tree while his toes hug the path. Peering down to what would be certain death, his straggly hair covering his face, he screams, "Help me!"

Throwing down my rifle, I race uphill. My feet push pebbles and stones over the side. I curse myself for starting a small avalanche, but keep running. It's so far to the bottom that I never hear the rocks hit. The soldier has one knee balanced on a rock outcrop. Otherwise, the tree is only thing between him and heaven. His eyes meet mine as he whimpers, "What do I do now?"

"When you feel me pulling back, let go of the branch." I grab the hem of his trousers and tug him towards the path, but my sweaty hands slip. He falls another inch. He's shaking, but says nothing. The branches crack slowly, sounding like the ticking of a clock seconds before the buzzer rings and it's all over. I lean over further and grab the back of his pack. My mind's telling me, one stupid move, and you're both mincemeat. With all my weight, I heave him backwards. The kid must weigh all of fifty pounds, pack and all. His body flies towards me like a released spring. We lay on the trail, panting and gripping the narrow ledge. Icicles of fear needle my heart. I'm shivering and sweating at the same time. When my breathing is back to normal, I scold him. "Soldier, next time, lead with your head, not your ass."

Tears build up in the corners of his eyes. Hell, he's just a kid.

I feel more anger at myself than him. "Are you okay now?" I ask, softening my tone and adjusting his pack so he's balanced.

He shoves past me without a word of thanks, kicking my rucksack as he stamps downhill.

I pull myself up, then stew in silence as I march recklessly towards our bivouac, punting rocks off the side until my toes hurt. It's only then that I realize the kid did me a favor. I haven't been thinking about Bob.

Below, explosions echo up the ravine. I pull my rifle into position, gripping it with both hands and releasing the safety. My heart thumps, already racing out of control. It seems the front echelon has encountered the enemy. There are only a few of us at the end of the column, and we're in a narrow draw. I can't see beyond the next rock face. So we plaster our bodies against the ledge and shimmy down. When the trail widens, we move into formation, flanking left, then ready to push forward for action.

Turning the corner, I see Pfeifer toss a grenade into the brook. A geyser of water sprays in all directions. I look for floating Japanese, but instead see a layer of fish floating sideways, their eyes staring back accusingly. Stomping towards Pfeifer, pissed at the attention he's drawn to the battalion, I grab him by the shoulder and spin him around: "You're going to be joining them any minute." I point to the stream.

My hand digs into Pfeifer's shoulder. Our eyes meet: mine bulging, his with concern. He gently releases each of my fingers.

"You bastard, the enemy's out there," I spit out. My stomach curdles. "Your stupidity may have exposed all of us." It takes my last ounce of sanity to keep my fists under control. Pfeifer looks at me like he thinks I'm joking, so I give him my most patronizing look before I walk away to get the sight and smell of him out of my mind.

"Drop it. You're not thinking straight. It'll get you killed," he says to my back, then walks away without trying to make it any easier for me.

The river draws me closer as if it will be soothe me, but it ends up jarring me further. I'm tied up in knots, frustrated and grieving. Even the serene sound of water spilling over the rocks annoys me. I want just peace and quiet. Instead, Preacher scrambles up from the bank, his black hair sopping wet and his helmet swimming with fish. Seeing me, he calls over, "Hungry, Harry?"

"What is going on around here?" I wonder. I thought we were fighting a war. They're treating it like a picnic.

Along the bank, smoke rises from scattered fires. Men wrap fish in palm leaves and bury them in hot coals. For now, there are no Japanese in sight—not even a single sniper. I realize we're not going into battle and while the irate energy drains from my muscles, the residual tension immobilizes me. Finally, I thrust my hands in my face and squeeze my eyes closed, hoping that when I open them, this insanity will be gone.

"Get something to eat, Flynn." I whirl around to find Hunter, eyes hard and square jaw fixed. It's an order, but it sounds more paternal than official.

I pull my pack off my back, far away from everyone else, and slip down to the stream. I close my eyes for a moment to shut everything out and let myself forget where I am.

When I open my eyes, I see the kid wading about two feet away from the bank. He's surrounded by dead fish that reflect miniature rainbows from the afternoon's light. He gingerly lifts one after another, discarding those with chunks of flesh blown away. Stripped down, he looks like he's forgotten to eat for a month. As he scoops water to cover the catch in his helmet, he sees me. Quickly, he looks away.

"Hey," I say, trying to shake off the anger that's burning a hole in my gut. "Looks like they left us some grub."

He stomps away, splashing water like a spoiled brat.

Downstream, naked men swim like carefree children while others sit on logs, checking for bug bites and airing out fungus-infected feet. We've stumbled upon a pocket untouched by the war, and everyone's soaking in every ounce of it. Returning to my pack, I see the kid has chosen a spot near me. "Guess we got stuck with the bleachers," I say, hoping to clear the air without saying I'm sorry. Then I add, "I'm Harry—Harry Flynn." But he ignores me again, and forces bamboo kindling into a feeble excuse for a fire. His sullen face lacks even a single stubble, and his stringy, blond hair hangs in his eyes.

"I haven't seen you before, and I know most of the guys from when I hand out k-rations. What've they got you doing, other than carrying that rifle?" I say, trying to smooth things over with him. Before I sit down, I pull out my knife to gut my fish. "I'll clean your fish with mine if I can share your fire." I don't need him hanging on me, but I feel sorry for the kid.

Slowly, his skinny shoulders relax. "Collin," he says, but doesn't look at me. "Air reconnaissance." He blows until the fire wicks up in the kindling. Finally, he says, "Thanks. I hate touching slimy stuff."

I don't say anything. Instead, I slice open the belly of the first fish in my lap and look down so he doesn't see me smile.

As the fire grows, I learn Collin's from Kansas—a farm boy, like me. Although he looks fifteen, it seems he's been around. He was stationed in the Pacific and saw some nasty action.

Lied about his age to get into the service, and now all he wants is to get out.

Over the next few days, Collin becomes my little buddy. He's more like a puppy than a soldier, getting tangled up in the bamboo roots and slapped in the face by their stems. He almost faints at the sound of a snapping twig and shadows me constantly, even when we reach the road south of Inkangahtawng, where we're to set up the roadblock.

"Over there, Harry," Pfeifer yells as he comes up from behind and points to the tree we need to saw. Pfeifer and I are back to talking. I can't stay mad at anyone, and he doesn't carry a grudge. We move in towards the towering trunk.

"You bastard," Collin hisses. He pulls out a cigarette to occupy his shaking hands. "This is enemy territory. You don't shout." He tries to strike a match, but can't.

Under his breath, Pfeifer says to me, "You've got to quit babysitting and let the kid grow up." Then he hardens his tone for Collin. "Boy, put that cigarette out and help." He points to a couple of guys who're hustling with axes, aiming to get the roadblock placed in record time so we can get out of here. "Clear the brush for those guys so they can fall that tree."

Pfeifer acts like a hardass, but he's really a good guy. He just shows he cares in a funny way. Growing up with "I know you can do better," as the only kind words spoken to him, would leave anyone feel unappreciated. We go to opposite sides of the tree, each grabbing a handle on the long saw.

This forest is infested with the enemy. Collin and I had scouting patrol this morning and took down three snipers our first five minutes. Collin about peed in his pants. One thing is for sure: stopping the Japanese from moving north into Shaduzup is going to be tough.

I look over my shoulder as each tree falls and the roadblock grows. My worst fear is to spot a truck with a platoon of Woodpecker machine-guns rumbling up the tarmac, followed by their artillery unit. Right now, all I hear are men grunting and the saws digging deeper into the trunks. Repeatedly, I push the saw towards Pfeifer, then pull it back. My muscles cramp, but Pfeifer doesn't let me stop. I understand why he wants to be in charge of everything around him. Once he told me that the worst thing that could happen to him would be for someone to let him know they cared. Said he'd get all confused, so he needs to do things his way, or he'll lose it.

Collin drags slash from the downed trees and piles it high. Pfeifer and I swipe sweat from our foreheads, then help drag the last log to top off the block. Finally, Preacher nods. We grab our gear and head deeper away from the road.

When we're deep in the jungle, Preacher lets us stop for a canteen break. The vegetation is impenetrable, so we're forced to spread out. Between the leaves and trunks, I only see bobbing helmets and hear splashing water. Collin asks, "Where's Hunter?"

Preacher answers before downing his water, "His unit set up another roadblock a half mile south from here."

Collin's under Hunter's command. He fidgets, and his lip curls like he's about to cry. "Hey, we'll regroup later tonight." I clap Collin on the back to give him some gumption. "Not tonight. I don't want to climb anything around here in the night," Preacher answers.

Screwing the canteen cap on, he points to the radio, then directs his attention to Collin. "Set it up. Let Hunter know we're done." He orders the rest of the platoon to dig in.

The command passes down, man to man. Soon, dirt flies as shovels loosen up the wet soil.

With watering eyes, the kid wordlessly begs me to stay near him. I pretend I don't notice, but drop my pack within earshot of the radio, then push the spade of my shovel into the soil. Pfeifer mocks me: "Is it just about bottle time?"

The drizzle that started while we set up the block now rains down in sheets. Mud splats in my face as I sling the load from my shovel over my back. Hell, I know Collin's a dumb cluck, but I wish Pfeifer would stop sitting on him. Be-Jesus, will these rains ever stop? Holding this block until the Chinese get here's going to be mental torture.

Collin readies the portable radio under a dripping, green parachute. The only thing he gets is static, so Preacher changes his command. "Pull the long-distance radio off the mule and crank it up. Try C.P. at Hsamshingyang."

Soon, the radio crackles. It's Merrill's voice. "C.P. to Blue Battalion, over."

Preacher answers, "Blue Battalion copy, Sir." Collin continues to paddle the portable generator that powers the connection.

"Intercepted enemy map. Shows their battalions moving north. Heading to attack flank of the X Force. Need new block at Nhpum Ga. Abort current objective. Where's Hunter? Over." Merrill sounds frazzled. His usual shrewd confidence is gone.

"Split up while setting up the roadblocks. It's raining like a dam broke down here. Over." Preacher looks like he's bracing for an unpleasant directive.

"OK. Let me worry about Hunter. Get out of there, now. We need you to move east.

Fast!" There's a static pause before Merrill nervously finishes his message. "Bad news from the Brits. We just heard Wingate was KIA in a plane crash en route from Burma to India. Over and out." The radio hums. Collin stops peddling.

Preacher drops the headphones. Unsteadily, he muses, "I liked Wingate. Why can't the jerks die?" He gathers his composure, rain bouncing off his helmet, then yells, "New orders from H.Q.: move out. And hustle."

Men turn their attention from their half-dug foxholes, soaked from the downpour.

Frustrated, some throw their shovels in the holes. Preacher shouts, "Get the wounded on litters and move. On the double!"

His anger builds while we pack up. "What am I missing? Why do we have to guard the Chinese artillery? Next, they'll ask us to roll out the red carpet so the X Force doesn't get lost on their way in to claim Shaduzup." He shakes his head, resigned to climb back up the steep slope we just slid down. "I said move out. Now! March until dark."

We form a column to retreat back east. I can't help but think it's Stilwell spouting orders from the safety of his warm bed, protecting his Chinese division to keep on Generalissimo's good side. We completed our objective, so we should hold our position. If you can't stick with a plan, why have one? Maybe there's more to the Wingate story than what we've heard. I've got a nasty feeling that this is a bad move. The rain's thick, and the mud's ankle deep. We may end up retracing the enemy's steps instead of our own. I grab Collin, who seems comatose. "Can't leave you down here for the enemy, little buddy."

CHAPTER 41

March 28, 1944

Ahead, the village of Nhpum Ga sits high, overlooking a valley to the east and another to the west. The north-south trail cuts through this settlement like a rift between two knolls. Both the west and east side are about fifty feet higher than the path down the center, which is where we've rounded-up the mules. Five native huts sit on the west hill.

After the three-day forced march, my legs are wobbly, and I'm exhausted from the thirty- two-hundred-foot climb to this peak. Collin bolts down the hill from one of the knolls, and practically tackles me.

"Harry, this is a great place to bivouac." He looks happy for the first time; his floppy hair is getting longer and forever in his eyes.

"Let's find Pfeifer," I suggest, ready to fall asleep while standing. We find him nearby, digging his foxhole like the rest of our men. Along the perimeter, dirt flies like we're in a windstorm, creating a network of fox-holes around the village. Pfeifer sees us, and spits out some chew, unable to disguise his dislike of Collin

With one eye sleeping and the other on trench duty, I open up a hole barely wide enough for me and my gear. Collin chips at the dirt with his shovel, periodically stopping to lean on its handle. Dreamily, he gazes below at the slow-flowing river.

I'm so exhausted, I don't even wake the next morning when the Japanese's shells blow craters in the path between the two knolls, killing about half of our mules.

March 29, 1944

Finally, the shell burst sets off my internal alarm. I'm wide awake with nothing to do but crouch deeper in my dugout. On one side of me, Pfeifer chews a biscuit; on the other, Collin bites his nails.

"Christ, I'm going to die from a concussion if they don't get me with a direct hit first," Pfeifer complains from his hole. The deafening explosions reverberate against the two knolls. "Harry, trade you a pack of fags for some coffee and a sugar cube."

"Coffee only. The sugar cube's mine." I toss him the cigs, which fly into Collin's hole. "Something hit me," Collin screams. From the rim of his burrow, I see him frantically searching, as though he'll find a grenade.

"Yeah, my fags. Give 'em back." I sigh and stretch out an arm.

"Can't you wait?" Collin's shrill scream hits raw nerves. "I'm going to be dead if I don't stay dug in." Only his bug-eyed head sticks above the pit.

"What a sap," Pfeifer smirks as I pull myself out of my hole to grab my cigs.

It irritates me how much of a prick Pfeifer can be to the kid. "Come on, Pfeifer, be happy he's around. When he's gone, you won't have anyone to bawl out." The stress gnaws at all of us.

I grab my gun and wait for their kamikaze squad to push up the hill. My heart thuds against my chest. All around me, men scramble back from their early morning piss and leap into their holes. The Japanese consistently pulverize us with their shelling, but we've got home advantage when they charge in with their shouts of "Banzai."

A blinding white explosion and dirt spray force me deeper in my hole.

About thirty minutes after the shelling begins, it stops. Those of us still alive prepare for the charge we know will come, and we are not disappointed. "Come on and get us, you yellow slant-eyes!" our guys shout.

The slope is so steep, we aim as soon as we see their five-point star. Some wear helmets; others just have field caps. Then we pull the trigger when we see the whites of their eyes. A red bead forms on their foreheads, and they tumble backwards. Within minutes, the slope is thick with dead Japanese.

"Harry, behind you!" Pfeifer yells over the murderous cries of "Banzai."

I swing my rifle around. The enemy had dragged himself up on his belly. With gritted teeth, he raises his bayonet, but is slammed back by the force of Pfeifer's bullet. "You ain't getting in my foxhole with me, you son of a bitch," I shout as I release the trigger.

Then I slip into a trance, where fate becomes my only logic. All around me, men in the Blue Battalion curse and lean out of their foxholes so they can get a better shot at the raving, suicidal Japanese. I scream unending obscenities as I stand up and recklessly let loose a stream of bullets, ignoring the fact that my own men are within range. But it feels good. Eventually, I duck back down into my foxhole, starving, gut aching from dysentery, and mouth foaming with saliva.

The charge stops, and my trance breaks. I curl into a ball and clutch my knees to my chest until my shaking stops. My mind focuses on everything and nothing; all at once. Even though the enemy has retreated for today, I know they'll be back tomorrow morning. I want to sleep this part of my life away.

A wad of paper hits me. Still drained, I force myself up and look over to see Pfeifer grinning from his enormous hole in the ground. "Where did you get your filthy mouth?" He watches me unfurl the papers he threw over. "Found those letters at our bivouac a couple days ago. You've got some reading left to do."

Even though the ink's been blurred by the rain, I recognize the letters. On top is an envelope from Ma. "Thanks for the bad news," I holler back as I open her letter, grateful that Pfeifer had more sense than me that night.

Harry, My Dear Boy,

Your sisters and I pray for you every day. We're doing just dandy, so don't you be worrying about us. It's you who needs God's protection right now. Ruth said she'd sent you news of Bob. He was a grand boy, and one not to be forgotten. But God knows what's best. Don't you be judging our Lord, for Bob's in a glorious place—one that he deserves, and better than the likes of what you're seeing. There's a time for everyone. This was his. Let him go in peace so he can rest. Father Ferguson sends his blessings. Your loving and devoted mother.

I close my eyes. Will Bob's death ever stop killing me?

When I let myself think again, I hear Preacher and Pfeifer chatting quietly. Seems a bunch of guys got wounded, and seven more men are dead. The Japanese have occupied both valleys, and they've blocked off the trails from the north and the south. We're surrounded, and our gunfire this morning gave away our positions. The Nips will be able to pinpoint our foxholes tomorrow, so shelling's going to be hell. It's time for the cavalry to charge in for the rescue.

March 30, 1944

The Japanese artillery opens when there's only a sliver of light on the horizon. This time, they target accurately. Rocks and shrapnel confetti fills the air. I dig in deep, praying no shells or shrapnel have my name on them, knowing that when their artillery stops, the Banzai will begin. Like an oath that the Japanese can't refuse or they'd risk losing face, we replay the same scene from yesterday.

It strikes me that the Japanese mind is methodical. At times like this, I find it hard to believe they have families, feelings, and fear. They're unimaginative students of war, and their unwavering belief in victory leads them blindly into death. We should use that overconfidence to outsmart them.

A warm wind sweeps through the ridge top, stinking of the decomposing Japanese and putrefying mule carcasses. It's insufferable. I can almost taste it.

I hear whimpering in the kid's pit. He hasn't talked all day. Pfeifer pulls himself out of his hole and asks, "What's up with little dumb-dumb?" It's obvious he doesn't want an answer. "I've got to get out of here. Maybe Doc needs some help."

Pfeifer doesn't know, but when we were climbing up to Nphum Ga, Collin tried to go AWOL. He hadn't seen me follow him until I squatted next to him. Collin just ignored me and sobbed. Finally, drained of emotion, he said, "I was crazy to sign up for this war when I didn't have to."

"But you must've made your parents proud," I said.

"Oh, I did indeed." His voice cracked. "I thought Uncle Sam would say no. Then I could brag that I tried, but was too young. I surprised even myself, getting assigned to air reconnaissance. Guess being a weird kid and playing with a ham radio was really stupid."

"Collin, this is no place for regrets. Even if you weren't ready then, you've got to be now."

"Before I joined the army, my neighbors didn't even know my name." He looked off in the distance at something that wasn't there. "There was one time, when I was in the South Pacific, I didn't hear a Nip sneak up on my foxhole? I dodged a piece of flying shrapnel, and I accidentally pulled the trigger on my gun. It blew the Jap's brains out of his skull. I got a medal that should've gone to someone else."

I placed my hand on his shoulder, not sure if he'd shrug it off or slap me away. He didn't move. "I never killed a man before the war, either," I said.

Defiantly, Collin looked me in the eye. Tears had streaked black tracks down his cheeks, but he was no longer crying. "You don't understand." He looked back to the empty space, his face strained. Then, in a barely audible voice, he said, "I've got a bad left ear. The Nip had just bayoneted my foxhole buddy, and I didn't hear a thing. When I looked over, I thought my pal was just sleeping. I let him bleed to death." The kid clenched his jaw, lip trembling.

"That's the way it works," I said, thinking of Bob, someone who had every right to live. "Life isn't like buying a lottery ticket, where you can decide if you want to play."

Collin pushed himself to his feet, then shouted. "Why let the cowards live? Isn't that what Pfeifer really wants to know? Don't answer. He's right."

When he walked back to the trail, he looked as though he was leaving a part of himself behind. Now I know which part it was.

"Harry." Preacher's commanding voice brings me out of my reverie. "Doc Winnie needs help. You got anything better to do?"

"Let me see…stay here and get riddled with shrapnel, then stabbed with a bayonet…or help Doc." I hoist myself to level ground. Before I leave, I put my canteen to Collin's cracked lips. It dribbles down his chin. "Well, that's one way to make sure you don't have to leave your hole to pee," I say, but even I can't laugh.

Preacher and I look at Collin, then each other. Without a word, we leave for the medic station. This madness is contagious.

I follow Preacher to the north end of the knoll past the rotting, maggot-infested mule carcasses. The smell intensifies. "Did you say the name of this place is Maggot Hill?" I gag.

Pfeifer is already at the medic station when we arrive. Doc shoves a bucket at each of us. "The water hole's down that slope. I'll take all you can bring up."

We look over the edge of a sheer cliff. "You've got to be a trapeze artist to get down there," Pfeifer says.

"Who says the army isn't a circus?" Doc answers as he twirls a scalpel in his hand.

So we slip and slide down two hundred feet through tangled vines to where a bamboo reed drains water from a spring leaking out of the hillside. I stand guard with a rifle, resting against a wall of moist soil.

Pfeifer lets his head hang in front of the natural spigot, gulping it down while it splashes freely on his face and bald head. "Have you ever tried to describe the taste of water?" he asks.

This question jogs a recollection of diving into the lake behind the farm house. I lick my lips, recalling that fresh taste and feeling it slide down the back of my throat, charged with fullness. "No, it never seemed to be something worth thinking about," I lie, fearing that if I admit it reminds me of a life I may never see again, my fear may come true. Pfeifer and I let the water's healing sound fill the buckets.

When I return to my hole at dusk, Collin is rocking back and forth in his pit. It's that time of day when the Japanese surge uphill to hurl grenades into foxholes, hoping there'll be men within. It's been a bad day. Twelve more men are dead and forty-two wounded.

"Hey, little buddy." I try to get his attention, but he either can't or won't listen. "Looks like you need a little boost." I pull out the sugar cube I'd been hording and offer it to him. He doesn't respond. So I pull myself out of my hole and crawl over on my belly to place it in his hand. Like dice, it rolls from his limp palm to the ground. His eyes are riveted straight ahead.

"Collin, we're not playing roulette," I joke, to keep from crying. Even the little things in life are losing their pull, for all of us.

March 31, 1944

Today, we lost the water hole, and the Japanese have stationed a platoon by the bamboo reed. So we just finished digging a shallow pit by the medic station to catch the rain. Even the slop buckets for pigs back home were cleaner than this, and the water tastes like decomposed flesh.

"What do I need water for?" Doc jokes. "No medicine for operating, no water to plaster the breaks. This means I get a vacation." Yet he continues his daily rounds, handing out jokes— the only thing he has left.

Above, I watch our fighter pilots strafe the valleys below, searching in vain for the well- camouflaged enemy. "I'm sure those guys would rather be anywhere else than keeping us company," I say as the planes make another run over the valley.

"So would I," Pfeifer answers.

We're surrounded on all sides. We've lost our water. Our air force is striking out. It's been days since we've had a food or ammo drop. We've had thirty casualties in the last two days, and over one hundred wounded. We just heard Merrill had another heart attack, and no one can reach Hunter. It's been raining hard all night. Is God mad at us?

"Good news, guys," Preacher offers as he squats down by us. "We can check off our second objective. The White team took Shaduzup." He waits for us to cheer, but all we can muster are lethargic glares. "They literally caught the Nips with their pants down. Our boys confiscated a truckload of fresh underwear, then ate the enemy's hot fish and rice.

"Can they make Maggot Hill their next objective?" I ask, ready to give up.

"I hope you told Osborne to get his skinny ass over here to break us loose." Pfeifer leans back against a tree, hands clasped over his head to control his nervous energy.

"They'll be here in forty hours." Preacher stares out over the socked-in valley as though he expects to see the column marching through the clouds. "Sam said they'd use their noses to find us."

Being trapped on this hill is making me claustrophobic, so I pull myself off the ground and scan the top of the knoll for a diversion. My choices are to either give myself a haircut with my knife or find out if there's any dope from C.P. I walk over to Roy, who's peddling the long- range radio.

"Any news on when H.Q.'s going to break us out of here? Or are they still farting around?" I ask, lighting up a cigarette for both of us.

"Still no word." He peddles at a slow, tedious pace.

We've been around each other for so long, there's no need to talk. I finish my smoke, then ask, "So where you from?"

"Los Angeles," he says. "And you?"

Instead of answering, I continue my questioning of this Nisei interpreter, "No, I mean your folks. Aren't you Japanese?"

"Yes," he answers pensively. "We were all sent to interment camps when the war began." With a hint of resentment, he carries on. "In my culture, we would never put our elders behind barbwire fences." He keeps peddling. I don't ask any more questions, but he's in the mood to talk. "My mother is still in Japan. I would worry about her if she was in Tokyo, but she lives in a small city in the south, Hiroshima."

April 1, 1944

It's been storming so hard, our foxholes are caving in. So I try to capture what rainwater I can in my helmet. Last night I lay awake, listening to it plop on my parachute cover. I couldn't get to sleep for hours after it stopped. Wish I'd had a good book and five gallons of water.

In the pale, gray light of morning, I hear Preacher clearing his throat with a raspy cough. "I'm so thirsty, I'm thinking about sucking the water out of the dirt in my pit," he says. "No more bad news today." I croak, then return my attention to my game of solitaire.

With a quizzical look, Preacher asks, "Getting a little sensitive lately, are we, Harry?"

Before I can answer, bullets fly in all directions around us. Preacher dives into Pfeifer's pit. We all duck, grabbing our weapons, expecting the enemy to pounce.

A couple Marauders scramble out of their foxholes and drag a body up the hill, then men start shouting at each other. Silhouetted in the early dawn, two men shove at each other. Standing on the knoll's bare edge, they're easy targets for the Nips. The unmistakable dull thud of rifle metal bashing against rock is followed by more arguing voices. A single bullet is fired into the sky.

"Shit, are they going to kill each other?" Pfeifer leaps out of his bunker, and races across the knoll, followed by Preacher, then me.

"Call Doc Winnie," a stocky man barks as he bends over the body.

"What's happening?" Preacher demands, but gets shoved out of the circle. He elbows one of the men and pushes back in. "Was there an accident?"

"He started it." A lanky soldier points a finger at the man crouched over the body.

The squatting man whips around. "I shot in the air. You shot to kill." He stands up and throws an empty punch in the air.

Another man screams, "How many Goddamn bullets do you need to kill a man? Did you both empty your rifles into him?"

"I saw you fire, too," replies a man with limp arms, whose eyes are riveted on the body.

Someone asks in a stunned, weepy voice, "Goddamn it, why wasn't he wearing his glasses? And who the hell'd he think he was, sneaking up on us from the enemy side?"

Everyone stares at the body. There's so much blood. What is this war turning us into?

Accusatory fingers turn into fists. A solid punch to the jaw and cracking bones lands one man on the ground. More soldiers join, and, within seconds, a tangled mass of bodies is kicking and wrestling in the mud.

I grab a thrashing arm, a jerking leg—anything I can put my hands around to separate the men pummeling each other. Instead, a drop-kick knocks me into the brawl.

"I'll beat the shit out of anyone who makes one more move. Then I'll have you court martialed," Preacher says, both hands on his hips. Men slump to the ground, their bodies bloodied and defeated. And it's only dawn. Then he whispers so only Pfeifer and I can hear, "They shot their Goddamn C.O. Fuck, can you believe it?" He isn't looking for a response.

As we walk back to our bunkers, I keep my distance from Pfeifer, who's like a pacing cat ready to pounce. He's the kind of guy who needs lots of space to operate. "I'm going go help bury the dead," he says casually, as if he were grabbing a cup of coffee. He walks to the perimeter with his shovel.

With the downpours, I doubt we'll get our airdrop of ammo

and water today. Still, I'm asked to put in a special request for five hundred gallons of water in plastic bags. I'm expecting zilch. Isn't it April Fools' Day? I go back to check on Collin. He's still comatose.

I slip into my foxhole, wanting to bury everything. But the last letter in my bundle stares up at me as it has a million times in the last couple of days. It's from Bob. I've been tempted to just toss it, because it's the last time I'll hear from him and I'm not ready to accept that. But that wouldn't be fair to him. I reach down to my rucksack and open the envelope before I lose my nerve.

Dear Harry,

Greetings from Italy. We surprised the Nazis by slipping into Anzio Harbor last week. It's only fifty miles to Rome, now, and I bet the Krauts are pissed. But we've had our work cut out for us the last few months. The enemy's been hunkered down in medieval castles built with five-foot-thick granite walls. I think you'd like it here, being the history buff that you are. (That's a joke Harry).

The food here is bland but the wine is worth the trip. What else do I have to talk about? Oh, the signorina! As Marco Fazio would say, they are bella, with more curves than these here mountainous roads. And what they don't tell their mamas, you won't get out of me.

So when are you coming to join me, Harry? Wouldn't it be great to tell our kids about the time we marched into Rome together? It's a shame what this war is doing to Europe. Looks like it once was a beautiful place.

I hear everyone but the British Chindits and Merrill's Marauders are snoozing in your neck of the woods. You need some action? My travel agent can get you a ringside seat to the hottest show in Italy.

By the way, Happy Birthday. January 5th, right? You're as old as me now, but in July

I'll turn twenty-one. Guess I'll always be the old man in the group.

Don't forget your old pal, especially if you find a good-look-ing dame. (You always could reel them in, you blue-eyed devil.)

Bob

Thunderstorms crash loudly. "Christ, not again!" I pull my ground cloth around my neck and cinch the parachute tight. Pudgy Bob with a sexy Italian? That, I can't imagine.

April 2, 1944

There's nothing to do but wait to be killed or rescued. My deck of cards is starting to mold with the rain. Roy got through to head-quarters and learned that the Orange combat squad got as close, but the Japanese are popping up like mushrooms in season. The enemy is dug in and camouflaged so well that our fighter pilots continue to strike out. We've been shelled every morning and ambushed with grenades every night. Collin's coherent, but won't leave his hole, not even to pee. Thank God it's been raining, or I'd be asphyxiated by the stink.

Pfeifer spits out, "Kid, one more squeak out of you, and I won't be held accountable for my actions."

"Pfeifer, does your foot have to fall out *every* time you open your mouth?" I ask. Still, I'm not sure if Pfeifer's strategy isn't the right one. Mine sure hasn't helped the kid. I'll be a raving maniac if this siege doesn't stop soon.

I hear a C47's engines approaching overhead. That means a delivery. "Duty and dinner calls, boys." I'm out and racing to the supply station before I even realize I don't have my boots on. I look up, expecting to see our military stork dropping green, blue, and white parachutes with food and water. But they continue north to the C.P.

Shuffling to a stop, I shout in vain, "You fucking morons! You missed your target!" Then I pick up a stone and throw it in the direction of the retreating planes. It's silly of me to think a battalion that's been under siege for days would be more important than field headquarters.

Then I hear a cheer rise up from the men.

Bulky chunks, dangling from double parachutes, float towards the command post. Fishing nets filled with metal parts drift awkwardly into the forward echelon air field. The Japanese aren't guarding the C.P., so there's no shelling, only the calm, swaying descent of a multi-ton weapon. Finally, Ledo has sent our C.P. some muscle artillery to decimate the enemy. Dare I hope we'll get ourselves out?

"You slimy slant eyes, wait till we get those howitzers assembled. You'll get a taste of Yankee medicine." Inside the stork nets are un-assembled parts to a 75 mm. A roar rises from the Blue Battalion. This losing team just sunk a three-pointer from the opposite end of the field to tie it up with seconds remaining. And we thought we were crushed.

More engines approach. I race back to my bunker, thinking this would finally be my unlucky day. Next to me, a cylinder crashes. I dive, fearing shrapnel from the explosion. Instead,

I look up to see the sky filled with a sea of green, blue, and white parachutes. Boxes of food break open upon impact. Men dance and trip over each other trying to get to the boxes. Even the horrors of the last few days can't rip off their mud-crusted smiles. Does this mean we get to live?

A man carrying a parachuted water bag pushes past Preacher. Preacher claps the man on the back and teases, "Don't tell the others when beer arrives." Preacher seems to be back to himself, his black hair flopping in his face. "I guess our maker's not ready to meet us."

Later that night, in the pitch dark of the cloud-covered night, Pfeifer calls over our foxholes, just loud enough for me to hear. "Harry, the waiting's driving me mad. When are they going to get us out of here? And if that sniveling parasite next to you whines once more…I don't know how much longer I can last."

I've never heard such desperation from Pfeifer. I don't have an answer and wish I could feign sleep. Eventually, I say, "Give it time."

Pfeifer answers, "Well, I'm glad you didn't tell me to 'hang in there.' I'd have a hard time finding rope."

April 3, 1944

The whole battalion is barely hanging in there; it's as though our fingertips are scraping down a cliff while we sink towards the bottom. If H.Q. can't set those howitzers up by tomorrow, the Chinese better get here to blast the Japanese out of position. I won't consider any other scenario.

Instead, I let myself hope, thinking about Ruthie and going home.

April 4, 1944

Our Vengeance dive bombers swoop down from the blue skies into the lush Tanai Valley and, like golden eagles, cruise over the jungle canopy looking for prey. But our fly guys still can't get those little devils out of their rat holes, and today, the Jap guns are honed in on our bombers. So we're still trapped up on Maggot Hill. I'm sick of this mountaintop straightjacket.

I listen to the rat-a-tat-tat as I rearrange supplies on our makeshift pallets of rock shards and rubble so they'll stay dry. There are sections for ammo, medicine, and rations. Food is always a great way to get my mind off the real problem. But my gums are bleeding from yesterday's food drop. "Just got off the radio. Get ready for another drop." Roy Matsumoto walks up to the supply station wearing a big smile that hints at something to come.

"I'm ready for this vacation to end. Maggot Hill mountain resort has lost its charm. I'd rather they bust us out of here than fill up these shelves."

"Well, someone intentionally leaked the news that a platoon of parachutists will be dropped tomorrow. That should keep the Japs' attention on the air. Meanwhile, our boys with flame throwers are going to push in on the ground."

"While we continue to fall like leaves in a storm, they keep revising yesterday's hare- brained plans," I answer, deflating Roy's enthusiasm. "Hopefully they'll find something that works before there are none of us left to rescue."

Roy shrugs, gives me a farewell salute, and stuffs his hands in his pockets as he walks away.

April 5, 1944

Morning breaks with the deep rumble of engines in the distance. It's broken suddenly by a staccato of bullets and whining bombs. The earth in the valley below erupts in geysers of dirt. Previously hidden by clouds, squadrons of Vengeance bombers flock into the valleys on both sides of Maggot Hill. Our rescuers have arrived.

"Hells bells!" Pfeifer begins to laugh hysterically and loosens his grip on his gun. "I thought it was a swarm of Franks. Looks like there's no need for a first or last prayer."

I let my head drop back against the wall of my pill box, tension cracking along each vertebra. Just as Roy had relayed, white, blue, and green parachutes drop on our narrow ridge top—only they're not parachutists, just more supplies. The enemy is fooled and keep their guns shooting at the boxes instead of our aircraft. Like piñatas, the boxes shower us with cigarettes and gum.

"Hey, Pfeifer, look at the pinball game below," I say as a platoon from our Orange Battalion floods Jap holes with sprays of fire and our planes soar above. The enemy scampers away like rodents, only to be taken down by the rat-a-tat-tat from our fly guys. The Japanese that don't get shot run for other foxholes.

A droning chant from the Blue Battalion erupts, and pulsates all around us: "Revenge! Revenge! Revenge!" The chant becomes part of the symphony of whining bombs, cracking shells, and stuttering bullets.

"Our boys just slaughtered half a dozen rats over there." We cheer and throw our helmets in the air.

"They're finally gonna get us out of this sardine can!" someone shouts.

After three hours of nonstop fighting, the smell of sulfur fills the air. A gang of men, including Pfeifer, Preacher, Doc, and I huddle around Roy, who's peddling the radio outside the C.P. "If they don't break through today, they never will," Doc says. I can't tell if he's confident we're on our way out or preparing us for our perpetual post in this hell.

"Blue Battalion 2 to Orange 3, over," Roy's voice is even and controlled.

"Orange to Blue, we've pushed the enemy in a mile tighter. But the game ain't over yet, boys. We'll be back tomorrow. That's a promise. Over and out."

I close my eyes for an internal replay, knowing I must've heard wrong. When I open my eyes, I see it isn't defeat paralyzing the men, but distrust. There's nobody up there who gives a damn. Why are they letting us die?

"It's time we sit on the bench and let the brass go toe-to-toe. I bet the match would be over by nightfall," I say as I skip a shard of shrapnel off a wave of rubble.

Night seeps in like routine, and tomorrow will begin as it has for the last week. I curl myself up in a fetal position in my foxhole, clutching a letter from Ruthie. I read the first sentence.

"I'm counting on you coming home." My tears have dried up with my hope.

April 6, 1944

"You devil. GAAAAh," Collin screeches with bared teeth, safely surrounded in his pill box. "Fucking bitch asshole shithead whore, GRRRRRR." Spittle from his cursing spews out in the air. Few can hear him over the earsplitting shelling.

Lately, Collin's hours of silence are broken with hours of piercing profanity during the morning attacks. I don't know where he gets the energy.

"Harry, you could take a lesson from that kid. What a vocabulary!" Pfeifer yells out as he presses flat against one of the walls of his pit to avoid the shrapnel that does most of the killing. "I'm still waiting for that lucky metal shard to slice his vocal cords. It'll save me some trouble."

I ignore Pfeifer's insanity. We're all anxious to see if the Japanese try to settle yesterday's score for our Vengeance squadron attack. Later, I haul my ass out of my crumbling bunker to collect yesterday's drop. First, I open the cap to my canteen, force Collin's clamped mouth open, and dribble some water down his throat. Like giving my dog back home some medicine, I force his mouth shut, then rub his throat so he has to swallow.

"Hang in there," I yell to Pfeifer, over the sucking sound my boots make in the mud. "And let me know if you need any rope. I'll be at the supply station."

At the supply hut, I grab my clipboard and review the checklist that always accompanies a drop. The papers are wet from the rain, and my writing goes askew from a folded sheet trapped underneath. So I rip out the offending paper, ready to toss it, but decide I'd better make sure it isn't important first. I strain my eyes, and bring the sheet into focus by tromboning it in front of me. It looks like some ancient hieroglyphic.

Looking over my shoulder, I clutch the paper closer to my

chest, as though I expect someone will catch me with confidential information. "Where the hell did I get this?" I wonder aloud. Then I remember picking a loose page of paper off the ground that day back in Walawbum, right after the three bigwigs' speeches. I start to read the letter from General Stilwell to Win, his wife.

Dear Win,

I'm wrestling with papers today, trying to reduce the manure pile. It made me think about everything I've got to deal with here. It's so hard to win this war with bozos all around me. Merrill's boys are a little scruffy, but they're good, solid citizens. I don't worry about them. Instead, I'm constantly laying the law down for the Chinese artillery, who don't know that building the road is what's best for them. They're always stalling and losing lives by being too timid. Or I'm standing up to the Brits, who are full of themselves, and butt in where they're not wanted.

The worst of them is Mountbatten. He says he wants to help—sure, help me slit my throat. Then the soft, old fool back home makes it worse by supporting Louis' Walla Walla to "achieve essential working accord." It's not just the Limies, though—Brown's Chinese tank battalion is like a flock of chickens, and Kinnison tells me what he thinks I want to hear, not what I ought to.

I'm no politician, but I hope the boys see me as a soldier's soldier. I'd be marching and bivouacking right next to them if I could. But they've got rules for generals, too.

Just in case I get bumped off, let me tell you that this war has made plain to me what a wonderful girl I married. After all these years, I still wonder why you accepted a bum like me. I'll never understand it, but I can sure pass on without regret.

Saw a movie last night—Jane Eyre. Corny as hell. Joe

It's pouring outside, and the tarp covering the supply depot sags. I'm alone and glad for it.

Can I, too, die with a clear conscience? I know I'd put my life on the line for any of these guys, and I know they'd do the same for me. Even if the worst isn't over yet, I feel like I've crossed my threshold. I don't have to worry, and I don't have to care. I've done my job, and I've done it well. What a relief it is to admit to myself that I've done something right.

April 7, 1944

"What the hell," I yell as I'm jerked out of my early morning sleep by the shaking earth. Explosions from Jap artillery are answered by angry detonations from our 75 mm Howitzers. Tallied hits based on puffs of smoldering fire in the valleys below show the Yanks are in the lead. Have my prayers been answered, or is this going to be another stalemate? These rollercoaster rides with victory only a shell away are losing their thrill.

Pfeifer props his elbows on the rim of his pill box and cups his chin in his hands to watch the fireworks below. "This is better than the Army-Navy game."

"Pass the buttered popcorn," I yell from my bunker, and taste it in my mind.

Looking over the edge of the knoll, I watch our artillery advance deeper into the valley, knocking out Nip machinegun outposts. Little Japanese figures scramble away from burning pyres. From the north, the guys in white hats charge in.

By noon, the valleys on both sides of the crest are smoke-covered, and we can't tell who's who. We're coughing from the sulfur and soot as it rises from the manmade storm below. Pfeifer and I decide to find Roy, knowing he'll have some dope on the score.

As usual, Roy is enveloped by a crowd of soldiers listening to the transmission. As we join them, a radio voice gives Howitzer trajectory directions: "Thirty-five degrees north of west, two hundred and fifty feet." A loud bang transmits through the air.

"Hey, that's Woomer the Boomer!" Pfeifer claps me on the back. "I knew he'd get us out of this."

Woomer's weapons platoon is manning the Howitzer within twenty-five yards of the Nip machine guns. He orders, "Deflection correct. Bring it in twenty-five yards, and if you don't hear from me, you'll know you came this way too far. Then shift it back just a little, and you'll be right on it."

The next round is released. The explosion over the radio waves rings in our ears. When the jostling metal and the clinging shells stop, I strain to hear a voice from the radio—any voice. At least I'd know which side lived.

"Things are looking up down here, boys." There's glee in Woomer's voice, followed by a fit of coughing. "Knocked out those little buggers on that one."

"I'll put fifty bucks on Woomer's next shot." Pfeifer pulls out an Indian rupee. "Make that one hundred." From his pocket falls a wad of bills, which are just glorified toilet paper these days.

"You can thank Merrill for the Howitzers. It was his last order before he went on his unfortunate vacation," Woomer shouts over the radio line. "The White team arrived last night after three days and nights of non-stop marching. Get ready! We're coming in for you boys."

April 8, 1944

Last night, before I fell asleep, something hard and angular continued to find soft spots in my thigh, my gut, and my groin. I dug in between the seams of my pants pocket and found the small, gilded Buddha. It was too dark to see, so I fingered its arms, legs, and belly, wondering whether the talisman would bring me better luck than it had its previous owner. This morning I awoke with the Buddha still in my hand. Maybe if I promise to change my ways, I'll be granted protection.

The orange globe on the eastern horizon rises quickly. I'm

dreading the next two hours of assault by the Japanese. *Will they never run out of supplies? If our guys can't break us out, do I care any more?*

There's an eerie quiet before the shelling starts. No breeze blows. No birds sing. An acrid sulfur smell lingers within the grey shards of metal that blanket the ground. The men remain stationed in their bunkers, not risking getting killed by the enemy or one of our own. Wisps of cigarette smoke rise like a leaking crevice in a volcanic seam.

Collin calmly steps from his foxhole. "Life is short; at least, I expect mine to be. And I've no one to blame but myself for not living the life in my dreams."

His voice grows in volume and projects over the entire knoll, as though he's giving a heartfelt sermon. The men listen, half interested and half because they can't shut out his voice. "I hate the life I live. It's filled with regret and scorn. Soon it will be over, but there'll be no one to mourn."

Collin hasn't uttered a single sentence in two weeks, and now he talks as though he's Plato or Socrates. *I'd feel better if he started shouting a stream of profanities. At least it would be the Collin we've come to know.*

The first shell of the morning crashes only a few yards from our holes. Shrapnel-laced mud pies fly in all directions. I compress myself into the smallest ball my body can make and wait for the others to come. The ones that follow reverberate in my ears, sparking light into my closed eyes. *Shit, they're too close today.*

"Get your pea-brain head down," Pfeifer shouts at Collin. Collin is standing up in his hole, preaching to his congregation. With mud-crusted hands outstretched and pleading, and his dirty blonde hair in his eyes, Collin continues.

"But what can I do
With no place to go
And things that I need
To climb that tall hill

I'm afraid it'll lead
Where I'll have no will."

Shells electrify the ground around us, spraying metal shards. At least one Jap gun is aimed at us, but Woomer answers their volley with a bigger bang. As the monsters battle below, my head bounces against the pit, soil dribbles in, and the sulfur almost suffocates me.

I shout to Collin, "Hey little buddy, Pfeifer's right. Get down. We'll be out of here soon."

But the kid's beyond hearing, his face is slicked with sweat, and he's soaking in the artillery fireworks. Like the pre-show to the big event, his arms reach high in expectation, his head tilts back, and tears gush from his eyes. I know then that he's a goner.

"Life can be lonely
You get trapped in a rut.
You talk to yourself
So they think you're a nut."

A big, squirming mass wriggles by; it's Pfeifer. "Hey Dumb-Dumb, the Japs don't know English," he taunts the kid.

Collin gazes down, benevolently, at Pfeifer.

But before Pfeifer can crawl any further, Collin takes one long step away from his hole and walks down the ridge to the enemy.

"No!" I scream. My cry is lost in the raining gunfire. Before I know it, I'm racing after him. That's when the big one hits.

I'm thrown in the air and land hard. The kid staggers and falls back. His head cracks on a rock. I close my eyes.

The next thing I know, I'm being dragged uphill and thrown unceremoniously into my foxhole. I won't watch Pfeifer toss Collin's body into his tomb, but I hear the thump. Pfeifer dives back into his pill box, and we wait for the explosions to end. I rub the gilded Buddha until my fingers bleed, then rub some more. Right now, I can't hear God at all.

I don't come out of my shell until sunset. My face stings and I have a headache from the rocks I landed on. I can't see straight, but I don't want my eyes to focus. I already know what I'll find.

Preacher and Pfeifer sit on the rim of Pfeifer's once-oversized foxhole. The downhill side is completely exposed now, and there's a crater fifty feet ahead. Pfeifer's clothes are bloody and his face and arms are gashed, but he's smoking a fag as nonchalantly as he would if he was sitting poolside.

"News from Roy Matsumoto: the White team is circling south," Preacher says quietly.

That night I fill in the rest of Collin's poor excuse for a foxhole. His dog tags jingle in my pocket. My grief is a parasite I know I'll live with forever. When there's more of a mound than a hole, I tie two sticks together with half of my shoestring, brace them with shrapnel shards, and hang his dog tags towards the valley–so he always has something beautiful to look at.

"Where's the good in goodbye?" I muse as I rub the Buddha in my pocket, wishing I'd asked for more.

CHAPTER 42

April 9, 1944: Easter

"Dear Lord, on this day of yer greatest miracle, we thank ye for life and pray for world peace." Father Stuart clasps his hands in prayer over a makeshift altar. He has taken off his Aussie outback hat and replaced his vest with a clerical stole. A pleasant breeze offers a false sense of comfort. The sun settles in the western horizon as it has for an eternity. But today's no ordinary day.

The grassy, rolling field surrounding the command post at Hsamshingyang is thick with thousands of kneeling soldiers from every denomination. Pfeifer's shiny, balding head; Preacher's floppy black mane; Sam's youthful, round face; Roy Matsumoto's thick eyeglasses; Mr. Doyer's slow, steady smile; Major Johnson's wild, red beard—they're all in this crowd.

Even the Kachin, Nau, is here somewhere, and we're all fused as one.

This is the best Easter of my life because I'm still alive. I'm not sure if it's real. Looking up into the cloudless sky, I blink back the tears that choke my throat, and swallow hard.

Throughout the gathering, scattered coughs attempt to mask heavy emotions.

In his Irish accent, the priest continues, "Why did these young lads need to die before our countries can make peace? Seems to me that fighting for peace is an oxymoron." Extending his arms in an open embrace, he says, "Peace comes when yer willing to listen to what ye don't understand; when ye let yer heart and spirit talk, instead of yer mind."

Digging my nails into my folded arms, I close my ears to shut out the grief. I picture Maggot Hill from early this morning.

"Harry, are you walking around in broad daylight, out of your bunker and out of your mind, for some particular reason other than to get killed?" Pfeifer had asked with a twinge of sympathy. He slumped against the wall of his crumbling foxhole.

The morning's enemy artillery bombardment hadn't started, and I didn't give a damn why it was late. "I got a Buddha in my pocket. The Nips dare not attack me," I answered, then continued to pace back and forth between Pfeifer's hole and Collin's grave.

"I thought you were Christian," Pfeifer commented, not one to let anything drop.

"I'll believe in any god that brings me luck," I said, fingering the gilded talisman before turning and walking from our knoll towards the path through the center of the village.

The decomposing mules and maggots had gotten worse, but my nose was deadened to the stink and my eyes ignored what I didn't want to see. Nothing had changed on the outside since yesterday: the supply tarp flapped in the wind, the central path still connected the north to the south, a cloudy sky cast bad luck over us all, and Doc Winnie's rows of litters continued to grow.

I couldn't look at the pain these men had to endure without wanting to break down. It reminded me of when Ruthie and I had gone to a movie and she had cried so hard, I had to take her home.

"How can you get so upset about something that's not real?" I asked.

"Don't you ever see grief in someone else that reminds you of yourself?" she replied. "I don't see anyone else who's like me. And I think everyone's suffering is their own business."

"No, there is no one like you. And you wouldn't want others knowing how you feel. But others welcome the sympathy. Can't you understand?"

My laugh was unsure, my feelings hurt. I told her I didn't know, but I did. I had been hurt too many times before. Still, she made me feel incomplete, because I couldn't open up my heart to suffering. But I feel it now, and it's crushing me.

Behind me, crunching shards on the path caught my attention. Pfeifer and Preacher approached me.

"Flynn, why aren't you in your foxhole?" Preacher demanded. His voice was stern, but he looked as apathetic as I felt.

I rolled my eyes with an insolence that warranted a good ass-kicking, then said, "If you don't mind, I'd rather get out of the enemy's line of fire than be buried in my ass-pissing hole." As an afterthought, I added, "Sir."

We all staggered forward towards the south, along the path, in the hot, muggy morning.

Probably pulled by the devil. I could hear voices.

"Sounds like God's coming to get me," I heard myself say distantly. Depressed and lathered with sweat, I thought, "So this is what it's like turning into a fruitcake." Who could blame my mind from straying from the world we were stuck in? "I'll let you know what He looks like when He gets here." I received vacant stares in response.

The reverberations in my mind grew louder. Cynically, I said, "It sounds like the saints are marching in with him." My high-pitched, and erratic voice frightened me, but it did sound like a battalion of stomping boots. There was huffing, grunting, snorting, and a sneeze.

"Saints sneeze?" Pfeifer whispered, breaking his silence. We reached for guns that weren't there, and, finding ourselves defense-less, crouched low.

From the southern bamboo forest marched a six-foot-four skeleton with a rangy red beard and eyes too big for its emaciated body. It looked a lot like Major Johnson. Two feet in front of us, it stopped and studied us like we were the ghosts.

I wanted to believe my mind wasn't playing tricks on me, but I didn't trust anything. So I froze like a cornered animal and just stared. No one else budged, either. The morning's rays sparkled off shrapnel shards in a rainbow of colors. Transfixed, I expected the apparition to dissolve in the sunlight's reflection.

At Maggot Hill, the only colors in my mind's optical kaleidoscope were grey clouds, black mud, and red blood. Yet, at that moment, out of the corner of my eye, I caught a rainbow of colors: lime green from supply parachutes, a pocket of royal blue skies peeking through, a bursting orange sun, and red hair.

Then the skeleton said, "Vacation's over, boys. Time to pack up and move on." It *was* Johnson! He paused to see if anything registered in our emotionless faces, then added, "We're here to get ya out."

Behind Johnson was Sam, then Osborne, then the whole White battalion. I stretched out my arm to touch them, but my feet wouldn't move. Nervous sweat prickled my forehead, but the Whites didn't vanish or evaporate. They just looked back at us, smiling dumbly. I closed my eyes, and my insides crumbled.

"After we cut off their supplies from the south, the Nips made a quick retreat. Want some hot breakfast? It's still cooking down there," Colonel Osborne said, and clapped each of us on the back. "Shit, you guys smell like you don't know how to dig a latrine."

"And you *look* like you've been hitting the bottle. It's time we take you out of here so you can sleep it off," Sam jabbed lightly.

As we marched through the village, a trembling soldier jabbered, "It's about goddamn time you got here."

"I had to take a few piss breaks," Johnson said. "Sorry we're late." Nervous laughter broke out among the men.

"Welcome to Maggot Hill Resort," another said, beaming like he'd just won the lottery.

A private from the Blue team grabbed a White soldier's chin between his hands and silently studied every pore of the man's face. Grinning with satisfaction he finally said, "Yep, you've got to be real. No ghost would be that ugly."

My eyes burned, and my lips struggled to hold down the gasp rising from my chest. Then I spotted Mr. Doyer, who came up to me, wordlessly touching me with his confident, caring smile. Eventually, he asked, "How are you doing, Harry?"

The lump in my throat snapped like a brittle rubber band,

releasing all the tension from the last two weeks. I wanted to say something clever, something that would hide the fact I could barely breathe. But I just smiled like I had no brain left.

Gently, Mr. Doyer slung an arm over my shoulder and asked, "Harry, where's your bunker?"

Instead of answering, I said, "I need to get the rations passed out before we leave. I've got to track everything."

Mr. Doyer led me by my elbow and said, "Let the other guys get that stuff later. You look like you need a shot of something strong. Now, tell me how your face ran into a meat cleaver."

"Aaw, I just tripped." The glib answer rolled off my tongue, but my cheeks were still raw from yesterday shelling.

"What you boys went through here was no small feat," Doyer said with concern. Too exhausted to joke, I asked, "Where do we go from here?"

Doyer smiled. "Are you speaking philosophically or literally?' He lit the cigarette I didn't want, shoved it between my lips, and pushed me into motion. "Either way, I'd say the only way to go is forward."

Father Stuart's brogue pulls my mind back to the Easter evening's sermon. "Lads, the cold, the hunger, the sickness, and the fatigue ye have suffered has changed ye into men. Tis a tough way to become a man, fighting the crusades of others. It's the ordinary man, trapped between earth and hell, who wins the war. And, while we can't choose when we die, let our death be worth our lives."

In front of the gathering lies a field of wounded men, their tortured eyes holding tough questions for God. I think of those who didn't make it and wonder why I was spared.

"But let God open yer eyes to the beauty that refuses to surrender." With a sweeping arc, the priest encompasses everything within the hills and valleys. Silver-tipped fruit pigeons swoop in for an evening's meal, cooing gently. Perfumed, yellow-fringed flowers rustle with the leaves. "Ye know that long after yer gone, this valley will be here. And the children of this country will walk in yer path. But yer struggle will not be theirs. God will hand them their own burdens.

Hopefully, the seed of peace will have been nourished by yer blood, and life's beauty will lighten their load." With that, the priest steps down from the altar to the injured. As he moves among them, he finishes the sermon with, "Let the war wait! Let us rejoice in life today! And tomorrow, give the Japs a good kick in the ass. In the name of God. Amen."

Watching Father Stuart bless the boys as he meanders through the network of litters, I realize I'll smell the stench of Maggot Hill for the rest of my life. Water will always taste better because I know its value. Nothing will be insurmountable, because I landed on my feet—okay, my face—when I thought it was the end. But it was only another beginning.

Finally, the tears break loose as my mind sees Collin's grave and what I said to him as I knelt by it for my final farewell. "Oh, little buddy, I wish you could've waited one more day."

CHAPTER 43

May, 1944

The Chinese didn't show up at Maggot Hill until April 22nd, about two weeks after we'd marched out. Rumor has it Chang Kai-Shek told them to make sure they could win, so they dragged their feet until the enemy was gone. Can't say I blame them, with the little training they've had and the fatalities they've suffered. But they've moved south now and can open a path for the road crew. I wash off my Maggot Hill days with my first bath in three weeks. How my priorities have changed.

After Maggot Hill, we marched north to Naubum where Merrill met us, having recovered from his heart attack. Seems the old commander still wanted a piece of the action.

With the Blue Battalion busted up so badly, we were reshuffled into the H, K, and M Forces, named after our commanding officers: Hunter, Kinnison, and McGee. Pfeifer, Preacher and I are split up. But I'm marching with Sam. I'm still not confident anyone knows where we're supposed to go, so I hope they'll figure it out before we march past our next objective.

The return to Naubum was faster than the march into combat—maybe because we knew the territory, or because we'd been seasoned. At night, when we bivouacked, I would throw up my tent and crawl in, just glad to be alive and above ground. I'd wrap my blanket next to me, pretending it was Ruthie that I draped my arm over. When I closed my eyes, I saw the sandy beach we'd escape to the summer before I shipped out.

Lying on our sides facing each other, I slowly dragged my fingertips along Ruthie's silky, supple arm from her wrist up to her elbow, then I'd massage her shoulder. When she let me, I'd fondle her while nuzzling her neck.

"Hey, Mr. Big Stuff, I hate to remind you, but we're in public." Ruthie eventually pulled back and adjusted her swimsuit.

"I can change that," I'd offer with a devious arch of my eyebrows.

"I'm sure you can." This time she teased, suggestively narrowing her eyes and smirking. "Instead, tell me what you'll do when you come back home to me," she had said.

"How explicit do you want me to get?" I'd asked.

"You know what I mean," she chuckled, her laugh warm and husky.

I took her tiny hand in mine and shared the dream I'd never told anyone before.

"I'm going to buy one of those corner grocery stores; freshly painted white with thick wood beams, a flower box out front, and a big picture window to show off the fresh-baked cinnamon rolls. We'll live on the second floor. You can raise the kids while I butcher the meat, stack the vegetables, and stock the ice box. Our customers will be our neighbors, and our neighbors will be our friends."

Her dreamy eyes said yes.

As I laid in my tent on the road to Naubum, the crickets outside buzzed and the moon shone brightly through my parachute roof. I realized it wasn't the manhood Ruthie brought out in me that I missed, but her arms, cradling me close, protecting the boy who wanted to be someone special. I had thought the two of us together would make one whole, she would fill in the parts I could never be. After Maggot Hill, I know that's not the way it works. But I've got a lifetime to create me. And only I can do that. Feeling the heavy weight of exhaustion, I let sleep slip in.

On April 28, 1944, Stilwell flew in to Naubum. We guessed it was to give us another mission, but hoped we'd be sent stateside. All fifteen hundred of us gathered on the air strip, the camouflaging dead shrubs and debris moved aside for our assembly. The Kachin villagers that we had celebrated the monsoon festival with only a month earlier hugged the perimeter. Women stood, holding children on their hips, bangles looped around their wrists, and the men displayed necklaces of ears chopped from dead Japanese soldiers. Darlington, with his arm draped around his wife's shoulder, and Fr. Stuart, surrounded by Kachin scouts, hung back among the villagers.

Old buzz-cut Stilwell smoked his cigarette in his holder, surrounded by a laughing Merrill, Hunter, and Kinnison. He spoke as though through a megaphone. "Gentlemen! Let me explain the third objective of Operation END RUN."

We stood at attention. I examined our ragtag crew with less judgment than I had three months ago.

"The full effects of the monsoon will be upon us in June, and the Japanese expect us to pack up and call it a year since it'll be next to impossible for planes to land in the rain. That's exactly what we want them to think." Stilwell punched the air with a fist. "I'm asking you to go in there one more time and surprise them at Myitkyina. Because if we take Myitkyina, we'll have northern Burma."

Men grumbled under their breath, and I agreed. We were bleeding out of our asses, we had Naga sores from leeches, and everyone had lost at least fifty pounds: we just wanted to go home.

Instead, we're climbing up six thousand feet due east across the Kumon saw-toothed ridges to the principal Japanese air base north of Rangoon, their northernmost railroad junction, and the navigational head of the Irrawaddy River. If that doesn't spell trouble with a capital T, what does? Operation END RUN.

CHAPTER 44

"Fresh Jap tracks." The words get whispered down from man to man. In sequence, we un-sling our rifles and load the chambers, preparing for the unknown. Dusk, with its shadows and rogue shafts of light, settles in. The H Force, along with a platoon of Kachin, have been following a tortuous path at a twenty percent slope for two weeks, and we just crossed a river about three hundred feet below us. Traipsing through mud the consistency of butter, my muscles cramp, and my blood pounds in my face. Jesus, when will my nerves get a break?

"Take five-hundred-yard intervals...and don't talk." We spread out, and instinctively follow the standard operating procedure that has served us so well in the past. The only sound is the soft stomping of the mules.

Ahead, the foliage hangs motionless. Rays of light filter through the jungle's thick canopy to its sparsely vegetated, acrid-smelling floor, blinding us and creating needless sparks of fear.

A band of forest monkeys break the silence with hysterical, unrestrained whoops, shattering our confidence. If there are any Japanese around, they'll have our position pinpointed now. The monkeys' apocalyptic ruckus ends almost as abruptly as it started. As the band leaps from branch to branch, broad, waxy leaves flutter in their wake, letting us know it's their jungle. Johnson hisses, "If I didn't need my ammunition for the Nips, those sons-of-a-bitches would be tonight's dinner for some lucky scavenger." His pants, in the spots on his legs where leeches have attached themselves, are blood-stained and almost the color of his beard. Yet he pushes forward, ignoring everything he can't change.

"We're moving," a voice commands succinctly. Ahead, Nau

raises a single fist, then pumps it up and down, emphasizing "on the double."

In single file, we pass a clearing with a rock pit, the fire recently doused. We march on in silence.

That's when the coward in me sneaks in.

It's not the whizzing of bullets, shredding everything in their path, that terrifies my every step. Or the whine from shelling that decides life or death instantaneously. It's the minute-by- minute, second-by-second hallucinations sketched in detail while I have nothing to tell my mind to shut up. I cringe at each corner, edgy with panic, and convinced a shrieking, obsessed beast will rip out my vitals and gouge my eyes in an ambush before I can finger the trigger. I'm dead from fright before the monster even sees me. All it has to do is smell my fear. The worst part is visualizing those I let down back home when they receive that single telegram.

Terror has a taste. It's brassy and metallic. But we don't all succumb to its bullying; some comfort themselves with the warm glow of a cigarette as darkness closes in, their minds churning for a way out. The image of Ruthie daring me to not quit is what saves me.

"Flank right," Sam says, dropping back to lead us into formation. There's going to be some action. I'm relieved, because reality is so much easier to fight than my imagination.

Ahead, in a clearing about two hundred feet off the path, a shadowy figure builds a fire, controlling the flame so it won't be seen. Men around the fire whisper in their harsh, guttural language.

A single rifle lets loose from the east, triggering others. They're answered by a deadly rip from our machine guns.

Instinctively, I look for a path leading to the opening, but instead crash through the brush next to it and belly crawl. If I see the path, then the enemy will know it's there, too. Bullets fly without prejudice.

Under a volley of machine gun fire, the enemy troops around the campfire pitch forward.

Some roll down a side slope, where they come to a stop and sprawl around tree trunks.

One heavy, clanging Japanese machine gun opens up on us. Shell fragments fly, lopping twigs and leaves off nearby shrubs and spraying dirt in my face.

I press my cheek against my rifle stock and wriggle in for a better angle. A bullet skims off the flesh on my arm, but I ignore it. Aim. Fire.

The Nip gunner topples backwards. "Got ya, you son-of-a-bitch," I yell. "Ollie got hit," we hear from behind. I look in the direction I last saw him. "Oh, God, it hurts. Don't leave me!" he screams, clutching his gut.

I remember Ollie's pleas from the night before: "Sammy, it don't make sense for our platoon to take that path. It's a setup. Listen to me."

Sam snakes over to him.

"You'll make it, Ollie. Calm down, buddy," Sam murmurs, wrapping his arm around Ollie's shoulder and lifting him so he can breathe easier.

"Mama," Ollie screams. "Oh, Mama, help me!" The young boy searches Sam's face for an instant, then his body relaxes.

"I'm so sorry," Sam sighs as he closes the young man's eyes. "You were right last night." Sam sits there, immobilized and cradling Ollie.

Some of the enemy retreats off the side slope beyond the fire pits while our men race towards a path in the opposite direction. Johnson stands and lets loose several rounds of bullets, taking down four in a row. "God, what a pretty sight," he remarks calmly.

Sam surges up. He reaches into his pant leg's side pocket and lobs a grenade into three scrambling Japanese. The ground bursts open, spewing rocks, roots, and bodies. "You asked for it!" Sam wails.

Quiet descends. We wait and watch for movement. After ten minutes, we're given the all clear I force myself off the ground with the help of my rifle. As I check for booby traps, I kick dirt on the enemy's smoldering fire. Men dig shallow graves for the dead and mark them with helmets and dog tags while others scrounge through the Japanese packs. One guy lets a rising sun flag drape open. Another piles up maps and compass-like equipment. I pull out a partially sheathed dagger-like sword from a ripped rucksack, and examine its edge. Sharp, very sharp.

"Move out!" The command reaches those of us still looking for a treasure or a reason to hold back. I tie the sword to my pack then catch up to the others. When we reach the top of Nam Hykit Pass, I see Sam standing alone in the bitter cold, looking into the vast expanse of jungle below a star-filled sky. I join him, unsure of what to say or if I should say anything at all. I'm sure he's thinking about Ollie. .

He jerks his head to let me know he doesn't want company, but says, "After all that, it's a beautiful night."

I shake my head in agreement. "Yeah." Pausing, I remember Father Stuart's plea to take pleasure in nature's beauty in spite of the war before I add, "Seems wrong, doesn't it?"

"All I know is, Uncle Joe's gamble better pay off."

We find the others resting with their packs still on, looking grim and unsure.

"Nau's been bit by a viper," Johnson explains, keeping his officer's level head. "If we don't get the venom out, he'll be dead in six hours."

I finish Johnson's unspoken words in my mind: "We've just been sentenced to purgatory until daylight."

It's pitch black, and we've been following a path only Nau can see. Without discussion, Johnson slashes the boy's Achilles tendon where the fangs penetrated and starts sucking. Nau bites his lower lip. In the valley below, Japanese campfires burn while we wait for Nau to recover—if he recovers. If any of us survive.

While we take turns extracting the venom, I imagine the enemy's fear and loss of confidence when we outsmart them, and it strengthens my determination. We must win, after all we have sacrificed. We must occupy Myitkyina, if that's what it takes to jumpstart the end to this war. Then we can all go home.

CHAPTER 45

It's past 02:00 hours, and an angry rain has been coming down since we stopped.

Johnson, Sam, and myself have been sucking this foul-smelling venom from Nau's stinking foot since midnight. If I don't keel over from hyperventilating between mouthfuls, it'll be from holding my breath to save my nostrils. And I thought Maggot Hill reeked.

Nau's copious sweating has subsided, and his dizzy spells have stopped, but the flesh around the bite still burns hot, and, every now and then, he grimaces from the muscle spasms. Unlike us Yanks, he is calm and stoic in the face of death. We need to save his life so he can help us save ours.

Hunter never gave the order to set up camp, so men are sprawled wherever they can find a spot, wedging themselves and their packs between trees or boulders, or just doubling up on the ground. The men sleep through the rain while Hunter and Osborne consult maps in the event we lose Nau.

The Allies' air reconnaissance charts are black with brown contours. It's like finding a tick on a brown dog—there's no way to know if we're moving from forested hills down to paddies, or from jungle cover to exposed marshes. We can't tell when we'll have cover or when the enemy will have an unobstructed shot at us. On the other hand, the Japanese drawings show forests in green, paddies in yellow, rivers in blue, and roads in red. Hunter and Osborne consult a Japanese map from our last ambush.

I think the Stilwells of the world also look at war as a black and brown board game.

They forget that six-thousand-foot climb up greasy switchbacks, and carrying sixty-five pound rucksacks through rice paddies while you're up to your waist in flood water; that mud is not a walk in the park. Men get sick and tired, and mistakes are made when machine guns are placed in the hands of weary, sleepless soldiers. Stilwell's biggest weakness is this oversight, and his decisions suffer from it. I tell myself that I'm not going to let Myitkyina be the last chapter in my book.

Just before Nau got bit, Hunter broke radio silence and sent a two-word message: "Cafeteria Lunch." Myitkyina is still a two-day march away, so I wonder what the code means.

"Your friend live?" a pallid Nau asks me, now that he's got nothing to do but talk.

I feel a smile push through my exhaustion. "I wondered if you remembered," I answer, thinking of him helping me pull Earl out from under that construction rig.

"How I forget when you shout at boss man Merrill? I think you dead meat," Nau says with a hint of humor. Though his face is thick and pitted from scarring leeches, he looks much younger than I originally thought he was—maybe because I now see the boy behind the disfigured face and body full of tattoos.

"My friend's name is Earl, and yes, thanks to you, we got him to the hospital in time," I say, wondering whether Earl is sleeping right now, or if Colonel Pick has him on graveyard duty.

Nau laughs quietly, "You bring him to Burma surgeon, no?" A sudden spasm wracks his body before he continues. "Burma surgeon teach me special English: fuck, shit, bitch."

"That's our man," I say, remembering a delicate length of ash growing on the tip of a cigarette hanging from Dr. Seagrave's lips just before he entered the operating circle, full of dedication.

With a sagging jaw and heavy eyes, Johnson gently lays Nau's heel on the bloodied rag we've been using as a footrest. "I'm no doctor, but I proclaim you healed. If we suck out any more, I'm afraid we'll inhale your brain."

We help Nau atop Hunter's horse and tie him on since he's so weak. The command to march passes along the living chain. So we don't get lost on the ink-black trail that's really not there, we place sticky mucus threads from phosphorescent glowworms on the rucksacks ahead of us to light the way. Like walking dead, we push onward to a spot where we can stop, rest, and drive again.

Later that day, Osborne shades his face from the noonday sun and demands, "There's to be no gunfire. The Japanese are not to know we're here. If you're spotted, use your knife." The dark circles under his eyes are not just dirt. "The enemy expects us to march into a village with a hail of bullets. But remember: we're not here! Any villager who sees us is to be captured and held until we reach our objective." His toneless order steels us for the marshland and conflict ahead.

Walking next to Nau, who sways from side to side on the horse as it inches down the steep precipice, I study the vast expanse of rice paddies that spread through the valley in front of us. Nau tells me, "I sleep like bird—on wing, ready to fly. Not like red-beard—he like bear in cave, only he roar in sleep." When we had bivouacked for the night, Johnson dropped like a rock and snored the rest of the night. Nau's joking is a good sign. He seems to have beaten the odds; the swelling on his foot is down, and his fever is no higher than anyone else's.

"Yeah, well, I knew you'd be dragging us through the swamps today," Johnson says. "So I guessed there'd be no time for a nap." His skinny, six-foot-four frame deftly leads Nau's horse by the reins.

Sam catches up to us, as excited as a boy released from class for recess. "Are you having fun yet?" he asks, sounding younger than his nineteen years.

Swamp and rice paddies stretch as far as we can see. Smoke rises from villages scattered among the wetlands. A land bridge, above the flood plain, connects them. Streams weave around the villages like fingers. We don't know where the Japanese are, but we know they're down there somewhere.

Surveying the land, Johnson says, "I see which path I'd take. Bet it's the same the Japanese would use. But probably not the one that Nau will have us follow."

"Walk trail of Red-beard and you get caught in game of hide

and seek," Nau says with a sly smile. Gaining strength by the minute, he points to a meandering channel. Lily pads float aimlessly down the center, and rows of rice beds branch out from the edges of the muddy water. "Like snake, stream wiggle. Japanese think white man take shortest path. So he look one way while we slip through other. Sucker play enemy." We're almost level with the marsh, but Nau's still on Hunter's horse and has a better view than us. Pointing to rising smoke in the distance, Nau adds, "Only one village must cross before Myitkyina. Not know if enemy there…yet."

Sam's the first to wade into the channel. Turning back to us, he says, "Guess it's time we sink or swim, boys." Unexpectedly, he sinks about two feet in the soft, mushy bottom and thrashes to regain his balance. Tempers are short, so we don't tease him. He pushes ahead before anyone can say anything.

I grit my teeth and move forward. The murky, tepid water seeps into my boots and up my pant legs. I imagine being barefoot and feel the slimy muck squishing in between my toes. As I portage through the green scum, innocently floating leeches hook onto my clothes. Soon they squirm to my skin, burrow into my flesh, and inject their anticoagulant so my blood leaks freely, like a broken faucet. "Nau, are you sure this is the best way to Myitkyina?" I ask.

"Any other way, you dead," he answers, and his serious expression silences more questions.

To our left, through a blind of bamboo, we hear the gentle prattle of children playing and water spraying. Deeper, agitated, female voices seem to scold the youngsters. I visualize squatting women scrubbing laundry while the children dig in the mud.

Hunter motions with his hand for us all to crouch into the stream. With only our helmeted heads above the water and our rifles held high, we look like a chain of stepping stones. Nau lies flat on the horse, blending into its hide. Thankfully, the Army had the sense to de- vocalize the mules and horses; otherwise, we'd have a braying hissy fit.

There's more giggling and the joyous sound of children screeching in delight. Then, like a bolt, we hear what we all fear.

"Kore wan nan desu ka? Kodomo tachi?" A man's voice asks curtly in Japanese. "Hai," a woman answers hesitantly.

"Nani?" The man insists. "Wakarimasen," the woman pleads. "Nani?" He yells.

"Hottoitekore!" She screams.

Petrified, I hold my breath. A lump grows in my throat.

The man's demands are followed by a burst of wild chatter, like a flock of birds lifting off from a pond. Then we hear bare feet padding on creaking boards, followed by racing boots pounding on the wooden planks.

The soldier in front of me slips and goes under. The splash seems deafening. As he thrusts his head back above the water, he chokes and struggles for air. We stare and pray for silence, thankful that his controlled cough sounds more like a gurgling stream. The Japanese shout and a woman cries. I can hear as many as a dozen of the enemy, so we stay frozen until the noise on shore fades, and they move away from us.

Hunter rolls his arm, motioning us to speed up. Hugging the bamboo thickets, we continue downstream, and don't stop until halfway through the night, outside a village four miles from Myitkyina.

CHAPTER 46

May 15, 1944

I scoop tepid, brown water out of a water buffalo wallow and throw in my instant ground coffee to hide the floating crap. The stream nearby is where everyone pisses, so this is all we've got. Last night we bivouacked in this soggy, miserable excuse for a camp outside the village we're to advance into today, and the mosquitoes ate me alive. "So we're going in today," Doyer says as we walk towards the C.P. He's always the first out of the sack and a reliable source of early information. "Still don't know if the village is occupied by the enemy, but we've got to take a chance that it's not if we're to get to Myitkyina on time."

"Doyer, the guys are dropping like flies from the heat and malaria," I say. "We need a break." The sun has barely crested the horizon, but I already feel like I'm baking in an oven.

"Think positive. Maybe the Japs are nearby, and those buggers like lemon better than vanilla."

Hunter and Osborne eat cold breakfast rations nearby at the C.P., under a rare palm tree.

We're under strict orders to not light fires. Doyer and I stay close enough to listen in on their conversation.

"The last group of Chindits finally made it across the Chindwin River," Hunter says to Osborne as confidentially as possible in this exposed wetland.

"Hasn't it been two months since the first Chindits were dropped behind the lines?

Where's this group been lollygagging?" Osborne asks, then

sighs. "Ah, hell, at least they made it before we start our attack."

Sometimes Stilwell has a point when he says the Limeys are a bunch of wimps. While we're always on the move, they set up base camps with barbwire fences and liquor drops that would put W.C. Fields to shame.

"Well, the Brits will have a hell of a time getting air drops in their new position with all the Japanese anti-aircraft guns," Hunter answers. "They walked right into the center of the enemy front."

I mentally cross myself. The only thing I can depend on is things going wrong, and that we won't have enough food, equipment, or men.

"All I ask is that the Chindits block the roads from the south so no Nip reinforcements can slip in," Osborne says. He looks up when thick drops of rain start to fall. "Keee-rist. Give me a break."

Hunter packs his coffee cup and finishes stuffing his sack while Osborne throws his on his back. "Pass the command, no talking. We're moving in on the village," Hunter orders. "Last stop of Operation END RUN."

I sling my pack over the bleeding sores on my shoulders that callus and break open again. But it's my stomach, boiling with acid, and my bowels, ready to run, that make me lightheaded. Putting one foot in front of the next, I move forward with a sick feeling about Operation END RUN. We're to capture the Myitkyina airfield when we've only got the Kachin V Force and our H, K, and M forces. If the Chindits aren't ready and the Chinese X & Y Forces hold back when we attack, this is going to be the suicide mission we thought it would be.

The drizzle builds to monsoon strength, and rain drips from my helmet, distorting my view. I'm boiling in my own sweat with this suffocating heat. I keep my rifle at the ready.

In the village, stilted huts almost create a vision of tranquility, except the thatch on the roofs has worn through, and useless bamboo siding flaps with the downpour. Other than the livestock under the huts, the town appears abandoned. Through the blur of the rain, the primitive shelters, naturally decorated with flowered climbing vines, seem inviting and not at all like a Japanese trap.

Whenever we move in for an assault, I ask myself, will I make it through this one? Will I be injured? Or go crazy? Then the worst thing possible happens, I think of Ruthie and my family.

"Your mom's not going to think any girl's good enough for her son." Ruthie said; stiffening as I led her into the dining room decked out with ma's finest china for my last supper before I shipped out.

"Harry, is that you, my boy?" Ma called from the kitchen, her Irish brogue always the strongest when she's at home. I can still smell her roast and those browned, melt-in-your-mouth potatoes.

"Yeah, Ma. And Ruthie's here with me." I called back to Ma before pulling Ruthie close. "I'm in love with you. It doesn't matter what Ma thinks."

"Oh, yes it does." Ruthie's eyes twinkled, but she wasn't laughing.

"Move in," Osborne commands. I focus on the snot-slick mud below. Around me, the whole battalion advances in a crouch from one bamboo thicket to the next. We press forward until we're about to charge into the village, then Osborne holds up a hand to halt us and waves Sam forward.

Sam, always the one volunteering his intelligence and reconnaissance squad, pushes ahead to check out the village before we attack. His men don't like his recklessness, and I think of Ollie.

We're to hold back until we get a signal from Sam's I&R team. Trusting someone else with the unknown is hard for me, so my mind wanders.

"Harry, I won't be having you talk nonsense to this girl. Pass the potatoes, please. With you going away and all, you'll be getting her all doe-eyed with promises you can't keep and leaving her with a cuddly little bundle you won't be finding out about 'til you're back." Ma poured the gravy over her meat, then took a huge bite. Red with angry embarrassment, Ruthie's hand shook as she sipped from the delicate china.

"Truth be known, you're the best thing that's happened to this boy," Ma said to Ruthie. "So, if you know what I mean, keep it that way." Ma gulped down coffee hot enough to boil tar off a roof, then said, "And he's the best mistake the Lord gave me." That's the closest Ma ever came to saying she loved me.

Chickens squawk in the village. A wailing child is abruptly silenced. I close my eyes for a second to catch the sound of the first inevitable bullet through the driving rain. Instead, I hear the thump, thump, thump of running feet. In response, the clicking of rifle locks echo down the column.

"It's Sam," someone warns, only seconds before Sam turns the corner. He grasps a grenade in his hand, but the pin has not been pulled. We hold our fire.

"A Nip platoon's moving out on the other end of town." Breathless, Sam gulps for air. "I don't think they saw us."

"What about the natives?" Hunter has moved up from the rear. "Did any get away?"

"Negative," Sam answers, still huffing. "I stationed men to guard all the trails." "And what about the streams? Isn't that how we got in?"

Osborne interrupts. "Lets move in and round up the villagers."

"Affirmative. On the double," Hunter commands. The entire H Force infiltrates the village. Sam was right—there are no Japanese.

Within thirty minutes, every villager has been interrogated by Nau, with his string of chopped ears hanging from his belt for all to see. The natives seem like a docile, friendly group, but we can never be sure.

At 14:00 hours, Hunter sends another radio message: "STRAWBERRY SUNDAE." Within twenty-four hours H.Q.'s to start preparing five days worth of food and weapons to be dropped at our objective, Myitkyina. Until then, we've bought food from the locals and butchered the calves and chickens. It's been days since I've eaten real food, and my belly growls.

We sit near the C.P. gorging ourselves until we ache. It's been another day of roller coaster nerves. No one wanted to fight, but waiting for the possibility was excruciating. As evening falls, I wait with Doyer while the others get final orders from Hunter.

"Roy, just after dusk, I want you to slip into Myitkyina and tap their lines," Hunter says. "See if they've got anything on us and whether they're planning any attacks in the next twenty- four hours." Then he looks at Osborne and Nau.

The swelling is down, and his fever is gone, but Nau's still weak. "Like ghosts in tree, I take my men see where Japs sleep, how many, and what guns," he says. I know Hunter wants to say no, but he doesn't. He's not in some safe office; he's in the trenches with his men when they charge and when they die. I wouldn't want Hunter's job.

"Good man," Hunter answers, and has the courage to look Nau in the eye. "Osborne, your men are to swing southwest and take the ferry. If the Chindits have wiped out the road and rail, we only need to worry about the Irrawaddy River. That leaves the air strip." He turns to Sam and Johnson for the last assignments.

"My men are ready," Sam says before Hunter has a chance to explain the mission. "If anyone can do it, we can." Sam looks like an eager puppy, but I know his men are going to rebel. They're sick of being the first for everything; first in means first to die.

Hunter looks to Johnson and says, "Then I want you to guard the villagers. We wouldn't want anyone to RSVP to the Nips."

Johnson, looking like a vicious Viking with his grungy, red beard, nods to accept the mission.

Before anyone can leave, Hunter adds, "I've called off the strike team so there'll be no planes strafing the runway. The Japs'll probably be hiding out in the forest until they think it's safe to return. Sam, your men are to walk the airstrip without you. You're to stay in camp.

That's an order. I can't have you fainting while on I&R. You've lost so much blood today from that damn dysentery, I don't know how you're standing. Now, I want everyone in place at 01:00 hours."

Sam's left speechless, and the two colonels walk away without a word. Now all Sam has to do is tell his men they're left to do his dirty work without him. Doyer and I watch the nineteen-year-old limp towards his men, puffing up his chest in a bravado I'm sure he doesn't feel.

"Who's fool enough to voluntarily put his neck in a noose?" Doyer asks, rubbing his chin as his eyes follow Sam.

"Clean your gun." I say. "Sam's boys are going to need help."

CHAPTER 47

May 16, 1944

It's 02:00 hours. Six of us crawl on our bellies to the edge of the unlit runway with our knives. It's bad enough walking through the jungle in the night, knowing some of the most deadly insects and reptiles in the world are underfoot. But as I elbow my way forward, barely an inch separating me from the ground, each leaf that's thrown up in my face becomes a striking cobra.

"Harry, grab your night vision goggles and tell me what you see," the sergeant in charge orders.

I reach in my pack and drag out the binocs. The gilded Buddha entangled in the straps falls in front of me. I pick it up, hold it between my thumb and forefinger, and rub it. "I'm holding on to you, buddy. You're my lucky fortune." Using high magnification, I scan the field.

"It doesn't make sense, Sarge," I whisper. "There's not a thing out there—no planes, no gunners, none of the enemy. Are you sure we're at the right place?"

The sergeant slithers over to me and hisses, "Hell, give those to me." He traces the length of the field with the binoculars, pausing every now and then, before he continues. "I'll be damned. They're probably asleep at the wheel in those huts."

He points towards a dark outline on the eastern end of the field. "Harry, I want you and Doyer to flush out the surrounding jungle. We'll check the buildings." Slinking away into the shadows on the north side of the strip, the sergeant and three others fade out of sight.

I doubt we'll find any enemy in the woods this time of night. They hide in the forest during the day to avoid attacks from our fly guys, but our boys usually don't fly at night.

Doyer rubs his chin, then says, "I think we just got assigned to rear echelon duty. So much for taking control of the area. Let's knock this out."

Hunching over, we take a few steps, then stop to listen. The night sounds of scampering rodents turn into muffled squeals as predators make their kill. Flying foxes swoop in and around roped vines in search of insects. We give grunting wild boars a wide berth. I yawn. Boredom is a terrible, attention-grabbing thief.

"What did you think of me the first night we met?" I asked Ruthie, one arm wrapped around her shoulders as we swayed in the wood swing on her front porch. I pushed her thick, black hair away from her eyes.

She considered my question for a moment, then said, "I thought you were a handsome jerk and the best dancer on the floor."

It wasn't what I expected to hear, so I laughed, a little hurt and a lot surprised. "And now?" I asked.

Without a moment's hesitation, she answered, "I think you're a handsome jerk, and I'm in love with you."

My body relaxes at the memory of those words. I push my hands deep in my pockets and let my pack sway on my back. Ahead, Doyer pushes a branch aside, and ducks under it. He scares up a small deer that freezes in place for a split second before leaping deeper into the brush. Jittery from the doe, my nerves start to cook. I wonder why we don't hear even a single Japanese patrolling the perimeter. I stop to pee, first kicking at the twigs on the ground. Got to be sure I'm not walking into a snake's nest.

By the time I move again, Doyer's out of sight, so I stop and listen to get a reading on his location. Overhead, the soft flutter of leaves fills the air. I expect to hear the deafening, inhuman monkey cries accompany the falling twigs, but I don't. I also gradually realize the scurrying sounds of night critters are missing. Just then, about a hundred feet ahead, a large mass drops from the trees, followed by a thud. Not sure what just happened, I keep still. The sound of wrestling and a stifled gag that follows leads me to Doyer, in trouble.

Something grabs my ankles, and I fall face-first into a web of spiders and tangle of branches. Millions of tiny legs race all over my body as I frantically lash out. The more I try to break free from the clutching vine, the deeper I sink into its thorns. Ripping through with blind strength, I finally crack its hold.

In the dark, a garbled "Kochira" is smothered as the two bodies grunt and thrash in the mud. I see an arm break free, knife in hand. It's only then that I remember I have no gun, and my knife is still in my pack.

Reaching behind as I hurry forward, I grab the Japanese dagger tied to my pack, and rip it free, ready to help Doyer and hammer the Nip bloody. But I can't tell who's who in the tangle until I fall on top of them and see Doyer's bald head on the bottom.

I raise my fist and smash the soldier under me again and again, striking with all my racing energy. Blood squirts from where the Japanese knife gouges the body beneath me. Frenzied, I stab and stab and stab until, exhausted, I slump over the limp body.

Shaken, but not injured, Doyer turns over the lifeless form. I stare at the dead man, face frozen in a permanent, silent cry. I have killed before, but with a gun. I stroke the dagger's curved hilt.

"My mind went crazy," is all I can say, while thinking how easy it was to slip into that other world.

"We better go," Doyer answers, regaining his nerve. "There are probably more on patrol."

We hide the body, but I know the face will never leave my mind. Continuing our loop, we zig-zag from tree to tree, trying to become invisible. Near the shacks, we hear whispering voices out on the tarmac. It's the sergeant and other Marauders.

"The huts are swarming with Nips," the sarge says as we approach him. "But they're not expecting us—too busy with a couple of geishas, if you know what I mean." I hear the raw smile in his voice as he baits us. "I always wondered whether they painted their whole body white."

"We don't need to know," Doyer says. "Glad you were there to enjoy it."

Like schoolboys, the others snicker under their breath. Meanwhile, I whistle softly, not daring to shout. "If you want to meet those young ladies tomorrow, let's get some azimuth bearings on this anti-aircraft equipment. When we attack tomorrow, we'll want our flyboys to help us out." We survey in coordinates for our fighter pilots, then return to camp just before dawn.

May 17, 1944

The morning sky is clear of rain and planes. We move in at 08:00 and by 10:00 we're on the airfield. Something seems to be missing: it's the enemy. At 10:30 hours Hunter announces over the radio, "IN THE RING." Then he crosses his arms over his chest and makes a three- hundred-sixty-degree observation of the Myitkyina air field.

"Roger," the radio replies. Then there's static. "Take your positions," Hunter orders.

The black tarmac is deserted of enemy forces. Marauders hug the perimeter, dashing from hut to hut, turning over crates, slicing open cargo boxes filled with Japanese supplies, and taking position behind fifty-five-gallon oil tanks. All day, the surrounding forest crawls with the 53-07th, as if we're hunting dogs sniffing out our prey. By 15:30, we've captured the Myitkyina airfield. Men are happy, but hesitant. It didn't feel like a fight, but the beginning of a setup, with Japanese snipers taking pot shots at us until nightfall.

Hunter radios H.Q. "MERCHANT OF VENICE" from the same huts where the geishas had diverted the Japanese interest only the night before. "They'll be sending us food, water, medicine, and ammo shortly," he tells us, but there's no relief evident in his face. "Harry, get some cover and prepare the site for those supplies."

On the open runway, flickering stars fill the vast sky like stepping stones to another world.

Is the clear, cloudless night a good sign? Pushing the dead soldier from last night deep into the recesses of my mind, I hurry to relay a radio message to Colonel Hunter. He stands alone on the tarmac, arms folded across his chest.

Around the bend of the Irrawaddy River, in the center of town and near the rail yard, the sounds of gunfire reverberate. One, two, three oil tanks explode. Flames soar skyward, a spectrum of yellow and orange fanning out from its shocking blue center. Near the oil explosion, an ammo stockpile erupts. The scorching fire swells further into the black sky, billowing smoke and soot.

"Sir," I say, watching the wavering blaze dance in the distance. "We just received word that the Chinese X Force is dug in outside the railway station. Looks like they've announced their arrival."

"Yes. Thanks, Harry." Hunter's eyes are riveted on the inferno, but his mind seems elsewhere. "You weren't supposed to go on last night's reconnaissance mission." I'm too exhausted to feel fear or disappointment. "Good job at getting the coordinates on the anti-aircraft guns. We need men who can take control and make decisions."

I heard those exact words two years ago, and my breath catches in my throat as I think about those days. From behind us, another explosion rings in the distance. We turn our gaze from the oil bonfire at the rail yard to the bridge target in the west.

"Most of those Kachin never saw a train or dynamite before the war," Hunter muses. "Now, we've got the enemy almost completely surrounded." He shakes his head, reflective rather than triumphant. "Is Operation END RUN really over? Or is this just the end of the first inning? " He has stripped down to a pair of baggy, pocketed fatigue trousers, and the sinews of his arms and trunk are unnaturally prominent. As though I'm not there, the Colonel asks himself, "Is this it, after four months of hell?"

"Not a single Marauder was killed at the airfield," I say. "This was too easy."

CHAPTER 48

Like Hunter predicted, everything went crazy after "MERCHANT OF VENICE." Two days after we took the airport, the loud hum of plane's engines approaches. I yell,

"Someone radio that pilot to tell him we've got snipers down here still taking pot shots and to stop farting around and land." Finally, a day late, the supplies arrived in Myitkyina.

The Dakota glides down the runway. The roaring motors and spinning blades eventually stop. Then it just sits on the tarmac. "We'd like a little help here," the pilot demands over the radio in a huff. "I got Stilwell and his gang needing some stairs. It's been a rocky ride."

I grab a wood crate and drop it at the rear door. "I suppose he'll want me to wipe his ass when he gets out, too," I mutter, then step up on the crate and pull the door off. Was I right!

"Soldier, what the hell took you so long?" Stilwell barks at me before turning on the charm and announcing, "Welcome to Myitkyina airfield, ladies and gentlemen."

I peer inside the plane, wondering who he's talking to. Instead of food and ammo, a dozen newspaper correspondents with fancy photography equipment all scramble to be the first out the door.

"Take it easy," Stilwell chuckles. "Nobody can send anything out 'til you get back to Ledo tonight."

One by one, they push out the door, handing me what they can't carry until I look like a coat rack. "I promised my son a Japanese flag as a souvenir," says a stylish man with a smart blue suit and flyaway blonde hair. "Do you know where I should go to find one? I don't want it too big." If he could see my rolling eyes, he'd know where I'd tell him to go.

I totter towards the huts and drop their load at the entrance. "Hey, take it easy, soldier," Stilwell growls at me as I enter the shack. "Go round up some grub and refreshments for our guests. By the way, why isn't Hunter here?"

"I'll tell the Colonel you've arrived," I answer. "And rats are the only food we've been able to dig up since we secured the site." I want to add that this was supposed to be a supply plane. So why should Hunter be here?

"Who cares what it looks like? Dress it up and make sure the drinks are a little exotic, if you know what I mean." He claps me on the back. Before I get out the door, he shouts, "And round up Merrill, Kinnison, Liu, and Sun for the press conference."

Gunshots ring out on the runway. Snapping bulbs into their cameras, the correspondents trip over each other: pushing to rush out of the hut.

I grab a Tommy sitting by the door. "Get the fuck out of my way," I scream. The reporters make a narrow path by the door, looking surprised at my rude behavior.

Lying on the tarmac, a soldier clutches his leg. "I'm fine," he shouts, then points. "Over there."

Seeing the reflection of the sun off metal, I spray bullets from the Tommy and take down the enemy in a tree on the edge of the jungle not fifty feet away. With the gun, I scan the perimeter of the runway around the hut, searching for the enemy. The flash from what feels like a million clicking shutters blinds me. Hell, I hope there was only one sniper out there; otherwise, they'll get great photos of my gushing blood.

"OK, all's clear," I yell, and sprint down the runway to the far end, where we've set up a temporary evacuation hospital. Along the perimeter and deep within the jungle, gunfire bounces back and forth like a deadly badminton game. A second cargo plane lands, and a third circles in the air.

"Winnie, you gotta help me out." I barge in while Doc prepares for surgery.

He pulls out his forceps, wipes them on the seat of his GI

shorts—the only thing he's wearing—and blows on them. "Must have abs'lute sterility for this operation." Then he uses the forceps to yank out a tick embedded in a less-than-comfortable spot on the soldier's reproductive anatomy. The soldier shrieks.

"I need alcohol!" I say, knowing Winnie has provided his patients some form of liquid support in the past when the end seemed inevitable.

"I hate to rush you, but we need this bed," Doc says as he helps the GI off the cot. "Harry, isn't it a little early for cocktails?" He approaches the GI on the next bed, who requires an amputation without morphine or anesthetic. "Sometimes I have to remind myself this isn't the American Civil War." This time, he takes his job seriously and starts the scrub down, then stops mid-motion. "Aren't you the supply guy?" he asks me.

"Stilwell arrived with guests who need entertaining instead of supplies," I say, throwing my hands in the air.

Hands dripping wet, he reaches into his medical box and hands me a gallon of antiseptic. "They distilled this so much, it'll burn your lips. I hear it tastes best with coconut milk and a twist of a juniper berry, which we don't have, so try bamboo."

By the time I return, Hunter's storming into the journalist-filled hut. Without any niceties, he charges up to Stilwell. "Where are my supplies?" he asks. "I got men out there fighting with one bullet left in their chamber and others dropping, unconscious, from exhaustion and starvation."

I lay out strips of rat meat before I start my bartender duties. A female journalist, munching on a sliver of meat, corners me while I chop the caps off the coconuts with a machete. She asks in a low, conspiratorial voice, "I hear soldiers use parachutes from the food drops to sleep in. Where can I find one?" A soldier or parachute? I think, but choose to let the noise crowd out her request.

"Why so much doom and gloom?" Stilwell sounds cheerful and ignores Hunter's question by offering him a cigarette. "Hell, we can tell the Limeys to stick it up their asses now. And they thought we couldn't take Myitkyina. Ha! Did you hear about SEAC's thirty-seven- page report, *How to take Myitkyina*? The art of war is killing me." A photographer positions his camera for a close-up of the General, who takes the attention in stride. "You had me sweating it out yesterday. Four hundred Japs against twenty thousand GI's! It would've been embarrassing if you hadn't put on a good show."

Nose-to-nose with Stilwell, Hunter shouts, "Four hundred Nips? Try four thousand, if we don't get that gap on the east side of Myitkyina closed. And our two thousand extremely sick GIs are quickly dropping down to two hundred since someone thought it prudent to replace our medical supplies with those bozos." He gestures towards the oblivious press.

Stilwell backs up to the refreshment table for a glass of composure. "Four hundred, four thousand, it's only decimal dust," he grunts, and takes a swig of the sanitized coconut delight. "Besides, you've got two battalions from the Chinese X Force to back you up."

I feel Hunter's exasperation as he clenches his fists. "Back us up? Right! After they set their compasses wrong, they opened fire on their own men. They backed up so far, they ran away."

"I heard they took a good shellacking," Stilwell hoots. Seeing the hovering press, he wraps an arm around Hunter and puts on his camera best. "These guys are so calm and brave, they ooze it."

While I lay out the hors d'oeuvres, which I hate to touch, and the thousand-proof aperitifs, I recall that the General had implied Mountbatten was a media whore. Now isn't that the pot calling the kettle black?

A little glassy-eyed and with goofy grins, the press wait, pen to paper, for Stilwell and Hunter to duke it out. All the guys are in civilian clothes with sports jackets, even in this stifling humidity, and if they're not chewing down on a cigar, then they have a cigarette hanging from their lips. We're packed tight in the tiny hut, so the rank smell of sweat and smoke is almost debilitating.

Kinnison arrives and tries to push through to Stilwell, but he's barred by the swarm of journalists. His K Force has been holed up at Charpate, a northern crossroad branching to the west and east. The settlement is nothing more than a slightly elevated rice paddy. "Sir," he calls out in a failing voice, trying to catch Stilwell's attention. He loses his balance and grabs on to the door.

My attention is drawn to a female journalist, her red lipstick and thick pancake makeup melting with the humidity. She suggestively licks her lips and shimmies up to a photographer half her age. Nauseated, I turn and notice Kinnison has made it to Stilwell's side. He's shivering through his sweat. Something is wrong.

I hear him report to Stilwell breathlessly. "Sir, we're holding the enemy back from the north at Charpate, and we've blocked the rail line leading out of town."

The same rail line with the bridge we already blew up the other night? I think to myself sarcastically. Then I remember that Pfeifer and Preacher are under Kinnison's command. I'm worried.

"Are you ready to kick their asses out of the Myitkyina rail station? Then Burma?" Stilwell asks so everyone can hear.

"Yes Sir. Can do!" Kinnison answers; collapsing against a chair rather than faint on the floor.

Hunter interrupts, spittle flying as he towers over the spineless Kinnison. "Is that the new strategy? Starve our boys? Hold their water and medicine in a dog bowl until they sit, roll-over, and pulverize the enemy, completely delirious?

"Gentlemen, gentleman," Stilwell cuts in with a stiff, conciliatory tone, and then glares at Hunter. "Don't be a spoilsport. Ledo hasn't forgotten your supplies." The General finally notices Kinnison, leaning against a wall for support, his face blanched and drained of emotion. "I can't have you dying on me, Kinnison. Get something to eat."

Out on the airstrip, a fifty-caliber battery, barely big enough to shoot down the Wright brothers' glider, is being hauled out onto the runway. "You think those toy trucks and that miniature anti-aircraft gun they're unloading are going to do us any good?" Hunter asks, hands on hips, and scowling.

A complaint rises up from the press as the leaders from the Chinese X Force, Liu and Sun, push the inebriated reporters aside.

Stilwell's attention is diverted to the newcomers. The hut shrinks even more as the crowd swells. I'm convinced I hear nails popping and expect to see boards fall off, leaving nothing but the shack's skeleton

"My men take Myitkyina railroad station," Sun boasts, pointing an emphatic finger at his chest.

Not to be outdone, Liu steps in front of Sun and brags, "Your men pick flowers. *My* soldiers kill enemy."

Sun's eyebrows rise in surprise before he says to Liu, "Enemy? My men kill one hundred enemy and three hundred your men." Proud of his conquest, Sun adds. "So I kill one hundred more than you."

Liu will not allow Sun to better him. He squares off his shoulders, and adds, "I kill three hundred total: but two hundred Japs. I kill most enemy."

"Boys, boys." Stilwell steps in and separates the two, putting an arm around each. "There was some confused fighting out there," he tells the correspondents. "But we've got it squared away now." He steers the two Chinese officers away from the writers and past the snacks and refreshment table, then, in barely a whisper, says, "I don't have time to chew you out right now. This is your lucky day." The General all but shoves them out the door. The Chinese fiasco is beyond belief. If the White Battalion killed three hundred of the Orange Battalion and the Orange wiped out two hundred of the White, we wouldn't be bragging.

It's only after the Chinese are expelled from the room that I notice Merrill has joined the crowd. He staggers towards Stilwell in something that resembles a two-step. The frisky female journalist sidles up and all but dances with him. Always a gentleman, the pipe-smoking officer politely answers her questions while clutching his arm. I doubt she is doing more than scribbling gibberish on her paper since she never takes her eyes off him. Merrill looks real bad. Why did he fly out with his heart problem?

Once he escapes the journalist, Merrill all but falls into Stilwell, looking like he's about to upchuck his lunch. "Joe, I've got some bad news," he says quietly. "Masters retreated from BLACKPOOL."

"That yellowbelly," Stilwell spouts before Merrill can finish.

"Dodging his duty again." The General shakes his head. "Shameful performance by the Brits. How will we block the Japs from the south now?"

Merrill leans against the edge of the food table. "Joe, you gotta listen to me," he pleads. "Masters' men were forced into a suicide position. They had to withdraw, or all of them would have been killed." Merrill pauses, and I feel a bomb about to drop. "Nineteen of his men were shot by their medical orderlies before they left. They were too sick to haul out and were beyond recovery. I wanted you to know before rumors started spreading."

Stilwell starts coughing uncontrollably, having just taken a long inhale from his cigarette. He grabs the already-unstable Merrill and glances around to see who is within hearing distance. Deciding it's only me and the two of them, Stilwell berates Merrill in a gruff whisper. "You dumb cluck. You don't spill the beans with intelligence like that in front of the press. I know you've been a little sick lately, but get a hold of yourself; you're slipping on the job." He lets loose with a bogus laugh—end of conversation.

Stilwell says no more, but does seem to chew over the news. I try to believe that he'd make a different decision than Masters and would find a way to get his men out. Pulled out of his reverie, the General clears his throat to make an announcement to the press, who have taken photos of everything from the geisha's cast-aside clothing to the spread of food and drinks.

"Let us show you around this place." Stilwell rounds the table and grabs my elbow. "This Lieutenant will be your tour guide." I groan, but obediently follow the command.

"Over here," I order the reporters and point to the side of the hut. "Line up like you did in kindergarten. We're going down to the evacuation hospital at the end of the airstrip. Remember, there are snipers out there, so don't clump up. Leave a ten foot space ahead of you." They do the exact opposite and glob together, making themselves easy targets for any gunman.

What a bunch of fucking idiots. Maybe I should just treat them like dogs. I start walking. "The tarmac is chopped liver from our bombs," I say, in case someone is listening. "Those Dakotas will land wherever they can. They're military transport planes: they can't brake on a dime, and they're not going to stop for you. So stay in line with me." The wind builds up into gusts as a gentle patter of rain slaps against the fan leaf palms edging the strip.

A lone photographer runs out on the runway to get a shot of a plane nosing in for a touchdown. His jacket flaps open and hat flies away as a blast of air from whirling blades blows towards him.

"Make it chopped liver and imbecile meat," I yell, secretly hoping that the photographer makes an example of himself.

A scouting Jap Zero slips in, the rising red sun emblazoned on its skin. Intent on getting a photo of the landing Dakota, the photographer doesn't see the enemy aircraft approach. He tap dances as it spits gunfire down the airstrip. Chunks of metal spray from our fighter planes on the ground. Some reporters run towards the jungle, and others let loose with their bulb-flashing cameras. Some stay in place and crouch on the open tarmac. The Zero tips its wing at the new anti-aircraft and waves goodbye without a scratch.

Within minutes, the Zero disappears behind the clouds. "That anti-aircraft gun they just unloaded is worthless from the first time you use it. What a piece of crap," I say. Pilots scramble out from hiding to assess the damage on their planes.

The bamboozled correspondents remain rooted in place, stunned or stupid. I scan the airfield. As I call, "All clear," I see that, instead of weapons, construction equipment: dozers, rollers, and dump trucks, are rolling out from a grounded Dakota. Incredulous, I ask, "Does anyone in Ledo know what they're doing? First Stilwell, then toy guns, now..." I trail off and do a double take Smiling largely and whistling like he's out for a Sunday stroll is a large Negro soldier, his biceps just about splitting his uniform sleeves. The mechanics around him reassemble a newly arrived bulldozer with a bulletproof blade.

The Negro halts mid-step as our eyes connect. "Harry? Harry, my man, is that really you?" he shouts. Without waiting for an answer, he half runs, half hobbles over to me.

I reach to shake hands, but Earl grabs me in a bear hug instead. "Gee whiz, I thought you was out fighting with Merrill's boys. Instead, lookee what we have here! A boy scout with all his little cubs." He snickers, then raises a questioning eyebrow, daring me to give an explanation.

"First Stilwell and his merry band of reporters this morning, and now you, Earl. What's going on? I thought this was a warzone, not a circus." It's great to see Earl, but I'd rather they be unloading ammunition and food.

"Are you calling me some clown?" Earl asks, only partially joking. "We knew you'd be needing us to fix up this here runway and bring you all those supplies you been crying about.

Why, we brought the whole gang, except Charming Charles— says they don't need no more radio operators out here. He's pleased as punch." Motors roar from another plane circling overhead. Earl glances over at his rig, where mechanics wipe their hands on their pants. The truck's motor growls into action with the turning of its ignition. "Looks like those grease monkeys done their work. Now, tell me where I can fill up this here rig with gasoline."

I cover my face with my hands. Do I cry? Do I laugh? What does Earl not understand about the word warzone? And where in the hell is Stilwell's merry band of tourists? I'll be dead if Stilwell finds them without their chaperone. Exasperated once again, my hands drop to my sides. In front of me is a crew-cut, red-head, his face smudged with grease and wearing an idiot grin.

"Surprise!" he says, landing a soft punch to my gut before wriggling his eyebrows in that Groucho Marx way that bugs the hell out of me. "Hey, you're getting a little skinny these days, Harry." He plugs his nose and adds, "P.U. You guys need a little soap?"

I return his greeting with a gentle left hook to the head. "Bernie, let me tell you before you ask, there are no Quonset huts for a shop. Look around—this is what you get." It's surreal.

Bernie can't answer, because the correspondents surround us. Their coconut delight seems to be wearing off. "Hey, you said you were going to show us the evacuation hospital. We don't have all day."

At the far end of the airstrip, a camp of parachute tents billows in the wind. The green, blue, and white give a festive appearance. What a sick joke the sight plays on me. Litters, cots, and blankets on the ground are packed with wounded men. A stream of profanity drowns out the moaning and screaming patients. Ah, I say to myself, that's a familiar voice; he must've arrived this morning.

"Just because this is a fuckin' shithole doesn't mean they need to treat us like crap." Seagrave's boisterous objection sets the reporters in jolly spirits. They think he's joking – he's not.

A flurry of Burmese nurses hustle about in their longyi. Finally, I catch a glimpse of the Burmese surgeon. He tosses a blood-crusted forceps in the air, followed by a rusted clamp. "Is this a hospital or a morgue? I don't expect sterile, but would like to see some exposed metal on the instruments." Seagrave doesn't see the swarm of reporters until he's poised with a jungle- clean scalpel, ready to cut. He gives us a dirty glare, then shouts, "Maran Lu, get these morons out of here." He turns back to begin the operation and adds, "This is one of those days I wish I was dead."

Maran Lu has always been a no-nonsense kind of girl, but now she's a true veteran of evacuation hospital nursing. As she stretches a parachute from one bamboo post to the next, covering the operating theatre, she scolds, "You no see blood before. I give you scalpel. Slice vein here…you get lots of blood. Shoo. Shoo." She waves the meek reporters away like they're mangy dogs, her long braid flapping down her back. They scatter like rats about to be caught, and then she notices me.

"Harry, I surprise at you. Know Daddy not like people gawk when he busy. He say too many bad words. Then they frown. Not like Daddy." It is so good to hear her sassy voice. Her tone softens when she asks, "You see my Earl?"

"*Your* Earl?" I ask, shock evident in my voice. Seeing her hurt face, I know I've overreacted. "Must be more to those choir practices than I thought." She blushes, but before she can chew me out, I hear a weak call from the horde of litters.

"Harry. Is that Harry Flynn making all that noise?"

I search the sea of weary, nameless soldiers for an outstretched arm or something that would lead me to the voice, but there's nothing. Forcing myself to do what I've dreaded since I joined the service, I look into the faces of each injured man. These are the boys of the 53-07 battalion, Merrill's Marauders, Galahad—and many are my friends. They don't look back; they think they're the lucky ones, soon to be going home.

Finally, the lantern-jawed, boyish good looks of Lieutenant Sam Wilson stand out from the others. I weave over to him. "So how's the Confederate historian holding up?" I ask, seeing the answer in his blood-soaked clothes. This boy, who selected his I&R platoon from men who held the world in contempt and thought life and death meant nothing, is showing a change of heart in his eyes.

"You must not have heard about our last patrol on the Irrawaddy," he says, as he looks down and shakes his head, his southern accent soft and unsure.

I wait for him to continue. "We were starving. So were the villagers. But they gave us some rice. My stomach had shrunk so much, I couldn't even eat a full cup. Later on, I found they gave us all they had. Then, when we were leaving, a formation of our fighter pilots roared in and strafed the hell out of them." The vacant look of a blocked memory fills Sam's face. "We went back after our guys cut out. One of the villagers grabbed me by the arm and led me to his dugout. There, sobbing and wailing, was a young woman clutching a toddler. The man lifted the girl from her mother, his hands reddened with blood that still flowed from the shot through the girl's back."

Sam looks up, his eyes red and swollen. "I did something I've never done before." It's as though he's giving me his last confession. "I crumbled in a heap and wept." He struggled with a couple of deep breaths. "Lord, I've taken it as far as I can."

I feel someone behind me. It's Doc Winnie. His eyes are not twinkling. "Sammy boy, you've got a simple case of typhus and malaria, and all the blood you've decorated your cot with is from amoebic dysentery. Time to go home."

Sam nods, knowing his tour of duty is up. Still, he's not ready to say goodbye to the Marauders and asks, "Harry, how's Pfeifer doing?"

"He's here?" I ask, the surprise in my voice revealing a sudden fear twisting my stomach. "That way," Sammy answers, jerking his head to point me to the far end of cots. "Thanks, buddy." I lay a hand on Sam's shoulder. "You gave it more than your all."

As I'm leaving, the soldier in the litter next to Sam asks, "Sammy, can I have your Tommy?"

I zigzag in the direction of Pfeifer's cot, thinking that's the nicest thing anyone could have said to Sam. He was so proud of his gun.

I pass by a soldier, his hand constantly wiping his shiny, domed head. I don't recognize him. Then, his goading voice asks, "Too good for old friends?" I twist to find Pfeifer.

"Did you go on some kind of a diet?" I tease as I crouch next to him. "You're skinnier than any skeleton I've ever seen." I want the joking to help him, but realize it's more for me.

Rather than answer, he gazes straight ahead and doesn't look at me. His eyes are unblinking, unwilling to miss anything, yet seeming to see nothing. "Why are you in the hospital?" I ask, expecting the usual, typhus, malaria, dysentery or wound.

"Not sure," he answers absentmindedly while stroking his bald skull.

I have no idea what to say if he doesn't know why he's in the hospital. He's not the kind of guy to fake it so he can go AWOL. Then I notice he's vigorously fingering something tiny in his other hand. He finally glances at me, follows the direction of my eyes, and gives me a familiar, snide Pfeifer smile. "You got your Buddha, Harry. I got my bullet."

I carefully open his hand. There, lying in his palm, is a single, 45 mm bullet—not gold, not shiny, but deadly. Without saying a word, my eyes ask him to explain more.

Pfeifer starts to tremble, and I take his hand in mine. "Harry, it was hell out there; worse than Maggot Hill. We thought we had 'em licked. Forced them to run like rabbits up the hill, even with all their artillery." If the enemy was on top of the hill, that meant the K Force was in a hole—a slaughterhouse.

"We outlasted them. We had to. We had no ammo." He looks to me for confirmation. "Remember those Banzais on Maggot Hill? I used to love 'em. Those bastards ran up that hill screaming with raised bayonets. Then we'd let loose with our Tommies. It was suicide." Pfeifer swallows, his eyes frightened by what only he can see, and whispers, "We had no ammo at Charpate, Harry. Only our knives. Do you know what it's like to be so close that you can smell the stink of a man's breath right before you kill him? " He starts to shudder uncontrollably. I hold his hand with the bullet tighter.

"It wasn't until I went to load my chamber for the last time that I thought, there's a bullet out there today with my name on it. Then I remembered you, Harry, and your damn Buddha. So I pulled out my last shell. That's how this bullet became my Buddha. And look, I'm alive." Pfeifer breathes deeply and reaches up to stroke his head. That's when I see the blood dripping from his hand. He's rubbed his scalp through his skin to bone. The cot under his head is soaked in red. I feel sick at the sight of his exposed, raw skull. Pfeifer's inability to admit what he's doing to himself terrifies me.

"It's shell shock, Harry," Doc whispers. I wonder how long Doc's been standing next to me. He patiently waits for my nod of understanding. Pfeifer's oozing wound has knocked out the last bit of strength within me.

Winnie leans over to check Pfeifer's pulse. Patting him gently on the shoulder, Doc says, "Hell, Pfeifer, today's your day. I'm giving you the last ticket on that plane to Ledo." Compassionately, he claps me on the back and quietly says, "Spreading democracy is hell, ain't it?"

Doc turns to continue his rounds. Lying on a litter next to Pfeifer is a green soldier, just off the plane this morning. His uniform is still creased, and he smells like the breakfast they serve in Ledo. He's got a gunshot wound in his upper thigh that's bleeding pretty badly. With a withering smile, Doc pulls out a scalpel and forceps. "This is going to hurt you more than me," he says. Two Burmese nurses assist by throwing the entirety of their body weight on the man. Without any painkiller or antiseptic, Winnie digs in. "I save my morphine for our boys coming back from a real battle."

The man screams, "What the fuck…what the hell do you think you're doing? Get me in an operating room." He shrieks, then finally bawls.

Holding up the bullet he has just yanked out of the soldier's leg, Doc tells him, "This ain't no Nip pellet." He tosses it to the solider. "Keep it as a souvenir from the war. Someday, one of your grandkids will ask why it's American made."

It's hard to stomach soldiers who self-inflict wounds so they can go home when others, like Pfeifer, move beyond what they don't want to do. They march. They kill. And some die.

"You know, I think about Collin a lot," Pfeifer confides, his faraway eyes seeing the kid. "Why that hour, that minute? If he'd waited one day, maybe things would have worked out for him."

"I feel responsible for what happened to Collin," I answer. "I know I'm just a supply officer, but he was a friend." Had we been in the States, we probably wouldn't have crossed paths, yet, because of this war, he'll be in my life forever.

"Harry, you don't give yourself enough credit," Pfeifer scolds, sounding stronger. His eyes are focused, and, although there's a nervous tremor in his hands, he's clasping them together rather than raking the back of his head. "You make your own decisions and stick with them. Other men see that and respect you. You're not your parents' trophy or God's puppet. And you don't fight because you want to, but because you have to."

The rain outside builds to a shower, and I hear the plane's engine rev up for departure.

The damn journalists' nagging voices approach me. I wish I could say, "There's your plane; hop on and leave me alone." Christ, I feel helpless. The minutes slip away as they load Sam and others onto the plane.

Seeing the injured being carried away, Pfeifer reaches with his hand to soothe his nerves.

I grab his fingers before he can cause more damage.

"They say you once had hair." I feel the body snatchers getting closer and know our time is running out. "Stop using that hand comb with all those calluses, and you'll get a thatch like mine." My voice cracks, and I hold both of his hands in mine.

The litter bearers hover over Pfeifer, waiting for a green light from the Doc. Finally, Winnie rushes up to us and says, "This guy is A-O.K. to go." Doc raises his eyebrows, ready to tell a joke, as usual. "Treat him as if he was family; that is, if you like your family."

As four men lift Pfeifer from his cot to the litter, the journalists see the bloody damage. I clutch his hands as we hustle around the whirling blades, knowing that once he's on the plane, he'll have to settle his own devils. Then I let go. I don't know if it's the flash from the cameras or the blur from my tears, but I can't see him any more. Doc grabs me by the shoulders and holds me back as the body snatchers hoist this last patient, the man who saved my life, onto the plane to India. I feel the rain wash the blood from my hands, but not the memories—never those.

I try to come to grips with the absurdity of the day, but my thoughts are warped and slanted. As clouds on the western horizon swallow the plane, I ask, "What day is it today?"

CHAPTER 49

June, 1944

Thousands of Japanese marched into Myitkyina from the gap in the east. In the south, the trap set by the Chindits had been breached at Mogaung, and the enemy flooded the town.

They're dug in at the Myitkyina rail station, and everyone knows they've vowed to die before they'll surrender.

It's dusk, and this is what I think about as I retreat to my tent to get some privacy. Our camp, in the jungle along the Myitkyina airfield, continues to be plagued by snipers, but I feel safer here than by the rail yard. The last letter from Ruthie came about a week ago. It's already dog eared, and some of the ink has bled from the seeping rain. I unfold it to read one more time.

Dearest Harry,

I've been sitting on my bed, pen in hand, for the last ten minutes, thinking about what to write that would make you smile and tear you away from the war, if only for one moment. But what do I have to say that would be meaningful? I feel so small and insignificant when I think of all that you and the boys have done for us.

Most of the entrants in the 4th of July parade this year will remind us about our boys overseas. How can we forget? I made a few dozen paper flowers with the girls at work for our company's float. Remember the little fruit stand at the end of the parade? This year, they've got the best tomatoes and corn. The Heirloom are sweet and juicy, and, with all the rain we've had, the corn is already taller than my knees. My friend Doris just had a baby, so I knitted her little one a tiny red, white, and blue sweater for the 4th.

Babies smell so fresh and pure. We're all waiting for our men to come home.

Won't your two years be up soon? What does it take to get you home? All I have to offer is my love, but love for you makes my life worth living.

Forever yours, Ruthie

There's so much to say that I'm not sure I'll write back. Merrill had a third heart attack and was flown out for the last time. Kinnison died of mite typhus. Only two hundred of the original Marauders are left, the others are dead or too sick to fight. The Chindits fared only slightly better. Yet the Japanese garrison grows daily. Doesn't anyone understand the saying: "An eye for an eye makes the whole world blind?" A death for a death, then nobody's left. Is this what Ruthie wants to hear?

The repetitive grinding from the generator pedal on the airfield's radio breaks my train of thought. I pull out a Chesterfield and strike a match. All we have to do is hand in our walking papers, and we'd be on a plane headed home. But as much as I hate this war, something's holding me here. I may sign up for another tour of duty with Osborne, Johnson, Preacher, Doc, and Doyer.

If we leave it to the paper pushers, this war will never be won, but in combat, all rules are thrown out. But the men in power seem to enjoy the insanity of war; they show no sign of wanting to be cured. And because of that, what's important to me is slowly being taken away: Bob, Reginald, Lester, Collin, Pfeifer, Sam. This has become a personal war. How can I write to Ruthie and tell her I'm not ready to come home?

Around the campfire, Earl and others poke fun at Bernie while they play cards. I slip Ruthie's letter into the side pocket of my haversack, then crawl out to join them.

"Who's feeling lucky enough to gamble against me tonight?" I ask the circle of men squatting around the deck. "I'll even throw in a genuine Japanese flag, fresh off the battlefield."

"Harry, I'd wager the Nip took one look at you, handed you that flag, and slit his own throat," Bernie imitates a knife severing his Adam's apple, then scoots over to make room for me to join the game. "You and your Marauders are a scary-looking bunch of thugs."

It hasn't occurred to me that, while Preacher and I call the new recruits and road crew pansies, they may think of us as social deviants. But how can you win a war without men like the Marauders?

"Let's get this game going," I say. "Have I already got you so scared that you're shitting in your pants?" Bernie lets out a loud fart and gets the last laugh.

Bernie deals the cards like he grew up in a smoke-filled back room in Chicago. Earl throws down the first bet. I raise him. Bernie folds. Lin sees my bet and raises it, confident.

"Hey, looks like you've been corrupting this innocent Chinese soldier while I was gone." Lin's cowlick gives the impression he's an adolescent, but of all my friends from Ledo, the war seems to have punished him the most. His fine, small, even features and wide cheekbones look as though they've been carved from marble. His face is lined like a man double his age, even though he's still in his twenties. He rarely unwinds, always worrying about his men—and with good reason.

Maran Lu's exotic looks are not ignored as she approaches us, pushing through the gawking soldiers.

"So, how's your girl?" I tease Earl. He ignores me, watching her get closer. Her slight frame appears even smaller when wrapped in her longyi, and her long, black braid makes me think of a school-girl.

She leans over to wrap her arms around Earl's neck. "What you win for me tonight? I think radio that sings songs day and night make me happy." It's plain to see they're mad about each other.

"Yeah, that's what I need, too." Bernie nods in agreement. "One for the shop, and one for my foxhole, cuz that's where I seem to be living. Damn those snipers."

"You don't like stuffing yourself in a custom-made dirt hole?" I ask.

"Hell, it's so little, I can't even pick my nose while I'm in it," Bernie says as he absentmindedly shuffles the unused cards.

Not far away, Hunter's voice carries over Bernie's whine. He's shooting the breeze with a cluster of soldiers. From the laughter, it seems someone's made Hunter the butt of a joke, but he's being a good sport about it. Then he moves on to check in on everyone along his path and give his pep talk.

"Evening, men and young lady." Hunter sounds relaxed, but the man doesn't know the meaning of the word. "I want to make sure everyone's keeping their rifles clean and ready with all the sniper attacks. Several of you are not assigned to a combat battalion, but you're all still soldiers. So keep those guns by your side." He notices me, then adds, "When you get a chance, go out with Flynn for some practice shots. I know it may be tempting, but don't use him as the target." He chuckles, then gives an informal salute before continuing his rounds.

The next day, before the sun has fully risen, a growl from Earl's sleepy dozer breaks the sweet sound of birds chirping in the tranquil morning air. "WHOA!" Earl pats the dashboard of his rig as though it's his thoroughbred preparing for a big race. The tarmac fills up with the road crew, digging out and replacing aggregate bedding and adding new layers of asphalt. Combat soldiers position themselves at the anti-aircraft guns, and gunmen patrol the perimeter for snipers.

Up near the hospital, sniper fire breaks out. Everyone's alert, but the planes from Ledo continue to land, so I'm out on the strip unloading the non-stop deliveries. "This goes to the H.Q. hut," I command a platoon from the road crew. "Set this aside for the hospital, then, once the snipers are taken down, bring it up there on the double." Another group of men drag the boxes off the runway to make room for more supplies. "Guard this with your life; it's a crate with 10-1 rations; they've got everything from cigarettes to quinine."

Then the telltale pop from a knee mortar bursts from the jungle. It scares the shit out of me. "DROP!" I shout. Without hesitation, all but one man hits the pavement. He looks bewildered up until the moment the fragments from the mortar fly and the horror of realization registers on his bloody face.

"Clear out!" I yell as I lift myself into a crouch, then prod the men from their prostrate positions and lead them away from the exposed field. With knee mortars, the enemy can shoot from a quarter mile away, in the jungle, at any angle. You won't know if you're in the line of fire until you're hit. "Bring your guns," I remind them.

"Take cover," I scream at the untested construction workers while grabbing the downed man by the shoulders and dragging him from the tarmac to the dirt. Another pop sounds further down the runway. The explosion has as much force as a 50 mm mortar. Freshly placed gravel and hot, sticky asphalt spray in all directions. Men shriek, and the air strip explodes with smoke. Fires erupt from bulls-eye hits on the construction equipment. The mortar shells fly in all directions. Everyone races away from the last blast until the next shell explodes in front of them.

"Get in your bunkers," I bark, unsure if that's really the best advice. With knee mortars, they can change the angle, so the first one hits ten feet in front of you, and the second blows you out of your foxhole.

The mortars stop, and I know what that means: "Banzai!" I screech. "Aim your rifles!" Japanese soldiers flood the tarmac and charge on our camp, masked by the smoke and flames. A will to survive is one of my better traits, so I sprint for cover, then dive into a foxhole next to Bernie. "Start firing," I command.

"I don't know how to load my gun," he whimpers, cowering deeper in his hole.

I feel sick at his stupidity, but remember I did the same thing my first time out. "Stay down," I order. Then I do what I do best—what Maggot Hill taught me: I rely on my instincts and prepare for the unexpected. Round after round, I lay down lines of bullets. My hands burn from the hot barrel.

I check out Bernie while I reload my chamber, then freeze. A Japanese soldier at the edge of the bunker thrusts his bayonet down. Bernie wails, "No!" Blood erupts from a jagged gash in his bicep.

The enemy soldier jerks the bayonet out and aims for one final blow. But Bernie grabs the barrel of the gun, surprising the Jap, and flips him over. In a wild rage, he heaves himself from the hole and aims at the Nip. "You bloody son-of-a-bitch. I'll teach you. You ain't gonna kill Bernard Roman that easy." Bernie pulls the trigger, but the chamber's empty.

He throws the rifle down and chases the Jap. Flinging himself on the Nip, the two men fall. Fists fly. Bones crunch. Blood erupts. Then Bernie encircles the man's throat with his bare hands and squeezes, and squeezes, and squeezes. The enemy's body goes limp and slumps to the ground. "You shouldn't have got me mad." Bernie towers over the body, hysterical.

I didn't see the next bullet coming; neither did Bernie. His incredulous eyes tell me this.

Before the Japanese can pull the trigger again, I nail him. But it's too late. Bernie's down. "Harry," he calls to me.

I crawl over to him under a steady volley of shells. "Hang in there, buddy." My voice cracks. Blood drenches his shirt, and I rip it open to find the bleeding. But the raw, serrated hole in his chest is too big for me to do anything about.

"Harry, I was just starting to get the hang of it," he whispers, the grease smudges on his face track with tears. He grabs my arm.

Men scream. Rifles click. Flames explode. But I'm in my own world and hear none of it, feel none of it, see none of it. It's as though I'm wrapped in a cocoon, holding Bernie tight. A light breeze chills me. The wind rustles in the jungle like an autumn afternoon back home.

"You're not gonna die, Bernie." I wipe the tears from his cheeks, leaving my own to fall freely. "Cuz you're a bad-ass motherfucker. Only the good die young."

His grip loosens until it's limp. Smoke billows on the tarmac, curling up to the sky until it feathers into wisps. Gently, I lower him as though he's sleeping, making sure there are no rocks or anything under his head that would make him uncomfortable. My body feels as taut as a strung wire. All I want is unconsciousness to wash this all away.

Abruptly, I decide I've got to find Earl and tell him. I know it's irrational, but my body is not listening to my mind. Without giving myself a chance to question my actions, I stride onto the runway, zig-zagging around craters and looking for his bulletproof dozer. I find it up ahead, inching towards camp. I speed up my pace, and a mortar explodes in front of me. The front of Earl's rig lifts in the air and snaps, while I'm thrown into a nearby trench.

Sometime later I raise my head, realizing I've been unconscious but not sure how long: seconds, minutes, hours. I force my pounding skull above the rim of the trench and look up.

That's when my memory returns.

Earl's body slumps over the rig's steering wheel, his unblinking eyes bulging in disbelief.

Sweat droplets trickle from his forehead down his dark, stubbled cheeks. It turns pink as it mixes with the blood from his nose and mouth, then drips off his rigid jaw. I'd need to leave the protection of the bunker if I were to touch him. So, instinctively, I wait.

"Move," I finally command my useless legs, but they don't respond. Instead, I sink deeper into the trench as the earth splatters around me from a spray of bullets. Inhuman screams from nameless men wail like sirens. My heart thuds in my chest and neck as I crouch tighter.

The cracks and bangs from the Nip artillery sound like 4th of July gone berserk. I'd like to get off this rollercoaster ride; this is no fun. Pain wrenches all sight and sound from my consciousness when my leg suddenly spasms. Then I remember Earl's body, sprawled in his trusty big rig, and know I can't leave him there.

As my gaze shifts further down the trench in search of help, a body comes into focus. My eyes instinctively close, and I see the afterimage of his face on the backs of my eyelids. I know that face too well, those wide cheekbones etched in marble.

"This isn't the way it's supposed to end," I howl, mourning Lin and all the others. Thick tears blur my vision. "We're supposed to win and go home," I choke.

PART III

MARS TASK FORCE - LOI KANG

CHAPTER 50

December, 1944

It's been six months since we first attacked Myitkyina in May. We fought there until August. The 53-07th was down to two-hundred Marauders. So they sent in the 124th Cavalry and the 475th Infantry to form the 5332nd Brigade. As we advance southeast, towards Bhamo, signs of civilization reappear. Instead of jungles, palm plantations flank one side of the trail and towering tea gardens the other. Fields of villagers pick the palm fruit for later crushing. On the opposite side of the road, as far as the eye can see, men with machetes climb the hillsides to trim the rows upon winding rows of three-foot-high tea shrubs.

"Is it only three years ago that the Japanese started this mess?" Preacher asks, sounding weary and ready to throw in the towel. "Instead of seeing the light at the end of this tunnel, I feel like we've just entered a new one."

Not only have the Marauders been replaced by the 5332nd Brigade—most of them green recruits fresh off the boats in Bombay—but FDR has cleaned house at the top. I used to think I had a handle on things, but it's slowly breaking.

"I've never been a Stilwell fan," I say, gut checking the others guys' reactions. They just keep marching. "He may have been a good soldier in the First World War, but he never walked in my shoes, and he should have if he wanted me to follow him. Still, that doesn't mean I like the way he was booted out." War has no mercy; neither does the press. In the end, Stilwell's greatest victory handed him the sword he fell on.

Before shipping it off to the printing press, the Signal Corps reporter showed me his rough draft report on Stilwell's removal as commander of CBI theatre. He told me, "Harry, I know they're going to cut out the good parts before it hits the press. I tried to add Stilwell's side. But I can't force editors to print the truth."

STILWELL RELIEVED OF SERVICE - Draft Press Release

The White House announced this week that General Joseph W. Stilwell has been relieved of his triple command in the Far East. He was replaced as Chief of Staff to Generalissimo Chiang Kai-shek; as Deputy to Admiral Lord Louis Mountbatten, Southeast Asia Commander; and as Commanding General of U.S. Force in the China- Burma-India Theater. After the beloved Lord Mountbatten and the Chinese military leader, Chiang Kai-shek, said the General bucked "the common good" and Tokyo Rose broadcast Stilwell's plot to oust the Chinese leader and make himself the Czar of China, the General's leadership was questioned.

There is conjecture in the U.S. that Stilwell was "relieved of duty" at the direct request of Generalissimo Chiang Kai-shek following differences over the conduct of China's armies. Later, when offered China's highest military decoration, the General told CKS to, "Stick it up his arse." Stilwell described CKS as a "paper tiger that should be spanked like a spoilt child," and charged him with "gumming up the Lend-Lease accounts so they couldn't be untangled."

This sensational development, marking the first time an American four-star general has been relieved in this war, was linked to announcements suggesting the division of the CBI Theater into two parts, British and American jurisdictions. Stilwell was said to have insulted the British, calling them "pansies," "quitters" and "garrulous pigfuckers". The General then accused his superior, "Grandma Mountbatten," of cutting his throat with a dull knife. Stilwell's response when questioned about the mutiny by Galahad in Myitkyina was, "I wasn't a rebellion. Those boys never backed down and never gave up. They were just worn out and had no more to give."

In an interview with General Stilwell, he said, "Whatever the Peanut thought of me, he should remember my motive was only for the good of China." Stilwell also admitted his refusal to accept S.E.A.C.'s top-secret tactical plans, saying, "Their cockeyed art of warfare was killing me."

Stilwell, often called "Uncle Joe" by others because of his disdain for ceremony and concern for the common soldier, said, "My only ambition was to win the war and get the hell home." The Ledo-Kunming Road, otherwise known as " Stilwell's Road," a critical supply link to China, is scheduled for completion in January, 1945.

We march two abreast on the relatively flat terrain—Knight, Doyer, Preacher, and me. December is cool and dry in Burma. In the brisk, clean air, swallows track our route, swooping in and out without fear. No one wants to talk about the past or speculate about the future; it's all painful and uncertain.

Last June, we lost control over Myitkyina. So many lives were sacrificed to get there, but the powers in charge were too busy fighting each other and accepted those deaths as a reasonable price to pay. I lost Bernie and Lin. Thankfully, Earl made it out alive. The bearing on his axle was so rusted that when the shell hit, instead of flipping the entire cab, it split in two. That's what saved Earl from being flattened under fifty tons of metal. I'd like to think my special chemical application of HCL to decommission the equipment, safeguarded other men in the same way.

That's what I need to believe.

Fighting through the monsoon was the mistake that helped the Allies regain Myitkyina in August. The Japanese never expected us to be so ignorant. Who in their right mind would dispatch three battalions of soldiers in two hundred inches of rain? In the end, we lost nine out of every ten Marauders. Too bad Stilwell never got it through his thick skull that wars should not be fought in jungles during monsoons, because supply planes crash in torrential downpours. And guerrilla warfare should be just that—small units used for hit-and-run assignments. Because of the Peanut, the Chinese artillery was not always there before we went into front line battle, so the Marauders had to fight alone.

Hidden among bamboo thickets along the ditch, small, Buddhist shrines with offerings dot the way. Most are stone or plaster. Mortar shells have left their scars; some are cracked and broken from random crossfire. Guarded within these tiny temples are sacred statues: the resting, the laughing, the sitting Buddhas. Only Pfeifer knew of my miniature Buddha. I compare it to its cousins along the path and hear Pfeifer's taunt in my mind: "Is that a Buddha in your pocket, or are you happy to see me?" Now he's gone.

"Ain't that disrespectful, the way them little, tiny temples have been smashed up?" Lieutenant Jack Knight drawls. Knight, a newcomer with the 5332nd from the 124th Calvary Regiment, was recently assigned to Burma.

"War values nothing but victory," Mr. Doyer answers.

Back in Myiktyina, domed stupas, flanked by guardian lions and lotus petal columns, suffered from our bomb attacks and mortar shells. Whole chunks of plaster gouged from the roof let sunlight stream in where there had previously been private corners for meditation. Still, the locals continued their daily visits, lighting candles and worshiping as though there was no war. It's painful to see what we've done to their religious monuments.

"Yep," Knight says; his gentle twang easy on my ears. "But we can't take credit for our wins if we don't accept the blame for our failures."

Knight, a plain-talking guy, is cut from the same cloth as Pfeifer. Despite his intense, narrow eyes; his Slavic nose; and thin lips—all giving the impression of a high-level predator— he's a likable guy. He came from a family with a strong sense of patriotic duty, and proudly introduced himself by saying, "If I can't live with glory for my country, I don't want to live without it." He would've made a hell of a Marauder, but he's definitely rounding out the 5332nd—or Mars Task Force—well.

My eyes flit back and forth, looking for any unwelcome movement. We're in the middle of enemy country, so talk is sparse. Up ahead, everyone turns onto a dirt road that winds around a rice paddy. We're to bivouac at the edge of the field tonight. Forests thick with undergrowth line both sides of the road, hemming us in. I don't like it. It's as though we're marching to our execution with nowhere to run.

When we finally stop, the men in the lead are already digging in and setting up their tents.

We find the C.P. where Roy's translating something in Japanese for Osborne.

"We got these off a captured Nip." Osborne points at the papers Roy's holding. "They plan on sending in reinforcements, so we better make sure we're not walking straight into their front." With that, we know we've just been handed an assignment.

"Let's do a little recon," Preacher says, dropping his large pack against a tree and grabbing his Tommy.

Nau joins us. He says, "I climb tree. Better in air than ground, where, like elephant, cannot hide behind a bamboo pole."

He shimmies up a tree while we continue along the trail. Preacher leads us south for a while, then cuts sharply to the east, into the dense undergrowth. "Harry and Doyer, go west," Preacher whispers. "Knight, follow me."

I spot a Japanese scout peering from behind a tree. Automatically, I raise my Tommy to my shoulder and blaze away, dropping him. Doyer moves to my right flank to fire at movement in the brush. Another enemy falls. Preacher and Knight come charging out of the woods onto the path, firing all the way.

"Got two more back there," Knight brags.

Nau is back on the ground, racing towards us with fear in his face but not his voice. He calls, "Get out now. We in hornet nest."

Shrieking Japanese close in on us. It'd take too much time to follow the road back, so Preacher consults his compass and pulls out his radio. "We're coming across the paddy from fifteen degrees northwest of C.P., about a hundred and fifty yards out. Give us some cover. Over." He holsters his walkie-talkie, then commands, "Run!"

Like spooked rabbits, we race across the open field. Shots crack, but we're out of their range. We just keep running and hoping nothing bigger opens fire on us.

As we stumble into camp, exhausted but exhilarated, Knight says, "That's the way I like to fight. Let them come to us." His dirt-splattered face can't hide his broad smile. "They can start it. We'll finish it." We quickly extinguish the Japanese platoon. No enemy reinforcements arrive.

The Chinese force landed earlier and are digging in next to us. They unload their mules and set up their artillery for battle. We eat our rations cold, without fires. No one talks. We can't even smoke, so we just wait. Looking up, I see the moon is only a shadow of itself.

Just before daybreak, the Japanese creep to within fifty yards of our perimeter. They use smokeless gunpowder, so the only way we can place them is if they make noise. By then, it's too late, and we've lost a man or two. We pick them off one by one, but at dawn, the enemy opens up with everything. After a couple hours of shelling, "Whistling Willie," their 150 mm mortar gun, can't knock us out. So they Banzai.

As they charge across the paddy, we mow them down. I don't let myself think of them as husbands, sons or fathers. One platoon after another race to their death, tripping over their fallen comrades as they advance. By late afternoon, the battle is over.

We search through the mutilated remains, looking for any living. A GI bends over to strip a decorative belt from a downed enemy. The Japanese soldier rises up with one last effort, his eyes wildly searching for a last moment of honor, and throws a grenade. The soldier picks it up to toss it away, but it explodes as it leaves his hand. When will this waste end?

As we pack up to move out, the radio squawks. "Bhamo taken. Japs broke ring set by Chinese, then retreated. Only fifty miles to the border. Goodbye, Burma. Hello, China."

CHAPTER 51

January, 1945

Before we pulled up camp this morning, I watched the skies for a mail drop. A Christmas card from Ruthie is all I wanted, but no luck. I'll have to reread the letter she sent several weeks ago. I sure miss her.

Harry,

At Thanksgiving a bunch of girls went on a hay ride. We even started a bonfire. Only, it wasn't much fun without our guys. Christmas is still a month away, but I've hung a stocking for you. I'd put myself inside it as a gift if that would get you home. Why haven't I heard from you? Don't even start thinking I'll let you go. Every day, I wait for you to come home. When I wake, I listen for your footsteps. At the faintest hint of your voice, I rush down the stairs, ready to throw myself into your arms. I'm not willing to admit what I don't want to believe. Where are you?

Your Faithful Girl Back Home, Ruthie

So when I wrote last, it was short. I had to let her know I was still alive.

Ruthie,

Every day I think about going home, to good cooking, laughs with the guys, and most of all, you. The end feels closer. Pray for me. Have a Happy 1945, and wish us a lucky one.

I love you, Harry

I should feel like I own the world. It hasn't rained for days, we had real chicken for dinner last night. I finally got rid of that damn athlete's foot, and I cheated death another year, but I can't dig my spirits out of the gutter. Today will pass the same as yesterday, slogging another fifteen miles deeper into enemy territory.

Nau steps out of our marching column and into an orchard along the edge of the dirt road.

He repositions his burp gun, then reaches up and pulls down a branch laden with oranges.

Overhead, the sound of whistling wings makes me cringe. I hold my breath, expecting a 150 mm howitzer shell to explode in my face any second. Instead, a hornbill, its large, yellow beak too big for its body, shrieks as it flies where it won't be disturbed by tromping boots. I let my shoulders relax.

"Try." Nau offers me a fruit, slipping back in line. "Taste like American ice cream," he tempts me.

I'm not hungry and haven't been for some time. Lately, I'd rather drink my meals. "Got any with whiskey flavor?" I ask, but I take the fruit. "Also, how do you know about American ice cream?"

"Missionaries come to village when I child. Tell parents I smart. Take me to capital city, Rangoon, where they teach English. They think I become priest. After six years, I go home to marry. Cannot be priest if married," he laughs, looking proud that he ended up with an education that didn't cost him celibacy.

I throw the orange rind into a ditch and tear off a couple of sections, then, surprised, say, "Hey, this I like! Almost as good as American made." I check to make sure he knows I'm teasing. Sometimes the message comes out wrong in translation.

Nau grins, satisfied, and says, "My land have beautiful mountains, rivers, trees, filled with ancient temples. Your country new, rich, strong. My country better."

"Well, granted, you probably don't have to pay taxes, but if things were that great in your country, we wouldn't be here," I challenge him with raised eyebrows.

With hands clasped behind his back, he reflects on my words. Then he kicks the pebbles on the road and says, "You right. Burma have many problems. Feuds between tribes and Burmese government start before I was born. Probably end after I die. But we must trust power of Spirit and have faith"

"Nau, I don't buy that missionary crap." The syrupy orange citrus scent on my hands attracts an irritating string of bees.

"Harry, believing in Spirit is good. It teach us to ask for what need. Brain only tells us to fight for what we want. So we fight till all dead. That is not answer."

"So what do you ask for?"

"I ask my people be left alone." Nau throws his shoulders back defiantly. I've never seen this side of him before, but, in the past, we always talked about *my* war.

"Well, that ain't going to happen. What's your next plan?" I ask.

Nau nods in agreement. "No next plan. Not easy to feel sorry for enemy when they put knife in back. How can I see light in man who doesn't honor light in me?" He looks at the dry ground, clasps his hands behind his back again, and continues to march forward in silence.

We start our climb to the east. I inhale the scent of cypress trees; they smell fresh and clean enough to eat. It's a sharp contrast to my mind, which has gone from diseased to rotten. Five days ago, we left Mr. Doyer along the side of the road. I was sure I'd see him again.

"Hey, you got me into this mess; otherwise, I'd still be on the road crew. You can't walk out on me." I hoisted him under my shoulder from the litter and hauled him over to a shady spot against a smooth tree trunk.

"I ain't actually walking out on you, Harry. If you notice, I'm flat on my butt." His fever was so high, he'd drained his own canteen and mine. It had to be mite typhus or malaria.

"I can't just leave you here. I'll wait a bit." I sat down in the dirt, and we watched the leaf-cutter ants parade in front of us for what seemed like hours. The sun rose high in the sky.

Finally, Doyer complained. "Harry, you know the drill. You have no choice. A light plane will fly down from Myitkyina, and I'll be back to Ledo by nightfall. They'll probably shoot me up with some sugar water, then, in a couple of weeks, stick a gun in my hand and send me back out. Count on it."

That's not what happened. This evening, they radioed the bad news. I didn't know I could sink any lower, but I did. Soon, those he loved will learn what we already know, and a telegram is no substitute for a son. I've pulled out my pen because I need to tell them what Joe meant to us, to me.

Do they know about his nine medals? Or how, in World War I, he was trapped in a cemetery with mortar shells shattering tombstones in all directions, and still led his men to safety? Then, in Lille, he fastened a telephone wire to himself, swam the Canal du Nord, and established the line on the far bank so that his comrades could pull themselves hand-over-hand to the other side. I bet they don't know that, when he volunteered for the Marauders at age forty-seven, he was told the age limit was thirty-eight but didn't take no for an answer. Then, at Myitkyina, he received an even dozen slugs of shrapnel in his legs, chest, and elbow. He was never one to brag, and he was always there to help.

Every soldier wants to be a hero, but it takes something exceptional to actually become one. Joseph Doyer was no ordinary man. I remember when I joined the Marauders, Joe immediately asked me how I felt and where I was from, and let me know what to expect. He didn't snow me or belittle me. After one eighteen-mile hike that made us all glad to hit the ground, Joe built a fire, cooked up some three-day rations, and fed a young soldier sick with Typhus. This war was hard on him, but he died as he wanted to in war times.

He was in the saddle that shaped his entire life, moving

forward to protect those he loved. Joe was a model GI and a father when some of us needed it most. I cannot put in words how much we'll miss him.

As I reread the letter, I know something's missing. The pen wrote the words, but my heart refuses to accept them. I want to just walk away. Isn't that what I did five days ago, when I left him on the road? I pushed myself off the ground and said, "I best be going. Can't be late for war."

Doyer didn't answer. He didn't even call out a glib farewell, pretending all would fine.

And I wouldn't let myself think it could be any other way. Damn him. Why didn't I say goodbye?

CHAPTER 52

It's 05:00 hours. There's frost on my poncho and ice in my helmet. I make myself get up and eat a cold breakfast before we start the forced march. The sultry voice of Tokyo Rose from yesterday morning's radio broadcast replays again and again in my mind. Why would an American-born Japanese woman flaunt her English by spewing enemy propaganda over the air waves?

"Hey there, boys. I mean, enemies. We know where you are. Are you ready for that air attack on the Hosi Valley? Don't worry if you're not; we are. Your wives and girlfriends back home already have new men in their lives, so they won't miss you. Now, relax and listen to Strike Up the Band by the Boston Pops. And by the way, that first convoy you sent out the other day will never reach China. That road won't get built."

Mist blankets the trees as the morning air warms. We've been climbing up a range of foothills on the west side of the Hosi Valley, following the contours rather than scrambling straight up. After we get to the crest, we'll drop down into a basin before we mount our final climb. If the Japanese are positioned on the eastern ridge, we'll be sitting ducks when we're down in the bowl, and our route to connect India and China will be blocked. But this is the farthest east any Allied troop has marched. We can't give up now.

"How the hell does Tokyo Rose know where we're going before we do?" I ask Knight, expecting to see planes bearing the red rising sun.

"Harry, don't let her get under your skin. Whistling Willie's calling cards are what you should be losing sleep about," Jack answers, unfazed as usual.

Sometimes I get nervous with that guy's invincible attitude. The enemy knows where we are and where we're going, and he responds with, "why worry?"

As morning turns into afternoon and then night, we don't stop, even to eat our lunch. We just march. Like the night Doyer and I were attacked, the wildlife has disappeared. I become obsessed with watching for Japanese tracks on the ground and Zeroes in the sky. Grey pushes up from the horizon in the east, lifting higher until a streak of white breaks through from the morning sun.

"Take a look at this," Knight calls back as we pass a recent enemy bivouac. Two Japanese corpses lie face-down, bare asses looking like a butcher had sliced out chops for the market. "What happened here?"

Johnson answers flatly, "Seen that before. Those are butt steaks." He keeps marching, but his head drops in disgust. "Desperate soldiers are the worst kind. They know it's too late to turn back and have nothing to lose." Finally, in the late afternoon, forty hours after we began, we're in the valley. Surrounded by a ring of foothills, cool air and moisture trapped in the basin supports a lush grove of trees. A gurgling stream offers our aching feet relief.

A boom-whaaow-bang from a 70 mm gun greets us, and I dive to the ground. On the eastern ridge, the setting sun silhouettes the enemy's granddaddy of guns, their 150 mm howitzer, Whistling Willie. Let the artillery volley begin.

Another disadvantage: our best tactical leader, Osborne, stayed in Myitkyina to update General Wiley, Stilwell's replacement. He said he had the flu, but I think it's typhus. Now that we've already realized Osborne's greatest fear—an intimidating Japanese barrier at Loi Kang— we need to find a way around or through their wall.

First, to protect ourselves, we quickly dig bunkers in the valley in the dark of night. The Japanese know we're here, so they release random shells—unlucky for those men in the line of fire. On our first night, the death tally begins. Welcome to the Hosi Valley.

Once our fortifications are built, Preacher, Johnson, and Knight huddle together, marking up a map with an impossible plan of climbing an eight-hundred-foot hill with a seventy-degree slope. We'll need claws to take that on. But if we can knock the enemy out at that pass, we'll open a route for the Chinese artillery to crush their blockade.

At dawn, Preacher and Knight take off to scout ahead of us for an easier trail to Loi Kang.

I join Johnson and Nau in leading Johnson's infantry platoon. We move forward quickly, edgy and trigger-happy. A whole battalion of the enemy could be screened by the undergrowth, and we'd never know it until it was too late. "Nau, climb the tallest tree around. Let us know if you can spot the scum," Johnson orders, no longer the wild-eyed, rangy, red-bearded Viking that rescued us at Maggot Hill. Nau steps deep into the jungle and is soon in the air.

Our pace slows as we approach the edge of the valley, where the sodden grass transitions into a rocky path leading up into the foothills, and the leafy cover thins. Sweat trickles down my face as heat from the morning sun penetrates through the foliage. Just as our column reaches the uphill climb, Johnson forms a quick body block and motions the platoon back in the woods.

Ahead, a Japanese soldier points a Nambu machine gun at Preacher's spine. Knight kneels on the ground, head bent, while a second enemy soldier holds the curved samurai sword around the back of his neck. Preacher and Knight are unarmed with their hands on their heads.

The Japanese commanding officer waves a rifle back and forth between the two GIs.

Then, eyes bulging, he screams in Japanese at Preacher. Eventually, in clipped English he asks, "How many?"

From our vantage point in the woods, we're close enough to see the spit flying, but the Japanese are too obsessed with their prisoners to listen for us. Preacher refuses to make eye contact; instead, he looks at the ground. The officer slaps Preacher's face, back and forth, infuriated or scared or both.

He motions the Nambu-carrying soldier to search Preacher. The soldier lowers his gun and aggressively rips Preacher's pockets inside out, as though he's afraid to touch Preacher, and any wrong move will give Preacher the advantage. He comes up empty-handed, except for a rosary, which he flings viciously on the ground. With trembling hands, he repositions his gun in Preacher's back while his eyes flit from one edge of the opening to the other. I sigh, relieved and thankful that Preacher left the marked-up map at camp.

With a jerky, erratic swing of his rifle, the officer moves over to Knight, and knees him in the face. Cracking bones are followed by squirting blood, but Knight remains silent. Frustrated, the officer shrieks, his wide eyes betraying his panic.

On the trail behind us, running feet approach. It's Nau. Johnson steps out and signals him to hide. Within minutes, the Kachin ranger is at our side, breathing heavily.

The samurai guard is directed to go through Knight's pockets. He hesitantly lays down his sword and kicks Knight in the stomach. He laughs anxiously, then, with caution, empties Knight's pockets. Once he is done, he recklessly repositions the sword, drawing blood from Knight's neck.

"What did you find?" Johnson whispers to Nau.

"Twenty men camped ahead where stream flows from hill."

"How far?"

"One hundred yards."

"OK. We've got to act quickly. I want you to climb that tree. When you get up there, wait for my signal to shoot the soldier holding the Nambu in Preacher's back. Harry, you take the samurai guard. I'll get the officer."

"What then?" Nau asks anxiously.

"Drop fast. They should all be dead by the time you hit the ground."

The Japanese officer screeches at his men, and the Nambu gunner's lip curls in anger. He levels the gun at Knight, eyes filled with hatred. He looks no older than Nau.

They argue back and forth. It seems the two enlisted soldiers are edgy, probably expecting us to arrive any minute. But the officer wants information from Preacher and Knight before they're killed.

As Nau climbs, Johnson says, "Harry, wait two seconds after Nau fires before you shoot.

I want them to aim for the trees. That'll give us the time we need."

The rest of our men hold fire. I position myself, gun against shoulder and eye level with the barrel. Johnson looks up. Nau looks down. Johnson nods and aims.

A single rifle cracks above, reverberating off the trees and bursting into open air. The Japanese behind Preacher drops to the ground. The others look up into the canopy, but they don't have a chance. Johnson and I pull our triggers simultaneously until the enemy is dead.

Stunned, Preacher and Knight finally recover and pull the guns from under the dead men.

They stumble towards us. "They've got a camp by the stream," Preacher yells, still dazed. "We know," Johnson answers, pushing the two ahead of him. "Get the hell back to camp."

Knight uses his forearm to wipe the flowing blood from his nose, "You couldn't have done that five minutes earlier?" he asks. His terrified voice betrays the calm in his words.

"Sorry," Johnson answers. "Just following protocol. I wanted you alive."

"We're outnumbered," Preacher calls back, fumbling between stumps and fallen logs in the path.

"Not when they get to our camp," I answer. But I think that was only their reception party. "They're trying to decide how many bullets to put on the table."

CHAPTER 53

After two weeks of stubborn fighting, we're still unable to advance into the foothills.

Every night, we sleep hugging our guns. In the mornings, the Chinese announce the start of the artillery fire with a bugle call. Without fail, Whistling Willie replies to their trumpet with craters in our camp. We're down fifty men.

"How did we break them at Maggot Hill?" Johnson asks, impatient and unable to stand.

Remembering the unbelievable relief I felt at the sight of that six-foot-four skeleton marching into our maggot-infested camp, I propose, "We starve them out."

So we huddle together and study the maps again. We've memorized every dip and curve on the valley floor, but the maps are useless unless we can get up the mountainside.

Knight's broken nose and swollen lip have not crushed his spirit. If anything, he, like Johnson, is blinded by determination. Preacher's daily dose of caution is also wearing off. I'm the only one looking for a practical plan.

"Isn't that a road near the top?" Johnson asks, pointing to a dashed line on the paper above a sheer drop off.

"Sure is," Knight answers, having trouble speaking around his mashed-up face. "Won't do us any good from here unless you plan to put us in that artillery barrel and shoot us there."

"The only way we'll get to China is to scale the face of that cliff and knock out the enemy's supply line," Johnson decides. "We'll need dynamite." The adrenaline surging in his voice jolts Knight and Preacher off their butts. I follow, thinking that desperate men make reckless decisions.

"I've done this only once before," Johnson says as we walk into the supply tent. "Have any of you worked with explosives?"

I mumble, "I'm not an expert, but we did this on the road job." I grab the dynamite sticks from the inventory and lay out everything we need with innate confidence. Just the sight of the detonator brings back disturbing memories.

When all the equipment is ready, Johnson commands, "Pack your guns, some rope, and the dynamite." Then he points towards Loi Kang. "We climb, set the explosives, and get the hell out."

It's only 09:00 hours. when the four of us reach the base of the eight-hundred-foot cliff. We look up until our heads can't tilt back any further. "I love this shit," Preacher jokes. "What Jap would look for us here?" No one laughs.

Our daredevil, Knight, squints one eye, cocks his head to the side, and says, "Not bad after that first landing."

A close-up view of the rock face looks better than what the map showed, even though anyone in their right mind would still walk away from it. But we're not in our right minds. The nearest outcrop is twenty feet up a headwall. After that, the grade is not as steep, and nature has scoured out some crevices for us to use as leverage.

"So, how do we scale that first twenty feet?" Preacher asks, sounding as skeptical as I feel.

Johnson rubs his beard and answers without hesitation, "We'll make a human ladder for the first reach."

I scoff, and Johnson shoots me a disciplinary look for questioning his authority. So I humbly offer, "Can I suggest someone climb that pine over there instead? We could make a tree- bridge from the trunk to the cliff if someone can loop a rope around that jagged rock on the ledge."

Johnson paces the distance between the tree and the cliff, then claps me on the back, saying, "Harry, the true measure of a man is how he gets himself out of a tight spot. Job well done." He opens his pack, then orders, "Rope up."

Cowboy Knight lassos a cinch between the tree and the rock landing.

We loop the climbing rope around our waists, grab our packs, pull ourselves up and over the tree, and tackle the cliff. For the next two hours, we haul ourselves up the wall in unison, like a machine.

From a bird's eye view, we're four specks on a barren, exposed precipice. Then Knight dares fate: "Do you think any honorable Zero would stoop to pick off such easy targets?"

Preacher grabs hold of an uneven crack and pulls himself higher. "Death is not on my schedule today."

About thirty minutes later, a Japanese plane circles the valley. Roped together in a vertical line, we freeze. The aircraft levels out and skims over the treetops, probably searching for our artillery. It completely ignores us.

Johnson's the first to reach the top. He listens, then pulls everyone else up. We stabilize our ropes on a securely embedded stone, then pull out the dynamite, wire, and detonator box.

The road swings out almost to the drop off, then cuts back in to form a hairpin switchback. It's all rock and no cover, except for a few sage shrubs along the side. If enemy trucks come rolling up this path, the only way out is over the drop off, the way we came up.

I think back to the last time I laid dynamite, outside Ledo. The rain and slippery incline almost sucked me into the flooded culvert. And my knife slipped, cutting my freezing hands until I couldn't control the bleeding. Now the air is so dry that grit settles in my eyes, nose, and mouth.

On the inside edge of the bend, I place the sticks. Preacher hands me one end of the wire before he rolls out a length to the edge of the cliff. It's like riding a bike; once you've done it, you never forget. I splice the line, then attach it to the dynamite cap. Knight and Preacher cover the wire along the road with dirt and gravel. Johnson sets up the detonator box by the brush. I hurry over to Johnson, cut the second end of wire, and start slicing off the covering. That's when we hear engines.

"Down the cliff," Johnson orders.

Preacher and Knight scramble over the edge while I continue to splice the wire and fit it into the igniter.

"Now, Flynn," Johnson demands and grabs my shoulder.

"Give me three minutes. We can't give up." There's confidence in my voice, but uncertainty in my heart. "You know we won't come back."

He nods.

"I'll make it happen," I assure him.

Reluctantly, Johnson ropes up and slips over the side.

A dust cloud swells from the truck around the bend. I know it will be in my face any second, but I feel an unexpected composure. It's like I'm not breathing, even though my body is panting. My fingers fumble as I wrap the wire around the igniter. "Damn it," I whisper. "Little Buddha buddy, calm me down. I don't want to do this, but I want to go home."

I see the cab of the truck nudge forward from behind the cut bank. It backfires, then rolls in reverse and out of sight. The engine revs up, and it advances again.

Finally, the wired sticks are in place, and I hide the detonator in the brush. The wire snags on a branch and slips off. "Damn it." I wrap the rope around my hand several times, knowing I'll have to come back, then lower myself down to a sliver of a ledge. The truck rolls up to the rim of the cliff and stops. The driver shuts off the engine. I hear two doors open, followed by Japanese laughter. The pee gushing onto the road makes me want to yell, "Get it over with." A striking match fizzles in the silence, and I smell cigarette smoke. Down the road, the rumbling of several large engines continues. They must be waiting for a supply caravan to catch up.

I dare to look down the sheer drop off and shake my head to let Johnson know I'm not done. The other three are roped up, but, like me, have little to no footholds and hug the cliff for dear life. At the bottom, the rope clutches the bending tree to the rock. I close my eyes and wait.

Finally, the truck doors shut and the engine starts. Before the lead vehicle has cleared the area, I scramble back up to the top. Down the road, the engines from the convoy grind with the lowering of gears. Dust billows as tires spin on the steep rise.

I shake uncontrollably, legs wobbling from exhaustion and fear. Stumbling to the detonator, I grab on to the brush to regain my balance. As I reach for the box, my hands shake and I almost drop it. The trucks inch their way up and around the corner in a cloud of dirt.

Frantically, I block all sound from my world and immerse myself in a bubble of calm. After retightening the wires, I gently level the detonator on the ground. The first convoy clears the hill. I push the T-bar down, loop the rope around my waist, drop over the side, and pray for a delayed explosion.

"Down. Down. Down," I scream. The rope pulls me towards the bottom as the others peel off the face of the cliff. A rotten piece of rock slips out, and I dangle by one arm, swaying back and forth like a pendulum until I find a hold and grab. I slide down the precipice, ripping my shirt, my skin, my face, until I land on a foot-wide outcrop. The rope continues to drag me down. With energy I never knew I had, I bump from one handhold to another, the fear gone, fate telling me that I've got what it takes to get home.

At first, the explosion sounds like a muffled drum roll, but it surges and swells until it reaches a deafening roar. A scree of bouncing rocks pummels my head and the rock face around me. Pieces of metal and fractured rock slide down the rock face. The others are on the ground and I'm almost to the tree when my rope breaks. But I can't stop my momentum or the quaking cliff. I fling myself onto the branches, hoping they're strong enough to catch me. The branches crack with my weight, but hold. I slip to the ground, feeling lightheaded and alive.

"And I thought you said you weren't an expert." Knight grabs my arm and pulls me up from the dirt, looking like he's had the time of his life.

"I'm not. I'm just scared shitless, and I want to go home."

CHAPTER 54

February, 1945

Knight's courage is contagious. Morale is pumped so high among the Mars Task Force that it's floating in the danger zone. Men play cards, joking and ready to eat metal so they can spit arrowheads at the Japanese. After we punctured that hole in the enemy's shield and obliterated one of their access roads, the other men have become anxious to take revenge. It's hard to tether them back; they're so sick of waiting for victory. I'm the only one digging in, but with everyone else spoiling for the big fight, I say nothing.

Tomorrow, we'll push up to Loi Kang. Everyone knows it's flirting with suicide to charge uphill from the valley, but we've run out of options. And we've heard the enemy is packing up under the cover of night, so the men think we've finally starved them out and expect to find spineless skeletons.

We'll jump off tonight at 18:00 hours. Earlier this week, rations were cut so the cargo planes could drop more ammo for the assault. Two large-scale pincer attacks are planned for dawn, one on the village of Hpa Pen, and the other at Loi Kang. Johnson's to lead the battalion to Hpa Pen with Preacher; Knight and I will take on Loi Kang.

"Grenades?" Knight asks. "Check." The men shout back. "Magazine clips?"

"Check." "Cartridges?" "Check."

"Be prepared to stare death in the face today," Knight says with relish, pacing among the enlisted men and making sure everyone's ready. "Remember shot control: one bullet, one kill." He grabs his gear. "OK, let's get this over with." It's too dark to see faces, but there's a hint of wild excitement as the men throw only their battle gear in their packs and move out.

At 03:00 hours, a barrage of Mars artillery fire provides the initial distraction we need to cross the paddies and reach the hill that leads to Loi Kang. Knight points to a rendezvous spot and then waves the men to start crossing. The first soldier takes off, with the men behind him laying down machine-gun cover. Finally, the last one darts out from our shelter, leaving only Knight and me.

Before we start our sprint, the men on the far side spray the enemy with bullets, forcing them to duck for protection. Just as we leave, an ear-splitting whistle descends from above.

Behind us, a shell from Whistling Willie thumps into the ground. I know the shrapnel is going to gouge my body any second, but I keep running with no choice but to hope the adrenaline will carry me until I disintegrate and never feel the pain. Knight races beside me, panting.

We reach the other side alive. Instinctively, we drop, cover our heads with our hands, and wait for the explosion. But nothing comes. When we look back, we see the dud: a twelve-foot vertical shell, its nose dug in the ground. I'm shaking uncontrollably and can't stand up. I gulp in air faster than my lungs can expand.

"I would've shit in my pants if I had anything in my stomach," Knight growls, and stalls to regain his nerve.

Soon after, we start the two-thousand-foot ascent from the floor of the valley to the pill boxes we spotted dug in at the top. If we can take out the anti-aircraft bunkers, our flyboys can say "Sayonara" to Whistling Willie. But trouble starts on our first three-hundred-foot climb. The danger is an ugly risk.

"Jack." I grab Knight before he advances any further. "This looks bad. There's another route, but it's longer. They'll expect us to take the shorter path. It may be better to take more time to get to the top alive. Think about it."

Knight shrugs off my hold. "Harry, the true measure of a man is not whether he survives the battle, but how many times he picks himself up after he falls. He's got to be convinced that whatever is pushing him forward is right. I can't give up what's driven me my whole life, even if I die because of it." He waves the men to move forward. I follow.

The enemy has foxholes dug in along the trail from the base of the hill to the crest. Our men begin to fall immediately, but instead of intimidating us to retreat in fear, the Mars Men only become more determined. We race up the slope from bunker to bunker and toss grenades into their holes. Obsessed with reaching our objective, we keep moving and don't look back.

Knight raises his rifle high, signaling a sighting of the enemy ahead. We crouch and wait for them to turn the corner. With our Tommies locked in position, we mow a half-dozen of them down. Another half-dozen falls, and the rest of their column flees into the brush. Our ammo feeds our craving for destruction and steals away our sense of mortality. We need to conquer Loi Kang. We want the enemy dead. We have to end this war.

In slow motion, I feel myself float away from reality. The air is a dense cloud of clotted blood, rank sweat, whizzing bullets, and thrashing bodies, but nothing touches me. I watch the Japanese as they spring from their foxholes and release streams of bullets. Beside me, Mars Men are slammed to their death, but it's as though the enemy sees beyond me—like I'm not here. I toss grenades in their pits, then, in a Banzai charge, trail Knight to the top.

This is no spineless opponent, but there's no turning back now. Our single thought is to reach the top. Only then will it be over. We stumble over bullet-ridden GI bodies, frozen mouths wailing for one final plea for life. But I hear nothing, say nothing. I let my gun talk for me. The enemy drops.

We're beyond reason as we approach the ridge. I see our target just as a shell explodes in front of me. A massive blow from the flying debris knocks me to the ground and hammers some sense in me. Looking around the battlefield, I want to cry; so many men have been killed. What kind of god pits his creations against each other and sits back to watch? The bile bubbles up in my throat, and my body retches, emptying my stomach, my brain, and my heart. I wipe the vomit from my mouth.

"Goddamn it," a soldier cries out as he falls to the ground and down the hill.

This is not where I want to die, but that isn't my choice to make. We're fighting with our balls, not our brains.

That's when Knight shouts, "Come on, boys, I found the anti-air-craft nest." Without waiting and under no cover, he charges towards the horseshoe cluster of pill boxes, tossing grenades left and right.

The first bullet strikes his shoulder and sends him reeling backwards, but he continues his attack. As I lay on the ground, a second bullet grabs his leg. Still, he staggers forward.

The other men follow blindly. I whisper to myself, "We're going to die."

My mind answers me in Ruthie's voice: "Don't you dare come home to me in a box." I remember the earnest plea in her eyes and hear the soothing patter of rain on the roof. "What will you do?" Suddenly, I know the answer to that question.

It wasn't until Knight was struck for the second time that I flashed on Maggot Hill and remembered the Japanese Banzai attacks. We took aim and watched for the whites of their eyes as they raced towards us, upright and rigid. Then we fired. But one Japanese soldier unexpectedly crept up to my foxhole to make a hit. If Pfeifer hadn't taken him out, I'd be dead.

"Drop to the ground," I yell. The hard confidence in my voice sounds alien.

But the men are mad with battle fever. At first they ignore me, looking for direction from Knight, but he's down with a third bullet. I shout again, "Hit the ground. That's an order." One by one, they drop out of sight from the Japanese trenches.

"Dying is not the way to win a war." I need them to think for them-selves, do their duty, and save their own lives. But time is running out. "Keep low so they don't see you and drag yourself to their bunkers. Then lob in the grenades," I bark, and crawl to the lead.

We slither past Knight, lying in the dirt, blood seeping from his face, shoulder, leg and gut. He's not breathing. I look away. If I live, I'll process that later.

"Spread out. Make sure every foxhole is covered. I'll give the signal when I get to the anti-aircraft bunker at the end. Then strike simultaneously," I order. My command passes along the line.

I wriggle up to the first pill box, listening to the enemy's frantic chatter. They're waiting for our charge. Reaching one arm forward, then the next, I heave my body up the incline to the next pit. I glance back and see the men setting up for the attack. Then I feel a presence slide up next to me.

"Private, what the hell do you think you're doing here? Didn't I say spread out?" I snarl through gritted teeth.

"Sir, looks like you need help. I'm your man," the young soldier answers, battle madness still in his eyes.

There's no time to change course. "Let's do it," I say. We drag ourselves the last ten feet.

Before I can give the signal, a soldier stands up and lobs the first grenade. I close my eyes as the spray of bullets pummels him. Have I done the right thing? There's no time for an answer. "Now!" I yell.

I rise from the ground to a crouch, locate the anti-aircraft gun, toss my grenade, then lunge downhill. Screams and smoke follow. Dirt, metal, and shredded, bloodied clothing lands on me. I scramble back up for another attack. One by one, we drop our grenades. The young private next to me charges the bunker—exactly what I said not to do—lobbing his grenade at the last moment. A bullet blasts through his chest, and he's thrown backwards, eyes wide in terror. My heart sinks.

The smell of burning flesh, phosphorus, aluminum, lead, and acid forms a cloud. By now, all the pill boxes have been hit at least once, but the enemy does not retreat. They rise and fire without aiming. Our men hug the ground as bullets ricochet off trees and rocks above them. We throw our grenades until there are none left. If we're meant to die, then we'll go out giving it our best. I'm so terrified, I don't think or act like a human anymore. That's probably why I'm alive.

Finally, it's silent. We break from that other world, dazed. Rising from the dirt, we stagger among the smoldering ruins of collapsed bunkers and mutilated bodies. Mars men gape silently at the massacre. The nightmare is over.

On the edge of the ridge, an explosion plumes into the sky. The tail of an American bomber dips a salute as Whistling Willie is engulfed in a black fire of revenge.

One of the Mars men falls to his knees and looks towards heaven with outstretched arms.

He screams at the top of his lungs in disbelief, "God saved us."

"No," I answer, hoping only I can hear, "Jack Knight saved us."

I sink to the ground and wrap my arms around Knight's body, rocking him back and forth. "Jack, you're the only man I've ever envied: you lived by your word." All that wiry tension that propels men forward has left a limp body behind. "You didn't have to pay the final debt for glory."

From the corner of my eye, I see a bloodied Japanese soldier stagger towards me. As slow as he is, I'm not fast enough, and I feel the cold slice of his samurai in my back. The suction as he pulls it out tugs my body towards him, and he prepares to spear me again.

The gash steals my concentration, and something inside screams, "You fucking idiot." I release Knight, twist around, push myself off the ground, and grab the ornate handle from the Japanese soldier. He just stands there, wobbling, and lets me ram it deep into his heart. I rotate it once then twice, feeling the grief consume me. I realize it's what he wants. Exhausted, I pull the steel out, and he crumbles to the ground.

Not strong enough to stand, I drop to my knees and prop myself against the hilt of his sword. His blood drips from my hands down the blade and onto the dirt. My eyes fix on his young face, scarred and anguished. Was he really ready to die? At the same time, I feel nothing towards him—nothing at all. I double over onto the ground. If this is glory, then I want none of it. Eventually, the smoke clears, and the world around me dissolves.

PART IV

WRAP UP

CHAPTER 55

The only thing that kept me alive that day in Loi Kang was my anger. I remember a hilltop reeking of phosphorous, vomit, and blood, and feeling emotionally empty with Knight and the young Japanese soldier's bodies lying next to me. I thought, "The only way they'll get me home in a body bag is over my dead body." Then I got mad and passed out.

"I was afraid you were going to sleep the war away," Dr. Seagrave says. He arches his eyebrows as he peers through his wire-rimmed glasses; his sunken eyes are heavy with dark circles. Then he grabs my wrist to check my pulse and calls out, "Maran Lu, we got a live one over here. Give him only water until he can sit up by himself. Then we're sending him back to Ledo. These beds in Myitkyina are reserved for sick soldiers." His lopsided half-smile shows his relief at pulling another soldier from the grave. "Harry, next time, don't turn your back on the enemy."

Maran Lu pushes the doctor away. "He my patient. You go find own trouble." As she turns me over to check my wound—her loose braid now a tangle of uncombed hair flopping in her face—she whispers, "Harry, you sweet boy. I take good care of you." The wound hurts like hell, but that's better than the alternative. Before she leaves, she confides, "Earl be happy you live. He no good at writing goodbye letters for friends' family."

All of March, 1945, I was laid up in Ledo. That's when Stilwell's Road was completed.

I hear it looks like a hardened scar through the jungle, undulating behind bends that wind to infinity. With the road done, I had nothing to go back to, so Uncle Sam recommended a desk job.

Because of my stupidity, I took the offer. In spite of it, in April, they sent me to Ceylon with a promotion.

CBI headquarters in Ceylon needs someone to manage the supplies for the gas lines they're building parallel to Stilwell's Road. With my knowledge of North Burma, I'm the man for the job. Now I realize how lucky I was to get an SOS position. But by resisting my original assignment on the road job, I just about bucked myself out of the training that will land me a good-paying position back home.

A familiar figure enters the hallway as I walk by in search of my new post in H.Q.'s main building on this tiny island off the tip of India. Closing the door to a room without any designation stenciled on the frosted glass, the soldier hesitates. So I tap him on the shoulder to see if the door leads to the SOS office.

"Harry?" Charming Charles asks as he turns to face me. His usual refined gentility is replaced with open-faced shock, which quickly changes to mischief. "You're to report to OSS?" He narrows his eyes to study me for confirmation.

"OSS? Hell no, I'm still with SOS. Or is SOS a part of OSS? What the hell is OSS, and where is SOS?" I grab hold of Charles' outstretched hand like a dog unwilling to release a bone.

"It's Office of Strategic Services," Charles cautiously answers, then points down the hall. "SOS is in the next corridor. What the hell are you doing here?"

"If the Japs can't get rid of me, do you think Uncle Sam can?"

"You're as skinny as a stray dog, but you're the same, Harry." Charles straightens his jacket and tie. "Get settled in, then meet me for a drink at the pub on Queens Road by the British Consulate."

It takes almost no time for Charles and me to pick up where we left off in Ledo. I hail from a long line of farmers, while Charles is a Stanford man, like his father. Our former lives are from opposite social classes, but war has a way of equalizing us all.

"Whatever happened to Schmidt?" I ask Charles while nursing a beer. There are no enlisted men in the British pub, with its panels of carved mahogany and mother of pearl ashtrays.

"Funny you should ask." He swirls brandy in the snifter cupped in his long, polished hands, downs it, then settles into the over-stuffed, velvet chair. "Remember the day Colonel Pick arrived and the transport truck went missing? I had you race off to the train station to fetch the Colonel."

I nod.

He leans over the table and whispers, "Harry, this is between you and me, because I know I can trust you." He waits for another nod. "Well, there was a tip-off that illegal supplies were being shipped from Delhi to Ledo. We weren't sure who it was, but we were absolutely certain there was a rat in the pack. So we started planting propaganda in our radio calls."

"Who's we?" I ask, seeing an interesting side of Charles that I won't blindly trust again, as I had in the past.

"You don't need to know." Charles dismisses my question. "Quite frankly, the way you were acting back then, you were a suspect. But the rat that walked into our trap was Schmidt. Seems he had an in with friends of the Fuhrer. We also got the guy in Delhi, but not before they had stolen and shipped out a year's worth of contraband supplies." With an upraised finger, he motions for another round of drinks. "We think it went down to Kohima or Imphal. Nasty business for the Brits back then. But I wasn't sorry to see that bastard get his due. Even execution was too good for him."

I tilt back in the chair and marvel at how quickly I've escaped my life of the last four years and put thousands of miles between me and that world. I recall the recruitment officer in 1942 telling me, "You have mighty fine handwriting, son. We can use men like you." The humiliation I felt at that time blinded me. I'm ashamed to say I used my authority to order explosives that could've hurt the very men I thought Stilwell was sending to their graves, and now I find out I almost got caught. Lately, the little girl with the wicker basket—and all of the men I lost—haunt me. Was I one of the lucky ones? Did I really get away?

CHAPTER 56

September 12, 1945

I look all around and find only white, luminous clouds, thick and infinitely layered. From my seat on the C87 cargo transport, I crane my neck to catch a glimpse through the few windows in the front of the fuselage. Where I sit, near the back, there's a six-foot square door on the port side, but no windows. Charming Charles, in his creased-to-perfection uniform, snores in the seat next to me. I'm exhausted, but I can't sleep. We're en route to Shanghai, and I'm scared shitless. The war is over, but do the Japanese in China know?

Like translucent spider-webs, the clouds outside the plane are teased into millions of swirling threads. I concentrate on the droning engines, hoping they'll lull me into a calm I can't find. I don't know how Charles can sleep through this; I've seen too much to pretend it's all over. So I pull out a piece of paper to write my final letter to Ruthie, in case I don't make it back.

What do I tell her? I wonder if she still has that sassy sway after three years. I loved her gutsy disregard for hoity-toity airs. What lights up her smile these days? Is it still me? I try to imagine how she looks when she sits down to pen her letters.

An air pocket outside bumps the jitters in me. I look over at Charles, still sleeping like he doesn't have a care in the world. Finally, I write what I can't say aloud to myself.

Dearest Ruthie,

Do you know how many times I've wondered if this day

would ever come? When I could say the war is over and I'm alive? That boy you sent off to combat in 1942 had little respect for authority. The simple, high-mindedness of youth egged me on. I had something to prove. But too many people, plus the war, got in my way.

Bob only saw the good in me. I never realized that the best of ourselves stays in our friends and family for those times when we need someone to remind us we've got what it takes. Now he's gone. But you're not.

The war showed me I had a lot to learn, and it wasn't from the generals. I always thought it was important for a man to be fearless, but I was wrong. Sometimes being frightened knocks a little sense in you, so you end up doing what's right, not what's heroic.

These last three years, I've remembered the tingle of your tears on my neck when we last hugged, and how your lip quivered when you walked away. How could you ever love a dope like me?

That image of you wouldn't let me die. I had to get home alive. But most of the boys I fought with won't be going home. Fate chose them and not me. I hope someday I can bury those desperate times and move beyond.

Through the plane's window, I see patches of blue sky breaking up the clouds. I have more to say but no way to say it.

The engines slow as we approach Shanghai, and Charles wakes up.

"Are you ready?" he asks as he rustles in his seat, finally looking tense.

"I can't be if I don't know what to expect," I say, then stash my letter. Before I tighten my seatbelt, I check to see that my gun is secured for the landing.

"So you heard about the coup to oust the Imperial House of Japan?" he asks, offering me a cigarette before pulling one out for himself. "Don't worry, Harry. They've seen our A-bomb. It's all under our control now."

"If the Japanese officers in Tokyo are ready to overthrow the Emperor for signing the peace treaty, I can only imagine what the foot soldiers in China are ready to do. They've run the country for almost ten years. I don't think they'll want to give it up that easy," I say, trusting the cigarette will eventually calm my nerves or boost my courage.

"I thought you were a Marauder, a Mars Man. Where's the backbone?" he teases, but I see the ashes on his smoke glow non-stop with his frequent inhales.

"It's not guts you're going to need—its smarts, in case we're walking into a trap. All I want is to go home."

"What are your plans?" he asks.

"Buy a house. Maybe get married. Start a jungle warfare training course. What about you?"

"Funny, Harry—real funny." Charles checks to see if I'm joking. "The OSS is disbanding.

I guess they're forming a special intelligence agency. Maybe I'll just hang on."

We're descending into an overcast Shanghai. All we can see is a mass of buildings, so I can't get any clues from the windows. I wonder whether they have anti-aircraft artillery aimed at us. Do they know they're supposed to surrender? Will they let us land, then pick us off one by one as we exit the plane, or will they send us to interrogation camps? Knowing the Japanese as I do, they're inflexible and predictable because they've been brainwashed to place honor above all else. Maybe they'll mow us down, then commit hari-kari. Why the hell did I get put on the first flight into China assigned to supply the transition operation? I grind out my cigarette, hoping it's pumped me with enough nerve.

The plane noses down to connect with the runway. Tires bump and brakes screech as we slow down. I grip my hand rests. No one speaks. The aircraft stops, and we're still alive.

After shutting the visors on the plane's few windows, the brass are the first out of their seats. They look at each other hesitantly, then the commanding officer speaks. "Men, there are one, two, several Japanese regiments posted on the tarmac to greet us. We're here to re-establish order in China, not fight a war. So once you're outside, the butt of your weapon is to rest on the ground. But be ready. You represent the United States of America. Remember that. Now, line up."

I stare at the door as we form a single-file to leave. Slowly, the cargo door opens. Out on the tarmac, hundreds of thousands of armed Imperial soldiers stand at attention. There are more than the eye can capture or mind can count, in full uniform, with cloven-hoof boots; samurai swords; and a flag with the red, rising sun waving behind them. But the Zeroes stand idle. The anti-aircraft are unmanned. And no one shoots.

The twenty-five of us line up along the length of the C87. My heart is racing, and my hands itch to level my rifle. I survey the grounds for an escape route, but where would I go surrounded by this field army? Then, without realizing what I'm doing, I look into the eyes of the enemy: first one, then the next. Each has a family and, now, a future, I think. Soldiers may be good men, even if they're not brave. And officers may have been heroic soldiers, even if they're not the best leaders. So why should I expect leaders to be more? They're only men.

Reaching into my right pocket, I grab my gilded Buddha.

At that moment, the flag with the red, rising sun is lowered and the stars and stripes are raised. The Imperial forces release their weapons and bow in unison. The Allied soldiers salute, except for me.

I tilt my head down, close my eyes, clutch my Buddha, and pray. I've lost so much to this war. Ask anything of me but compassion and forgiveness. Not right now. Not yet.

Flashes of faces and places from the last three years cross my mind. Most I'll never see again. I clutch my gilded charm tighter, craving a better future for all of us. Give me strength one more time, so the light in me can find a way to honor the light in you.

It's then I realize what I must tell Ruthie: the Harry Flynn she knew is never coming home.

HISTORICAL NOTE

I would be remiss if I did not pay tribute to all those serving in the China-Burma-India (CBI) Theater. In writing this book, it was impossible to show every contribution from the Americans, British (Chindits in particular), Africans, Australians, Indians, Kachin and Burmese to the CBI effort. Also, I want to note that through fiction I placed individuals in scenes where they may not have been in real history because I was unable to find documentation identifying their exact locations during all the battles. An example of this is including Logan Weston with the 2nd Battalion in Nhpum Ga. But the major events in this book all happened. Unfortunately, I had to limit the number of characters in the story so as to not confuse the reader. Many men who should have been showcased for their valiant service were not even mentioned. I hope the fictional characters represent, in some way, those I could not re-create as individuals in this book.

Without the commentaries from personal diaries, biographies, historical novels, and web sites, I would not have gotten a glimpse into the heroic actions, passions or mistakes made by those who lived behind the Forgotten Front. Although many of the characters were real-life people living through WWII in the CBI theater, there are no scenes that use actual verbatim accounts from documented history books. I used the following references:

www.cbi-theater-1.home.comcast.net/cbi-theater

www.cbi-theater-1.home.comcast.net/cbi-theater-1/roundup/

www.cia.gov/library/center-for-the-study-of-intelligence

www.history.army.mil/books/wwii/marauders

www.hoover.org/library-and-archives/collections/east-asia/
featured-collections/joseph-stilwell

www.marauder.org

www.Wikipedia

Baines, Frank 2011 Chindit Affair: A Memoir of the War in Burma

Briscoe, C.H. Dr. 2002 Kachin Ranger: allied guerrillas in
WWII Burma

Calvert, Michael 1952 Prisoners of Hope

Hawkins, Richard Unpublished Diary

Ogburn, Charlton Jr. 1956 The Marauders

US Government Signal Corp Maps